THE RETURN

BOOK THREE OF
THE TRIALS AND TRIUMPH TRILOGY

KENNETH E. NOWELL

VERO HOUSE
PUBLISHING, CORP.

The Return
Book Three of the Trials and Triumph Trilogy
Copyright © 2012 by Kenneth E. Nowell
Printed in the United States of America

Vero House Publishing, Corp.
5460 Corsica Place
Vero Beach, FL 32967
www.VeroHousePublishing.com
Telephone or fax: 888-292-7160
Email: admin@VeroHousePublishing.com
Paperback ISBN-13: 978-0-9828279-9-4; ISBN-10: 0-9828279-9-7
Digital ISBN-13: 978-0-9886539-0-0; ISBN-10: 0-9886539-0-7

Library of Congress Cataloging-in-Publication Data:
Nowell, Kenneth E.
       The Return – Book Three of The Trials and Triumph Trilogy / Kenneth E. Nowell.
       p. cm.
1. Fiction - Religious; 2. Fiction - Thriller
Title
813.6-nov16
ISBN-13: 978-0-9828279-9-4;   ISBN-10: 0-9828279-9-7

The author and publisher recognize and accept that the final authority regarding apparitions, miracles and prophecies rests with the Holy See of Rome, to whose judgment we willingly submit.

DEDICATED TO GOD'S GIFT OF BETSY,
WITHOUT WHOM THIS BOOK,
OUR FAMILY AND MY LIFE
WOULD NOT BE COMPLETE.

WHAT HAS BEEN WILL BE AGAIN,
WHAT HAS BEEN DONE WILL BE DONE AGAIN;
THERE IS NOTHING NEW UNDER THE SUN.

ECCLESIASTES 1:9

> **History doesn't repeat itself.**
> **It rhymes.**
> Mark Twain

Chapter 1
Earth
66 million years ago

IT WAS AN AGE when predators reigned. For 163 million years, the most dangerous of dinosaurs had triumphed during the trials of life. Small mammals survived, but only as long as they remained unnoticed.

The dinosaurs had thrived on conquest and had risen to rule over the plants, the animals and the planet. Eventually, they became a threat to all God's creatures, and it seemed that nothing on earth could challenge their supremacy.

The creatures of this primordial planet lacked reasoning minds and could not appreciate God's gift of life. Love and self-sacrifice were absent among such base animals because their impulsive instincts rendered them incapable of freely choosing their destinies. Unable to gain wisdom, they valued only slaughter and dominance.

So, when God looked down upon His tumultuous and violent world, He judged it incomplete and desired change.

Change occurred in a split second.

A ruinous rock found its target near what would eventually become Mexico's Yucatan Peninsula. Only a moment earlier, the asteroid – over six miles in diameter and larger than Mount Everest – had been hurtling through space at 40,000 miles per hour. Now, however, the dreadful object had vaporized upon impact in the future Gulf of Mexico.

Earth shuddered and the unprecedented consequences were global and cataclysmic.

The impact unleashed the energy of millions of nuclear weapons.

Earthly debris – larger than city blocks – bombarded the planet's surface. Now, in the aftermath, earthquakes and tsunamis jolted to life, ravaging the land, while smoke and ash dominated the air.

The resulting blockage of sunlight eventually caused plants to die, which led to the starvation of herbivores, which initiated the extinction of land-bound carnivores.[1]

Ultimately, the dinosaurs were doomed.

Yet, nothing on earth could have challenged their supremacy.

EVENTUALLY, God would complete creation[2] with His most beloved species, made in His own image and likeness.[3]

To mankind, He would offer Paradise and, there, all creatures would live in interdependent harmony. The sun and the moon, the cedar and the flower, the eagle and the sparrow, would demonstrate that, even among countless diversities and inequalities, no creature is self-sufficient. For that reason, they would rely on one another, to complete and to serve each other.[4]

Above all other species, however, man would be created good,[5] in friendship with his Creator and in harmony with himself and the creation around him.[6] Uniquely, God would reveal His wisdom to man, both Spiritually and intellectually, and He would respect man's liberty to choose his own destiny.

So, with infinite love, God offered mankind three extraordinary gifts: first, conscience, so that whenever the prudent man would listen to it, he would hear God speak;[7] second, freedom, so that with man's rational mind he could master his actions[8] and be responsible for his choices;[9] third, dominion, so that man would reign over the visible creation in peaceful happiness.[10]

To no other creature would He offer such loving generosity.

So, for a time, man and woman would revel in the joy of God's company. They would immerse themselves in the pleasures of

Paradise. They would live without worries, enjoying the beauty of the Lord's creation and exercising dominion over it.

Then they would want more.

Then they would seek to become like gods.[11]

66 MILLION YEARS LATER

Before I come as a just judge,
I am coming first as the King of Mercy.
Before the day of justice arrives,
there will be given to people a sign
in the heavens of this sort:
All light in the heavens will be extinguished,
and there will be great darkness over the whole earth.
Then the sign of the Cross will be seen in the sky...
Prophecy of Jesus Christ,
from *The Diary* of St. Faustina

Chapter 2
Providence Hospital
Washington, DC
July 13 - The Third Day of Darkness

THE DARKNESS continued to linger and the earth shook like rarely before.[12] Hideous voices howled through the atmosphere, sounding too demonic to be human. From nearby hospital rooms, however, some patients joined the hellish chorus with defiant screams of coarse and blasphemous curses.

The moments had stretched into hours, the hours into days.

Cradling her newborn closely, Angela Concepcion had trembled in her unseasonably cold hospital bed.[13] For two days, now, fear had almost paralyzed her. But she had desperately tried to hide the anxiety she felt. She did not want these horrifying hours to traumatize her child.

"Agent Anderson?" she called out, again and again.

She heard no response.

Initially, she pulled the covers tighter, but they could not shield her from the harsh memories that continued to race through her mind.

She was no longer proud of her worldly honors while rising to the highest office in the land. Instead, the president remembered her life's unrelenting rejections of God's love. From Him, she had received every grace imaginable. To Him, she had returned nothing.

During the first day of Darkness, she marveled at the destructive lifestyle her choices had produced, and she was astonished at how stubbornly she had clung to her materialistic ignorance, oblivious of anything that had truly mattered. As her disturbing memories streamed, she grew horrified at how much good she had avoided and how much evil she had embraced.

She trembled in anticipation of a just God's judgment.

By the second day, the blinding blackness had become so dense that it could be felt, and it pressed in on her like a suffocating blanket. To her, it seemed an apt metaphor for her lifelong habit of shielding her sight from all things Spiritual.

However, she was now gaining clarity. This time of blindness had actually opened her eyes, allowing her to perceive reality without the deceptions of sensorial pleasure.[14] More powerful than the Darkness, she learned, was the light of Truth.

So, as she reconciled herself with God, she perceived the world in a completely new way. For the first time, in a long time, she was filled with hope.

Once she made the effort, her transformation evolved so easily and quickly that she smiled at its simplicity. She humbly and sincerely asked God to forgive her for everything she had done wrong.

Then ... He did.

She heard no lectures. She experienced no punishments. Angela felt only the invigorating joy of total forgiveness. Now, she knew that her life would never be the same and, even under these seemingly dire circumstances, she became filled with hope and trust.

She had accepted her inheritance as a child of God, a daughter of the King. In that grand scheme, even the American presidency meant little.

This must be the Three Days of Darkness, she thought. It was one of those odd beliefs that her mother had shared with her, even though the younger Angela had often dismissed it as a superstition of fools.

Along with those memories of Elizabeta, long-forgotten prayers returned to Angela's mind and she put them to good use. Whenever the dense, oppressive fog pressed in on her, Angela fought back. She drew her baby closer and whispered, "Don't worry, *chiquita*. God will protect us." Then, she returned to praying the ruby red rosary that she recently had dug out of a box of memories. A lifetime ago, it had been a gift from her mother to the faithful child that she once was.

Each time, the effect was immediate as demons screeched a fearful retreat, the disturbing, distant screams quieted and the earth's quaking tremors eased. Angela had never imagined that her prayers could carry such power over demonic forces. However, she quickly corrected her thinking, remembering that it is not her power that they fear.

So, that holy strand of beads became her reliable weapon against the unseen evil, and the power of prayer became tangible to her for the first time in her life.[15]

Yet, even with that confidence, Angela did not dare leave her hospital bed. She would wait it out with her little *chiquita* resting calmly in her arms.

She's amazing, Angela thought. *What a tough little cookie.*

The new mother admired her baby's simple needs, finding complete comfort from nothing more than caresses, prayers and occasional nursing.

Oh, if only my life could be so uncomplicated. Angela wondered, *What will the world be like when the light returns?*

Elizabeta had once told her that the end of the Darkness would bring a brief time of peace – a thought welcomed by Angela. However, she had also said that many would die during the Three Days because their consciences would not be able to bear their shame.[16] After a lifetime of opportunities, those who had relentlessly rejected love would be unable to draw upon God's mercy during the hour of justice.[17]

Angela now realized that the Darkness should not have surprised anyone. Jesus had promised, "Immediately after the distress of those days the sun will be darkened, and the moon will not give its light; the stars will fall from the sky, and the heavenly bodies will be shaken."[18] Clearly, global distress had preceded the worldwide Darkness, just as had been foretold.

Christ also prophesied that before His return, the world would be like in the days of Noah and Lot.[19] Of course, those were sinful times ... and these were, too. It was now clear to Angela that Jesus had described the 21st century, a time when technology had empowered the unprecedented advancement of every cardinal sin.[20] So, like in the days of Noah and of Lot, the evil ones had been swept from the earth. The good had been left behind.

Recent newspaper headlines had proclaimed warnings from alleged visionaries in the tiny villages of Garabandal and Medjugorje.[21] But those little articles had been buried deep into the newspapers, alongside UFO sightings and other incredible tales. In fact, most of the world had become conditioned to dismiss anyone who spoke of the end of the Age. Only kooks or pranksters announced such silliness.

But the warnings had registered with Angela, perhaps only subconsciously. Consequently, these events had been traumatic, but not overwhelming. Though Angela's mind raced with uncertainties and questions, she did not fear. Her newfound love for God and her daughter cast out fear.[22]

She had only seen her baby for a brief, glorious moment. What a beauty she was: big brown eyes, surprisingly thick, dark curls and a smooth olive complexion. Angela marveled at the memory.

Such a special little girl, born on the eve of a new world.

The proud mother had intended to use a pair of grandiose names, worthy of a president's daughter. But then she decided for simplicity.

Born on the eve of a new world? I'll name you Eve.... My little Evie.

As she rolled onto her side, snuggling the unseen infant between her tummy and a pillow, Angela whispered, "How many of us are left, Evie?"

Soon, her mind slowed and, for the first time in three days, Angela yearned to sleep. Before her eyelids closed, however, Evie giggled and the light returned.

"MADAME PRESIDENT!"

The soft but emphatic words startled Angela as she stopped shuffling down the hall and clutched Evie even more tightly. The president turned and stepped over one of the bodies that littered the hallway and peered into a shadowed room. On the floor, next to a bed, she saw her lead Secret Service agent.

"Anderson?"

"Yes ma'am," the lanky agent answered as he rose to his feet and dusted off his pants.

The electricity in the hospital had not returned, but slight rays beamed around the room's window blinds, allowing Angela to discern that the agent was standing next to someone in the bed. He appeared to be dead.

"What are you doing in here?" she asked.

"I was outside your room when it went dark. Then I heard this old guy scream. I didn't want to leave your door but then he started crying. So, I felt my way over here to help him or … I don't know."

"You were with him the whole time?"

"Yes, ma'am. I tried to get him to pray with me." The agent shook his head. "But he was too proud … all the way to the end." He drew in a deep breath. "But I think helping him is what saved me."

Angela looked down at the shadowed corpse and frowned when she recognized the face. He had been famous, wealthy and one of her top contributors. During the Three Days of Darkness, however, his worldly connections had carried no weight.

"I could have been like him." Anderson added, solemnly, "From now on … well … I'm not gonna blow my chances, this time."

Angela offered a nod of understanding.

Anderson moved closer to admire new, innocent life. "She's a beauty."

Angela smiled as she brushed a finger across Evie's cheek.

Then the agent's training kicked in. "I have to get you two back to the White House."

ANDERSON PRIED OPEN the emergency room's sliding doors and led the president out, onto a quiet 12th Street. As Angela struggled with holding her baby while securing her open-seamed hospital gown, she marveled at the beauty of the striking blue sky and puffy white clouds, above. Inhaling deeply, Angela immediately appreciated that the air seemed purer, cleaner. Washington was like she had never experienced before: quiet and peaceful.

However, when her gaze drifted downward the president was confronted by a confusing scene. The streets were not only congested but all traffic had stopped, as if frozen in time. In many cars and taxis, the drivers had simply expired at the wheel. Other vehicles were unoccupied, apparently deserted when their drivers sought safety from the demons of the dark. Yet, though bodies were scattered on the grounds of a nearby park, and here and there in the street, the sidewalks were mostly empty.

"Please, wait here," the agent instructed.

Angela watched as he slid into the closest vacant vehicle in the southbound lane. The key had been left in the ignition and so he attempted to start it, but with no success.

"Must have run out of gas, idling," he shouted as he jogged to another empty car. Again he tried, but failed.

"Try that one," Angela shouted, pointing to an old, flatbed cargo truck in a delivery zone parking space.

Anderson nodded and trotted to the truck, opened the door, and was startled when a dead man fell out. Looking down at him, the agent shook his head with sympathy and frustration, knowing that there was nothing that could be done now to help the man. So, he dragged the body to a grassy area, returned to the truck and slid in, behind the wheel. He found the key in the ignition. However, Anderson sighed deeply when he saw that a heavy piece of equipment occupied the passenger seat. Still, the truck's engine started on the first try.

Soon, he was lifting the president and her baby onto the flatbed. "I'm sorry, Madame President, but you'll have to sit back here." Then, a moment later, he slowly advanced his VIPs down the wide sidewalk, headed to the White House.

As they drove, Angela stood behind the cab, marveling at what had become of her city, her country, her world.

Anxious eyes peered out at them from windows, along the way. Corpses were strewn across the landscape, especially in the most dangerous parts of town. All roadway traffic had stopped and it seemed no one had ventured out of their homes yet.

Then Anderson startled Angela when he yelled out the window, "Hey lady, get out of the way."

Angela looked ahead and saw an old black woman, standing on the sidewalk. She wore a backpack and hunched over her cane while tugging on the leash of a small, scraggly dog.

The agent honked his horn but the woman just waved him off as she waited for her puppy to do his business.

With the truck at a standstill, Angela yelled ahead, "You need a ride?"

"No way!" Anderson shouted. "I'm responsible for your safety. We can't pick up strangers."

The old woman looked back, smiled and nodded.

"Come on," Angela said. "My driver will help you up."

Soon, the truck was rumbling slowly down the sidewalk with the passengers sitting on the flatbed. Nothing was said, at first, but Angela felt a little uncomfortable as the old woman kept nodding and smiling at her while petting her dog.

Finally, the woman spoke up. "I know who you is."

Angela sighed and shrugged her admission as she stroked her baby.

The black woman let out a loud cackle, exposing her decaying teeth. Then her dog barked a couple times, showing his appreciation for her happiness. "You is the pres'dent!" Then, as she looked at her dog, she chortled, "Teddy, we is sittin' wit' the pres'dent of these United States!" She laughed again and Teddy howled along with her.

"My driver will take you home," Angela suggested, changing the subject.

She chuckled again. "Lady, I ain't had no home goin' on twenty years, now."

Angela observed the woman quietly, for a moment. "Then why are you so happy?"

The old lady frowned at the question. "Don't you know what just happened? We been blessed."

"You think?" Angela said, with a hint of sarcasm. "A lot of people are dead."[23]

Again, the woman studied Angela's ignorance, then mumbled to Teddy, "People say she so smart." The woman raised her eyes and spoke directly to the president. "Lady, there's bad people in the world... at least, there was. I ain't got no sympathy. They done made their choices."[24] As they rolled along, she pointed at a corpse on a grassy slope. "You see dat man?"

Angela nodded.

"He done killed six women ... prob'ly more. One of 'em had a baby not much older than yours. He use ta brag, ohhh, he use ta brag that they ain't never gonna catch him." She turned serious. "But God sho' did."[25]

Angela thought about the old woman's difficult life on the streets, so close to her own comfortable home at the White House, yet a world away.

The old woman continued with her philosophy on life. "Dese days, people be callin' evil good and good evil.[26] Why you think dat is?"

Angela shrugged.

"I ain't stupid. I go to the library and get on the computer. Some people there just watchin' smut,[27] but I read the news. And I tell ya, the world done flopped upside down. For you politicians, the problems get worse and worse but the trips and parties get bigger and better."

"Look," Angela sympathized, "I can make sure you're taken care of."

The woman fingered her gray hair away from her wrinkled, ebony face and stared at Angela suspiciously. "Yo gonna help me?"

Angela did not understand the question. "There's a lot of government programs out there."

"Dat's what I thought," she said, shaking her head.

"No, look. I'm trying to help you."

"Stop makin' out like yo some kinda Mother Teresa! Yo wanna help me? Then help me yo'self! Don't send me off to some desk monkey and then walk away all puffed up 'bout how good you is."

Angela did not know how to respond.

The old woman became more animated. She waved her fingers in the air and said, "I remember what you said. Oh, yeah, you is gonna make everything perfect!" She shook her head and snorted. "Lady, you may have a "Perfect World" in the White House but we ain't seein' it on the street, yet."

The president listened more closely.

The old woman pursed her lips, squinted her eyes and studied whether Angela was worth the effort. Then she continued. "Ya know, my boy's a politician and he says gov'ment's gonna care for me, jus' like you." She shook her head. "Love sho' has grown cold dese days. Sho' has grown cold."

Angela regretted how she had neglected her own mother, through the years, drawing selfish comfort from the illusion that government assistance would provide for her every need.

"Lady, America don't lack money." Her voice dropped to a deep whisper. "It lacks soul."

For Angela, the task ahead was beginning to seem too big for government to solve. She agreed with the old woman. Selfless love would be the only solution to the problems facing America and the rest of the world.

But her mind was closing down. She had been through too much over the past three days, without sleep. Spiritually, she had come far, but was still struggling.

As she glanced around at more of those who had not survived, her intellectual nature returned. "Maybe it wasn't God," she mumbled to herself. "Maybe there's a natural explanation."

Just then the truck turned a corner and Anderson slammed on the brakes. For the first time, out of the shadows of the numerous office buildings that had surrounded them, a mysterious light shone down upon them.

Angela and the old lady rose to their feet.

"Praise God!" the woman shouted. Then she asked, "You call dat natural?"

Angela was stunned into silence as she stared at the fulfillment of prophecies: God's permanent, miraculous Sign.[28] Directly ahead, a Cross dominated the blue sky, crystalline in appearance, ruby red in color, and so incredibly large that it seemed the whole world could witness it.[29]

The president blinked and squinted, adjusting her eyes to the unfathomable object and the light rays that beamed down from it. At the heart of the Cross, flames raged, but with no apparent kindling. Its expansive beams were translucent yet radiant, and its beveled edges were so straight that intelligent design seemed obvious. For Angela, the extraordinary features of the awesome Cross left little doubt that its origin was supernatural, and that only almighty God could have created it.

Angela heard the old woman's babblings, but wasn't listening.

"You see? There He be, looking over us. Gonna be hard to ignore Him, now."

Angela's eyes remained locked on the sacred object but one thought would not leave her mind. *I have to find John Malek.*

Later, Angela vaguely remembered hearing, "We gettin' off here" and, when Angela's amazement finally subsided, the old woman and her dog were gone.

The president knocked on the window and the truck began rumbling down the sidewalk, stopping only when their path was blocked by bodies. Then, each time, Anderson would get out, move the corpses out of their way, and resume his unlikely transport of VIPs.

To Angela, the slow journey home seemed eerily dream-like. Only days ago, she could not have imagined being driven through Washington like this. She yearned to return to the secure protection of the White House and she longed to tell Fred everything that had happened to her and his new baby girl.

"Oh, Fred," she sighed. But then she again scanned the urban landscape, contemplated the awesome death toll for those who had refused to reach out to God in the Darkness, and tried not to jump to conclusions.

INSIDE THE WHITE HOUSE residential quarters, Angela frantically rushed through the first floor. Here and there she came upon a body. At the moment, however, only one person concerned her. She needed to find Fred … alive.

She worried that the homeless woman had been right: all those with too much pride and too little love could not have survived the Darkness.

Hoping to avoid disturbing the sleeping baby in her arms, she whispered loudly, "Fred? Fred?"

No one answered. The White House was eerily quiet.

Angela bounded up the Grand Staircase and searched through the residence level. She glanced into the Treaty Room and then headed down the center hall, rushing past the Yellow Oval Room until she found their Private Sitting Room, empty.

Then, when she entered the Presidential Bedroom, she gasped. Fred was on the floor, curled into a fetal ball.

"Oh, Fred," she sadly scolded. "Couldn't you sacrifice just a little of that pride? Couldn't you show God just a little love?"

Now, the White House was empty and silent, a vacuum of lifeless memories.

In her loneliness, Angela sat on the bed and contemplated the awesome task ahead. She was numb, too exhausted to feel anger or fear ... until the cell phone on the dresser vibrated ... the one that only received calls from Evan Thas.

The training and education of the great saints,
who will appear towards the end of the world,
is reserved for the Mother of God.
These great saints will surpass in holiness
the majority of the other saints
like the cedar of Lebanon surpasses the lowly shrub.
St. Louis de Montfort

Chapter 3
Miguel Castro Castro Prison
Lima, Peru
July 13

FINALLY, Pedro Lopez managed to snatch the burlap sack off his sweat-soaked head and gasp the stale air. He squinted downward and grimaced at his bloody wrists, the result of a painfully exhausting effort to free himself from the bindings of his interrogation.

Now, the light had returned.

As he scanned the surroundings in his cell, the Lima prison was strangely quiet, and he heard only a constant drip. At his feet, the little Honduran was not surprised to see the lifeless bodies of his interrogators. They had been passionately repulsed by Pedro's every mention of God, but they had been happy for the opportunity to crack him. Each knew that breaking a famous Imperfective, like Pedro, could launch a Patroller's career.

He struggled to untie his feet from the chair and, when they were finally free, he turned and surveyed the intended instruments of his interrogation: a large, leaky water bucket and a car battery. Pedro thanked God that the Darkness began just before the tortures.

Before the Latter Day Apostles left India, John had established a global, viral communications strategy for them. As the twelve travelled the world in pairs, they encouraged each newly converted believer to develop twelve new disciples of his or her own. Then, just as the original Apostles had done in the first century, Latter Day messages were quickly transmitted by word of mouth through that international chain of believers.

For the faithful, it was the only safe means of messaging because Evan Thas had gained control of – or, at least, the ability to monitor – telephone, Internet and mass communication networks.

Until the Darkness arrived, the evangelizing pairs had been making remarkable – even miraculous – progress while crisscrossing their assigned territories. In their wake, each left dedicated converts who were determined to resist submission to the centralized power of the global Perfectives.

For months, now, Patrollers had become increasingly omnipresent. Fortunately for Imperfectives, though, they were easily avoided because they always stood out in crowds with the sleeves of their bright blue shirts sporting chevron insignias over Titan bulls eyes. However, their searches had become even more intrusive, lately. Their inspections had been tolerated prior to boarding airplanes because the threat of terrorism seemed to establish the need. Patrollers now, however, regularly demanded pat-downs before entering sporting events, malls, grocery stores, theatres, and hospitals. Even random searches on the streets were beginning, with attractive women complaining most about being subjected, arbitrarily, to the groping.

However, Imperfectives who had refused to receive a Titan implant, were particularly singled out for harsh treatment. For them, almost anything might be confiscated as a dangerous weapon, including belts, pens and even purses. Then, whenever a harmless item was seized, the offending Imperfective would be denied access, arrested, or even sent to a mental institution, depending on the Patroller's mood. The inconveniences and persecutions made life extremely difficult for Imperfectives. Still, many brave believers refused to surrender their faith to the popular will.

The increasingly notorious Latter Day Apostles were the resistors' role models, as they criss-crossed their territories, proving that some can get away with defying the Perfective Agenda.

For example, the lanky Canadian, Chippy, and his Jamaican comrade, Henry, had found welcoming audiences across North America after leaving the tragically impenetrable community of Semiazas California.

Booker and the resurrected Muslim convert, Qurban, had found that their effectiveness had been advanced by the gift of tongues. When they travelled across Africa and the Middle East, they were understood by every listener, regardless of his native language. They had become particularly effective at calming the envy and hatred in the hearts Islamic extremists.

Samir and Rodney, trekking across India and China, had introduced believers to deep Spiritual ecstasies, just with the touch of their hands. And Father Alonzo and Ricky Zipp spanned Europe and the Former Soviet Republics with such dynamic preaching that few doubted their prophetic warnings.

However, the affable Australian, Ozzy, was not as pleased. He had been asked to traverse his homeland and the nearby Pacific islands. For that responsibility, he had been happy to comply. However, Jin was becoming an increasingly uncooperative partner.

Ozzy remembered how John had warned that Jin would encounter the most difficulties atoning for his sins as a leading abortionist, before his conversion. Now, it seemed that the man's heart was not in his work, and Ozzy worried that if anyone might backslide, it could be Jin.

Still, whenever Ozzy took the lead, and Jin kept his mouth shut, they had been admirably successful at bringing people to God.

No pair, however, exceeded the effectiveness of Pedro and Worthington.

For over eight months, now, they had evangelized the Gospel across Central and South America. In each town, the unlikely partners made quite a spectacle, together, and the power of their words seemed to move people to conversion like never before. They had become very convincing and, consequently, very notorious.

Their infamy had necessitated, for them, a tactical variety of evasions from those who followed in hot pursuit. Consequently, the Perfective attempts to slow their evangelization efforts actually had caused the opposite effect. Their need to move along quickly had insured that they never lingered for long in a town. So, their territorial coverage had been astonishingly wide-ranging.

Because of the threat of arrest from pursuing Perfective Patrollers, their ministries tended to be hit and run affairs. Each time, they would sneak into a city and try to attract attention in areas that were congested with pedestrian traffic.

Typically, they began by pretending to be part of a circus act. Worthington – the intimidating, tattooed hulk – would lift little Pedro, who would stand on his palm, high above his head. Then, after Pedro attracted attention by shouting an invitation to hear an important message, Worthington would flip him into the air and catch the small performer like a circus monkey. The amusing theatrics always brought a smiling crowd toward them. Then, without delay, Pedro would spread the good news of the Gospel.

Even John would have been amazed to witness Pedro's transformation. The little man had always seemed too humble to make a lasting impression on anyone. Now, however, his fiery passion mesmerized audiences.

He assured them that Jesus Christ loved each of them so much that he was willing to submit to a torturous death to prove it. The message resonated with most audiences because they knew that these two evangelists were also risking their lives by professing their faith. This kind of preaching was no longer tolerated by the increasingly powerful Patrollers.

In town after town, Pedro warned listeners to resist the growing control of Titan and to disconnect from submission to global governance. He predicted that very difficult times were approaching and that everyone should stockpile food and water to prepare for a retreat to a more simple and holy life. More importantly, he begged his audiences to repent of their sins, to pray ceaselessly,[30] and to spread God's love. Ultimately, he assured them, the trials of this life are nothing compared to the glorious eternity God will share.

Typically, Pedro would next amaze the audience with a healing, proving that Jesus Christ is truly the greatest physician. Then, as quickly as they had appeared on the scene, the Latter Day Apostles would disappear into the crowd, before Patrollers could catch them.

It was a pattern that had worked brilliantly … until they reached Lima, Peru.

A SHROUD OF SILENCE blanketed the prison. Pedro rose from his chair and inspected the pockets of his primary interrogator. Then he found the keys he wanted.

When he got to the cell door, he reached through the bars and fumbled with the lock until the bolt slid open.

"Worthington," he whispered as he stepped into the hall, "where are you?"

Pedro tread softly, forging ahead even though the shadowed creepy calm disturbed him. He knew that the prison had been emptied of inmates before his arrival. In fact, Thas had granted pardon to any prisoner, anywhere, who would prove his value as a Patroller. So, here, as far as the holy pair had been able to discern, they were the only inmates.

Lopez shuffled from cell to cell, believing that Worthington had to be nearby. His interrogators had deliberately tortured the big man within Pedro's hearing range, probably to instill greater fear. So, before the Darkness, Pedro had heard the Patrollers angrily demanding, "Who is God's son?"

Worthington defied them by refusing to say what they wanted. "Jesus!" he'd answer, and then Pedro would hear growls of pain from the tortures. Later, Pedro only heard soft moaning, in response.

"*Amigo,*" the Honduran whispered again, "I have the key. We were saved by the Dark…"

Then he saw him.

Pedro fumbled to unlock the door, flung it open and rushed into the cell. Inside, Worthington was slumped over, tied to a chair, and his sack-covered head was submerged in a bucket of water. Around him, his torturers lay, dead.

Pedro snatched his head out of the water and ripped the bag off, but Worthington's condition was obvious. Gazing upon the bald, flame-tattooed head, the little Honduran tried to understand the point of such senseless cruelty. However, it only confirmed for him that evil truly exists in the world and must be confronted.

Pedro breathed a long sigh, dropped to the floor, and prayed, sitting next to his unlikely friend and partner.

"Oh Lord, you are the Great Miracle Worker. You have the power to heal, the power to raise from the dead. This good man has more work to do, here on earth. We need him, if we are to complete Your mission. So, if it is Your will, Lord, I will be Your instrument of resurrection. Please, Lord, tell me what You want because I only desire to accomplish Your will."

Pedro waited for an answer, but none came. His body was numb from all that he had experienced over the past three days. Initially, he had emerged into the light with renewed Spiritual confidence. However, this tragedy was another major blow to his addled mind.

As he looked around the room, he saw that a video camera had been set up to tape the tortures. That explained why Pedro had heard the interrogators taunting: "Smile for Highest Holiness." It seemed just one more confirmation that the man who called himself Pope Jesus II was every bit as evil as he seemed.

Pedro continued to wait for God's answer, but his exhaustion was catching up with him. He slowly slumped over until his cheek rested on the cold, concrete floor. Then he descended into a deep slumber.

No eye has seen,
no ear has heard,
no mind has conceived
what God has prepared
for those who love Him.
1 Corinthians 2:9

Chapter 4
Paradise
Eternity

W HEN PEDRO AWOKE, he lifted his cheek from the cold, stone ledge. His drowsiness suddenly disappeared, however, when he sensed danger. He quickly sat up and slid back, away from the edge of the roaring precipice.

Pedro rose to his feet and marveled at the awesome world around him.

Almost within reach, tumultuous waters raged over jagged rocks before plunging off a towering cliff. Wide eyed, Pedro leaned over the edge and gazed into the misty abyss, but for only a second. Then he hopped a step back, for a safer view of the dazzling panorama.

The chubby, little man's heart pounded when he surveyed the turquoise pond, below him, that shimmered as it welcomed the torrential waterfall. The lake stretched to the base of verdant foothills that rolled and climbed toward granite cliffs. There, a stone mountain rose into snow-covered peaks that seemed to poke at cotton ball clouds floating in a bold blue sky.

Closer, but across the roaring rapids, Pedro saw large, colorful fruit accenting a lush green forest and he reached out to touch flowers, nearby, that seemed to explode with color, like fireworks. Their spectrum of colors was like none he had ever before seen and they appeared to be constantly changing in hue, saturation and brightness.

Those sights amazed him, but his other senses also were overwhelmed.

When Pedro touched a shimmering blossom, he experienced more than its soft texture. He felt its beautiful life, and perceived its joy at giving him pleasure. His eyes widened and his smile broadened from the splendor of its life. Then he sniffed the flower's fragrance and nearly swooned from its intoxicating range of aromas.

Around him, the raging waters were not just roaring. He listened more closely to its comforting rumble and detected a tune that seemed natural but beautifully musical – almost symphonic.

The amused apostle laughed without restraint, celebrating the pleasure of his exquisite environment. But when he wandered into the nearby flowers, Pedro quickly quieted.

There, in the distance, just beyond the glistening undergrowth, he glimpsed a wolf and then slipped behind the broad trunk of a towering tree and observed. The predator appeared to be focused on prey and, indeed, a small lamb soon came into view.

Pedro wanted to shout, hoping the disruption might save the sheep. But he also knew that the wolf might turn on him, instead.

Closer and closer, the silent predator waded through the tall, golden grass.

He prepared to pounce.

Pedro had to act.

"Run! Run!" he screamed.

The sheep and the wolf turned his way, but did not seem to care. Then the wolf sidled up to the lamb and began licking its soft, woolen fleece, as if to groom him.[31]

Pedro flinched when he heard a loud, baritone laugh. He recognized it immediately and jerked around to witness his friend, emerging from the rapids.

"You're all heart, Pedro."

"Worthington!" Pedro could not believe what he saw. "You look … great!"

Indeed, the big man's weathered face had been transformed: the tattoos across his bald head were gone, and even his scars and wrinkles had vanished. He appeared younger, fitter, healthier and happier, and his face radiated confident joy.

As Worthington emerged from the depths of the roaring waters, his white, silky clothes seemed to dry, immediately. "That's what we love about you, brother."

"We?"

"Here, everything is 'we,' because nothing is without God."

Pedro offered a handshake, but Worthington accepted with a bear hug.

"This is amazing!" Pedro marveled. "Am I dead?"

"No, you still have important work left."

"Then, why am I here."

"To make a decision."

"About what?"

"You'll see. I have a lot to show you but not much time. You ready for this?"

The little man began to nod but, before he could finish, Worthington grabbed him by the shirt and hurled him off the cliff.

> And it was given to him to make war with the saints
> and to overcome them; and authority over every tribe
> and people and tongue and nation was given to him.
> Revelation 13:7

Chapter 5
Northern Russia
The day before the Darkness

THE PLUNGE was unlike anything Pedro had ever experienced; exhilarating but without fear. He and Worthington hit the surface of the water, but immediately found themselves falling through dark arctic air, until a mound of snow broke their fall. As Pedro tumbled down the snow bank, he could not control his laughter. Then, finally at rest near railroad tracks, the small man examined himself for injuries.

"I feel dirty," he complained. "Ooooh."

"We're not in Paradise, anymore."

"Then where?" Pedro asked as he hugged himself to resist the cold.

"A valley in the Khrebet Mountains ... Siberia."

"Why here?"

"Because it's one of the coldest places on the planet." Worthington rose, brushed himself off, and led his partner down the railroad tracks. "Come on, I want you to see what was happening just before the Darkness arrived."

Silently, they walked through a dark, barren landscape, lit only by the full moon on reflective snow. Finally, Pedro asked, "Where are we going?"

"Soon, you'll understand."

Pedro trudged through the snow a while longer before adding, "I'm really glad to see you, Worthington. Man, when I found you in that prison cell..." Then, the little friend grinned as he offered a more amusing take on the story. "I thought: *Thanks amigo! Now, how am I gonna carry your big butt outa here to bury you?*"

"Wait," the big man warned, "here it comes. Hide over here." He grabbed his friend's arm and pulled him behind nearby shrubbery. "It'll slow before it hits that curve."

A seemingly endless train approached and began to rumble past them. Then, after watching for a while, Worthington suddenly shouted, "Lets go! Stay close," and bolted toward the slow moving caboose.

Adrenaline rushed through Pedro's veins, propelling him toward the train as fast as his little legs could carry him. When he reached the last car, Worthington was dangling from the back. Then he reached down and pulled his partner on board.

Their train continued to rumble along the tracks as they clutched whatever would provide support, and shivered in the bitter, wintry wind.

Ten minutes later, the rail car slowed and Worthington said, "Come on," as he jumped off, rolling into the snow. Pedro followed his lead, and then trailed him to the moon-shadowed side of a large, dense bush, where they squatted in hiding.

"Watch," Worthington instructed.

Eight men with handguns emerged from one of the railcars and began unlocking the side doors of dozens of cattle cars. Pedro knew they had to be Patrollers – the only ones, these days, who were allowed to have guns. Then the men began sliding the doors open.

Inside the shadowed railcars, Pedro saw what looked like thousands of men, women and children – many without coats or even shoes – huddling against the cold.

The Patrollers began shouting, "*Kazhdyy iz! Kazhdyy iz!*"

Men seemed to understand the orders. They jumped out of the cattle cars and women began handing crying children down to them.

"Who are they?"

"Those who witness the Word of God."[32]

"The Perfectives are doing this?"

"Yes, they are masters of efficiency. They have no patience for concentration camps or even gas chambers. Instead, they simply transport their enemies into the wilderness and let them freeze."

"Why do they see us as enemies?"

"Because evil's greatest threat is a person of faith. They are Satan's soldiers, we are God's."

Pedro lowered his head in prayer as he listened to the anguished cries of women and children.

Worthington continued, "Few of them will survive the Darkness. But, for those who do, they won't have ignorance as an excuse again."

Pedro's head popped up when a prisoner began shouting, in English. "In the name of Jesus Christ, I command you to stop!"

"Look!" Pedro nudged Worthington and pointed at the man who was bravely defying the Perfective Patrollers. Standing at the door of his railcar, Ricky Zipp radiated authority. Pedro could see that he had completely transformed from the weak and addicted person he once was.

"I do not fear for my life, but I am concerned for your souls, if you do this. Do not commit yourselves to an eternity in…"

Suddenly, a gunshot echoed through the canyon, a Patroller lowered his gun, and Ricky dropped to the floor of the cattle car.

Pedro and Worthington then heard someone say, "Ricky!"

In the railcar, out of the shadows, a man emerged. He knelt beside Ricky and attempted to inspect the wound in his chest.

"It's Father Alonzo," Pedro whispered.

Then the little man's heart raced when Worthington stood up and began to yell, "Father, there's nothing more you can do. Come with us."

Pedro could not believe that his partner had acted so recklessly. He felt certain that their lives were now in danger. But, as he watched, nobody except Father Alonzo seemed to hear.

The priest looked up but, before he hopped out of the railcar, he gave a final blessing to Ricky.

§§§

THE UNLIKELY TRIO shuffled along the snow-covered tracks in the mountain-fringed valley. In the past, Worthington had always deferred to the priest. This time, however, he became their guide, with Alonzo's approval, because the cleric realized that their new leader no longer occupied his mortal form.

Worthington warned them that time was running out for repentance and that those with lukewarm indifference would soon be overwhelmed by evil. He stressed that Pedro and Alonzo would soon learn their crucial roles in the final conversion of souls.

"Why us?" Father asked.

"Except for you two," Worthington responded, "the Latter Day Apostles are all dead, now."

Pedro gasped.

"That is why God's merciful patience has expired… why the Darkness is necessary. The Three Days of Darkness will shake up the world… provide a final warning."

"What about John?"

"He is safe, for now." Worthington said, "But Patrollers have been rounding up people of faith. In New Zealand, they killed Chippy. They captured Jin and he gave up everything he knew."

"Torture?" Father asked.

"No."

"But he's dead?"

"He couldn't live with his betrayal. He hung himself in prison."[33]

"Worthington," Pedro begged, "we need you back here. Please stay to help us."

"That is a decision you will have to make."

"What do you mean?"

"I told you in Paradise. God allowed you to witness it in order to make a wiser decision."

Pedro's face brightened. "Father, you wouldn't believe Paradise. It is the most amazing…"

Worthington interrupted, "Still, you saw nothing compared to the awesome presence of Almighty God."

The priest silently walked with them and listened.

"So, what decision?" Pedro asked.

"Decide whether I stay here with you, or remain in Paradise."

"No, I want you to decide."

"That's not what God wants."

"Well, what do you want?"

Worthington said, "I want only for God's will to be done, and God wants you to decide."

Pedro remembered the wonders of Paradise and realized that it must have been a great sacrifice for Worthington to come back to these horrors even for this short period of time. Slowly, as they continued trudging through the snow, he accepted that he could not snatch his holy friend out of heaven to send him back to this hell on earth. Worthington had earned his eternal bliss.

Father Alonzo asked, "You mentioned our roles in the conversion of souls…"

"Find John," Worthington stressed. "He has very important information for you."

Pedro begged. "Why don't you tell us?"

The big man stopped, turned and asked, "After twenty centuries, why do you think John – the Lord's Beloved Apostle – chose to reveal himself at Holy Sacrifice Monastery?"

They responded in unison: "Sister Clarita?"

Worthington offered a sad smile, turned and continued walking.

As they approached a mountain tunnel, Pedro asked, "Worthington, when will Jesus Christ return?"

"Only the Father knows."[34] Then, sensing their frustration, he added, "Immediately after the distress of those days the sun will be darkened, and the moon will not give its light; the stars will fall from the sky, and the heavenly bodies will be shaken."[35]

Pedro said, "Yes, the Darkness."

Worthington continued, "When you see all these things, you know that it is near, right at the door."[36]

The two students nodded their understanding.

Then, standing near the entrance of the dark tunnel, the big man asked Pedro, "Now, what's your decision?"

"*Amigo*...." He shook his head. "Selfishly, I want you to stay with me. But I can't do that to you. I love you too much to make you come back."

For the first time since they left Paradise, Worthington's smile reflected joy and peace. "We thought so."

Father Alonzo extended his hand and said, "We were blessed to know you."

As Worthington returned the handshake, he responded, "Some day you will realize that you were *my* blessing."

Then, the big man turned to the tunnel and led them into the darkness of slumber.

I invite you, little children,
to become peace where there is no peace
and light where there is darkness…
The Queen of Peace,
Our Lady of Medjugorje[37]

Chapter 6
Miguel Castro Castro Prison
Lima, Peru
July 13

FROM THE DARKNESS OF SLUMBER Pedro raised his cheek off the cold, concrete floor. As he slowly lifted his head, he frowned at the dead interrogators around him and remembered the evil that they had done to his friend. Still, his mind could not release the weird but realistic dream he had just experienced.

Then he noticed someone more familiar.

"Father!"

He jumped up, rushed across the cell and knelt beside Father Alonzo.

"Father, are you okay?" he said as he jostled the priest. "Father?"

Alonzo began reviving. He took a deep breath and then opened his eyes.

"Where are we?" he asked.

"In prison … Lima, Peru. This is where Worthington and I were interrogated. This is where they killed him."

"Are we safe?"

"I think they all died in the Darkness."

The priest sat up and noticed that the cell door was open. "Let's get out of here."

"We gotta bury Worthington, first."

Pedro turned to the chair where the big man had died.

"Where'd he go? They had him tied to that chair. I fell asleep on the floor next to him."

Father Alonzo thought for a moment and then offered, "You

know, there have been instances of saints being preserved into the next life."

"They didn't die?"

"Right. Scripture says that Enoch, for example, was translated into heaven so that he would not see death.[38] Elijah was greeted by a chariot of fire and brought there by a whirlwind.[39] Blessed Mother also experienced a corporeal assumption into heaven."[40]

"Maybe God took him."

The priest looked around at the instruments of torture. "Let's get out of here. This place is disturbing."

Pedro removed a cluster of keys from the belt of one of the dead interrogators and then followed the priest down the hall.

"Pedro, did I ever tell you about the first time I met Worthington?"

"No, Father."

"It was in a place a lot like this. I was walking past his cell and he was just sitting on his bed, holding a coffee cup."

"Yeah."

"I shouldn't have stopped, but that hateful glare caught my eye. Anyway, I guess he didn't like that I noticed him. So, he splashed his cup all over me."

"Coffee?"

"No. Urine."

Pedro hooted as he unlocked a door that led out of the building.

"Hey, it wasn't *that* funny."

When the diminutive partner swung open the door, however, the laughing stopped.

The two men walked out into the prison recreation yard, perplexed at what they saw. Before them was a fresh mound of sandy soil.

Pedro said, "It looks like a…"

"Yeah."

The two men circled the mound and then read what had been fingered in the sand: a "W" under a Cross. Pedro grinned, remembering his complaint to the big guy about finding his body: *Thanks amigo! Now, how am I gonna carry your big butt outa here to bury you?*

The last of the Latter Day Apostles raised their gaze to the awesome red Cross in the sky, and found comfort from it. Their friend's Spiritual life had begun in prison, and his physical life had ended in one. However, Pedro felt joyful that he had allowed his friend to stay in Paradise and he laughed out loud when he saw, written in the sand, "Thanks *amigo*".

The pair realized that they were not there to mourn a death, but to celebrate a homecoming.

Then, a beautiful breeze blew through the prison yard, and took the message with it.

**If you want to get rich,
start a religion.**
L. Ron Hubbard
Founder of Scientology

Chapter 7
Archbasilica of St. John Lateran
Rome, Italy
July 15

BROTHER DANIEL MITCHUM knew he was lucky to be alive. During the Three Days of Darkness, he accepted the truth of how misguided he had been, promoting a gospel of envy and resentment. He continued to harbor a hangover from his disturbing Illumination of Conscience.[41]

Still, his strength – and weakness – was a pliable personality, and wisdom had not yet become his priority.

As Mitchum adjusted himself on the concrete bench in the shadows of St. John Lateran, he studied the Perfective Patrollers who stood guard at the towering, bronze doors of the archbasilica. They appeared untrained, out of shape and unshaven. Uniform blue shirts were their only indication of authority.

Pretty pathetic police force, he thought. But Mitchum realized that their inadequate professionalism was offset by abundant fanaticism.

In fact, the Patroller who had retrieved Mitchum from his home yesterday had acted equally unprofessional. With thuggish insistence, he simply demanded that the popular preacher pack whatever he needed. "Dr. Thas wants to see you in Rome."

"Are you kidding? Airlines won't be flying for ... who knows how long?"

"His private jet is waiting."

The bulky goon did not appear to be willing to accept a polite refusal. So, Mitchum added one more incredible episode to an already amazing string of events.

Now, groggy from the unexpected 5,000 mile journey, he could do little more than anxiously sit, while waiting for a mysterious command performance before the mercurial Evan Thas.

So, Mitchum passed the time nervously monitoring his trademark appearance. With the back of a hand, he dusted his white suit, removing any speck that might offend a critical eye. He licked a finger and wiped away a scuff on his shiny, white shoe. He tightened the knot on his thin, white tie and adjusted the tuck of his matching shirt. Finally, Mitchum adjusted the *pièce de résistance*: his lapel's bright, red carnation. It was a synergistic ensemble – presenting an impression more dazzling than the sum of its parts, more credible than the content of his character. With this look, he had become known to struggling masses as "The Great White Hope."

The preacher gazed up, over the grassy lawn, marveling at the enormous ruby Cross that continued to loom over the earth. Then, as his eyes lowered, he watched Patrollers who had been mobilized to collect and dispose of corpses.

Zealots, he thought. At first he wondered how so many sleazy Patrollers had managed to survive the Three Days of Darkness. Fanatical loyalty to Dr. Thas appeared to be their only quality.[42] But, since the Darkness, he had learned to withhold judging others. "Maybe they're not so bad," he mumbled. "They're just followers."

Perhaps that was why Evan Thas had been able to mobilize his forces so quickly in order to deal with the global tragedy. It was almost as if he had been ready for it. Just hours after the light returned, XBC's global networks – both radio and television – were broadcasting again. They had become the only source of news.

For Mitchum, the dramatic rise of Evan Thas, the Three Days of Darkness and the ever-looming Cross were almost too much to comprehend. However, as he soaked in Rome's warm sunlight, Mitchum could not help but marinate himself with a sauce of self-congratulation for his own amazing history.

In only ten years, the rabble-rousing firebrand had risen from obscurity to national acclaim as a powerful preacher of a very harsh gospel. He professed that his meteoric career had been miraculous and that his growing popularity was proof of God's approval.

However, he was wrong on both counts.

A decade ago, Mitchum was an obscure taxi driver in Atlanta. He had been one of the only white men employed at the company and, from that experience, developed a compassion for the travails of his African-American co-workers. It was that ability to empathize with the downtrodden that would become one of the two keys to his future success. In fact, empathy was the virtue that saved his life during the Darkness.

One scorching, Atlanta afternoon, Mitchum picked up a dapper passenger at the airport. He did not recognize his famous rider as he loaded the polite, black man's suitcase in the trunk. At first, the only detail that caught his eye was that the passenger's gray suit seemed to match the color of his hair. But as he pulled away and headed to the Interstate, Mitchum repeatedly looked in the rearview mirror, nagged by the suspicion that the man might be famous.

Suddenly, a dark sedan swerved to pass them. Mitchum glared angrily at the aggressive driver but the car's windows were too dark to see through. Then the back window opened and a pistol appeared in the shadows.

The nightmare began.

In the corner of his eye, Mitchum watched flashes popping from the barrel.

Shattered glass rattled his ears.

Lead smashed against steel and anything else in its path.

Mitchum slammed on the brakes, throwing the car into an uncontrolled spin across lanes of the highway.

Oncoming vehicles blared their horns, skidding and swerving to avoid collision.

When the taxi finally spun to a stop in the grassy median, Mitchum's heart was pounding. He examined himself to find that his only injury was from a bullet that had grazed his forearm.

Then he heard the passenger, choking on his own blood.

Daniel jumped out of the car and swung open the back door. The man was slumped over, struggling to breathe. Blood gushed from his neck. Mitchum feared that removing the old man might add to his injury, but quickly decided that he would suffocate if something wasn't done. So he awkwardly cradled the bloody body, maneuvered it through the door and laid it out, on the grass.

Then the gurgling stopped.

Daniel screamed his anguish, realizing that moving the man might have killed him. Then he recognized the famous face. He pulled the bloody body close, sobbing that he failed to save an American icon, a true hero of the non-violent, civil rights movement.

The distraught taxi driver did not notice when a stopped motorist snapped a picture at the crescendo of his agony. That jarring image, however, would forever scar the minds of those who viewed it on the covers of magazines and newspapers, around the world.

Soon, Mitchum was swept into a whirlwind tour of talk shows and photo sessions. So, he mustered every ounce of his limited business acumen, hired an agent and then a publicist. Within a year he had sold the rights to his story for a book and a major motion picture. Eventually, he produced two more books, a DVD documentary, and countless magazine articles on the tragedy.

It was not long, however, before the empathetic opportunist realized that preaching the gospel according to Daniel would become his most enduring and profitable venture. With minimal theological training, and even less prayerful meditation, he parlayed his popularity into a mega-church. Then, when that booming venture seemed too small for his growing ambitions, he went national with his own television show on XBC News.

Behind the scenes, Evan Thas nurtured his rise with generous publicity. Though they had never met, personally, Evan admired the preacher's ability to stir up controversy and wanted to channel and control that talent. So, with each of his rants, Daniel soon learned that it would be promoted in proportion to its ability to offend or outrage. The good student quickly grasped the network's unspoken golden rule: Passions precede profits.

As a modern-day Pied Piper, the tune of Mitchum's sermons had vaguely resonated with Christian notes. But his lyrics encouraged resentment, blame, envy, and violence.

His sermons always included the chant, "Share the wealth," to which his audience never failed to respond, "or lose your health!" For that reason, he had developed a particularly strong following among prisoners, anarchists and various types of anti-capitalists and, whenever he toured the nation, vandalism and clashes with the police inevitably followed in his wake.

Moderate American politicians had dismissed Mitchum, in the beginning, as a harmless, publicity-seeking blowhard. Now, however, he was too big to ignore. The master-opportunist had parlayed a tragic chance encounter into a powerful, new human rights movement.

That talent for opportunism was the second key to his success. It was also the vice that nearly cost him his life during the Darkness.

"Okay, he's ready to see you," a scruffy Patroller shouted from the steps of the church.

Mitchum rose from his bench and trotted up the marble steps, between two Corinthian columns. As he approached, four Patrollers struggled to open the towering bronze doors that had once provided entrance to the ancient Roman Curia in the Imperial Forum.

Mitchum knew that if Dr. Thas had intended to intimidate him, the plan worked. Passing through the doorway that rose six times Mitchum's height, the grandeur of the dazzling nave assaulted his senses. He eyed the shining inlaid marble floor that stretched far into the distance. Overhead, an ornate coffered ceiling seized his attention with its intricate carvings and shimmering, golden accents.

Directed by a Patroller, Mitchum proceeded ahead, alone, through the seemingly empty building. As he listened to his own footsteps, echoing in the cavernous cathedral, he was awed by the beauty. His eyes scanned intricate mosaics of Biblical stories, marble columns supporting amazing arches, and an expanse of detailed craftsmanship that glorifies God as no other place he had ever seen.

Proceeding forward, he noticed that giant, marble statues of the apostles flanked his long journey toward the altar. The image of St. Bartholomew was particularly disturbing, to him, representing the saint's gruesome martyrdom. Mitchum paused to examine the large knife that the saint held along with a sheet of his own skin.

Soon, Mitchum realized that he was not alone. Ahead, he saw Evan Thas, decked out in full papal regalia and sitting on the papal throne of the archbasilica. At his right hand, Faridah Shabaan reclined in a similarly ornate throne, with coordinating vestments.

Mitchum stopped when he had approached as far as he believed appropriate. Then he waited to be recognized.

Silently, the pair continued staring into the distance as if they had not noticed him.

The normally assertive preacher was speechless for the first time in his life. To him, Thas looked buffoonish, almost like a boy, costumed as a Halloween pope. Precariously teetering on Evan's head was the papal tiara, a shimmering, gold, triple crown – adorned with rubies, emeralds and sapphires. It appeared far too heavy for Evan's slight build and the patch over his right eye seemed wildly out of place, especially with its black-and-white bulls eye, representing the mark of Titan.[43]

Finally, Mitchum blurted out, "Dr. Thas, I am…"

"No, no," Faridah interrupted.

Again, Mitchum stood silently as they continued to stare into the distance. Moments slipped by while he observed that Evan's sweaty face was losing its makeup, revealing burn-scars that looked worse than they appeared on TV. In shocking contrast, however, the increasingly famous face of Faridah Shabaan was even more beautiful, in person.

Then Mitchum regained his nerve. "I don't know what to say."

Faridah offered, "If you wish to speak with Pope Jesus II, you must address him properly."

Seconds ticked away until Mitchum asked, "How?"

She answered, "Highest Holiness."[44]

Mitchum breathed deeply and then offered, "Highest Holiness, I am Daniel Mitchum…. I was told that you want to see me."

"Yes, Brother Daniel," Thas responded without delay. "I desire to bless you beyond your ability to imagine."

"Uhhh … okay," Mitchum fumbled a response.

Again, silence.

"Uhhh," Mitchum finally asked, "is there something you want me to do for you?"

Thas did not hesitate. "You will be my prophet."[45]

Prophet? Mitchum mused. *Wow! This guy really has flipped out!* His jaw clamped down as he struggled to restrain a laugh and his cheeks tightened to prevent even the slightest smile. After all, Brother Daniel had heard alarming tales of Evan's ruthless response to ridicule.

Suddenly, the pretend-pontiff did not look so clownish. His one blue eye tightened and focused on his subject. With one wrong move, Mitchum imagined that he might share the fate of St. Bartholomew.

"So," Thas prodded, "do you accept?"

The wary opportunist answered: "Absolutely, Highest Holiness!"

Thas snapped his fingers and two bulky guards suddenly emerged from behind broad columns. Without a word of explanation, they grabbed Mitchum by the shoulders and hustled him out. Then they tossed him into the back of an unmarked van, sped across town, and delivered him to Rome's XBC News studio.

Of all tyrannies,
a tyranny exercised for the good of its victims
may be the most oppressive.
C. S. Lewis

Chapter 8
Rail line to France
July 15

FROM COLOGNE, the disguised medi-vac railcar rumbled southwest, shortly after John Eben Malek had concluded respectful funerals for five heroic martyrs.[46] John regretted that Pope Innocent had disregarded his last scroll that had warned the pontiff to remain in Rome.[47] However, even the Beloved Apostle would obey the wishes of the Vicar of Christ.

Now, John had risen to that rank, becoming Pope Peter II,[48] the true pontiff. It was a great honor for him to finally lead Christ's Church on earth, but that title had plunged him into more deeply dangerous waters.

So, he knew not to linger in the German region of Westphalia,[49] realizing that he could not afford to remain a stationary target, there. More than anyone, John understood the wicked resourcefulness of Evan Thas and his determination to annihilate the last vestiges of God's one, holy, catholic and apostolic Church.[50]

So, John and Henri Blanc traveled together, alone, not wishing to place the lives of others in jeopardy. They had been assisted on this journey by devout Christians who had not only survived the Three Days of Darkness but had been invigorated by the knowledge that almighty God had illuminated their consciences with His presence. Now, believers here and around the world understood the power of prayer and the joyful peace and Spiritual prosperity that awaits anyone who accepts it … and keeps it.

Early on, the exhausted Blanc had slept briefly while John dictated their route to the train's engineer. Now, he had roused himself awake but still felt the numbness of three sleepless days. In prayerful silence, the holy pair sat on the bunk beds that Pope Innocent and four cardinals had occupied, shortly before their deaths.[51]

Eventually, Blanc asked the question that would not leave his mind: "Why me, Holy Father?"

John nodded, "It is impossible to teach a man that which he thinks he knows."[52]

The answer did not make sense to Blanc, so he let the pope continue.

"Henri, even with all your brilliant accomplishments, still, you humbly long to learn."

The French priest added, "So, why do you think I will become this ... this so-called Great Monarch?"[53]

"Think?" John asked, almost smiling.

Blanc scratched his head.

"Alright," John sighed. "I suppose some secrets may now be revealed."

Blanc leaned forward and listened.

"Recent events should not be surprising," John said. "These are the times that have been foretold. It is only surprising that many are surprised."

Then John described a detailed summary of accurate prophecies from sacred Scriptures and holy saints over that past two thousand years.[54] They foretold how evil would proliferate, near the end of the Age, in ways that could not have been possible without the rise of modern technologies. Indeed, he maintained, the destructive flames of the seven cardinal sins had been stoked by many 20th century inventions.[55] The Internet, for example, had burdened many souls with lust, provided a means of communicating and coordinating terrorist acts, and popularized false beliefs. Movies and television shows encouraged pride, greed and boasting. Popular magazines flaunted promiscuity and materialism, and bestselling books contained enticing tales of spiritual deceptions, amusing violence and sexual perversions. News sources encouraged some viewers to envy and others to develop the sense of hopelessness that is known as acedia. Even children had been lured into sloth as video games, television shows and other forms of entertainment deadened their healthy ambitions.[56]

John described prophecies that predicted natural disasters including the extreme earthquakes, tsunamis and volcanic eruptions that had been the focus of many recent headlines. He pointed out that, long before "global warming" was feared, prophecies predicted that the seasons would become unpredictable in the latter days.[57]

He explained how the rise of militantly atheistic communism, extreme secularism and the raging wars of the last century had been foretold. Then he talked about the prophecies regarding drug addiction and violence, widespread abortions and the breakup of the family. Even the global economic collapse and crippling Church scandals had been predicted.

All were the tainted fruits, not just of Satan's focused fury over the past century but, more importantly, of mankind's choice to believe Satan's lies and to follow his leadership.

"You should realize," John said, "that the general timeframe has been announced. Less than two weeks after the sixth and final apparition of Our Lady of Fatima, the October Revolution of 1917 ushered in communist control of the future Soviet Union, the world's most ruthlessly anti-theistic government. Our Lady had pleaded with the young Fatima visionaries to request prayers for the conversion of Russia[58] before it could 'spread its errors throughout the world ... raising up wars and persecutions against the Church.' However, the Red Dragon of communism[59] did, indeed, proliferate its errors, wars and persecutions throughout the 20th century, worse than at any time in history.

"Then, over a span of twelve weeks in 1981, three fortuitous events occurred. First, President Ronald Reagan – a staunch anticommunist – was nearly assassinated. He and the agent who protected him soon professed a belief that God had saved their lives for a greater purpose.[60]

"Next, roughly six weeks later, Pope John Paul II survived an assassination attempt on the anniversary of the first Fatima apparition. He was saved by unexpectedly leaning out of his vehicle to bless a pilgrim's Fatima card, just as the first shots were fired.

"Finally, after another six weeks, The Queen of Peace appeared and spoke to the young visionaries of Medjugorje in communist-run Yugoslavia. She eventually revealed that her appearances to them would be among her last."[61]

"But Soviet-style communism is dead. That threat has been eliminated."

John responded, "'Peace, peace' they say, when there is no peace."[62]

"So, you believe an aggressive Russia will revive?"

"The goal of Soviet communism was global control, established by any means necessary. Today, a number of groups share that ambition.[63] Only Evan Thas is capable of achieving it. You see, Henri, the century-long arc of evil, that began with the prophecies of Fatima, will end with the secrets of Medjugorje.[64] Inevitably, however, Blessed Mother's Immaculate Heart will triumph."[65]

"So," Henri interrupted, "why was the Darkness necessary?"

"Jesus Christ warned us, 'As the weeds are pulled up and burned in the fire, so it will be at the end of the age.'[66] God does not warn us to entertain Himself. He means what He says. So, how many warnings must He give before His patience wears out? I suggest to you that there are hundreds of warnings in sacred Scriptures, thousands of warnings from holy saints, and billions of personal warnings that He has placed on the consciences of His beloved children. Those who had irretrievably rejected God did not survive the shame that their consciences discovered in the Darkness. They had freely chosen to advance through life, alone, without God's protection. In the end, they learned that they are lost, without Him."

"So, all of us who are left," Blanc asked, "are destined for heaven?"

John shook his head. "Sadly, no. Our Lord also spoke of a farmer, sowing his seeds. For one reason or another, many of those seeds failed to bear fruit. Some others, however, rooted deeply in rich soil and produced a hundred-fold crop.[67] This is a lesson of life. The seed of faith must be protected and nurtured. Holy life is not grown by accident. It is not maintained without effort. In fact, in order to succeed to holiness, one must become a warrior: a Spiritual warrior. For our struggle is not against flesh and blood, but against the rulers, against the authorities, against the powers of this dark world and against the spiritual forces of evil in the heavenly realms.[68]

"Both before and after the Darkness, three types of Spiritual warriors exist. First, some put on the full armor of God, taking their stand each day against the devil's schemes. They draw protection from the truth and righteousness of the gospel of peace. Their faith shields them from the evil one and they wield the Word of God like a sword.[69] These warriors, you can trust with your life. They will live fearlessly, defending God and His people on earth with heroic virtue."

"And the others?" Father Blanc asked.

"Some Spiritual warriors are not fit for the battlefield. They imagine themselves ready, but live in ignorance, stupidly wandering into enemy traps, oblivious to the signs and warnings that are sent to protect them. With God's mercy, they were spared during the Darkness. This time, however, they live with the knowledge of the Truth and, with knowledge, comes responsibility.[70] Still, it is dangerous to rely on them in battle because most will flee at the first sign of opposition, just when you need them most."

Blanc nodded.

"Teach them, if you can. But beware of hollow words. Take them into your confidence only if assurances of faith are accompanied by holy works such as prayer, Scripture study, humble service, fasting, and the Sacraments. For a person is justified by what he does and not by faith alone."[71]

Henri asked, "And what about the third category.

John sighed. "Most of them are gone, now. So, they are few in number, but still powerfully evil. They will influence those who can be convinced to embrace the ways of the world. Those recruits foolishly think they are battling for themselves but, in fact, become slaves in Satan's army. The ones who survived the Darkness are permanently and completely possessed by the evil ones. Because of that, they have no consciences to restrain their actions, making them immune from the deadly shame of the Illumination of Conscience."[72]

"Evan Thas is one?"

"Yes. However, with the demise of so many who had been drawn willingly to his evil leadership, Thas has been crippled. Now, he must work even harder to deceive the Spiritually gullible and ignorant warriors."

"So, why don't you just speak out? Publicly condemn him!" Blanc's anger rose. "Surely the world will accept that you are the rightfully elected pontiff. They will respect your leadership." Henri raised his eyes in exasperated prayer: "Dear Lord! This is your Beloved Apostle! Make people understand!"

John smiled. "The Great Monarch will do that."

Suddenly, a voice spoke out from a speaker in the railcar. "Holy Father? I'm sorry to disturb you."

John was surprised by the communication because he knew that their destination was at least three hours away. He pressed a button on the intercom. "Yes, Francois, go ahead."

In spite of the engineer's extensive, secret training, he spoke with an uncharacteristically nervous tone. "I ... uh ... don't believe we should continue to Avignon."

Blanc whispered, "Avignon? I thought Paris is the second stop on the papal evacuation route."

"Paris is still in flames,"[73] John answered. "Avignon will be safer."

Henri felt relieved to hear the news of the change because he knew that Paris had descended into riotous anarchy shortly before the Darkness.[74] The reports of vicious massacres, there, had reminded the priest of the horrors of the French Revolution.[75] For many, however, the increasing anarchy only improved the popularity of the wonder-worker, Evan Thas.[76] They reasoned that a firm but competent dictator might limit freedoms but, at least, would restore order and security. [77]

John spoke into the intercom, "What's happening? Why divert our course?"

"I was able to pick up XBC Radio News and ... uh ..."

"Go ahead," John prodded.

"Well, they said that ... that you are why God took vengeance on the world." He worked up his nerve to add, "They put a million dollar bounty on your head."

John sighed. "Alright. But we will continue as planned."

"That's not all, Holy Father. I just received a call on railway communications. The man asked a lot of suspicious questions."

"A railway official?"

"No, a Perfective Patroller. He said he's in charge of train routing on the line, now."

"Do you think he suspects ...?"

"Maybe. He wanted to know why we're moving without authorization."

"What did you tell him?"

"I lied. I said I have to get to Avignon to see my dying mother."

John contemplated how much attention he might draw by diverting course. Then he answered, "We'll continue to Avignon."

"Uh, Holy Father?"

The hesitant engineer's seemingly endless bad news provoked a frown from John. "Yes?"

"Should I confess that lie?"

"Certainly," John grinned. "Your sins are forgiven." Then he added, "Francois, you're a good man."

But Blanc was not amused. He asked, "Why do we have to worry about our safety? I don't understand. You said that the remaining evil ones are few in number."

John's smile slowly disappeared. "And powerfully evil," he added. Then his eyes locked in on Blanc's, emphasizing the importance of his warning. "For many, this will appear to be a time of peace.[78] However, there is nothing on earth more diabolical, more dangerous, more inevitable than the coming malevolence that will be propagated in the name of a god."[79]

The war ... made possible for us
the solution of a whole series of problems
that could never have been solved
in normal times.
Adolf Hitler

A CHUNKY LITTLE *NONNA* dusted Daniel Mitchum's forehead with a powder puff. Then she held up a small mirror and let him examine her work.

"A little more here," he advised, pointing at his shiny nose.

The Italian nodded and dabbed it twice.

Mitchum took the mirror but, this time, lingered to observe as he practiced his various facial expressions. He raised an eyebrow of suspicion, pursed his lips in disappointment, and then widened his eyes in shock.

Mitchum approved, "Okay," as he handed the mirror back to her.

The makeup lady set it on a table and removed Mitchum's disposable bib, tossing it into a nearby trash can. Then he rose out of his chair, straightened himself to performance height, and exercised his mouth with every possible movement.

From a nearby booth, a producer announced, "Three minutes."

Daniel closely examined his immaculate white suit for unwelcome lint. He adjusted the jacket, around the collar, and straightened his red carnation boutineer. Then the preacher rose to the podium for his most important sermon.

Standing tall, Mitchum cleared his throat and scanned the large cameras and darkened studio behind the bright lights.

"Do you need a teleprompter adjustment?" the unseen producer asked through a speaker.

"Uh, no," Daniel said as he pulled a copy of the script out of his coat pocket. "I read it a couple times. I'll be fine. I like the spontaneity of winging it."

The producer's tone was now sharp. "You're joking. Right?"

"Uh, no. I do my best work when I improvise."

Mitchum heard what sounded like muffled curses from the control room, but the microphone had been switched off. Then the producer's voice transmitted over the speaker again but, this time, in rapid-fire mode.

"You listen to me. You are not winging anything. Every word in that speech is calibrated for maximum efficiency. If it says 'The sky is green,' you say 'The sky is green.' I don't care what color you think it is. You're gonna read from the teleprompters exactly as Highest Holiness has written it ... and God help you if it doesn't sound sincere. XBC News is broadcasting to 184 countries with simultaneous translations in 62 languages." His tone became even more hostile. "Do you understand me? You read it exactly as written!"

With seconds ticking down to the live broadcast, Mitchum could not argue. "Okay ... okay." The producer's angry demand, however, had disoriented him. So, during the next few moments of uncomfortable silence, the star of the show massaged his battered ego by planning to get the producer fired. Mitchum also thought about how rudely those patrollers had hustled him over here. *They gotta go, too!* After all, if anyone was indispensable in successfully promoting the Perfective Agenda it was Mitchum, himself. Evan's scarred appearance limited his effectiveness as a spokesperson.[80] He needed someone more charming, convincing and attractive to convey his message, and Daniel saw himself as the perfect candidate. He lived for the attention he received from every crowd, camera or mirror.

Finally, the studio lights blinked and someone in the control room announced a countdown until the cameraman finished it, silently, with hand signals. When the cameraman pointed at Mitchum for the start of the broadcast, the preacher found that his voice had locked up. So, he swallowed hard, stared into one of the teleprompters and finally blurted out the words it scrolled.

"Peace on earth…. Good will toward men.[81] Blessed is he who comes in the name of the Lord."[82]

He cleared his throat. "I am Daniel Mitchum, prophetic oracle for Highest Holiness, Pope Jesus II, who offers you solemn assurances of peace and safety.[83] Highest Holiness has rendered judgment on the world and you have been judged sufficient. Now, accept his everlasting reign and receive his blessings."

Mitchum corrected himself: "I mean, his *everlasting* blessings." Then he continued.

"Highest Holiness will point the way to the promised land that is within reach and we must follow his guidance in order to recreate that Paradise, that Perfect World.

"First, the remains of those who were judged insufficient must be collected and buried as quickly as possible. However, the leadership ranks in governments and even in the Legion of Babylon have been decimated. So, considering that this immense task addresses the disposal of more than two billion bodies, it is clear that no existing government has the resources to manage the global effort. Therefore, the supreme pontiff is placing the worldwide resources of his Church behind this humanitarian cause. Catholic churches, schools, hospitals, monasteries, and convents will be converted into disaster recovery outposts from where Perfective Patrollers will manage the worldwide disposal efforts in each locale.

"Second, Pope Jesus, as the Church's universal bishop,[84] hereby declares a moratorium on the administration of Sacraments because they would only distract from, and delay, a quick resolution to this current crisis.[85] This temporary measure has become necessary because the people have lost faith in a clergy that has discredited itself.[86] Their nuns rebel and their cardinals betray.[87] They are corrupt, every one. So, because the Catholic Clergy have been deemed unworthy to lead, Highest Holiness hereby appoints members of the Perfective Patrol to serve as both secular and religious leaders who will guide us to the Perfect World."

Mitchum was beginning to relax a bit and his tone became more confident. "Third, working together, for the greater good, you will be rewarded with generous incentives. Patrollers will recruit volunteers from the general population. Those volunteers will then scour their communities in order to locate and dispose of human remains in designated landfills. Then, whenever a property has been cleared of the dead, a Patroller will certify that the ownership of that property transfers to the person who accomplished the clearing. One small requirement exists, however. Property cannot transfer to anyone who refuses their Titan implant. After all, Highest Holiness cannot protect those who refuse his protection."

It was a bold plan, but Evan knew that disorganized governments around the world would find it hard to deny property to those who believed they had earned their property rights. Just as Evan had gained popularity with the violent redistribution of Church property, this transfer of wealth would be even further reaching, and more popular.

To listeners around the world, the Titan implant requirement seemed perfectly understandable and they greeted Mitchum's news with the enthusiasm of a gold rush. The concern over so many deaths quickly transformed into a celebration of new-found riches. Most people hurried to become Titanized and then claim their prizes.

It was widely perceived that, over the past year, Dr. Evan Thas had eased the world's tensions when he brought the viral pandemic somewhat under control. Even though the virus had recently wiped out the college of cardinals – the hierarchy of the Catholic Church – still, people were beginning to accept Evan's argument that God the Father had lashed out at those men only because they had opposed His son, Evan Thas.

"Fourth, and finally," Mitchum continued, "a new age of peace and prosperity is upon us, if only we remember that cooperation insures safety and defiance invites destruction."

Mitchum smiled broadly and the screen faded to black. He was pleased that he had apparently accomplished Evan's requirement: "Always give them a show that they will never forget."

However, Evan was even happier. He knew that the most watched broadcast in history had prompted every viewer to wonder, *Is he really the Messiah?*[88]

> ... the Church will go through ordeals
> that are beyond description.
> Pope Pius IX
> 19th Century

IRON WHEELS suddenly squealed as the disguised medi-vac train grinded to an abrupt stop. Hidden inside, the two stow-aways quickly braced themselves to prevent being thrown for-ward. Then John reached for the intercom button.

"What happened, Francois?"

"Holy Father," he shouted, "we must reverse course."

"Wait," John demanded. "If you do, it will surely draw more at-tention to us. What is wrong?"

"I can see the station, ahead. They must know you're on board. A mob is waiting." The train remained still, poised to reverse direc-tion. Francois added, "There's thousands ... no, tens of thousands."

John sighed, but his mind found peace. He reflected on the love he had felt for each of the holy apostles and how, one by one, they proved that even horrifying tortures cannot break the Christian Spirit. John, alone, had been preserved from martyrdom ... at least, until now.

"Your Holiness," Blanc urged, "there's a bounty on your life. Please, tell him to reverse course."

"They're running toward us," the engineer screamed into the in-tercom. "What do I do?"

John recalled those early years, mourning the deaths of so many holy Christians. He remembered how the beheading of John the Baptist stunned even Jesus. He thought about the crucifixions, beheadings and stonings that others had suffered with Christian dignity. He resolved to accept his fate, however God allowed it.

"Holy Father, if they surround the train we won't be able to escape without running over them. Please," Francois begged, "let me start moving!"

John shook his head and spoke into the intercom: "You have done your duty. Leave, now."

"No!" the engineer snapped back, angrily.

"Francois, there is no reason for you to die. They want only me. Go in peace."

The rumblings of the rabble outside grew louder. Fortunately, however, the crowd did not know which railcar John occupied.

The ancient apostle slowly rose from the bunk and pointed to the back of the car. "Those will be appropriate. Please bring them to me."

Blanc turned to a deceased cardinal's vestments that were hanging from a hook. He exhaled, loudly, and then obeyed.

As the mob grew more tumultuous, outside, Henri assisted John with all the reverence of preparing for high mass. Both of them knew the significance of choosing the cardinal's red robes: a declaration of willingness to die for the faith.[89]

When he was fully robed, John turned to Blanc and gripped both of his shoulders. Henri's face tightened as he struggled to maintain his composure, but his eyes began to well up and his shoulders trembled.

"Henri, if I fail to speak the truth, I betray it." Then John added, calmly, "The gates of hell shall not prevail."[90]

Blanc wished he could still believe those words.

"When I open the door," John directed, "escape quickly. They will be after me. Do not look back. The future of the Church is on your shoulders."

The priest sighed loudly.

"A few cardinals were too old or sick to attend the conclave. They, alone, have survived to elect a new pontiff. Find them and preserve the future of the Church."

Blanc now wept openly. But he nodded his obedience.

"Henri," John said as he reached out to raise the priest's chin. "Bold courage is paralyzing fear after humble prayer. Do not worry for me. I have longed for this day."

John raised two fingers and gently stroked them across Henri's forehead as he blessed him. Then, with a sense of the calm that only Christ can bring, he added, "Today, I shall be with my Lord in Paradise."

Abruptly, the ancient apostle turned, jerked a handle downward and slammed open the railcar's side door.

The deafening tumult jolted Blanc with an adrenaline rush that triggered his flight instincts. The priest dove out of the railcar, into the crowd, knocking down three men. But before they could respond, he was on his feet, again, bulldozing through the dense mob. With heightened focus on survival, Henri heard nothing, relying only on his sense of sight in order to escape. He shoved, bumped and clawed through the mob.

Soon, however, the wall of humanity closed in too tight. Henri's progress stopped, his frustration peaked, but his ears opened.

The roar was not from an angry mob. These people were cheering.

For the first time, Blanc raised his eyes to study their faces. They were smiling, applauding and some even cried tears of joy.

Blanc turned to observe the object of their adulation.

Standing in the open door of the rail car, Pope Peter II looked down upon the roaring crowd with stoic humility.

Henri was struck by the immovable Spirit within this great man and felt deep humiliation that he had fled from the defense of the Lord's apostle. Now, as the subject of cheering approval, John exhibited no hint of pride or self-congratulation. His face radiated only the same peaceful determination that it had shown moments earlier, when he was preparing to die.

Clearly, this throng had no confusion over good and evil. They knew that the awesome object that lingered over John's head was not the "t" of Titan. It was the Cross of Christ, and John was His Beloved Apostle.

Then, just as the throng began to quiet, someone shouted, *"Vive le pape!"* and the crowd unified, thunderously: *"Vive le pape! Vive le pape! Vive le pape!"*[91]

> Rome will lose the faith
> and become the seat of the Antichrist.[92]
> Our Lady of La Salette

Chapter 11
XBC News, Studio 2B
Rome, Italy
July 15

FROM THE STUDIO CONTROL ROOM, Evan and Faridah watched the video monitor as Mitchum finished his broadcast. All in all, he was not displeased with the performance.

However, she was not impressed. "I could have done better," Faridah complained.

Evan nodded. "Probably."

"You should have let me make the announcement."

"No. We don't want to overexpose ourselves."

She wasn't buying it. "You don't seem to be worried about overexposing yourself."

He spun his rolling studio chair toward her and took her hand. "Dearest mother," he said with a hint of sarcasm, "don't confuse visibility with power. Inevitably, blame will become our shield.[93] Every chess master needs pawns to sacrifice." His single blue eye stared deeply at her. "And when the game really kicks in, we won't be playing a board game, anymore. Then, we'll need warm bodies to toss to the lions." He patted her hand. "Trust me. You won't envy good Brother Mitchum's celebrity when…"

"Excuse me, Highest Holiness," a Patroller interrupted, holding a cell phone. "XCyst satellite surveillance has an alpha-level message."

Thas reached for the phone but found his papal vestments constrictive. With an angry huff, he said, "Wait!" Then he jerked the bulky pallium and chasuble over his head and threw them on the floor, revealing just jeans and a t-shirt, beneath.

Thas took the phone. "Yes. What is it?"

He listened for a moment and then directed, "Okay. Patch it through to me. Let me take a look."

Evan clicked on the speaker and watched the video. A few seconds later, the screen lit up with live video streaming. It showed a train and a crowd, at a train station.

"Tighten in on the guy in red," he ordered into the phone.

Faridah growled, "He's still alive!"

"Looks like he's speaking to the crowd." Evan asked the technician, "Can you isolate his voice?"

The man on the phone answered, "I'll try."

As a variety of garbled sounds emerged from the speaker, Evan asked, "Where is he?"

"Avignon."

Evan and Faridah watched the video screen closely as the man in red raised his hands and the tumultuous reception quickly quieted. They all waited silently to hear John's words. Then they waited some more.

"Dammit!" Evan growled. "Get the audio going."

"It's on," the technician answered. "He's not saying anything."

They observed as John stood quietly and seconds passed into minutes.

Finally, the unnatural silence broke when John shouted in French, "How did you spend that moment?"

His wise old eyes scanned the crowd. Then he continued, "Did you focus on me, imagining how I might solve your problems or bring you hope for the future?"

He shook his head. "I tell you, if you did not spend that moment with God, you wasted it."

Faridah offered a derisive snort.

Again, John paused until they joined him in prayerful silence. Then he continued. "We have been called to share in the holy sacrifice of the Lamb." He continued with a mysterious verse. "The snorting of the enemy's horses is heard from Dan; at the neighing of their stallions the whole land trembles. They have come to devour the land and everything in it.[94] Anyone destined for captivity goes into captivity. Anyone destined to be slain by the sword shall be slain by the sword. Such is the faithful endurance of the holy ones."[95]

Evan smiled as he comprehended that John had made the mistake of puncturing the crowd's ballooning enthusiasm.

John observed, "You enthusiastically welcomed me because I am a novelty."

The audience listened closely.

"But I am only a man…. I cannot solve your problems…. I have nothing to offer you."

Thas laughed, sensing that the crowd's elation would now turn to disappointment, maybe even to violence.

"I have nothing to offer you…" John repeated, "except the Gospel of our Lord and Savior, Jesus Christ." A contented smile transformed the apostle's face. "And with that," he shouted, "I have everything to offer you!"

The crowd erupted with cheers.

"Turn it down," Thas snapped to the technician on the phone. "You don't need to blast me!"

John raised his hands, again, and quieted them. "Every moment passes, but some are more important than others. In just one fleeting moment, you may decide to love … or to hate. You may choose to conceive life … or to kill it. You may select the path to heaven … or hell. Yes, every moment passes, but some are more important than others."

John waited until anticipation silenced everyone. Then he shouted, "This is your moment!"

Again, they screamed their approval and support, waving their hands in the air and stretching them up toward heaven.

"Rejoice!" he continued. "For you have arrived at the great and glorious mission of your lives!"

John nodded his approval of their heartfelt enthusiasm.

He continued as their cheers escalated. "Blessed are you who have been chosen to defend God's one, holy, catholic and apostolic Church! From the foundation of the world, your names have been written in the Book of Life.[96] You are the children of the King, the servants of the Lord!"

"I can't stomach much more of this," Evan grumbled to his mother.

John shouted, "Blessed are you when people insult you, persecute you and falsely say all kinds of evil against you because of the Lord. Rejoice and be glad, because great is your reward in heaven, for in the same way they persecuted the prophets who were before you."[97]

"Go ahead. Wipe them out!" Faridah snapped, with a brisk waive of her hand.

"No," Evan answered. "Then he would die a martyr." Thas thought for a moment, resenting that John seemed to have support even without applying fear and greed as motivators. This kind of leadership made no sense to him. *Why would anyone follow a man who asks for sacrifice?*

His mother pressed on. "As long as he is alive, the Perfective Agenda is in danger."

"True," he nodded. "But John Malek is not the problem."

Faridah returned a silent, puzzled frown.

"The problem is not Malek," he repeated. "The problem is their faith."

Evan breathed deeply and pondered his options.

"For now," Thas asked, "does he serve me better as a martyr or a pawn?"

"If you kill him, you won't have to worry about him anymore."

"To every thing there is a season," Evan quoted the Scripture. "The question is not whether to kill him, but when and how."

Faridah's eyes tightened as she fathomed his dark logic.

Finally, he made himself clear. "A ssspectacle," Thas hissed, "will earn me the greatest glory."

Faridah smiled. She understood the power of theatrics.

"We know where he is. He's a sitting duck. So, let them invest their faith in John Malek." Evan beamed. "Then I will crush their devotion with the greatest show on earth."

I saw an angel,
and he touched the sinew of his hip, like Jacob.
He [the Great Monarch] was in great pain,
and from that day on he walked with a limp.
Blessed Anne Catherine Emmerich

Chapter 12
Avignon Papal Palace
July 15

POPE PETER II removed his red cardinal's vestments and neatly laid them on the old poster bed. Then he donned a simple black cassock. It was not the appropriate clothing for a pontiff, but he was not yet comfortable with papal regalia. After 2,000 years of simplicity, John preferred ... simplicity.

As he looked around the papal apartment, where he had been escorted, John remembered the tumultuous years that had disturbed papal residency during medieval times. By 1309, Rome had become an inhospitable home for Pope Clement V. So, he and his entourage relocated to Avignon, eventually leaving his successors with the task of building the Old Palace on the Rhone River. By the time of its completion, the lavishly decorated gothic structure was one of the most magnificent buildings of the western world, and Avignon had become a major trading center. Seven popes claimed residency there until 1377, when the last of those pontiffs finally was able to return to Rome.

Over the following decades, however, Avignon served as the residence of papal opposition, from where anti-popes attempted to rule. Eventually, even after returning to the control of the Roman Catholic Church, the structure became surplus property that fell into disrepair. The palace was later reduced to a military prison, after the French Revolution, causing further damage.

Now, even after significant 20th century renovations, John could see how centuries of neglect had marred the old papal apartment.

On the walls, the preserved dark frescoes were visible, but high-ly damaged. The coffered ceiling that was once bright with ornate detail, now appeared blackened from fire. However, the colorful, square floor tiles retained their original luster. They added to the drab room almost whimsical diagonal splashes of orange and tur-quoise along with occasional tiles that displayed contrasting *fleur de lis* and checkerboard patterns.

John sat down at a nearby table, and examined the meal he had requested. He broke apart the crusty French baguette and poured water from a pitcher. Then began to consume his sole source of sustenance for today. However, before he could take a second bite, someone knocked at the thick, carved door.

"You may enter."

"Holy Father, am I disturbing you?"

"No, Father Blanc. Please come. Have a seat."

Blanc limped in with a large book and sat at the table.[98] The priest had obviously not recovered from the injury he sustained when he jumped out of the railcar in Cologne. John knew well that he never would.

"Are your accommodations adequate, Henri?"

"Certainly. More than adequate."

"Good. We may be here for a while. Once again, Rome is an un-welcoming home. As you saw from our reception at the train sta-tion, we will be more safe, here."

"Holy Father, that is what I need to talk to you about."

"Yes … go ahead."

"At the station, you said something that made me think."

"I should hope so."

"No … I mean, made me think about a threat to our safety."

"Go on."

"Why did you say: 'The snorting of the enemy's horses is heard from Dan; at the neighing of their stallions the whole land trembles. They have come to devour the land and everything in it.' I mean, I realize it is from Jeremiah, chapter 8, but why choose that passage?"

John shrugged, "I simply spoke as I felt guided by the Holy Spirit."

"So, you don't know what it means?"

"I was referring to the antichrist … that he will be a destroyer."

"But how will he destroy? Do you know that?"

John thought for a moment and then said, "No."

"Holy Father, I may understand how."

"Let's hear."

"XCyst Industries controls a variety of top-secret, extremely powerful technologies."

"I see that you never lost interest in your old specialty."

"That's true, Holy Father. When you mentioned the destroying stallions, I began to piece together a puzzle that now seems to make sense."

John listened closely.

"The N1656 pandemic is believed to be mankind's greatest challenge. Yet, media reports have been sketchy regarding the symptoms and causes of the virus. Pretty much all we know is that Evan Thas has been responsible for moderating this so-called 'existential threat.' Reporters have justified the lack of detailed coverage, ostensibly, because they did not want to sensationalize the horrible effects and create a panic. Also, there has been so much other bad news to report regarding political and economic instability that much of the coverage has been unquestioned."

"True."

"But, think about it. We personally saw the symptoms from the outbreak at the conclave. We saw how this alleged virus attacked Pope Innocent and the cardinals."

"Alleged?"

"Yes. That was no virus."

"Then, what was it?"

"Acute radiation exposure."

John reflected on the observation with a deep breath. "How, then? These outbreaks have occurred all over the world."

"Precisely. That is what has thrown everyone off the trail. How could it be transmitted so quickly and lethally without affecting others who soon came into contact with the victims? We're living proof that it is not a virus."

"Perhaps. Or living proof of God's protection."

Blanc opened a large atlas and put it on the table in front of the pope. A map of the world spanned both open pages.

"Watch," Blanc instructed. "Something has been mysteriously killing fish and wildlife for a few years, now." He began marking dots on the map with a pen. "The death toll is quite alarming. Over 500 birds in Louisiana, 100,000 drum fish and 5,000 red-winged blackbirds in Arkansas, thousands of fish in Florida, hundreds of starfish in South Carolina, 100 pelicans in North Carolina, and two million dead fish in the Chesapeake Bay. Across the Atlantic, 40,000 crabs in England, 100 tons of fish in Portugal, scores of birds in Sweden, hundreds of doves in Italy, 12,000 antelopes in Kazakhstan, 150 tons of red tilapias in Vietnam, and multiple incidents killing thousands of fish in the Philippines and Australia, as well as 10 tons of fish in New Zealand."[99]

"What was the cause?"

"Some suggestions have been ludicrous, even going so far as to claim that thousands of birds were simply scared to death by fireworks. However, I believe radiation exposure is the cause. That would also explain how Thas has been able to find vast fortunes of lost treasure. Basically, he has used a variety of spectral technologies, including X-rays."

"So, what does all this have to do with stallions?"

"Rumors have circulated for years that XCyst Industries controls top-secret satellites that are code-named for various horses. Let me see, there's White Appaloosa, Red Thoroughbred, Black Arabian and Glass Andalusian."

The pontiff frowned. "How do you remember all these facts?"

Blanc responded with a tone of mild reprimand. "Holy Father, I developed the Cyst-Blanc supercomputer. I have a peculiar mind."

John laughed. "You certainly do."

"Now, lets test your memory," Blanc countered. "Do those code-names mean anything to you?"

John thought for a moment and then shrugged. "I don't think so."

"They should. After all, you wrote the prophecy."

John shook his head at the upstart's humorous audacity. "Then educate me, Dr. Blanc. Or should I start calling you 'Your Holiness?'"

Father Blanc answered seriously. "I believe that Jeremiah's destroying stallions are also foretold in the Book of Revelation. Whether or not Cyst and Thas meant it that way, their satellites fit the prophecies. White, red, black and pale; they are the four horsemen of the Apocalypse that the antichrist will use to dominate through slavery, war, famine and death."[100]

"Still, I see no common thread. There is no pattern, whether regarding the victims, times or places. What makes you so sure the virus … or whatever … comes from satellites?"

"There is a pattern, Holy Father." Blanc drew a smoothly oscillating line on the map, starting at Louisiana, north through the eastern U.S. states, curving over the Atlantic and then down between England and Sweden, through Europe and over Kazakhstan, then through Indonesia, Australia and New Zealand before curving up again, back to Louisiana."

John saw that the line followed near every fish or wildlife killing that Henri had dotted on the map. "So, what is that line?"

"The typical path of an orbiting satellite."[101]

John sighed. "Father Blanc, I am a man of faith, not science. What does this all mean?"

"Holy Father, we are in danger. Everyone is. The antichrist has weaponized space satellites."[102]

The two men sat quietly for a moment, gathering their thoughts, contemplating the threat.

Finally, Pope Peter asked, "So, what do we do?"

Blanc did not hesitate. "I must prepare. You must pray."

> An open enemy
> is better than a false friend.
> Greek Proverb

Chapter 13
Vatican Papal Apartment
July 17

THE PATROLLERS' frenzied dash to claim other peoples' property accelerated the pace of corpse removal after the Darkness, as well as Perfective Patrol recruitment and Titan inoculations. The world's population reduction – disturbing, at first – now presented the benefit of a redistribution of wealth. The only requirement for taking advantage of that bonanza was joining the increasingly popular Titan team.

For Evan, however, the speed of change still was not fast enough. He was haunted by the realization that he could no longer count on the offspring of Mercedes Dare to extend his life. His time, it seemed, was running out far too quickly and his increasingly erratic behavior was beginning to concern even his own mother.

So, with the greatest of frustration Thas tried to remain calm as he handled an unforeseen telephone call just four days after the Darkness.

Before answering his private line, Thas noticed that the caller identification screen displayed a mysterious group of symbols. That led him to believe that the call was not only encrypted but from a satellite phone. The mystery was irresistible. He answered and demanded, "Who is this?"

"Evan, my friend," a heavily accented voice responded, as jovial as it was insincere. "Or, now that you got promotion, should I call you Pope Evan?"

"Vasiliy." Thas did not hide his regret. "I thought you were…"

"Dead? Oh, no." A moment of silence passed before Melnikov added, "You don't sound happy to hear the good news."

"Well, we tried to locate the leaders of the Legion of Babylon..."[103]

"They are all gone."

"That's what I thought. And when we found no trace of you, we assumed that you had met the same fate."

"Oh, no, my friend. I am too clever for that."

"Apparently. So, why are you calling?" Evan's mind raced with all the reasons that Melnikov had become such a threat, shortly before the Darkness. The Russian oil billionaire – *that disgusting toad* – had engineered control of the Russian *Duma* much the way that Evan had previously mastered dominance over the U.S. Congress and White House. Then he had cobbled together a Russia/China/Arab alliance that seemed to be, increasingly, at odds with Evan's priorities for the Legion.

After the Darkness, Evan had been comforted by the expectation of pursuing his own goals without the interference of the ambitious Russian. Now, however, Thas could not afford to reveal his true disgust for the man. Melnikov was not one to take lightly. Nor was he one to smack down, because he certainly would have a revenge plan in place, ready to be executed in the event of his untimely death by unnatural causes.

"We should coordinate efforts," Melnikov suggested.

"Absolutely. I will make sure you are copied on all tactical and strategic communications."

"I do not believe that that will be enough to satisfy my alliance."

"You mean 'our alliance,' don't you?"

"Of course. We all seek perfect world." The words almost dripped with sarcasm. "But many of my – I mean, 'our' – friends believe that we will never have Perfect World as long as Israel exists."

"I understand, but we have to set priorities. Israel doesn't rise to the top of the list, right now."

"Evan, you approved troop preparation and mobilization before Darkness. We have forces soon ready to attack. China will back out if they begin to think that we are not serious partners."

"But the Darkness disrupted the timeline. Vasiliy, I'm trying to deal with a couple hundred countries, right now." He added, sarcastically, "So, I kind of have my hands full."

Evan was surprised to hear the determined Russian back off: "I understand. You are very busy, these days."

Maybe he mellowed in the Darkness, Thas thought.

"I will speak to our partners," the Russian offered. "I will … placape?"

"Placate," Thas corrected.

"Yes, I will placate them…. Buy you some time."

Evan had to consider the odd exchange for a moment, but finally offered the words that he never thought he would utter: "Thank you, Vasiliy."

> ... I announced to you the seven crises,
> the seven wounds and sorrows of Mary
> which should have to precede her triumph and our cure,
> namely: 1. Inclemencies of seasons and inundations
> 2. Diseases to animals and plants 3. Cholera over men
> 4. Revolutions 5. Wars 6. An universal bankruptcy
> 7. Confusion...
> Venerable Magdalene Porzat

Chapter 14
White House Oval Office
July 17

NORMALLY, cabinet meetings were not held in the Oval Office. But these were not normal times. Only a handful of cabinet secretaries had survived. Even Vice President Laugherly was gone and not yet replaced. Consequently, the leadership team had shrunk enough to assemble here for an emergency brainstorming session.

As they settled in around the table, each cabinet official contemplated the ominous times in which they lived. Every one thought they had witnessed the ultimate devastation back when the Great Quake of California hit, triggering a nuclear release and evacuation of the west coast. Now, that emergency seemed to be just another line item on a long list.

Natural disasters, epidemics and wars had steadily increased, in recent years. Social instability reigned as riots erupted from the envy and anger that now dominated human relations. Talk of faith and virtue were no longer tolerated in public. Instead, it was ridiculed, attacked or punished as a threat to the Perfect World Agenda.[104]

Then the Darkness delivered a climactic crescendo to the planet's plagues and problems. No one doubted that a supreme being had intervened and left mankind a signature for his warning. But was the awesome object in the sky the Cross of Christ or the "t" of Titan?

Angela and her leadership team knew that they were steering a course though uncharted, turbulent waters. Societal protection entities – from law enforcement, to criminal and civil courts, to military defense – were now undermanned and impotent. Even before the Darkness, the watchdog role of the media had virtually disappeared as so-called journalists had dominated the airwaves with the Perfect World agenda. Consequently, political debates were no longer conducted with traditional decorum, because dissenters – those who argued against the centralizing control of Evan Thas – were demonized as "Enemies of Perfection."

Now, Thas controlled the world's only operational broadcast company. He transmitted his messages, globally, through a series of sub-satellites that were controlled by the master-satellite known as White Appaloosa.[105] Though its standard communications capabilities were well known, this orbiter offered a major innovation: it was equipped to broadcast over the full audio/video airwaves spectrum, overriding competing broadcasts on every other channel. That novel capability allowed Thas to monopolize the airwaves with his messianic message, along with any other news that he deemed appropriate.

Each day, XBC News and Entertainment transmitted his messages to 184 countries, while simultaneously translating them into 62 languages.

The only other remaining source of information and news for the masses was the Internet. However, the technological tentacles of XCyst Industries had long dominated that medium, through their CyBot search engine and data storage capabilities. So, using data-mining and filtering techniques, Thas had established an ability to restrict or close down websites that were deemed non-compliant with the Perfective Agenda.

Still, like a cat toying with a mouse, Evan did not always close down non-compliant websites. Instead, he would let them continue to operate, knowing that spying on their communications would prove more beneficial to his cause.

Most of Angela's cabinet members did not realize the extent of Evan's global tentacles. They did, however, know that the world was in need of a savior.

So, with a heavy heart, Angela called the cabinet meeting to order. "Ladies and gentlemen, I want to thank you for responding to this call to serve your country under the most extreme of conditions. I realize each of you would rather be home, tending to your family's concerns and preparing for an uncertain future. Our work, here, however, will provide a better future for us all."

The president scanned her long list of priorities and mumbled to herself, "Oh, where do I start?" Then she acknowledged the Labor Secretary. "Larry, what's happening in the economy? How can we return a sense of normalcy to the workplace?"

The nervous, labor lawyer fumbled through some sheets of data, in front of him. "Madame President, we haven't had enough time to put together a detailed report, but I can tell you what anecdotal evidence I've been receiving."

"Go ahead."

"In short, the American economy has ground to a halt. Roughly a third of the labor force was lost in the Darkness. So, it's been hard to get the survivors to resume a normal work schedule. Machinery and equipment are all working fine, but when workers return to their jobs, they often find that their workplaces are dysfunctional and frustratingly undermanned. We hear that absenteeism is crippling businesses, hospitals, schools, factories, you name it. Adding to those frustrations, some suspect that they won't be paid for their efforts." He shook his head. "It's a real mess, out there. Then there's the problem of the Perfective Patrollers."

Angela perked up. "Yes, what about them?"

"They're not showing up for their old jobs because the rush to claim property has kept them busy with corpse removal."

The Attorney General spoke up. "That's an issue I want to discuss, Madame President. Thas has no legal basis for declaring that ownership rights transfer just for cleaning up someone's property."[106]

"Yes," she said, "but at least they're eliminating a potentially devastating health hazard."

"Still, this is a nation founded on law," the Attorney General continued, "with long-standing inheritance rights. People are being dispossessed of their legal property. We can't let them get away with that."

Angela sighed. "We can, and we will."

During an extended moment of baffled silence, some cabinet secretaries wondered if the political rumors were true: Thas really had been President Concepcion's puppet-master.

"Madame President, I know the law and I can tell you…"

"And I know Evan Thas," Angela interrupted. "Didn't you see how his Patrollers plundered the churches and synagogues? You go after them and your property will be next."

"But that's illegal and…"

"He is not dealing with your kind of law, anymore!" she snapped. "Thas is counting on the law of the jungle, now, and his followers are the alpha-predators. They are better organized for this crisis than we are."

The Secretary of the Treasury chimed in. "They certainly are." He was the administration's most prized recruit, from the prestigious international banking firm of Tepley Thor. Whenever he spoke, everyone listened. "It's almost like Thas was prepared for a meltdown. He's got his digital currency program just about ready to roll out, worldwide. When I first heard about it, I thought it was ludicrous. Now, I'm not so sure."

"So, update us on that," the president requested.

"If he gets his way, the single global currency will be called the Titan. The plan requires everyone to surrender their dollars, or Euros, or … whatever … into an account that is converted to digital Titans. In other words, no physical money, every financial transaction will be electronic."

"I don't know. Consumers want to touch and hold their money," she argued.

"Today, only a tiny percentage of monetary exchanges are conducted in cash."

"But surely Thas can't overcome resistance to such a massive change," she said. "People have faith in their existing currencies."

"That is changing," the Secretary of Treasury responded. "We're hearing about long lines and, worse yet, bank runs every time a financial institution opens its doors. Here and around the world, confidence in banking systems and national currencies is collapsing. People simply can't get at their money."

"Well, why not?"

He felt that a lesson in banking and finance would be helpful. "Madame President, I'm sure you realize that banks can lend out roughly ten times the amount they have on deposit. So, for example, when John Doe deposits $1,000, his bank turns around and lends $900 of it out. That money then makes its way into other banks that lend $810 of it out ... and on and on. After a little while, that $1,000 in real money balloons into $10,000 loaned into existence. So, the system is not designed for a panic, because the banks do not actually hold enough cash. When everyone, including John Doe, demands a cash withdrawal, the ugly reality becomes clear."[107]

"That's a Ponzi scheme!" she barked.

He offered a guilty shrug. "Banks, the Fed, every financial institution on the planet operates that way."

The Secretary of Education listened closely. At cabinet meetings, she had always felt a bit out of her league, especially since she had failed to gain support for Angela's education agenda from teachers' unions. So, she wanted to prove that she had something to contribute. "What about FDIC insurance?" she asked. "Just let them cover the losses."

Angela offered a searing, "Where do you think that money will come from ... the insurance fairy?" The questioner wanted to crawl into a hole.

"Confidence," Angela insisted to the Treasury Secretary. "People need confidence in their currency."

"Madame President, people are confused, right now. They're desperate. I think they're ready to buy into all the hype about the Perfect World."

"How can Thas protect against fraud, counterfeiting, theft?"

"He claims now that those N1656 inoculations not only fight the viral pandemic but have a secondary purpose: providing identity validations.[108] That capability is a natural fit for securing financial transactions. Spokesmen for XCyst Industries make a convincing case that the problems you mention would be eliminated when financial transactions can be tracked digitally. The program would also make existing currencies and coins unnecessary and, consequently, worthless.[109]

Then the Attorney General jumped in. "I'm hearing that hyper-inflation is becoming a concern. Even when a store finally opens, its inventory is not being replenished. Price gouging is rampant. Pretty soon, people will be without access to the basic necessities…. By the way, what's gold trading at now?"

The Treasury Secretary answered, "Being quoted at over $18,000 an ounce."

"That's what I thought," the Attorney General said. "Good luck with that. I heard one guy could only negotiate a loaf of bread for a gold coin. Then thugs followed him home, robbed the rest of his gold and killed him. People are starting to realize that they can't eat precious metals. The rich are becoming so worried about roving gangs that they're throwing their jewelry, gold and silver into the streets to placate mobs and discourage break-ins."[110]

The Labor Secretary added, "I heard that Michelangelo's *Pieta'* was dumped in a Roman landfill after the ransacking of the Vatican. What value does something like that have today? Nobody wants to look like they're bucking the Perfective Agenda, supporting religion."

"This is unbelievable," Angela groaned. "We can't even get the mail service running. God help us if we're confronted with war."

"Yes ma'am," the Secretary of Defense, finally spoke up. "God help us. Our technologies are operational but manpower is lacking. You can't just drop a foot soldier into a Stealth fighter and expect him to fly it. We'll do the best we can but, frankly ma'am, our defenses are vulnerable."

"So, Secretary Broderick, what's the situation in the Middle East?"

"The forces surrounding Israel seem to be in a holding pattern. We believe they're evaluating relative disadvantages after, and as a result of, the Darkness. The issue is not whether their execution capabilities were set back. Everyone's was. But rather, how much compared to Israel's? If either side sees advantage, they may strike without warning."

"Nuclear?"

The rugged, former general responded with greater gloom than he had ever shown in battle. "Madame President, the computers may decide that question."

"Computers? What are you talking about?"

"Madame President, every country is ratcheting up defenses. The bio-weapon strike on the Saudi Royal Family was a warning for every national leader. Now, with civil unrest everywhere, they are all on edge, and I can assure you that every one has established an Automatic Decapitation-Response Protocol."

"Automatic? We don't have that."

"Yes we do, ma'am. Our ADRP was established long before you took office."

"General," she said, angrily, "I want it clear that I, alone, give the order before any attack."

"But what if you have twenty seconds to respond and you're in bed, or… otherwise indisposed. Ma'am, with all due respect, what if you're already dead? Hell, the way that crazy virus hits, the occupants of this room could be wiped out in the blink of an eye. Then who's gonna defend the rest of America?"

"So, you're saying the computers take over?"

"Madame President, these protocols have not been established lightly. The brightest minds in the world have incorporated redundant protections into our command and control systems."

She argued, "That's what they said about computerized stock trading. You remember the flash crash of XCyst stock? A lot of people got crushed in that computer-driven collapse."

"Yes ma'am," he nodded, "but if the nukes are flying, and you're not responding … at least the computers know what to do."

The room was quiet for a moment as the president assessed the relative dangers.

"For everyone's safety," he continued, "computers won't waste time on philosophical or theological debates. All they understand is their binary language: if this, then that. If we're not responding to a nuke attack, then they respond to it."

"So, you're saying they'll fall like dominoes, automatically countering enemy aggression. When Iran's nukes fly, then Israel will respond in kind, then Pakistan, then India, then China, then Russia, then us."

"Frankly, ma'am," he responded solemnly, "America won't be waiting that long."

She threw up her hands. "How did we ever get to this point?"

"Madame President," the General spoke hesitantly, "that's actually not your biggest concern, right now."

"I don't know if I can handle more news from you, right now," she answered angrily. "But go ahead."

"Dr. Thas and his companies have technological tentacles into America's military industrial complex. We need him on our side."

The Education Secretary spoke up. "Are you kidding? You want us to work with that lunatic? His gangs of Patrollers are really scaring a lot of people. They're taking over."

"Believe me," the General added, "XCyst Industries has more firepower in their arsenal than you've seen, so far."

Angela asked warily, "And you think he might turn it all on us if we don't cooperate with him?"

"I don't have the least doubt about it," Broderick answered. "That's why I say he is too powerful to have as an enemy."

The President seemed to disengage from the conversation and drift into deep thought for a few moments. Slowly, she ran her fingers across her forehead, back and forth, over the three concentric circles of her Titan implant. She remembered how much blackmail material she had given Thas and his minions during her repeated Titan analyses.[111]

Just like the Patrollers were learning now, she had understood that the better she tested on Titan, the more Thas would trust her and the more he would empower her. She felt embarrassed by her past eagerness to earn his trust.

How stupid! she thought.

"Madam President?" the General prompted. "He'd be a dangerous enemy."

"Oh, yes," Angela responded as she roused back. She pulled her hand from her face and answered, "Dr. Thas will not be an enemy."

Character is destiny.
Heraclitus

Chapter 15
Choteau-Agusta, Montana
July 21

ERCEDES DARE removed the bottle from her baby's mouth, laid him in a crib, and nestled soft bedding around the sleepy boy. He needed his rest, but she could not resist lingering over him while softly stroking his tummy. She was at peace with possessing far less than she had ever wanted, but far more than she had ever deserved.

Here, miles from anyone, Mer had learned to enjoy the natural, rustic beauty of her father's hunting lodge. She believed it would be the perfect place to raise a son, away from the masses of humanity from whom she once sought admiration and approval. Now, her garden, her water well, and her baby were all she needed … except, of course, her merciful God.

Mer had never succumbed to serious evil. But during the Darkness, she discovered how petty, venal and stupid she had acted most of her life. Like many others, today, she was still trying to make sense of those historic three days. However, no explanation seemed plausible if it did not include God's almighty power.

The year had begun, for her, with so much false promise when she imagined that Evan Thas would be the man of her dreams. Then, disaster engulfed them on the island of Nauru and her dreams morphed into a macabre nightmare. For a few months, it seemed as if she had been sucked into the vortex of a catastrophic whirlwind.

Evan had suffered injuries so severe that they may have scarred not only his body, but his mind. First, he had appeared to take Mer's apparent miscarriage in stride. But then he lashed out at her, venomously, when he discovered that she could not bear more children. The shock of his irrational cruelties eventually delivered her into the grip of suicidal depression.

Then, a month ago, Ashley Adams arrived, carrying a baby.

The story she told Mer was alarming, disgusting and believable.

Nurse Adams had witnessed Evan's assembly line of cruel and dangerous human experiments on the secluded island. She said that he had become obsessed with the goal of mutating life from what God created to what he preferred.

Nothing on the island, she claimed, was more lucrative than the harvesting of human organs, bones and tissue. After only a few years of incubation in synthetic growth hormones, each fetus would mature to adult size and yield millions of dollars in profits.

However, she explained that Evan had been unable to benefit from his own bioengineering advances. His extraordinary genetic profile prevented his body from accepting transplants, unless they were from his own offspring. Yet, even after thousands of attempts, no one had conceived a child for him ... that is, until he met Mercedes Dare.

Mer, had shuddered with outrage when Nurse Adams told her that the baby in her arms had been prepared for just such a fate. Then the woman dropped an even bigger bombshell: the baby was Mer's son. She said that Evan had planned to nurture his growth, in a world of sensory deprivation, until he chose to harvest his son's organs.

Suddenly, Mer realized that what seemed to have been the most horrible tragedy of her life, actually, had been her greatest blessing. The explosion on Nauru had ended her foolish relationship with a rich but hideous monster and saved her son's life. For that, she could thank the heroic actions of Ashley Adams. So, in an *homage,* of sorts, Mer named the boy after the nurse, calling him Adam.

As Mer set the bottle on the table next to Adam's crib, she marveled at how easily she had lost her desire for career advancement and had adapted to this simple life of peace and prayer. Without a doubt, the Darkness had been traumatic. However, it had invigorated her soul as, perhaps, nothing else could. Now, she understood that love is our purpose in life.

Evan Thas, however, had other priorities.

When Mer heard a car, outside, she thought it unusual. After all, only her parents occasionally visited, but they were out of town.

Mer slipped over to the window and peaked through a crack in the blinds. She gasped when she saw a white, stretch limousine.

Her mind raced. *Oh, dear God, no!*

With her father's assistance, Mer had tried to prepare for this possibility. She knew it would not be wise to overreact. So, she quickly tried to harness her emotions. *Okay, calm down. Calm down. He doesn't know about the baby.*

Mer quickly slipped out of the bedroom, gently closing the door behind her. Then she bolted to the kitchen and pulled out plates and silverware. Hurriedly, she began to set the dinette table but paused when she heard her boy cough. She froze, waiting for another stirring from the infant, but heard nothing … until the sudden knock on the door.

The young mother breathed deeply and ran her fingers through her hair. Then she approached the door, looked through the peep hole and swung open the door.

"Evan!" she exclaimed with the best faux smile she could muster.

Mer was not only shocked by the visit but surprised by his appearance. He wore a tailored, dark suit and held a bouquet of white roses. However, for the first time that she could remember, he looked small and nervous, fidgeting with the flowers. As she gazed at his scarred face, she wondered, *What was I thinking?*

However, she was wise enough to keep that dangerous thought buried within herself.

Evan cleared his throat, "Hi Mer." He adjusted his eye patch and thrust the roses at her. "These are for you."

"Oh, uh, thanks," she said as she clumsily took the flowers. "What are you doing here?"

"Well, I … Can I come in?"

She whispered as if confiding a secret, "Evan, I put the dog in the bedroom. He gets pretty destructive when he hears people in the house…"

Thas didn't budge.

"But … sure. We just need to be quiet."

Mer led him to the dinette where she pretended to admire not only the flowers but the weighty vase.

"Waterford?" she asked as she stroked the cut crystal.

"For you, only the best."

Mer placed the flowers at the center of the table, trying to smile as she discretely positioned herself on the other side of it.

"They look very nice, there," Evan offered.

"Yes, they do," she answered, hiding her true opinion that a crystal vase was completely out of place in the rustic cabin. Then she made herself busy, setting the table. "My parents are coming over," she lied. "I don't have much time before they get here."

After a moment of tense silence, he said, "Look, Mer, I think we had some misunderstandings and I just want to put that all behind us. I think I overreacted when you said you can't have children."

"Yeah." Her eyebrows raised, indicating that she still felt wounded. "Frankly, you did."

"But then I realized: I'll rebuild Eden Village. So, we'll get you fixed up, good as new. Then we can have kids!"

"That would be wonderful," she feigned excitement.

Evan nervously busied himself, rearranging her place-setting. "You think that's wonderful? Just wait till you see what I have planned. Mer, Titan will be phenomenal."

"That's … great."

"People are still boggled by the Darkness. It's given us the perfect opportunity to centralize power. For two years, now, XCyst has laid the groundwork for a single, digitized world currency. Everything's all coming together fast. Within three months, every monetary transaction will be channeled through Titan and no one will be able to buy or sell without it.[112] I've really got this thing figured out."

Then he began rearranging the next place-setting. It seemed such an odd quirk, to Mer. She remembered that, once before, Thas had exhibited the same compulsion, onboard his jet. When the flight attendant had arranged the knife and fork in a cross pattern on the plate, he scolded her for not setting them parallel. Now, again, he was removing the knife from under the neck of the fork, and placing them side-by-side as he continued to ramble.

"Mer, the world is ripe for the picking and I want to share it with you. But this time, I'm delegating responsibility to take a lot of weight off my shoulders. I have the Patrollers to help me."

He moved closer to her.

"See, this crisis has opened a lot of doors for me. My biggest enemies are gone. People need a savior."

That observation added to one of her growing uncertainties. Intuitively, she had thought that the earth had been cleansed of evil during the Darkness. So, she was baffled by the fact that Evan still survived. She wondered if, perhaps, she had judged him too harshly. Today, in his nervousness, he seemed harmless, almost boyish. Maybe Nurse Adams had lied.

"Mer, don't you remember what a great couple we made? How happy you felt? You were my queen and everybody knew it."

Inwardly, she had to admit that those were the happiest days of her life … at least, at first.

"I want my queen back. I want to shower you with gifts, travel the world with you."

Though Mer's soul had been elevated by a sincere faith and a pure heart,[113] she had never worked to correct the errors of her conscience.[114] She had not yet learned that a holy life is not achieved by accident, and she was still vulnerable to Evan's lying persuasions because she had never sought guidance from sacred Scriptures or "the Church of the living God, the pillar and foundation of the truth."[115]

So, Evan counted on the fact that she could be easily swayed. As always, he was articulate and convincing. He knew how to bring out her nurturing instinct, whenever he wanted.

However, he did not know that she now had a higher nurturing priority.

As he took her hand, she wondered aloud, "How did you find me?"

Evan smiled, raised his crippled hand and gently stroked her hair from her forehead. Suddenly, however, she realized that he was not admiring her face, but the mark near her hairline: Titan's three concentric circles.

She pulled away and stepped back. *He can find me, anywhere!* she thought.

Her response angered Evan and his boyish charm disappeared. "Look, we need to make babies."

"Shhhh," she whispered. "the dog'll go nuts if he hears you." She was flustered, but knew she would have to respond. "Kids? I just … it's all so sudden." Then she added, "I don't have a TV. But I heard you're … like … pope something or other, now."

"That doesn't affect us. I can change the rules whenever I want."

Attempting to remain calm, she shrugged her uncertainty. "I guess you can."

Evan sensed her discomfort but did not realize how deeply fearful she had become. To Mer, the demand revealed his true intentions. He was not interested in her. She was only important to him because he desired the eye, the hand and the skin of a donor son.

"Come on, Mer," he reached toward her as he moved around the table. "Let's get back to old times."

She felt trapped when her back touched the wall. She heard her heart pounding when he tightly pressed against her and embraced her, warmly. Then, when his molten face brushed against hers, she cringed.

He whispered in her ear, "I can't bear to lose you." They sounded like words of love, until he added, "You know too much about Titan."

The implied threat sent shivers down her spine. *So typical,* she thought. *Always revealing the carrot and the stick.*

Mer flinched when the phone rang and her fears multiplied when she thought that her baby might start crying.

"I have to catch that," she said as she quickly pulled from Evan's embrace. "I'm expecting a call from my father."

Mer answered the phone. "Hello." A telephone solicitor was on the line. "Hi Daddy." She paused and then looked at her watch. "You're kidding. I barely have time to brush my teeth." She paused again and added, "Well, don't worry about it. I'll be ready." She nodded with a smile. "Love you too. See you in a few minutes."

Mer hung up the phone with a grin. "Parents. Always unpredictable." Then, when she heard their son stirring in the bedroom, Mer offered a toothy smile and quickly took Evan's arm, suggesting, "Please promise you'll call me tomorrow." She led him to the door and apologized, "I wish I could visit, now. This has been such a wonderful surprise."

He seemed pleased at her response, offering, "I will. I'll call you tomorrow."

Then, before closing the door, she attempted her best imitation of a schoolgirl crush. "I am sooo looking forward to getting back with you."

It was the wisest lie she ever told.

LATER THAT NIGHT, Mer was deep in thought as she warmed a bottle of formula in the microwave. But while the timer ticked down, she could not stand still. So, she paced around the dinette table, jotting notes regarding her mutually exclusive options: run or stay.

She knew that, by tomorrow, she would have to decide.

On the one hand, staying could be dangerous for herself and especially baby Adam, if he were eventually discovered. However, as she considered Evan's mercurial nature, she suspected that she could count on him to quickly grow tired of pursuing an unreciprocated relationship with her. At that point, Mer and Adam might find an opportunity to quietly fade away, out of Evan's life forever.

Fleeing, on the other hand, would most likely enflame Evan's passions, turning him into the determined and dangerous pursuer of an unending nightmare.

Frustrated, Mer tossed her pen and notepad on the table. Then she expressed her irritation in the only way that was convenient. She snatched Evan's roses out of the crystal vase and dumped them in a trash can, under the sink. When she returned to the dinette, she abruptly rearranged a set of silverware, back to the cross-shaped pattern that she preferred.

"I'll do it however I want!" she sneered at Evan's compulsive aversions.

Just then, she heard baby Adam rousing in the bedroom.

"I'm coming, hungry boy."

She grabbed the formula from the microwave and headed back.

Mer clicked on the crib-side light, carried her baby to the rocker, and sat with a sigh. As the rocker creaked, back and forth on the old plank floors, little Adam slurped the formula ferociously.

The new mother reminisced about her own parents and wished they were with her, now. More than ever before, she trusted their advice. She marveled at how much they had changed through the decades: once rowdy hippies, now humble Christians.

If only she had listened to her father's warnings, early on. He claimed that Evan was a horribly bad person, but she refused to even consider the possibility. Now she knew.

Mer had grown up resisting his warnings, seeing them as the products of an overly zealous Christian or an overly protective dad. She knew that he meant well, but he seemed almost paranoid about protecting his family, and Mer felt that his elaborate security schemes were practical, only in theory.

When Adam finished the bottle, she burped him, then laid him in the crib and turned the light out. She lingered over his bed for a moment, listening to his contented breathing and the soft sound of a million crickets, outside.

Mer whispered a heartfelt prayer: "Dear God, please bless my baby." After a gentle stroke of his face, he went for his thumb and she headed back to the kitchen.

Approaching the dinette, Mer decided to continue evaluating her options, on paper. But as she reached for her pen and notepad, she noticed the plate. On it, the knife and fork were parallel, again.

She thought, *What in the world…?*

Then she heard, "Dad was a no-show."

Mer froze for only a split second, but it seemed like an eternity. Suddenly, with both hands, she snatched the leaded crystal vase, swung around, and uncoiled like a batter aiming for the bleachers.

The vase smacked Evan's temple with a loud, dull thud.

It all happened so fast, she felt like a nightmare had just thrust itself into her consciousness.

Panting, Mer braced herself, preparing to bludgeon him again. But he did not attack. Thas could only respond with a brief, vacant stare. Then he collapsed on the floor.

Mer threw down the vase and ran into the kitchen. She opened a drawer and grabbed a butcher knife as Adam began crying in the bedroom.

She wanted to run to his crib, but she had a more urgent matter at hand.

As Mer approached Evan, her heart pounded. She understood the enemy that she had just created. Now, her life and her baby's life were in danger.

Clutching the knife, Mer slowly slid closer. She knew that, if the roles had been reversed, Evan would not hesitate to execute his form of justice. She wanted to kill him. She needed to kill him.

Adam was now screaming and Evan moaned, loudly. The escalating cacophony reverberated in her head, pushing her to the brink.

Inching ever closer, panic squeezed Mer's mind as tightly as she squeezed her knife. It seemed there was no other way out. With just one sharp slash at his neck, she could make it all go away.

Her anger boiled as something, deep in the recesses of her mind, urged her to move closer, to reach down, and to satisfy the rage that was bubbling over.

Closer! Do it, now! the voice demanded. *Closer! It's your only hope!*

She yearned for her father's protection. Then, suddenly, the fog of fear lifted and she remembered her salvation. If the Darkness had taught her anything, it was that there is always another choice. So, as Mer grabbed her crying son and escaped through the back door, she chose to pray.

SECONDS LATER, Evan recovered his senses and struggled to his feet. He cringed as he rubbed the throbbing, bloody bruise on his head and staggered around the house. He searched for Mer, realizing that she could not have gone far, but appeared baffled when he discovered the crib in the bedroom.

Thas made his way to the front door and yelled to his limo driver: "Hey! Where'd she go?"

Behind the wheel, the dull-witted Patroller roused awake. He opened his door and yelled back, "Huh?"

"Where'd she go?" Evan shouted.

"Uhhh, I dunno."

"Circle the area," Thas demanded. "Find her. She's on foot."

Evan slammed the door and rushed to the back of the cabin while pressing a sleeve to his bloody forehead.

As he stood on the back porch, Evan studiously gazed over the garden and the grassy plain that extended to the distant mountains. The full moon highlighted the landscape, but he saw no one.

She must be hiding inside.

Thas imagined that she might be in the attic or the crawl space or even in a closet. However, he did not care to look for her. After all, the end result would be the same, regardless of where she hid. So, when the driver returned, Thas ordered, "Get the gas out."

It was Evan's Plan B, prepared in advance.

The Patroller removed two plastic tanks from the trunk, brought them into the cabin and, together, they methodically doused room after room with gas. Then Thas flicked a lit match into the crib and left.

The conflagration grew quickly and brilliantly under the full moon while Evan savored his role as judge, jury and executioner. As the flames raged higher, he marveled at their intensity and prepared to enjoy Mer's screaming attempt to escape.

But it never happened and, after a while, Thas grew bored with the blaze.

On the long drive back to the airport, Evan comforted his throbbing headache with large quantities of vodka. He also found satisfaction in knowing that Mer would never betray him again.

TWO WEEKS EARLIER, a large object was buried in the garden. If an unknowing stranger had happened upon it, he might have mistaken it for a make-shift casket in a shallow grave. This container, however, was not designed to inter the dead, but the living.

It was the product of her father's security paranoia: a large freezer, buried horizontally, vented for air circulation and camouflaged on top.

Now, while flames engulfed the cabin, Mer and Adam reclined inside the small, white bunker.

The boy was content, crying no longer. He even chuckled when Mer's flashlight beam flitted across a few provisions that had been preserved, inside.

As minutes became hours, Mer's pleading prayers turned to prayers of thanks, and she began to find hope that they might survive.

However, she also realized that one more problem had to be addressed.

Mer rested the baby at her side and fingered along her face until she felt the concentric circles of her tiny Titan implant. Then she cringed as she raised the knife and sliced her forehead, first vertically and then horizontally. With tears streaming, she growled as she peeled the skin back and dug around, under the flesh, until she found and removed the implant. Then she smeared the blood-covered device on the refrigerator wall and crushed it with her knife.

> We must never lose sight of the fact
> that we are either saints or outcasts,
> that we must love for heaven or hell.
> There is no middle path in this.
> St. John Vianney

JOHN WAS PLEASED to watch Father Henri Blanc and his men work furiously each day to stock and fortify the papal palace. As he observed the effort from a distance, it became obvious that the priest was a natural born leader, pushing his men to excel while giving and receiving complete respect.

The laborers clearly admired that Blanc never slowed down and never acknowledged the obvious fact that his leg injury was causing him considerable pain. Yet, they all remained joyful, more than any workers John had ever observed. Without a doubt, the Three Days had convinced them of God's existence, and the realization that they were children and heirs of the Almighty King had presented them with a fulfilling new purpose in life.

Blanc was similarly optimistic. As he studied the monumental structure of the Avignon palace, he took comfort in the fact that the fortified walls were as much as 18 feet thick. However, the possibility of siege warfare required that the castle become self-sufficient. So, he organized many of the men for planting crops on the perimeter of the grounds. Bus he also mobilized men to stock the basement shelves with tons of canned foods, medications and bottled water, enough to maintain its residents for at least a year.

Still, he knew that the most likely attack would not be conventional. So he applied his scientific background to address his suspicion that their greatest threat was from the sky.

Blanc assigned men to monitor Evan's XBC broadcasts in order to gauge the timetable for the attack that they knew would soon come. Fearing that their telephone, television and radio equipment would be wiped out with an electro-magnetic pulse, Blanc designed a protection against such an attack. He instructed his men to encase the papal apartment in chain link wire, establishing a Faraday enclosure that would neutralize EMP exposure, inside the apartment. The relatively simple barrier would preserve their ability to communicate with the outside world, even after an EMP attack.

More importantly, however, he organized a group of competent followers to purchase and transport tons of lead ingot to the site. Then he instructed them to build massive bonfires upon which cauldrons were placed with ingots inside. The fires raged, but the men had to wait until the lead exceeded its melting point, 302 degrees Fahrenheit.

Then, the cauldrons were removed from the fires and the race was on.

Blanc had organized a pulley system in which buckets were filled with molten lead, quickly raised up to the roof and then poured and spread on the flat rooftop, before it could harden. The men found that working with the hot, liquid metal was not only exhausting but dangerous. Still, they forged ahead enthusiastically and without complaint.

Many pilgrims had decided to stay, often living in tents on the grounds once the rooms were filled. They tended the fields, planting crops for a self-sustained lifestyle.

The women of the community tended to the workers who sustained burns or were overcome by the heat of the raging fires. They also prepared meals and made sure the men received enough water to stave off dehydration.

Every effort was a family affair. Even the children participated by hustling food and water to the workers. They cheered every time a bucket of lead made it to the roof.

The order for the ambitious roof project was conceived when Henri Blanc finally pieced together a jigsaw puzzle of scientific clues. He had wondered how Evan Thas had been able to discover so much buried and sunken treasure in recent years. He had also found that the notorious N1656 virus did not seem to follow a normal virological pattern. So, he began to evaluate whether the pandemic might actually have a manmade source. It did not take long for him to deduce a probable cause. X-ray radiation penetrates all uncompressed gases, as well as some solids and many liquids. So, X-rays, diagnostic radiography and crystallography could identify items such as gold, silver and jewels. Under such widely dispersed discoveries of lost treasure, the obvious delivery system for the X-rays would be an orbiting satellite. However, there is also a deadly side effect to excess electromagnetic radiation from X-rays. The effects appear much like the symptoms of the so-called N1656 virus.

So, Blanc ordered the installation of an effective shield against satellite-delivered X-ray radiation: a leaden rooftop.

It was a scientific puzzle that few might have figured out and, as John watched from one of the papal apartment windows, he marveled at Henri's intellectual and organizational talents. However, his amusement was interrupted when someone knocked at the door.

"Yes. You may enter."

"Holy Father, I am sorry to interrupt you." The young Frenchman, barely more than a boy, dropped to his knees and motioned the sign of the Cross.

"No, no. Please stand. I am just a man."

The boy stood but kept his hands folded. He tried to catch his breath. "Holy Father, you are not just a man. You are Christ's..."

"Please," John softly interrupted, "what do you need?"

"A nun is in the chapel ... in the confessional. I was trying to lock up but she refused to leave."

"Why?"

"She says she won't go until you hear her confession."

"Did you recognize her?"

"No, I've never seen her before. Her French was not very good."

John remembered the bounty on his head and suspected a trap.

"Did she sound sincere?"

"Oh, yes. Definitely."

John sighed. "Show me where she is."

JOHN ENTERED THE BOOTH, sat down and shut the door. He did not feel safe with this stranger in the empty chapel but he would not refuse to hear anyone's confession. For a moment, in the darkness, he smelled the scent of aging wood and dusty upholstery. Then, realizing he could delay no longer, he slid open the wooden window barrier.

Through the metal grate, John observed the shadowed form of a kneeling nun. Her face, however, was lowered in prayer. A white coif and black veil concealed her identity ... perhaps deliberately.

"Yes," John whispered, "confess your sins."

She did not respond.

John looked more closely, into the shadows. He studied how her shoulders trembled and he listened to her labored breathing.

"Go ahead," he prodded.

Finally, she whispered, "Somebody wants to kill me."

John inhaled deeply. "Sister, that would be a matter for law enforcement. You need to report it."

Her sobbing grew louder.

"Is that all?" he asked.

A moment later, almost to herself, she whispered angrily, "I'm such a failure!"

He tried to reassure her. "Confess your sins. Christ's peace will comfort you. How long has it been since your last confession?"

She slowly sighed. "I don't know ... decades."

John wondered, *Has she lost her mind?* "Sister, I'm quite sure it hasn't been that long. Go ahead and..."

"I sold my soul!" she snapped.

"What?"

"Ahhh," she groaned, "it wasn't written on paper or even said out loud. But I knew what I was doing."

"So," he whispered, "what do you want?"

She raised her head and he gasped when he recognized her face.

"I want to buy it back."

My three main goals
would be to reduce human population
to about 100 million, worldwide,
destroy the industrial infrastructure,
and see wilderness,
with its full complement of species,
returning throughout the world.

Dave Foreman
Earth First! Cofounder

Chapter 17
Avignon, France
August 21

IN THE DARKENED CONFESSIONAL, President Angela Concepcion removed a black veil and white coif, revealing her full face to the pontiff.

"The disguise was necessary," she explained. "My visit with you must remain secret."

"So, why are you really here?"

"To make amends. I realize, now, that I have sinned. I want to ask forgiveness and offer penance."

"Please, confess your sins."

Angela unburdened herself, telling a story of prideful self-deception. She explained how her early leadership in the abortion movement had established the foundation for her political career. That early success, she claimed, whet her appetite for power and fame. So, it did not take long before those political allies began to entice her into advocating for increasingly radical legislation. Over time, she had championed partial-birth abortion bills, mass-sterilization projects, and the proliferation of abortion-inducing drugs. She had attacked legislation to protect the lives of infants born after botched abortions. She had opposed limitations on euthanizing senior citizens and protections against the growing problem of gendercide.

She admitted that she had turned a blind eye to the horrific human research of XCyst Industries, including embryonic stem cell research, human cloning and transhumanist genetic experiments.[116]

In short, Angela claimed that she had blindly promoted the initiatives of Evan Thas, accepting the Legion of Babylon's claim that "reducing the world's population by 95% would be ideal."[117]

During the Darkness, however, she said that she had experienced a transcendent realization in which she finally understood the gift of life and the gravity of her role in making mass murder convenient. She had been confronted by many thousands of souls – not angrily, but lovingly. They were the ones who had perished under the programs that she had advocated, and she realized that joy on earth had been diminished by their absence. She was deeply ashamed that she had played a significant role in depriving them of what she should have protected: life, liberty and the pursuit of happiness.

The president admitted that even though Evan Thas had been a major factor in leading her more deeply into sin, she could blame only herself. However, she felt that she now must act decisively in opposing the evil that Thas continued to propagate.

"So," John interjected, "is Thas the one who wants to kill you?"

"If he doesn't now, he soon will."

"What do you want me to do about it?"

Without hesitation, she answered, "Take my daughter."

"What?" John was stunned. "I don't understand."

"To atone for my sins, I deserve the ultimate penance. I will put an end to his evil, but I can't bear the loss of another innocent life."

"You think Thas will want to kill her?"

"Once I turn on him, absolutely."

John thought for a moment. "Why me?"

"I have always placed my trust in men. Not anymore."

John asked, "How long will we keep her?"

Her mind seemed to drift. "I had such high hopes for Evie ... the next generation of American leadership." Then she shook her head as her eyes welled with tears. "I don't believe I will be back for her."

President Concepcion breathed deeply and then placed the coif and veil back on her head. "I must go."

"Wait," John said.

"Yes?"

He raised his right hand to bless her with the Sign of the Cross. "I absolve you from your sins in the name of the Father and the Son and the Holy Spirit."

She whispered "Amen," and rose from the kneeler.

"Madame President?"

She stopped and listened.

"I need something from you, in return."

Cautiously, she asked, "And what would that be?"

"I must speak to Prime Minister Emunah ... with absolute confidentiality."

She thought for a moment, then responded, "That can be arranged."

JOHN REMAINED in the dark booth for a while after the president left. During that time, he prayed that God would grant her wisdom, and the angels, security.

Finally, remembering that he had a busy day planned, John left the confessional. But just before exiting, he heard a sound. John retraced his steps to the back of the church. There, on the last pew, was an infant in a woven basket. She wore a pink cotton jumper and was sucking down the last drops of her bottle.

John also noticed something around her arm. He reached down and pulled out a ruby red rosary. It was the one that had sustained Angela and her daughter during the Darkness. It was also the one that Elizabeta Concepcion had given to her own daughter, a lifetime ago.

> The task of the proletariat
> is to create a United States of Europe,
> as a foundation for the United States of the World.
> Leon Trotsky

EVAN WAS NOW DRIVEN by a renewed intensity. As he recovered from the concussion he had suffered at the hands of his former lover, Thas focused all his energies on the next phase of his diabolical agenda. He surprised even himself at the global scale of his organizational productivity and, consequently, had no regrets about Mer's fiery fate.

He looked at the bright side: she had taught him to trust no one.

So, skillfully managing his vast resources and enthusiastic followers, Thas methodically pursued his unification efforts for the Perfect World Agenda. He delegated far-ranging responsibilities to competent teams of trusted underlings. They, in turn, relentlessly drove his strategies for the Titan global currency as well as centralized control of the world's defense, public health, justice, and social services.

He had been secretly maneuvering to displace the power of the Legion of Babylon since most of the original members had been lost in the Darkness. But his old partner, Vasiliy Melnikov, was being equally duplicitous by attempting to resuscitate the once-powerful institution with his own hand-picked team. Thas did not see much upside, anymore, from allying with the Legion. However, neither did he want them as enemies.

For his public declarations, Evan cleverly crafted the talking points that would entice most people. His words were as fluid as water, but his policies as solid as rock. Each day, Thas effectively coordinated media themes that elevated his allies or blamed his enemies. The issue of truth was not important, only believability. His informational campaigns undermined the credibility of once-respected institutions like judiciaries, police forces and military branches, while elevating the appeal of replacing them with Perfective Patrollers. He promoted the idea of shaming, in the media, anyone who stood for the old traditions of familial cohesion, national patriotism, and religious faith. His transformational ideas then infiltrated the scripts of the news anchors, actors and comedians who were employed by his media monopoly at XBC News and Entertainment.

Then, whenever his lackeys successfully pushed one of Evan's priorities into the public consciousness, he would commission an opinion research poll on the subject so that the foregone conclusion of the poll could be promoted to create the impression that practically everyone believed the clandestine lie. Consequently, for those without deeply ingrained principles, everything associated with Evan was becoming fashionable. Everything he despised, they learned to hate.

For every perceived advancement, Thas took credit. For every perceived setback, he assigned blame. So, day by day, he was achieving his goal: incrementally and methodically driving global, centralized control into his own hands.

Before the Darkness, he had cynically encouraged the theft of Church assets. After it, he shrewdly took credit for the world's greatest transfer of wealth. Perfectives now found themselves with material possessions that they never dreamed of owning. So, a media campaign was established to publicize happy Patrollers who claimed, "I love my Evan yacht," "Thanks Evan, for my mansion," and "This is my favorite Evan car." Consequently, the media manufactured image of a benevolent redistributionist propelled his popularity.[118]

Evan's compliant media enabled him to become so comfortable with lying that he frequently contradicted himself, without challenge, even when his recitation of so-called "facts" proved at odds with well-known events or common sense. Still, he spouted lies so convincingly that many people deferred to his judgment, even when he had no real evidence or expertise to support his conclusions.

Once-respected award committees vied for favor from the world's supreme leader. Over the course of just two years, Evan had won the Euclidian Award for scientific excellence, the Middleton Medal for humanitarian outreach, supreme recognition from the Pacifica Freedom Alliance for achievements in equality, as well as the Unified World Harmony trophy for distinguished contributions to human advancement.

With each award, a frenzy of reports covered the globetrotting celebrations of Evan and his stable of star-struck celebrities. For reporters and entertainers, alike, centralized power remained popular... as long as they remained in Evan's good graces. He was particularly pleased that some of them had even scarred their faces as an *homage* to their pop culture icon.

Thas had become a public cheerleader for global unification of every major organization. But whenever officials dragged their feet, he was a private bully for it. If legislatures failed to pass his desired laws, he had regulations promulgated, instead, that accomplished the same goals. Whenever those regulations were resisted, he shamed resistors in the media. The incurably defiant, however, were packed into freight trains and sent to the wilderness.

This was a time of unparalleled persecution.

Many of those exiles, however, did not die in the wilds. In fact, they thrived. Though they clustered in simple, hand-crafted huts, or tents, or caves, they managed to live comfortably. Though they found nourishment only from hunting, fishing, farming and foraging, they did not suffer from hunger. They realized that they lacked nothing of importance. So, their families bonded in love, their communities lived in peace, and their God showered them with Spiritual blessings because He had become the focus of their lives.

The Lord richly rewarded their faithfulness and, for those who sought no earthly pleasures, heavenly ecstasies became common.[119] Here, God honored His promise: "In the last days, I will pour out my Spirit on all people. Your sons and daughters will prophesy, your young men will see visions, your old men will dream dreams."[120]

I do not love the bright sword for its sharpness,
nor the arrow for its swiftness,
nor the warrior for his glory.
I love only that which they defend.
J.R.R. Tolkien

Chapter 19
Papal Apartment
Avignon, France
August 29

AFTER MORNING MASS, each day, Pope Peter returned to his balcony where he risked possible assassination as he addressed religious pilgrims in the courtyard below. Still, he was prepared to accept God's will, whatever the outcome.

Today, overlooking the throng, he encouraged them in the faith and requested that they return home with a commitment to a simpler, more prayerful life.[121] As always, Father Henri Blanc listened while pecking away on his keyboard, inside the papal apartment.

The ancient apostle understood the deterioration of modern relationships. He warned the crowd that technology was endangering the personal associations that God had planned for each of us. Television, movies, video games, and the Internet had led to idolization of attractive celebrities, talented athletes and charismatic politicians. But their media-manipulated personas, he charged, were diabolical illusions designed to diminish the appeal of the gifts of friends, family and faith.

Even with today's youth, social networking had become an addictive enticement to meaningless chatter, producing a seemingly endless array of acquaintances, but rarely a true friend.

The Great Deluge of this Age, he claimed, was the technological flood of the senses, drowning out Spiritual thoughts; and though the flood of Noah's Age had caused physical death, the flood of this Age was even worse, producing Spiritual death. For most, communion with modern music or entertainments had displaced communion with God. Every moment spent with technology was a moment spent without God.

"No projected or printed image, no moving music, can transmit love," he warned them. "Love can only exist in the personal relationships that God has given you. Do not fail in those precious relationships."

Listening nearby, Henri felt that John might be harboring resentments for Blanc's important contributions to the technological Age. Still, he knew and was determined to prove that technology can also be used as a force for good.

John continued, urgently requesting that his listeners begin to spread the Gospel, not only within each family, but to whoever would listen with an open heart. Most importantly, however, he proclaimed that the glorious Cross in the sky was mankind's last warning to seek, speak and live the Truth.

"Speak Truth," he pleaded, "with love in your hearts. Some will accept, so nurture their knowledge with love. Some will ignore, so pray for their conversion with love. However, some will scheme and attack. They will fine you, imprison you, and send you off to mental institutions. But do not lose the faith. Denounce them with love. Defy them with love. Disrupt them with love."[122]

A respectful hush had descended upon the crowd. They focused on John's every word.

"We must return to the practices of the ancient apostles. In the early days, professing "I believe in one God" was not tolerated. The emperors could not condone any religion that ignored their pretended divine nature.[123] Also, Rome had expanded and prospered under the presumed protection of the ancient pagan gods. So, Christian professions were deemed acts of sedition, and getting caught with such a written declaration became a crime, punishable by death. Consequently, believers learned to transmit the profession of faith verbally, from town to town and generation to generation.[124]

"Likewise, the life of the faith now must be preserved by word of mouth. Soon, our Bibles will be burned. Our books will be destroyed. Therefore, you can no longer rely on the written word spreading the Gospel for you. You must communicate it, yourself. You must live it, yourself.

"You can no longer expect governing authorities to lead with charity and justice. You must be charitable and just, yourself. Still, beware who you trust. For, in this Age, whoever is not with us is against us, and whoever does not gather with us, scatters."[125]

Pope Peter II blessed the crowd and then added, "A malignant tumor is sickening the world.[126] It must be removed. Many ignored the danger of the growing cancer. Yet, they disregarded it at their own peril. So, just as surgery is preceded by concern, and accompanied by pain, removing the world's malignancy will be trying. However, the human body and the Body of Christ will only reach their glorious potential once the cancer is gone."

The crowd remained quiet, hoping for more.

"Though France has a long and glorious history, it has not yet risen to its greatest glory before God. That day will not arrive until you are led wisely."

Inside the papal bedroom, Henri Blanc raised his eyes from his keyboard and listened more closely.

"Throughout the centuries, a Great Monarch has been prophesied for France.[127] In the Latter Days, he shall be led by the Archangel Michael and unite the faithful,[128] assemble great armies and expel tyrants from his empire.[129] He shall subject all the East,[130] and rule Europe like Charlemagne.[131] He shall regain the Holy Land, convert the world, and bring universal peace."[132]

The words fell on Henri Blanc's ears harshly. He had not been warned that this announcement would be made. He stood up from his computer and began to pace, contemplating the future that was being thrust upon him.

John continued, "Restore the monarchy and France shall rise to greatness before God![133] My faithful friends, I present to you, today, a descendent of Constantine, Pepin,[134] Francis I,[135] and Louis IX."[136]

John turned to the open door and said, "Henri, it is time."

As the priest joined him on the balcony, John said, "I present to you Father Henri Blanc, your future king!"

Only a few pilgrims applauded. For a long, uncomfortable moment Henri felt embarrassment. But then more and more began to express their full support.

John continued, "Take this message to every French city, village, field and valley: France's greatest days are ahead! France shall lead the world's faithful when France is led by the Great Monarch! Demand a referendum and it shall be so."

The courtyard reverberated with cheers and applause.

However, watching from above, Father Henri Blanc was not moved by the crowd's festive attitude. He was a man of peace who would be thrust into a world of war, and he feared that this jubilant crowd would lose their enthusiasm as soon as the tumor resists removal.

Wisdom matters little to fools,
and madmen care little for sanity.
So, speak to everyone in his own tongue.
Baltasar Gracian

WHEN PRESIDENT CONCEPCION finished describing her five-point program on stabilizing the economy, she darted away from the podium. She ignored loud questions from XBC reporters: the only approved journalists, these days, as dictated by Perfective Agenda regulations. Before she reached the door into the west wing, though, one shout caused her to stop abruptly.

"Times Square lights are dark!"

Angela turned to see who had yelled that odd expression. As her eyes scanned over the journalists and guests who were heading out the Rose Garden, she remembered that the original remark had come from Huntington Cyst, the first time she met him.

Back then, Huntie was at his peak, Evan was on the rise, and Fred was stealing her heart. Angela, however, was just the lowly New York Secretary of State. So, she was thrilled to be invited to such a high-powered meeting.

But, that night, Cyst and Thas were aggressive in handling their newfound political neophyte. From their meeting room, high above Manhattan, Cyst had badgered her with, "Madame Secretary, I saw you looking down admiringly on Times Square. Someday, those lights may go dark. If and when they do, are you up to the task? Will you have the balls to take control and set things right?"

"Absolutely," she had responded, firmly.

But he had not been reassured. He hammered her with, "If not, you can take your principles and uncertainties all the way to the unemployment line. I don't side with lovable losers."

They had dangled the presidential apple before her and she gobbled it, peel, seeds and core. No matter how dire the circumstances would get, she would let them lead.

Since that meeting, however, Angela and Evan were the only ones who had survived. Yet, the odd shout that she had heard came from a woman.

Who could it be?

Near the last row of chairs, a woman stood with a toddler, sleeping in her arms. When their eyes met, the young lady nodded and gave a faint wave.

The president's hand went up and she abruptly motioned for her to approach.

"It's okay," Angela said to Agent Anderson. "I want to speak to her."

When the blond woman arrived, the president asked, "What does that expression mean to you?"

The young lady answered with a question. "Do you know who I am?"

Angela studied her face. "I don't think so."

She asked, "May we speak, privately?"

"Let's step inside … just for a moment."

The woman did not budge. "Madame President, I would rather speak out here. The Rose Garden offers greater privacy."

The president laughed. "Don't be ridiculous. Nobody wiretaps the White House."

"Nobody?"

Angela studied the attractive young woman's quiet determination. Then her gaze fell upon the boy who was now awake and smartly studying his surroundings. He looked vaguely familiar with his pale complexion, bright blue eyes and wispy red hair.

She thought, *He resembles…*

Angela gasped and then whispered, urgently, "You're Evan's girlfriend!"

The president grabbed the woman by the arm and pulled her

across the grass to a more secluded area of the garden. "I read that you were both dead!"

Mercedes Dare ignored the comment and proceeded with her own agenda. "Madame President, whenever we travelled together, Evan enjoyed his vodka... excessively. During those long trips, he told me a great deal about himself: about how he thinks, about his plans. I learned a lot about Evan ... a lot about you."

"Why did he trust you?"

"He let his guard down with me because... because he knew I was in love with him." Mer rolled her eyes and shook her head over the embarrassing admission. Then she gathered her reserve and added, "More importantly, he let down his guard because he judged me to be spineless, dependent and naïve."

"That's a pretty harsh assess…"

"You, too."

"What?"

"He believes that about you, too."

Angela reacted angrily. "Well, I don't really care what he…"

"Madame President, I do not say that to be provocative. I am trying to help you learn how your enemy thinks."

"My enemy?"

"Absolutely."

Angela thought for a moment and then said, "Go on."

"Let me ask you: Going forward, how do you plan to handle Evan?"

"Well, I've been trying to avoid him. He called, shortly after the Darkness, and I didn't answer it."

"That has only worked because he has bigger fish to fry, right now. But when he finally forces a communication and presents his demands?"

"Demands? I... uh…" Her tone became forceful. "I will let him know he's dealing with the President of the United States!"

Mer restrained a sad smile. Evan was right: Angela was naïve.

The young woman's hand slowly reached for Angela's face and brushed aside her bangs. There, on the president's forehead, was the mark of Titan.

The president resented the intrusion into her personal space. She reached for Mer's hair. "What about you?"

But when Mer's forehead was revealed, Angela saw only a scar, in the shape of a Cross.

"You... you cut it out?" The president thought for a moment, then added, "Okay, I'll get rid of mine. I'll have a plastic surgeon..."

"No," she snapped. "If you do that, you won't last a day. I only survive because Evan thinks I'm dead."

The president contemplated her diminishing options. "Then, what?"

"Madame President, he knows your instincts from your Titan analysis. So, he expects you to resist his leadership, now."

"And I will. I won't give in."

She sighed, "Right now we need heroes more than martyrs. I assure you, sooner or later, you'll give him what he wants ... or you'll give him your life. Even your daughter is not safe."

Angela was lost in a torrent of tumultuous thoughts.

Mer added, "Speaking of that, where is she?"

The president snapped back to life. "None of your business!"

"I only ask because she needs protection."

"She's with relatives," Angela barked. "So, don't worry about it!"

The young woman tried to soften the tension. "I understand. I'm just trying to be..."

"So," Angela demanded, "what do you suggest I do?"

"Become his biggest fan. Play on his preconceived notions. He thinks you are spineless, dependent and naïve, so pretend you are. Then, if you want him to avoid you, barrage him with an endless stream of needy requests. If you want him to stay away, beg him to come back to Washington."

Angela asked, "But what if he does?"

Mer's voice turned icy. "Kill him."

The president drew a long, slow breath and then exhaled.

"You might be the only capable person who can get close enough. But you won't have the opportunity until you regain his trust."

The president was doubtful. "How?"

"Think. Think like Evan. How would he answer that question?"

Angela paused for a moment and then responded, "Find his motivation and then use it against him."

"Right. And what motivates him?"

Angela snorted, "Paranoia."

"That certainly is one of his weaknesses," Mer nodded. "So, plant the seeds of paranoia in his camp."

Angela dredged up another memory, "His favorite strategy is divide and conquer."

"Right," the young mother observed. "You have been learning, haven't you?" She adjusted the infant in her arms. "I can't regain his trust. He thinks I'm dead. But you can. Only then will he be vulnerable."

She looked at the sleeping toddler in Mer's arms. "So, that's his son? He looks so much older than Evie."

"The incubation growth hormones accelerated his development. I pray he won't suffer adverse side effects."

"Is he safe?"

"Evan doesn't know he exists."

"What if he finds out?"

Her answer cut like a knife. "He'll dissect him for body parts."

"What?" Angela recoiled.

"Evan is a freak of nature; one in a billion. His body will only accept transplants and skin grafts from his own offspring." With anger, Mer continued, "I am also a freak of nature: the only woman who has ever been able to conceive a child with him."

"Ohhh, now I understand," Angela thought aloud. "I always wondered why the king of biotechnology had to inhabit the body of a crippled, molten ghoul."

Mer looked down on her child and shook her head as her eyes welled up. Trying to make sense of the world, today, she softly moaned, "He's such a smart, loving little boy."

Reminded of her own daughter, Angela sympathized.

Mer's eyes darkened. "But he's the son of evil incarnate." She growled, "Will he be a monster, too?"

"Stop it!" Angela snapped. "He's an innocent child of God!" Then she added, "...no matter who his father is."

With that passionate defense of life, Angela realized how much she was beginning to sound like her own mother. It was a startling discovery, for her, but one she liked.

"Of course," Mer nodded, "you're right."

For a moment, the president pondered the seemingly insurmountable obstacle this young woman faced. Her plan to remain in control of her child, while evading Evan's increasingly sophisticated surveillance technologies, seemed too risky. Successfully living off the grid would be challenging for anyone, but especially a young mother. Sooner or later, they would be discovered.

"Why did you come to me?" the president asked.

"The enemy of my enemy is my friend."

"The best of friends." Angela sighed. "The worst of enemies."

Mer looked more deeply into the president's eyes. "I need him ... neutralized." She added, "We both do."

Angela realized the serious implications of the request. So, her protective instincts kicked in. "Surely, you won't mind a full body search. I need to determine whether you're wearing a wire."

"Go ahead."

One more test was in order. "We have to search the boy, also."

"I understand."

The unwavering responses reassured Angela. She studied the young woman's face. "Never mind. I trust you."

"So, do you see what needs to be done?"

The president responded evasively. "I have some ideas." Then she offered, "Look, I know who can protect your son."

Mer responded with a sad snort. "There is no man on the planet who can protect him."

Angela said, "There is one."

The answer intrigued Mer, but not enough to relax her maternal instincts.

"No," she responded adamantly. "I will never give up my son."

There is a time for everything…
a time for war and a time for peace.
Ecclesiastes 3:1 and 8

A S JOHN SETTLED IN at his small dining table to prepare notes for tomorrow's announcements, he prayed for the Spirit to speak within him. But before he could open his Bible, he heard a knock.

"Yes?"

An armed guard opened the door and Father Henri Blanc limped into the room.[137]

"Father, come in."

Blanc offered a respectful bow and said, "Your Holiness, I'm sorry to bother you. I have a request… a private request."

"Yes? Come in." The pontiff waved a hand and the guard shut the door as Blanc shuffled toward the table.

"I have come to ask your blessing, Holy Father, for an undertaking of utmost gravity."

John studied the priest's serious demeanor and surmised, "You are ready for war."

"I am…" he corrected himself, "we are, Your Holiness."

The pope exhaled a long sigh. He thought for a few moments, without noticeable movement.

Blanc watched him with concern. He did not realize that this approval would be so difficult for the ancient apostle. Surely, he had seen and even participated in just wars of the past. After all, defense of life against evil attackers is not condemned in the faith.

Then John asked, "Of course, you realize that what you start, you may not be able to stop."

"I do. But Holy Father, we continue to receive reports that Patrollers are slaughtering people of all faiths. Our priests are particularly targeted. They have gone underground and continue to offer the Sacraments, but they are hunted and eliminated whenever they are caught. Patrollers, themselves, are claiming to be the only ones authorized to administer the Sacraments."[138]

"Are you familiar with the requirements for a just war?"[139]

"I am."

"Have you prayed on it?" He added, more emphatically, "Have you prayed, harder than ever, for wisdom?" Then, even more urgently, "Have you sought God's guidance? Have you seriously contemplated the horrors of war and whether you can avoid them?"

Blanc did not hesitate, but neither did he revel in the words, "I have."

John sighed again. Henri noticed that the ancient apostle's eyes seemed different than usual. Uncharacteristically, they were welling with tears and exhibiting, perhaps, even a hint of fear.

John reached out and took Henri's hand. "Join me, for a moment."

The priest sat on the bench, next to the pontiff. Together, holding hands, they bowed their heads, in prayer. Then John whispered, "Where two or more are gathered in Your name, there You are in the midst of them.[140] Holy God, guide us."

A moment later, the pope suddenly twitched with a slight gasp and, when his eyes popped open, Blanc could tell that his uncertainty had disappeared. In fact, he beamed with the enthusiasm of having received a revelation.

"Are you alright, Holy Father?"

John responded with a contented, "Yes … I am." Then he added, without hesitation, "I bless your efforts in the name of the Father, the Son, and the Holy Spirit."

"Amen," Blanc responded, but quickly added, "Holy Father, there is another request I must make."

"I will do whatever I can."

"We'll need to use this table."

"Certainly. I will have the guards move it to wherever you want."

"Uh, no, actually, we need to use it here."

"Here?" the pope asked dubiously. Then he gave in, simply accepting Blanc's request on faith. "Certainly. You may have whatever you want, wherever you want it."

"Thank you, Holy Father." Then, with the enthusiasm, Henri asked, "May we start, now?"

John nodded, with a shrug, "Of course."

Blanc rose from the bench, quickly shuffled to the door, opened it and directed, "Okay, bring it all in."

John watched with interest as a group of men carried into the room a wide variety of computer equipment. They all seemed thrilled to be in John's presence but were too shy to do anything more than work hard for him. So, on and around the table, they set up a dozen computer servers, assorted network hubs, a few video monitors, and a couple of keyboards, all connected with a jumble of miscellaneous cabling.

It was all so much more than John could understand. What does that have to do with war? However, he admired how Blanc took the lead, instructing the men every time they encountered difficulty in setting up the system.

As the knowledgeable men silently proceeded with their work, John remembered the stories of Blanc's legendary brilliance. Perhaps, Huntington Cyst could never have become so successful without his early partner's assistance. After all, the Cyst-Blanc supercomputer was at the heart of most of the greatest successes of XCyst Industries. John thought, *Maybe that's why Henri is so determined to confront Thas. The evil genius achieved his success on Henri's coattails.*

After a while, Blanc finally appeared pleased with the results. He gratefully dismissed the men and then sat at one of the keyboards and began tapping keys in rapid-fire succession. "This will take a few hours," Henri said. "I hope you don't mind."

"No. That's alright."

John continued watching as the priest pecked away and data streamed across his monitor. But a question kept nagging at him. "Why do you have to do that here?" the pope asked.

Henri continued typing as he answered. "We surrounded the papal apartment with chain link wire: outside the four walls, below the floor and above the ceiling. It's called a Faraday shield and it will protect our equipment if Thas chooses to use an EMP against us."

"An EMP?"

"Yes, an electromagnetic pulse. Very rarely, that kind of disruptive radiation can be produced naturally. But I'm more concerned about electromagnetic radiation from a nuclear explosion that would knock out all of our computers. As simply and economically as I can, I'm trying to protect our equipment from that threat."

John silently accepted that the science was beyond his understanding. After a long while, however, his curiosity emerged again. He could not see how all that time on the computer could be worth the effort. "What are you doing?" he asked.

Blanc stopped typing and looked up. "Holy Father, more than anyone, you know the lesson that the ancient Romans learned."

John shrugged.

"They built an unprecedented network of roads so that their soldiers could march out of Rome to conquer the world. After a while, however, those same roads were turned against them as invading barbarians marched into Rome, on them."

"So, what does that have to do with this?"

Henri grinned. "I'm hacking into a Cyst-Blanc supercomputer."

John thought for a moment, and then he understood. "Are you sure you're really a priest?" he laughed.

Blanc smiled, resumed typing, and said nothing more for three hours.

When he finished his task, he felt a deep sense of accomplishment. His mind was exhausted because he had not executed this kind of work for a long time. In the old days he had done it to prank friends or to undermine competitors. This time, however, he was firing the first shots of a just war.

THAT NIGHT, families huddled around their television sets to view the latest pronouncements of Pope Jesus II. Worldwide, it had become a mandatory and mostly unwelcome exercise, each evening. However, few complained publicly because it seemed that those who did, often caught the N1656 virus. Those casualties helped to reinforce Evan's claim to some kind of supernatural assistance.

So, fear had become his greatest motivator and the main ingredient in maintaining universally high television ratings around the world. He demanded that everyone watch because he so often changed the laws[141] of the Perfective Agenda. People learned that missing a broadcast was risky because Thas chose to make horrifying examples of lawbreaking Imperfectives whenever the opportunity presented itself. Consequently, the slightest deviation from each new law could subject an individual to arrest and imprisonment by the Perfective Patrol. Even children had been taken from their parents when they failed to remember the basics of the Perfective Agenda.

Tonight, Thas planned to deliver his message on the peace that Perfect World Unity would bring. He wanted this important speech to demonstrate the softer side of Pope Jesus, for everyone who would cooperate. His poll-tested theme was designed to comfort the masses: "A few freedoms lost, but a Perfect World gained."

Yet, the presentation began much like the others, with a pompous antipope on his papal throne, emphasizing that everyone must comply with his laws, precisely as dictated. Soon, however, bored viewers in 184 countries witnessed a surprising switch.

The video feed abruptly changed to security camera footage of an oceanfront pool at night. A date stamp in the lower, right corner revealed that the scene was from Christmas Day, twenty months ago.

As Evan droned on about how scientists all agree that he is the only man capable of setting mankind back on the right path, the video showed a balding man in a wheelchair, rolling down a pool ramp, into the water. When the man rolled around, facing the home's floodlights, the famous face of Dr. Huntington Cyst was revealed.

For a moment, Cyst sat in waist-high water, sipping from a crystal tumbler.

Unaware of the video glitch, Thas continued to explain that worldwide survey research had found near unanimous trust of his leadership.

Then, the surveillance footage showed another man, emerging from the shadows.

Cyst appeared to welcome him with a smile. He set his drink down at pool's edge and motioned for the man to join him.

In Evan's broadcast studio, however, Faridah Shabaan ran out of the control room and attempted to get her son's attention. But, as had become increasingly common, he ignored her.

So, Evan rambled on about his caring benevolence while the video showed the shadowy man, kneeling at poolside. Then the man abruptly grabbed Cyst's head and shoved it underwater.

The deadly struggle did not last long. It began with Cyst's arms flailing and splashing. Then he pulled the attacker into the water. But the headlock was too strong and, eventually, the Prophet of Technology was motionless, underwater.

In the broadcast studio, Faridah frantically gestured to Evan the cut sign, with her hand jerking across her throat. Still, he continued preaching his Perfect World Agenda, as determined as ever.

Then the video showed the shadowy man as he lifted himself out of the pool. After taking a last look at his victim, the man leaned over, picked up the tumbler and finished Cyst's drink.

By now, Faridah was desperate. She watched a studio monitor, helplessly, while Evan continued reading from his teleprompter.

However, the world was watching the mysterious murderer as he turned to walk back toward the house. Then, just as he neared the camera, he jerked his head back to sling wet hair out of his face.

The video paused, freezing the image of the red hair, blue eyes and white, pasty face of Evan Thas.

Faridah knew she was making a dangerous decision, but she was desperate. So, she snatched a cable out of the control panel for the satellite uplink, setting off an alarm.

Immediately, Thas erupted with obscenities, shouted at his mother. He jumped out of his throne and charged toward her, grabbing her by the collar and raising his fist. But studio hands screamed that she had tried to protect him.

As the alarm continued to sound, they explained that their system had been hacked. Evan lowered his fist and dropped his mother to the floor. Then he went on a rampage, trashing the studio and blaming everyone, but himself.

To Thas, it now seemed that he was warring against the entire world.

In this battle, however, he had only confronted the genius of Henri Blanc. Though a frontal assault on the Cyst-Blanc supercomputer was pointless, years ago, Blanc had programmed a "back door" in the operating system. He alone knew of its existence.

The priest had understood the cult of personality that Thas was meticulously promoting for himself. Evan's monopoly of mass media had unleashed a relentless barrage of propaganda, extolling his allegedly unlimited virtues. So, Blanc simply punctured the bubble of the world's ballooning hero worship, and crashed Evan's illusion of invincibility.

Henri had executed a technological ambush using the weapon that Evan feared most: the truth. In one brief instant he dismantled the image of Pope Jesus II from feared, god-like king, to sinister, murdering hypocrite.

For Henri, the first strike succeeded, exactly as planned.

For Evan, however, such audacity could not go unpunished.

Chapter 22
Avignon Palace
September 5

Q UIETLY, TOGETHER, the pope and the priest worked on their projects. John penned his lengthiest scroll though, this time, he would not be having it delivered surreptitiously to the ruling pontiff. This inspired epistle should be shared publicly, for the betterment of mankind.

At the table, next to him, Henri tapped away at his keyboard, attempting to disrupt Evan's control systems. So far, the brilliant priest had temporarily disabled Evan's universal translator, countermanded various orders of his and confused the schedules for some of his most trusted underlings.

The chaos Blanc had created was upsetting Thas but he was even more furious that his experts had not been able to trace the source of the mischief.

A knock on the door of the papal apartment interrupted the hard-working pair.

"Yes," John called out. "Come in."

A Dominican sister in a white habit entered, carrying a toddler.

"Evie!" John exclaimed as the infant's face broadened into a smile.

"Paapaa," the chubby girl squealed when the nun approached him.

"No, no," John mildly corrected the sister. "Let her crawl to me. It's good for her muscles."

Sister Francis placed Evie on the floor and everyone watched as the infant tried to decide what to do.

"Come to me, Evie," John coaxed. "Come to Papa."

The spectators were quiet with anticipation. Then they erupted with laughter when Evie bolted ahead on all fours, heading for Papa's outstretched arms.

John snatched her up with a lunge into the air and then nestled the laughing baby in his arms for a bear hug.

"Sister, did you already change her diaper?" Before she could respond, he added, "I mean, I'm willing to change her if its necessary."

"She has a clean diaper, Holy Father."

"Has she had a chance to play with her alphabet blocks today?"

"Yes, she just did."

The nun turned toward the door.

"Oh, and one more thing, sister."

She turned back to the doting pope who was bouncing Evie on his knee.

"Have you read a story to her today?"

Sister Francis nodded.

"Well, what? What did you read?"

The nun pursed her lips at his micromanaging of her childcare.

He offered a good natured scold as he stopped bouncing the toddler. "Now, sister..."

"The Garden of Eden, Holy Father."

"Good, good. One of my favorites. Okay. I'll take care of her now, sister. Thank you."

The nun offered a nod and then departed, shaking her head with a smile.

John asked, "Father, can you give me a hand?" as he slid his scroll away.

Henri immediately understood and assisted John with the baby food on a nearby table. The priest handed him a white towel, a small spoon and a plastic container of baby food.

"Smells pretty good," the priest offered as he popped the top open.

"Homemade butternut squash," John said proudly. "Evie's favorite."

As John began feeding Evie, he softly sang *Ave Maria*.

Henri studied their mutually amused interactions and was moved by what a truly outstanding man John was. *So full of love,* he thought. *A living contradiction to today's world.* John had never married, but would have made an outstanding husband. He had never fathered a child, but would have been among the best. He was strong enough to snap a man's neck, but never even uttered a harsh word. It seemed every room was improved by his presence, every conversation, by his knowledge. So, it was not surprising that John had become Jesus' most beloved apostle. He alone remained with the Lord, all the way to His death on a cross. He, along with Peter and his brother James, were the only ones to witness Christ's transfiguration. Still, this most important of men, had retained such humility that even a child responded to him with joy.

John was always at his best when he was with Evie. So, as he wiped her mouth and set aside the empty jar, he bounced her on his knee and urged, "You can sing too. Come on. Sing for me: Paaapaaa, Paaapaaa."

Evie smiled at him, quizzically, and then burped.

The pope and the priest hooted their approval and praised Evie for her talent.

These were the moments they treasured most. Even in times of darkness, nothing could rob them of their joyful appreciation of innocent life. Also, nothing could rob them of their faith in God's ultimate reward.

The furies of hell are now set loose.
Divine punishment is inevitable.
Teresa Neumann
1936

Chapter 23
Rome, Italy
September 10

THE ANTI-POPE, named Jesus II, had refused to explain to the world the incriminating broadcast that showed him murdering Huntington Cyst. Because of his control of the media, Evan felt that the embarrassing episode would eventually fade into a forgotten memory. As always, he possessed the luxury of fabricating realities that people would believe.

So, maintaining his message focus, he originated a steady flow of comforting communications from his studios in Rome. Bad news was always announced by Daniel Mitchum, but Evan delivered the good. However, realizing that Mitchum's feather-light credentials hindered his credibility, Thas chose to add *gravitas* to his resume' by naming the charming, smooth-talker Chief Global Correspondent for XBC News.

To the struggling masses around the world, Evan broadcast daily messages of hope and peace on XBC News and Entertainment's global networks. The elaborate productions were designed to hide Evan's sinister side as effectively as his abundant makeup hid his facial scars. In them, he preached his Perfect World philosophy, elevating science over superstition, and offering the enlightened elites an opportunity to become like gods.[142]

Evan used every weapon in his arsenal of rhetorical conquest. Concepts and phrases were chosen not for their descriptive accuracy but, rather, for their poll-tested likelihood of manipulating the minds of the masses. In fact, the most often repeated talking points of the Perfectives did not convey the truth, but its opposite.

Consistent with his CyBot data mining research, Thas utilized the language that most moved his audience. Now, he was emphasizing nurturing themes of love, caring and service. His words were far removed from his actions, but they were a necessary sedative to calm jittery nerves before the coming cruelties.[143]

Also, to the leaders of the Perfective Patrol around the globe, Evan communicated ceaselessly by verbally dictating major initiatives that were then transcribed, translated and distributed to appropriate Patrollers and Legion leaders. With those communications, he effectively delegated responsibilities and set up performance metrics for the purpose of achieving his strategic objectives. Specifically, he targeted five major areas of potential resistance: political, economic, social, technological, and legal. His goal was nothing short of domination over each target.

Such historic span of control could not have been possible without XCyst technologies, including the universal translator that allowed him to communicate directly to the Perfective leaders in every country as he pressured them for quantifiable results regularly. Those who failed to advance the agenda were quickly replaced. Those who posed a threat to the agenda were also quickly replaced, after being liquidated.

The Perfective Patrollers were primarily responsible for monitoring obstacles for the Perfective Agenda, worldwide. They, alone, were aware of the truth behind the so-called viral pandemic and they used that knowledge ruthlessly. Many times, a single report from a Patroller, alleging that a person had become a threat, resulted in quick liquidation. Consequently, the Patrollers, themselves, sought ways to prove their complete loyalty to Thas, even tattooing themselves with the mark of Titan: three concentric circles.[144] In fact, with the help of Evan's monopoly on broadcasting, that fad was becoming a very popular fashion statement with the young. For Patrollers, however, the tattoos had a more significant purpose: helping to insure that they would never be accused of insufficient zealotry for the cause.

Even major movie stars and professional athletes had been recruited to hype the Perfective Agenda and praise Highest Holiness. Already, they were learning that their beauty, talent or skill would have little monetary value without attachment to the media monopoly of XBC News and Entertainment. These days, fame was impossible to maintain without Evan's sponsorship.

So, with ruthless precision, Thas erased whatever aspects of human history he found objectionable. Then, utilizing the resources of XCyst Industries, the manpower of the Perfective Patrol, and the leadership of the Legion of Babylon, he set out to create the Perfect World as he dreamed it should be.

> If you don't make up your mind,
> your unmade mind will unmake you.
> Eli E. Stanley Jones

Chapter 24
Vatican City
September 10

"WE ARE NOT READY," Evan insisted into the phone as he paced around the papal bedroom. Vasiliy Melnikov was not deterred. "We have everyone we need: Russia, China, the Arabs, even Iran."[145]

"You left out America," Thas grumbled.

"Yes, of course. Land for free, home of the braves."

Evan knew that Melnikov deliberately botched the words to the national anthem just to annoy him. But he refused to let the manipulative troll goad him into distraction. "Vasiliy, we have to evaluate how much of our military leadership has been lost."

"We don't need leadership when we have millions of soldiers ready to devour Israel like vultures on carcass."

"Why the rush?"

"Why the stall?" Melnikov's tone was no longer friendly. "I have made representations to our partners. I have people in my own country who will lose credibility if we back down."

"We're not backing down, just delaying."

"Not good enough!" Vasiliy snapped. "Soldiers are mobilized. Yet, week after week, you stall. They can't wait forever. Iran is threatening to nuke Israel if we keep delaying. If that happens, our Muslim friends will be very upset. They want to take Jerusalem without damage to their holy places." He shouted, "You think we are not ready to attack? Israel is not ready to defend!"

Melnikov heaved a sigh and calmed down. "My friend, you understand technology. I understand oil.[146] When the Saudi oil reserves were contaminated, many of our partners benefited from the rising price of crude. But Israel has discovered massive oil reserves, enough to disrupt our control of world markets. If we're not careful, the Jews will soon dictate world oil prices. They could pump enough to make prices … how you say … plummet."

"I know all this, Vasiliy."

"Then let me tell you what you may not know. If light sweet crude hits $120 a barrel again, our partners will blame you."

Melnikov let Evan absorb the threat for a moment and then added, ominously, "Do you understand me?"

Thas did not respond to the obvious.

"So, ending the Jewish state, now, would prop up world oil prices, provide stability in Middle East and Russia, and make the Arabs and Persians forever grateful."

"I understand…" Evan tried to cut him off, but the Russian refused to yield.

"Then there is China. They have opposite problem. They need cheap oil to keep regime in power and economy going. So, we have the answer for their problem. We allocate Israel's new oil production for China while restricting supply to rest of world to maintain current market prices. You see? Everyone wins. As you say in America, 'It's a no brain.'"

Thas ignored his broken English. "Vasiliy, I have plans for Israel. But I have my hands full, right now, in Rome. Give me more time."

Melnikov was adamant. "I cannot afford to lose face."

Evan thought for a moment and then asked, "What else can I give? What else would buy some time?"

The Russian answered more quickly than Evan had expected. "Give me control of Red Thoroughbred."[147]

"What?"

"After all, you let *Roscosmos* launch the satellite. Why can't a Russian control it?"

"Shared control?"

"Evan," Melnikov grumbled with frustration, "our partners are losing faith in your leadership. They are not comfortable with this … pope act. Your media monopoly, fostering a cult of personality, makes them suspicious that you will not share spoils. You are beginning to look weak, my friend, and that is dangerous. Our partners are men of action, and they are ready to act. Evan, they believe you are becoming … obstinacious?"

"Obstinate," Evan corrected.

"But if you give me exclusive control of satellite, it will make them realize that you are not stonewalling them. Then, leave it to me. I will stall them for several weeks, maybe months."

Thas knew the impatience of the partners that Melnikov surprisingly had been able to bring together. The coalition was too important to allow splintering. However, the Russian was far too slippery to trust.

Putting Red Thoroughbred in Melnikov's hands would be extremely risky. That satellite had been designed to dominate 21st century warfare. It was capable of analyzing troop movements and the potential lethality of every weapon in the theatre, including chemical, biological, nuclear and conventional. Consequently, it could quickly make balance-of-forces calculations, enhance first-strike capabilities, as well as evaluate and map optimal attack routes.

So, control of the satellite was a major concern. However, one other thought kept nagging Evan. He wondered, *How did Melnikov survive the Darkness?*

Then Thas pieced together how Vasiliy had effectively imitated many of his own tactics and strategies. In a surprisingly short period of time, he had expanded his oil influence and fortune into control of key Russian politicians and oligarchs. That accomplishment made him a heavyweight, now, on the geopolitical stage.

Evan was supremely irritated with the mysterious Russian. *He copies my moves. He seems to know how to manipulate me.*

Then a startling thought struck Thas. *Has he studied my Titan analysis?*[148]

Huntington Cyst had prepared Thas for the Illumination of Conscience by teaching him how to extinguish his conscience.[149] Apparently, Melnikov had learned the same technique. Evan began to believe that Melnikov must have been granted access to his detailed Titan analysis. It was the same source for information that Evan had used so effectively against others. Now, Titan had been turned on him.[150]

Huntie must have given him my analysis!

The revelation made clear to him that Melnikov was more dangerous than he had previously realized.

"Just give me control codes," Melnikov pressed. "Our communication is secure."

With access to Evan's Titan analysis, Thas knew that the Russian would be able to predict his moves. It was an intolerable vulnerability. So, as Evan saw it, he now had no choice but to become unpredictable.

He had always despised confusion but, for the first time, he could not trust his own judgment.

"Go ahead, my friend," the jovial Russian prodded. "Make everyone happy. It's a no brain."

"Er!" Evan snapped. "It's a no brain-ER!"

> **We are not interested in generals**
> **who win victories without bloodshed.**
> Carl von Clausewitz

"**I**T IS VERY GOOD," Agent Anderson said as he returned his porcelain cup to its saucer. "What do you call this tea?"

"Lovely, isn't it?" the president mused as she sniffed the aroma. "*Bai Lin Gong Fu* ... a black tea from *Tai Mu* Mountain in *Fuding* Province."

He admired the way Mandarin slipped from her lips as if from her native tongue.

Angela savored another sip, and added, "Unusual flavors, don't you think? Hints of toasted nuts, spice, lemon ... even toffee."

Then, as they sipped, the conversation hit a wall.

For a few moments each of them hoped the other would say something ... anything.

Anderson wondered about the point of this unusual hospitality. He had never before shared off-duty pleasantries with the president, especially in the Oval Office. The formal setting was unsettling for him. After all, he knew more about American beer than exotic Chinese teas.

He thought, *Heads of state sit on this sofa ... not Secret Service Agents.*

"I never had a chance to formally thank you for protecting me, after the Darkness."

"It's just a part of my job, ma'am." To Anderson, the comment seemed odd. Why did she say 'me'? Why not 'us'? Then he realized that he hadn't seen the infant in quite a while.

"Of course you protect me every day, but that was something special."

His expression gave away his thoughts.

"Oh," she added, "and, of course Evie. The world's so crazy, these days, she's staying with relatives. Keeping her out of the public eye is safer."

He nodded as he sipped.

Angela smiled. "You know, I feel terrible to mention … but I can't remember your first name." Then she laughed nervously, with embarrassment.

Agent Anderson had been trained to interpret body language. To him, she seemed insincere, almost as if she was baiting him for something.

Still, he feigned ignorance. "Randall," he answered, "although most of my friends call me Randy."

She poured him another cup. "Then … may I call you Randy?"

He did not immediately respond.

When she stopped pouring, the president studied his face, while adding, "After all, we are friends, aren't we?"

She was definitely trying to manipulate him. However, it did not seem like she was doing it from a position of strength. There was almost a pleading quality to her question.

"Of course we're friends, but I don't think…"

"Good. Then Randy it is."

They sipped quietly for another moment until she blurted out, "Randy, may I ask your advice?"

"Yes."

However, she stalled again. "Would you like a crumpet?"

"No ma'am."

"They're absolutely delicious."

"No. No, thank you."

Angela nibbled on her savory griddle cake, a moment. Then she set it on the plate and asked, "What would you do if you knew that someone was bringing great evil into the world? What if you knew that he has been - and will continue to be - responsible for the loss of many lives?"

She waited, silently, for his response.

He tried a dodge. "I guess … I'm glad that those kinds of problems are above my pay grade."

She mulled over his answer and then asked, "What if you knew that the only way to save lives – millions of lives – would be to kill him?"

"Hmmm," he hesitated. "That's a lot of 'what ifs.'"

"What if it's true," she countered sternly, no longer playing games.

Anderson sighed. "Absolutely true?"

"Positively. If you were in my shoes, what would you do?"

He rustled in his chair and then offered the only advice that seemed logical. "Well … I guess I would kill him."

She breathed a sigh of satisfaction. "Then, I can count on you," she declared.

He was astonished that her words had not conveyed a question but, rather, a statement.

"Count on me for what?" he asked with alarm.

"Randy, your country needs your help. It's time for patriots to answer the call to arms."

He wanted to drop his teacup and run for the door.

"Wait a minute, Madam President. I answered a hypothetical question. I said: 'If I were in your shoes, I would kill him.'"

He hoped she would crack a smile and let him in on the joke.

But she didn't.

The agent responded with an incredulous laugh and his voice cracked from the stress. "I'm not in your shoes."

Angela remained calm. "What if I told you that he killed Vice President Blight?"

"Then … report him to the authorities."

"Randy," she blurted, "if I don't cooperate, I'll be next."

Anderson fingered his hand through his hair. He had no suitable answer. Finally, he ventured, "Look, we can double down on security. You have the best protection in the world. Nobody can get at you."

She softly laughed at his naïve faith in the Secret Service. "Today, not a person on the planet can count on anything more than the illusion of protection."

Anderson had to stand firm. "Madam President, I am not a hit man."

He watched as her face saddened. He could see that she regretted having invested so much into the conversation, with no result.

Her eyes welled with tears. "And you think I am?"

**In the end,
we will remember not the words of our enemies,
but the silence of our friends.**
Martin Luther King, Jr.

Chapter 26
Arnietsk, Russia
September 11

V ASILIY MELNIKOV briefly gazed out a wall of windows
that displayed the stunning Ural peaks of northern Russia.
Then he cleared his throat and returned his attention to a
video monitor that displayed the encrypted video conference he
was hosting.

Using XCyst simultaneous translation technology, the world's
richest man greeted each new member of the group. The new Legion consisted of ten of the planet's most ambitious, surviving power players.

The guests were honored that Melnikov had invited them to such
an exclusive strategy session. Until recently, they had not been considered top-tier players on the geopolitical chess board, and Evan
Thas had shunted them to the back of the bus. Now, amazing new
opportunities were opening up for each of them. The Darkness had
eliminated the Legion's A Team, so to speak, allowing a new generation to be lured into another foolish attempt to centralize global
control. In crafting this re-creation of the Legion, Melnikov's standards had not met previous levels excellence.

Today's meeting had been prompted by a major new development in the news: Israel had just struck Iran's nuclear weapons facilities with bunker buster bombs.

The Russian had hoped for everyone to meet, in person, at his
mountaintop castle. However, an ugly murder of the his prime
minister, there, not too long ago, discouraged these notables from
taking such a risk. To them, a video conference seemed safer and
certainly more expedient.

"My friends," the jovial toad announced, "welcome to Legion of Babylon 2.0."

Melnikov observed proud nods from most of the monitor's nine faces. He continued, "Our friend, Evan Thas, could not participate today but he wishes a welcome to you ..."

The new President of the People's Republic of China interrupted, "We do not have time for cordialities. Soldiers await their orders. I am not pleased that Dr. Thas has refused to participate. He does not seem to have our interests in mind. Why do we need him?"

"Yes, the Jewish problem will be our first order of business. But regarding Dr. Thas, I am pleased to announce that he has put war satellite, Red Thoroughbred, under my control as a gesture of good will and support for new Legion."

The Grand Mufti of Saudi Arabia declared, "Then why delay?"

Melnikov did not respond, immediately. He knew that inviting this man to the Legion had been done against Evan's advice. After all, as a religious leader, the Mufti might be compromised by loyalty issues.

But Evan, himself, had made the invitation necessary. His pretense of leading a worldwide Church had threatened to alienate people of other faiths. Besides, as Vasiliy had reasoned, the Mufti was highly motivated to accomplish one of the Legion's major goals. The accumulated wealth of Saudi Arabia had been placed at his disposal with ultimate revenge in mind: destroy Israel for its perceived role in attacking the Saudi Royal Family and causing the loss of Saudi oil reserves.

"Not just yet," Vasiliy answered.

Legion members grumbled at that response.

"Not just yet, because I promised Dr. Thas we would wait a few more weeks until he has time to mobilize full resources of XCyst Industries at our disposal."

The head of the U.S. Federal Reserve Bank said, "That's fine with me. We have a few more stability issues to sort out before a world currency can be introduced. War can wait."

"I don't agree," The United Nations Secretary General interjected. "A significant block of U.N. member states have reached the end of their patience. They have troops at the ready who will suspect an Israeli conspiracy if delays continue. Israel's unprovoked aggression warrants international solidarity."

The head of the *Sintilabra* Drug Cartel[151] – another wild card – mocked those words: "Unprovoked aggression warrants international solidarity." He shouted, "Attack!" Then, with a flip of his hand, he suggested, "Be done with it."

"Mr. Melnikov," the Chinese president warned, "you may not realize the urgency of the situation. Millions of soldiers have been armed and mobilized since before the Darkness. Most of them are upset, now, for being called away from their homes during the crisis. Further, they are bored, without an immediate outlet to vent their warrior instincts." He added, more ominously,

"An armed and angry but idle force is a powder keg, ready to explode."

"I understand," Melnikov conceded. "Our Russian troops have been similarly inconvenienced."

"We need that satellite reconnaissance," the prime minister of Turkey added. "Red Thoroughbred exposes their weaknesses and allows us the element of surprise."

"Correct," Melnikov said. "But I agreed not to engage the satellite until Thas is ready. I promised to vote for delay."

The comment received widespread disapproval, just as Vasiliy had expected from the members that he, himself, had chosen.

"I understand your anger," the clever Russian said. "But we must never initiate hostilities without moral high ground. Iran has its provocation, but we need something more." He thought for a moment and then added, "My friends, I believe I heard that Israeli Defense Forces have begun raping Palestinian women..." Melnikov embellished his lie. "...and murdering Palestinian babies." He reflected, sadly, on his story for a moment. "Yes ... I am quite certain I will be reading about it in tomorrow's newspapers."

Now, his audience listened closely. No one wanted to interrupt the pretext narrative.

"So," he continued, "I can see why you and all right-thinking people of world are outraged that this Jewish infection continues to scar great land of Palestine."

Still, they remained silent.

"I understand your frustration. In past, our people rioted, protested and stormed embassies. What has that gotten us? Nothing. Zionists continue to control world." The Russian's impassioned words began to rise to a crescendo. "Our goal is honorable. We seek justice for Palestine. So, who will now stand up for the victims? If we do not protect the women and children of Palestine, now, who will?"

"So," Melnikov concluded as he calmed down, "the Legion must decide now. I will honor my promise to vote for delay. But I am only one voice in a democratic body. If you outvote me… well then…" he shrugged his shoulders, "Surely, Dr. Thas will understand."

In the latter days,
the Holy Ghost will make His heat and light
more strongly felt in the hearts of the faithful;
they will find therein a renewal of faith
and they will the better know and love
the Father and the Son,
and especially our Eucharistic Lord...
and anoint souls for the conflict of those days
which will be marked by all the fury of Hell.

Lucie Christine
aka Mathilde Boutle

"WELL, AT LEAST let me accompany you," Father Blanc offered. "You need protection. You shouldn't go to Rome alone."

"No," John said as he laid folded clothes into a suitcase on his bed. "You stay here, for now. Besides, I won't be alone. I'll be with Evie."

Blanc was not amused. "Your Holiness, I will do what you say, but your plan makes no sense. You can't travel on public transportation. Your safety..."

"I can't take the medi-vac train because they know about it, now. We will be safe. I feel God's protection. Besides, I'll have others there to protect me."

"Holy Father, you directed me to fortify this palace for your safety. We drilled water wells and accumulated massive stores of food. We've made modifications to prepare for conventional battles and siege warfare. We even secured the facilities against many types of weapons of mass destruction."

"You are right that I had you fortify the palace in that way. But it was not for my protection.... It was for yours."

"What?"

"Soon, you will face attack. But your enemies will be ineffective, because you will be prepared and they will be leaderless in Europe."

"Leaderless? What about Thas?"

"Rome has always been a stepping stone for him."

"To where?"

"Jerusalem. The prophecies foretell that he will rebuild the Temple and rule from the holy city."[152]

"Holy Father, news reports say that Jerusalem is surrounded by armies that have broken away from his leadership. Within days, it will be under the control of his enemies."

John responded with a cryptic comment: "They marched across the breadth of the earth and surrounded the camp of God's people, the city He loves. But fire came down from heaven and devoured them."[153]

At times, Henri could not discern whether John was speaking personal opinion or Divine Revelation. So, he persisted. "Why must I stay? Why must you go?"

"Henri, you have wisely engaged the enemy using nonlethal means, as a first resort. However, that restraint will not suffice. You must prepare for military war. I must prepare for a Spiritual one. My future is in Rome. I have no need to hide."

"How long should I avoid an offensive attack?"

"For now, your enemy has an overwhelming technological advantage. Maintain your defenses, and pick your skirmishes cautiously. When the balance of power shifts, you will know."

He sighed and returned to his previous insistence. "Holy Father, Patrollers will be everywhere at the train station. They'll spot you, right off. It is too dangerous."

John smiled. "Just like you, my mother, Solome, continually worried for my safety." Then he added, pointedly, "And that was two thousand years ago."

Is God less powerful than the devil?
It is necessary to go forward without fear
and without trepidation. God is with us,
and He will be victorious.
Fatima visionary
Lucia dos Santos

Chapter 28
Avignon Train Station
September 11

TWELVE OLD NUNS had studied John's instructions and passed his standards. They were different in many ways, but shared a few commonalities. First, none of them had left Avignon's cloistered convent in years. Second, they had never before worn such bright, gaudy clothes and hats. Third, they were thrilled to be chosen to assist Pope Peter's clandestine journey to Rome.

Just as planned, when they streamed into the train station they became the focus of attention, fumbling with their heavy suitcases and bumbling through the crowd. The normally quiet and polite ladies had been instructed to be loud, uncultured and rambunctious. So, they pretended to be Americans.

Following close behind them, John was inconspicuous, wearing sunglasses and casual clothes in bland shades of beige. In his arms, however, he carried little Evie who sported oversized sunglasses, a big, floppy hat and a jumpsuit of dazzling neon colors. As loudspeakers reverberated announcements through the station, no one noticed his face. Everyone smiled at hers.

The always hectic train station was even more chaotic than usual. Undermanned staffs had not yet returned rail service to its previous efficiency. So, travelers were more numerous and more adamant about avoiding the delays and cancellations that had become common since the Darkness.

Still, John's entourage progressed quickly through the revolving doors, toward the ticket counter, coordinating their movements.

Not far from the entrance, he spotted a pair of men in bright blue shirts. On their shoulders he noticed distinctive chevrons under Titan bulls eyes. They were obviously Patrollers.

Suddenly and loudly, two heavy nuns confronted them.

"For goodness sake, where are the bathrooms around here?" said the first. "Don't you people believe in bathrooms?"

The other woman added, "No ice. No bathrooms. I thought this was supposed to be a civilized country."

The Patrollers offered directions but the ladies wouldn't listen.

"I can't understand you," one shouted. "Doesn't anybody speak English around here?"

The other nagged, "I told you we shouldn't have come to France!"

John and Evie successfully slipped past them but slowed as they approached four more Patrollers. John paused at a kiosk, pretending to be interested in their merchandise until he heard, "Help! Somebody stole my purse!"

Then he quickly darted over to the ticket counter.

"Deux billets pour Rome s'il vous plait," he requested as he looked down to count his currency while cradling Evie in his arm.

When he laid his money out on the counter, she handed him two tickets and he thanked God that they still accepted the old currency. Fortunately, the long-promoted Titan digital currency was not yet in place.

The unfriendly clerk never made eye contact with John and neither did anyone else until he and Evie had safely maneuvered to the boarding platform. There, one man caught his eye and seemed to recognize the pontiff. But his wife distracted him when the train arrived and John safely slipped into another railcar, along with his garish escort team.

So far, everything had proceeded as planned. However, during the course of the journey, more ruses became necessary. One angry nun was detained for slapping an inspector after a pat down and another diverted a particularly pesky Patroller when she slipped on her spilled soft drink.

So, at times, the journey had been amusing.

The destination, on the other hand, was not.

These are the evil times,
a century full of dangers and calamities.
Heresy is everywhere,
and the followers of heresy
are in power almost everywhere...
But God will permit a great evil against His Church:
Heretics and tyrants will come suddenly and unexpectedly;
they will break into the Church...
They will enter Italy and lay Rome waste;
they will burn down churches and destroy everything.
Venerable Bartholomew Holzhauser

Chapter 29
Vatican City
September 11

JOHN HAD EXPECTED that his homecoming would not be happy. After all, he would never forget the martyred saints of the Sistine Chapel. What he was seeing now, however, shocked him. When he, Evie and the sisters had first slipped into Rome, he sensed something was different. He could smell it in the air. So, as soon as he had securely deposited the child and her saintly nannies in a safe house near the outskirts of Rome, he ventured alone into Vatican City. To the nuns, it seemed a dangerous and unnecessary exposure, especially since Evan Thas still resided in Rome. However, John assured them that nothing would stop him from following wherever the Spirit led him.

In his hand, he carried the scroll that contained his final epistle to the Church, his longest ever. In his heart, he carried a very important message that would be delivered at the Vatican.

Now, standing on the front steps of the basilica, he viewed the origin of the unholy odor. Spanning the length and breadth of St. Peter's Square, almost rising to the peak of St. Peter's memorial obelisk, was a smoldering mountain of Perfective plunder: the ashen remains of the Vatican museums and archives.[154]

Gazing the sinister smoke as it rose toward the awesome red Cross in the sky, Pope Peter remembered Father Blanc's concern that the Perfectives were beginning to erase all references to God from the Internet. John also had heard that Patrollers had been seizing Bibles and other holy books. Now, he could see the result of such confiscations.

It was a diabolical holocaust of Christian knowledge. Before him lay the cooling ashes of the world's greatest collection of Christian writings and art. Where the Goths, Huns, Vandals, Normans, Saracens, and Ghibellines had failed, only Evan Thas had succeeded. The sack of the Eternal City was complete.

Now, just as vultures depart when the carcass is cleaned, Perfectives no longer patrolled the grounds of the Vatican. Everything of material value had been stolen. Everything of Spiritual value had been destroyed.

Their grand plan was now clear. The Perfective Patrol had been perfectly extinguishing all vestiges of Christian history, whether preserved physically or digitally.

John turned to enter the basilica, and proceeded with caution.

The building's interior was dark, lit only by beams of sunlight that streamed in from broken windows. Inside, he noticed shattered stained glass, former frescoes that had been painted over, and mosaics that had been hammered beyond recognition. Everywhere, statues had been toppled and crushed.[155]

As he walked, he saw that the marble Pieta' and the bronze St. Peter were missing. Even Bernini's magnificent spiraling *baldacchino*, that had canopied the main altar, was gone.

Every holy image had been destroyed, all salvageable metal had been hauled away for melting, and every sacred object had been defiled.

Worse still, John was disturbed by the suspicion that the toll of human death, here, must have been high. Yet, he knew that this slaughter of the innocents would go unreported by XCyst's media monopoly. These days, no one was allowed to even catalog those deaths. For the seekers of a Perfect World, the lives of Imperfectives held no value.

Carrying his scroll, John made his way out a side door and down a cobblestone alley until he found the Secret Archives. The door had been battered open and precariously dangled from one hinge.

He squeezed his large frame through.

There, John hoped he might find the prefect, Mosignor Bolaka. But the building was empty, not only of people, but of its precious contents. As he wandered through lengthy, ornate rooms he noted that every bookcase had been cleared.[156] He knew that every book, codex and scroll had been burned.

After a lengthy walk, he finally found the inconspicuous steel door he was seeking.

John remembered that the combination had been established with the Trinity in mind. The code was simply 3-3-3, a number that represented complete perfection.

As he turned the dial, he also reflected on the Titan symbol. *Three concentric circles,* he thought. *Zero, zero, zero: Symbol of complete nothingness.*

The heavy door squealed open. He stepped in, onto a metal grate, and then began descending down one flight of stairs after another.

His footsteps eerily echoed in the dimly lit shaft and he was concerned that he might be alerting someone below that he was approaching.

Still, he had no fear. He knew that the worst an enemy could do was to kill him and, as far as John was concerned, that eventuality was eagerly anticipated and long overdue.

When he finally arrived at the storage bunker, far below ground, John was shocked to find the vault unguarded, and the door ajar.

His melancholy eased as he felt that, perhaps, this surprise was an encouragement from God. After all, he believed that he had been called to deliver his last scroll to the archive vault. However, his task would have been impossible if the door had been locked.

This bomb-proof enclosure had been equipped with a state-of-the-art security system, including an access control system that required a series of biometric inputs.

He marveled at the fact that the fourteen inch thick door was ajar.

John heaved open the monstrous slab of metal. He clicked on the light and stepped inside.

The shelves were empty.

Every one of the 1782 scrolls that John had delivered to reigning pontiffs over two millennia had been removed. Most certainly, they were now destroyed.

The ancient apostle remembered his first one. He wrote about it in the Book of Revelation: "I was caught up in the Spirit on the Lord's day and heard behind me a voice as loud as a trumpet, which said, 'Write on a scroll what you see and send it to the seven churches...'"[157] Few had ever learned that many scrolls had followed.

Here, the inspired private revelations[158] that had been regularly dictated by God through John had been preserved. They had guided the one, holy, catholic and apostolic Church and insured that the gates of hell would not prevail against it.

John knew how carefully the Catholic Church had protected those works of inspired wisdom. Patiently, each pope had preserved them for the day on which the Beloved Apostle approved their release to the world. Now, they were gone, and John knew that Patrollers could have only gained access to the sacred scrolls by one means: torture.

John had known that those continuing instructions contained nothing more than could be found in the Scriptures. Still, every pope had treasured the advice and found clarity in their simplicity.

With all this protection, no one ever dreamed that the scrolls could have been destroyed so easily. This storage vault even had humidity controls and air filtration that protected its contents from attacks by weapons of mass destruction.

He observed that the Patrollers had plundered with single-minded purpose. They had left everything else behind. On the wall still hung photographs of succeeding popes pictured with the same man in his early thirties: John, himself.[159] They had also left stores of food and water. None of that was worth destroying, only the holy scrolls.

The shameless destruction of those inspired messages depressed him, and John sighed as he placed his last epistle on the shelf.

He thought, *Maybe somebody, some day, will benefit from it.*

Then he turned and quickly left, not bothering to shut the door behind him.

WHEN JOHN RETURNED TO THE BASILICA, an exhaustion overwhelmed him, unlike any he had ever felt before. It was more than a physical depletion. For the first time in his lengthy life, he was Spiritually spent.

As he collapsed onto the steps of the once-great altar, the demons haunted him with paralyzing anxieties of hopelessness and despair. His every inadequacy was flaunted. His soul was taunted with trepidation and doubt.

This was his dark night of the soul.[160]

Throughout the centuries, John had witnessed the horrendous persecutions of the Roman Emperors but, still, the Church survived.

He had endured the plundering and pillaging of the barbarian hordes but, still, the Church survived.

He had experienced the wave of Islamic warriors that swept across Christian lands and enslaved its people but, still, the Church survived.[161]

His whole, long life, he had witnessed and condemned the relentless attacks of heretics and apostates but, still, the Church survived.

Then, he watched helplessly as the 20th century unveiled unprecedented forces of evil that provoked world wars and invented weapons that made possible the destruction of all mankind but, still, the Church survived.

The Church, no matter how small, had always provided John's

support network. Now, however, he felt alone.

Where are God's allies on earth? Why are good people so indecisive?

It seemed that with each recent warning, mankind had first focused on God's chastisement but soon grew lukewarm again. The loss of the Saudi Arabian oil reserves had plunged the world into economic chaos that warned against a faith based on wealth. The earthquake in Semiazas California showed the fury of natural disasters and warned against embracing decadence and materialism. The N1656 viral pandemic had warned against forgetting the fragility of our short lives. The disaster on Nauru had warned against manipulating human life.

Most obviously, the Three Days of Darkness had opened every survivor's eyes to their sins and God's mercy. Still, a majority quickly grew lukewarm in their faith again, even dismissing God's permanent Cross in the sky as the symbol for Titan.

After each chastisement, mankind had simply returned to its former ways, depending only on man's ingenuity to rebuild whatever was lost, even bigger and better.[162] Unfortunately, however, lost souls cannot be rebuilt.

John wondered: without the uncompromising, visible guidance of the Church, how could mankind avoid a headlong plunge into hell on earth?

Tears were not adequate. Moans would not suffice. No human response to suffering could lessen the awesome burden of loss he felt.

Have You forsaken us, God?

Why was I chosen to lead the Church to its ruin?

How could mankind be so blind to the lies of Evan Thas?[163]

The ancient apostle reflected on how many times, over twenty long centuries, he had risked his life to deliver those scrolls. Producing, protecting and preserving them had always seemed like a great and holy mission. Now, what good had they accomplished?

John felt everlasting blame for the lives of every holy person who had died assisting his efforts. Their sacrifices had all come to naught.

A demonic spirit of nihilism had annihilated all he held dear.[164]

Now, without the guidance of the Magisterium of the Church people would fill the theological void with every conceivable interpretation of God's revelation to man. No longer would they rely on twenty centuries of accumulated inspiration and knowledge. The eternal truths would be reduced to passing fads, adjustable to each new generation and to each new perspective. Without the authority of the one, holy catholic and apostolic Church, the ancient apostle knew that the easy paths of Satan's heresies would soon become the popular routes away from God.

Lying prostrate on the cold, marble floor of this den of destruction, John felt nothing but failure. He had fallen so far since those heady times with Jesus Christ, twenty centuries ago. Then he had approached each day with unbounded optimism, even asking the Lord to allow him to sit at His right hand in Paradise. Jesus had warned John that he did not understand what kind of service and sacrifice that honor would require. Certainly, he had not.[165]

The ancient apostle was drowning.

Drowning.

Drowning.

But he stiffened when he heard the creaking sound of an opening door at the front of the church.

Suddenly, as he sat up, John's heart filled with emotions, none of them good. The thunderous anger of his youth returned, the rage that he had long ago mastered.[166] He was ready to fight and, unlike ever before, he was willing to kill.

"Who's there?" The pontiff's growl echoed through the basilica.

For a moment there was no response.

John raised his large frame erect and demanded, "Show yourself, damn you!"

Still, no answer.

"Speak! or I swear I will…"

"Holy Father?" someone implored in the distance.

John listened carefully. *That voice sounds familiar.*

Then he heard another man shout, "*Juanito?*"

§§§

THEY HAD NEVER BEFORE seen him cry such voluminous tears. John wept with shame and then cried for joy as he reunited with Pedro Lopez and Father Michael Alonzo. At this moment, no one on earth could have lifted his spirits more than these two men. They reassured him that all was not lost.

They described how the Latter Day Apostles had accomplished miraculous conversions around the world and, even though their accomplishments would never be widely known in this life, there could be no doubt that the Gospel was being spread and the Sacraments were being celebrated, secretly but certainly.

John had lost track of his mission. But now he remembered. Even with the total destruction of churches, Bibles and religious freedoms, the faith would survive. So, the ancient apostle's holy perspective returned and he felt clarity of purpose, again.

Their joyous reunion, however, was brief, because Father Alonzo insisted that they quickly move to a more secure location. He warned John of how vicious the Patrollers had become.

As they hustled the pontiff out of the basilica, Pedro happily babbled about his amazing visit with Worthington in Paradise. But his tone became solemn when he announced that they were the only two Latter Day Apostles left.

"I sensed it was so," John responded.

Then, as they scurried through the colonnade of St. Peter's Square, the little Honduran explained that Worthington had directed them to find John.

The ancient apostle slowed his pace. "Did he say why?"

Pedro answered. "He just said something about an important message you will give us."

John smiled and stopped abruptly, near the mountain of ash. "Oh, how I have longed for this day," he whispered.

"Come on," Father Alonzo urged. "We need to leave."

"No," John answered adamantly. "It is time."

They recognized the seriousness of his tone and drew closer.

John asked, "Why do you think I came to Holy Sacrifice Monastery?"

Pedro said. "Worthington asked us the same question."

"Well, why?"

Father Alonzo answered, "Because of Sister Clarita?"

"No," John responded. "She was an important and holy saint … but not as important and holy as you."

The two men laughed.

"I would be honored to hear that," the priest said, "if I didn't know you're joking. Holy Father, she bore the stigmata of Christ!"

John asked, seriously, "Do you trust me?"

"Of course!"

"Then fill your pockets with these ashes."

They frowned.

"Do it now."

Reluctantly, the two men slowly dug their hands into the warm black heap."

"Go ahead. As much as you can possibly fit into all your pockets."

The pair felt humiliated to be wasting valuable time on such a dirty, demeaning and pointless effort. But they obeyed faithfully.

When their pockets were bulging, John asked, "Are they full?"

The two embarrassed men nodded.

"Well done," the Vicar of Christ approved. "These holy ashes will last for the rest of your lives."

"Holy Father," Alonzo pleaded, "I don't understand…"

John interrupted. "There is a lot you do not understand. But you will." He continued. "The faith is not preserved in the churches, holy art, or even the sacred Scriptures. As you can see…" he pointed at the mountain of ash, "all that is being destroyed. So, from now on, the faith must be preserved in men's hearts and on their tongues."

The pair listened closely.

Then he charged them with an impossible task. "This will be your responsibility."

"What?" they blurted out, in unison.

John continued. "Pedro, where did you grow up?"

The little man answered, "Honduras."

"More details. Where did you go to school as a child?"

"Uh ... I, uh," Pedro floundered. "I can't remember."

"What's your mother's name?"

He responded with a baffled frown.

"Your father's?"

Still no answer.

John turned to the priest. "Father Alonzo, tell me about your childhood."

"Well, like what?"

"Anything," John answered with a knowing smile.

Alonzo's eyes revealed deep thought, but his silence communicated his confusion. He had no memories of his childhood. The Lord had clouded them.

John reached toward the ash heap and buried his thumb into it. Then he extended his hand toward Pedro and marked a Cross on his forehead. "Remember that you are dust, and to dust you shall return."[167]

Pedro's eyes widened, he gasped loudly and swooned, almost unable to remain standing.

Then John reached toward Father Alonzo. The priest pulled back, defensively, but John persisted, placing an ashen Cross on his forehead while saying, "Remember that you are dust, and to dust you shall return."

Immediately, full knowledge was revealed and Alonzo began laughing. From the depths of his soul he felt overwhelmed by a Spirit of joy, bubbling and percolating out of him, uncontrollably.

Suddenly, the minds of the two men could hardly contain a deluge of extraordinary new memories from their extraordinary ancient lives.

Pedro and Alonzo were, and had always been, Elijah and Enoch.[168]

The Arabs can fight, lose,
and return to fight another day.
Israel can only lose once.
Former Israeli Prime Minister
Golda Meir

Chapter 30
Jerusalem, Israel
September 11

PRIME MINISTER REBEKAH EMUNAH convened an emergency meeting with her Political-Security Cabinet ministers. In heated debate, many of them voiced strong opinions while she listened patiently. But she had never responded with a plan of her own.

Rebekah had been confused and distracted from the secret, secure telephone call she had received from John Malek this morning. His message had caused her to start questioning what were once her certainties.

Recently, Israel had taken out Iran's *Shi'ite*-controlled nuclear capability – a strike that even their *Sunni* neighbors privately welcomed but publicly condemned. So, at least one major threat to Israel had been removed from the strategic equation.

Still, each of her cabinet officials was exhausted, having endured a soul-stirring Illumination of Conscience only to recover to the continuing dread of endless war. The massive forces that had amassed on their borders had not dispersed. They maintained a holding pattern, seemingly waiting for orders to either attack or disband. So, the prospects for war had become clouded with uncertainties, particularly since every person on the planet was now forced to consider whether the great Cross in the sky might actually be from the Prince of Peace.

The new equation was now especially hard to calculate for Rebekah. Normally, American satellite reconnaissance would be a welcome addition to Israeli defenses. However, Evan Thas had become so dominant in the U.S. space program that shared American intelligence had become highly dubious. Consequently, none had been requested. America, no longer, could not be trusted as a defense ally.

The prime minister knew that many of the top leaders of the attacking forces had not survived the Darkness. However, the soldiers themselves had lived because they were not irredeemably evil. They were just followers. Consequently, it remained to be seen whether the surviving enemy leaders would still order the invasion, or whether their forces would even follow their dictates, now.

To the prime minister, that could be the key to success. Ground forces were essential for taking Jerusalem because the Arab Muslims would not allow air bombardment of the holy city that contained the Dome of the Rock and the Al-Aqsa Mosque. The Islamists viewed their mission as similar to the role of pest exterminators. The land and buildings were to be protected, only the Jews were to be eradicated.

During the heated cabinet debates, some Israeli ministers argued that God had just proved his almighty power and that He would lead Israel to another great war victory. They reminded her of the heroic initiatives that General Moshe Gideon[169] had seized during the Six Day War and the Yom Kippur War. Both miraculous victories had been won against seemingly overwhelming odds because of the element of surprise. So, they advised Rebekah to attack without delay, even advocating nuclear first-strikes.

Emunah silently rose from her chair, walked to the window and opened the drapery. For the first time, the conference room became quiet. Outside, the awesome mystery in the sky loomed. Still, even as she pondered the significance of the enormous ruby Cross, Rebekah struggled with her uncertainties until the secure cabinet telephone buzzed, followed by a voice on the intercom.

"Prime Minister, the director of Mossad has asked to speak with you. Will you take it?"

Rebekah picked up the telephone. "Yes. Put him through."

She listened for a moment and then hung up the phone.

She directed one of the ministers, "Turn on the TV."

On the screen, an image appeared of Evan Thas, ridiculously adorned in papal regalia, standing amidst the desolation of St. Peter's Basilica. "At my urging, the opposing parties have agreed to seven years of peace."[170]

Israel's defense minister grumbled, "We didn't agree to anything."

Rebekah waved him down. "Let's hear him speak."

Thas continued, "This period of peace is my gift to the world and, if everyone embraces Titan, this will be the beginning of a new age of peace."

The defense minister inserted, "We can't trust that lunatic."

Thas continued, "Whenever you look to the sky, remember that the symbol of Titan is watching over you. Only through Titan can we achieve health, safety and security. With Titan, we will achieve the Perfect..."

"I can't listen to this," the interior minister interrupted. "He's an abomination."

The words struck Rebekah's mind like a hammer.

The internal security minister rejoiced. "This is wonderful news. It's a complete humiliation for our enemies. After backing down, this time, they'll never be able to muster a force like this again."

"That's why I don't believe it," the defense minister declared. "It's a trick. They want us to stand down from high alert. We have to strike now, and it needs to be nuclear this time."

"Russia won't tolerate it," the interior minister said. "They'll respond in kind."

"That's why we hit Moscow first."

The normally quiet treasury minister spoke up. "No. That's insane. You'll set off a war like the world has never seen. Nobody will survive."

Around the table, the ministers argued: "We're backed into a corner. We have no choice."

"No. We can negotiate with Thas. He's a businessman, after all."

"We have to strike first."

"He can help us broker a permanent treaty."

The debate stopped when Rebekah screamed, "Look at him!"

They all turned to the television screen.

At the high altar, where Bernini's magnificent bronze *baldacchino* once stood, a macabre buffoon pretended to pontificate wisdom to the world.

"He is the abomination that causes desolation,"[171] she groaned as she raised a remote control and paused the video. "If we trust him, he will destroy all of Israel."

The telephone rang again and a woman announced over the intercom, "It's the Director. He says it's urgent."

Rebekah picked up the phone. "Yes. What's happening?"

She listened for a moment and then slammed down the phone.

"Turkey closed off Ataturk Dam. The Euphrates is drying up."[172]

The room erupted in angry condemnations.

The defense minister growled, "I told you it was a trick!"

The prime minister covered her face with her hands and pointlessly paced in circles. "Noooo," she moaned. Then she looked up and mumbled, "It is a confirmation."

"What are you talking about?" a minister asked.

When the room finally settled down, she admitted softly, "I have spoken to the Mystical War Counselor."

The defense minister dismissed her comment. "This is no time for fanciful legends or silly stories from General Gideon. You expect us to rely on ghosts?"

"He is not a ghost, but a man."

Some around the table demanded, "Who?"

"He has been known by many names. Recently, he was John Eben Malek. Now, he is called Pope Peter II. There was a time when he was revered as the Beloved Apostle."

"This is insanity."

"I know it sounds crazy, but it's true." She heaved a sigh and then reached into her briefcase. Some ministers frowned when she pulled out a Christian Bible.

She turned to a bookmarked page and read, "Two thousand years ago, the Mystical War Counselor wrote these prophecies:[173] *'Then I heard a loud voice from the temple saying to the seven angels, "Go, pour out the seven bowls of God's wrath on the earth." The first angel went and poured out his bowl on the land, and ugly and painful sores broke out on the people who had the mark of the beast and worshiped his image."* She interjected, "Think about it: the mark of Titan; the N1656 virus that causes these kinds of sores. Thas is responsible!"

She continued reading, *"The second angel poured out his bowl on the sea, and it turned into blood like that of a dead man, and every living thing in the sea died. The third angel poured out his bowl on the rivers and springs of water, and they became blood."* She added, "He's behind all the baffling fish kills around the world."

The health minister interjected, in agreement, "We haven't been able to find a natural cause."

The prime minister continued, *"The fourth angel poured out his bowl on the sun, and the sun was given power to scorch people with fire. They were seared by the intense heat…"*

"Actually," the health minister added, "that's a good description of the symptoms of N1656. I've always doubted that it's actually a virus."

Rebekah resumed, *"The fifth angel poured out his bowl on the throne of the beast, and his kingdom was plunged into darkness. Men gnawed their tongues in agony and cursed the God of heaven because of their pains…"*

Some of the men and women around the table tightened their focus on the prophecies, realizing that they would not still be alive if they had not repented their sins during the recent Darkness. Their faith in God had immeasurably grown, since then. Many less fortunate, however, had died in anguish.

Now, listen to this prophecy, Rebekah emphasized. *"The sixth an-*

gel poured out his bowl on the great river Euphrates, and its water was dried up to prepare the way for the kings from the East."[174]

A couple of the ministers gasped.

"Behold, I come like a thief!" she continued. *"Blessed is he who stays awake and keeps his clothes with him, so that he may not go naked and be shamefully exposed."*

The ministers sat with uncomfortable silence.

"Then they gathered the kings together to the place that in Hebrew is called Armageddon."[175]

Each of them knew what that meant.

"So, these prophecies have been fulfilled, and I don't think it is a stretch to say that each one has a connection to Evan Thas."

The defense minister blurted out, "We don't have time to waste. We will be overwhelmed by this time tomorrow. We need to attack now, hard and fast, with targeted, limited nuclear strikes."

"I would agree with you," Rebekah answered, "but the Mystical War Counselor does not."

The minister screamed his frustration, "Then what?"

She returned to the window and pointed at the looming Cross in the sky. "How can you make sense of what we are going through without acknowledging that? We are the promised race, the Messiah's people, and He shall be a conquering Savior."

"Please," the interior minister interrupted, impatiently, "what's your point?"

"But He first came as a sacrificial Lamb." The prime minister appeared weighed down by a heavy burden. "I have prayed with all my heart, mind and soul that I would never have to make this decision."

The defense minister sensed that she might be ready to trump his limited nuclear strategy. He prepared himself for her declaration of an immediate nuclear blitzkrieg.

She turned to the Cross in the sky and groaned, "Oh, Jesus! Why me?"

The ministers grew uncomfortable with the uncharacteristic focus on Jesus.

Then she sighed and closed her eyes, meditating for a moment as she attempted to overcome her emotions. She opened her eyes and said, "It all makes sense to me now: rely on the words of Jesus."

"The Mystical War Counselor gave me this Bible." She picked it up and turned to a bookmarked page. "This is the first of what I read, *'When you see Jerusalem being surrounded by armies, you will know that its desolation is near. Then let those who are in Judea flee to the mountains, let those in the city get out, and let those in the country not enter the city. For this is the time of punishment in fulfillment of all that has been written.'* [176] Ministers, that day has arrived," she declared. "We must evacuate Jerusalem immediately."

Shouts erupted around the table: "What?" "Are you crazy?" "That is insane!"

Ignoring their protests, she turned to another bookmark and read: "Jesus warned us, *'So when you see standing in the holy place 'the abomination that causes desolation,' spoken of through the prophet Daniel – let the reader understand – then let those who are in Judea flee to the mountains. Let no one on the roof of his house go down to take anything out of the house. Let no one in the field go back to get his cloak. How dreadful it will be in those days...'* [177]

Unanimously, her cabinet howled their rejections of her decision, with condemnations of utmost disrespect: "We will never abandon our homeland!" "You stupid, weak woman!" "I will die fighting before I give Jerusalem to our enemies!" "You're mad! Where would we go?"

Rebekah did not appear angry. Instead, she calmly reached into her briefcase and removed sheets of paper. She placed one in front of each minister.

They were letters of dismissal.

The cabinet became even more belligerent: "Traitor! You can't do this!"

Rebekah Emunah's steely determination had returned. "It is within my authority to dismiss any minister."

"You fool, we're on the brink of war!"

"Your objections are duly noted."

"The *Knesset* will overrule this outrage!"

"They will have that opportunity … after the evacuation."

**Jerusalem will be trampled on by the Gentiles
until the times of the Gentiles are fulfilled.**
Luke 21:24

**Chapter 31
Jerusalem, Israel
September 11**

THE RAREST OF SIRENS reverberated throughout Jerusalem, horrifying the population. This particular alarm was not a warning to seek protection in the city's plentiful bomb shelters. Instead, the distinctly ominous sound signaled an imminent attack from a weapon of mass destruction. It did not matter whether the coming devastation would be from chemical, biological or nuclear means, the frantic population had been trained to know that evacuation would be their only chance for survival.

Everyone responded. Women gathered their children. Men gathered supplies. They loaded whatever could fit into their cars, or carried whatever they could on foot, and fearfully fled the holy city as quickly as possible.

No one knew whether these moments would be their last.

But they weren't.

Three hours later, all roads into Israel were packed with military transport vehicles from Russia, China, Turkey, Iran, Sudan, Ethiopia, Libya, Jordan, Saudi Arabia, and Armenia.[178] Their destination was the ancient city of Jerusalem. But by now, it had become a holy ghost town. [179]

> No one has been able to strike terror into others
> and at the same time enjoy peace of mind himself.
> Seneca

E VAN GLANCED at the caller identification on his cell phone. The incoming call indicated an encrypted communication.

"Again? That woman will not leave me alone!" he growled to Faridah.

Evan connected the call.

"What do you want, Angela? I'm really busy right now."

"I should say you are," she responded with an offended tone. "Why didn't you tell me you were ordering the invasion?"

"What invasion?"

"Evan, we know your troops are moving on Jerusalem."

"What are you talking about? Your intel is wrong."

"Don't feign ignorance with me. There's no doubt."

For Evan, the news was a shocking bombshell. However, the one feigning ignorance was Angela. Her encryption experts had recently deciphered messages between members of the new Legion of Babylon, indicating a mutiny of Evan's leadership. She wanted to be the first to communicate the betrayal to him so that she might regain his trust.

"So," she asked, "you're saying you don't know anything about this?"

Evan did not answer.

"Melnikov's fingerprints are all over this operation. So, we just assumed you gave him the orders. The whole Legion's in on it."[180]

His mind raced with violent scenarios of his revenge on the traitors.

Angela pretended to think out loud. "Ohhh, I guess that makes sense, now." Then, acting alarmed, she added, "You know, we tracked the source of your computer hacking to Arnietsk Russia. I think Melnikov's out to get you. Evan, are you sure you're still in control of the Legion?"

Standing nearby, Faridah grew concerned as Evan's face turned red and his breathing became labored.

Angela was on a roll, dishing out the kind of mental anguish that had always been Evan's specialty. She was playing with fire, but loving it.

"And I hate to bring this up," the president added, "but are you aware that your mother is placing phone calls to John Malek?"

Thas growled, "What?"

"NSA intercepted three separate communications but it appears that they have some kind of code language worked out. I'll let you know if we decipher it."

Thas was lost in a dark fog of rage.

Angela asked, innocently, "Evan, are you okay? I'm just trying to keep you informed."

Faridah backed away from her son, unaware of what had been said, but fearing the look of his furious face.

Then, for the umpteenth time, Angela asked, "Evan, when are you coming back to Washington?"

He shouted, "Whenever I get around to it!"

"But we can coordinate…"

Thas disconnected the call and slammed the phone on the table.

"I told you Melnikov's a Judas!" he screamed at his mother. Then he hurled his crystal tumbler of vodka across the papal bedroom, barely missing her, crashing it into the fireplace.

"Evan," Faridah scolded, "taking it out on me will not accomplish anything. I'm on your side."

Evan's gaze darkened and he stared at her with a look she had never before seen. "That's what Mer said, too."

From the small dinner table near the window, Faridah wondered about the disturbing changes she was witnessing in her son. Physically, he had gained weight, consuming more food and vodka than seemed possible. Psychologically, he had begun to exhibit signs of paranoia and obsession.

She considered whether alcohol was at the root of his decline. However, she had no doubt that the deadly incident at Mer's cabin had changed him forever.

In the past, she had always revered his unique role in history. Lately, however, he seemed to be detaching from reality. She had tried to rationalize his apparent delusions, accepting them as a clever part of his eccentric plan to stay in the spotlight of the popular culture. Now, though, he seemed to be believing dangerous fantasies.

Faridah uncovered the plates on their small table and suggested, "Come on. Let's eat."

"No!" he shouted like an obstinate child. "Fix me another drink."

Reluctantly, she rose from the table and walked to the bar that they had installed in the papal bedroom. She poured him another vodka, but by the time she delivered it to him he was back on the phone, talking to another underling. These days, he spent all his waking hours issuing orders.

"I just found out Melnikov double-crossed me," he barked into the phone. "Turkey cooperated. The invasion began without me. The whole Legion's in on it."

He listened for a moment as he snatched the drink from Faridah and gulped it down.

"I don't need excuses," he snapped. "How quickly can I get back in control of Red Thoroughbred?"

Evan motioned for another drink and handed the glass to his mother.

"That's not good enough!" he shouted. "Then, how can we disable it?"

Faridah had warily observed the dramatic decline of her son ever since he had returned from Montana. He was morphing into a bitter and contorted version of his old self, now becoming reckless with his drunken words and actions.

"We don't have much time. If we can't disable it, then we need to warn prime minister Emunah. I'm not gonna let Melnikov get away with this ... this ... betrayal." Thas shouted, "Can you believe it? He's the one who advised me to declare an age of peace!"

Faridah handed Evan another drink, but he dropped it when he heard more bad news.

"What?! That doesn't make any sense! Why would they evacuate? They're gonna give Jerusalem to their enemies without a fight? You've got to be wrong!"

Faridah backed away, uncomfortable that her son was descending into one of those dangerous dark moods that frightened even her. She did not like that he no longer wore his makeup or eye patch whenever she visited with him. His bare, molten flesh made her uncomfortable, and his vacant eye socket repulsed her. Worse, still, his dark rages made him appear even more ugly. But what could she say?

Evan growled into the telephone. "I will punish him ... and all the traitors!"

Then the voice on the other end of the call said something that completely changed Evan's belligerence. He paced the room as he listened for a few moments. Then he sat down and slowly smiled.

"You're right," Thas said. "Yeah ... I can't believe I didn't think of it." The underling filled in a bit more information and Thas responded, "Okay. That's exactly what we'll do. I'll contact you tomorrow morning."

Evan ended the call, but his mind was still on his plan. After a moment, he looked up at his mother and mused, "An army of deer led by a lion is more to be feared than an army of lions led by a deer."[181]

She nodded, pretending to understand his meaning.

Then Thas added, "Make sure the studio is ready for me to make a major address tomorrow morning."

"Now?"

"Yes. Go now. I'll broadcast at 10 AM."

Warily, she asked, "So, is everything okay?"

His glare did not reassure her. He answered darkly, "It will be."

MOMENTS LATER, Angela tapped a pen on her desk as she nervously scrutinized the grandfather clock in the Oval Office. Then the phone finally rang.

It was her NSA Director. "Madame President, she's on the move."

"You're certain they are not together?"

"Yes ma'am. GPS coordinates from each of their cell phones indicate that they are at least 1,000 yards apart, right now."

"Good."

The president disconnected and placed another call.

FARIDAH SCURRIED across the *Cortile del Belvedere* in the direction of her chauffeur-driven limousine. In any other city, she would have felt unsafe in a darkened courtyard, alone. Violent crime in Vatican City, however, was virtually nonexistent.

For some unknown reason, she felt pressured to please Evan. So, her biggest concern was to avoid delay in executing his directive.

However, she had learned how undependable Perfective Patrollers had become. They excelled at snitching on neighbors or claiming Imperfective property. Yet, they were not so reliable when work was required. So, she wondered if her driver would be at his post when she made it to the car.

Before it was in view, however, her phone rang. Faridah slowed her pace, pulled it out of her pocket and examined the screen.

"Who would send me an encrypted call?" she wondered as she connected. "Who is this?"

Angela asked, "Do you recognize my voice?"

The question startled her. Faridah was not allowed to screen calls from the President of the United States. She answered, hesitantly. "Yes."

Immediately, Angela's voice became electronically enhanced to sound guttural and masculine. "Good. We need multiple layers of protection to secure this communication."

Faridah asked, "Why are you…"

Angela interrupted, "Do not ask anything. Do not say anything. I assure you that you want to hear what I have to say."

The president continued, point by point, in rapid-fire fashion. "You know that your son is in need of organ, bone and tissue transplants; that his companies have the biotechnology capabilities to accomplish such operations, but that his extraordinary genomic profile dictates that the only acceptable source material would be from his own offspring. You know that he has attempted to conceive with countless women but that only one has succeeded: Mercedes Dare. You know that Dare has been advised by her doctors that she is no longer able to bear children. Answer with one word only. Do you understand?"

Faridah did not hide her irritation at the game-playing, and brusquely answered, "Yes."

"You do not know, however, that your son's doctors have advised him to move to Plan B, because they have found that it is not exactly correct that his body will only accept organ, bone and tissue transplants from his own offspring."

Faridah listened intently as she slowed her pace.

Angela lied, "They have determined that your body will provide acceptable source material."

Faridah stopped walking.

"Answer with one word only. Do you understand?"

She could barely choke out, "Yes."

Then the connection went dead.

On that day,
I will make Jerusalem a weighty stone for all peoples.
All who attempt to lift it shall injure themselves badly,
and all the nations of the earth shall be gathered against her....
On that day,
the Lord will shield the inhabitants of Jerusalem, and...
I will seek the destruction of all nations
that come against Jerusalem.
Zechariah 12:3,8,9

EVAN CONCEALED HIS BOILING RAGE under the pure white vestments of the supreme pontiff, below the golden crown of the Vicar of Christ, behind a molten mask of confident calm. No mere symbols of authority, however, could sufficiently revive his rapidly fading reputation.

Evan's precious Cyst-Blanc supercomputer had been hacked and, consequently, every CyBot web search now produced the incriminating murder video first, regardless of what was being searched. Thas could not find the origin of the sabotage, but suspected Melnikov of the betrayal that was turning him into an object of suspicion and scorn.

The cameraman's hand extended into the air, showing five fingers, then four, three, two, one. A worldwide audience lingered around their television sets to hear the news.

Pope Jesus II cleared his throat, adjusted his crown, and began his worldwide broadcast.

"My children. I must share with you a few matters of great urgency and importance. Many of you have seen the video of the death of Dr. Huntington Cyst. I am sure it has been disturbing for you to witness. He was a great man, the Prophet of Technology. He was a voice crying out in the wilderness: 'Make straight the way for the Lord.'[182] Indeed, he has served me well in preparing the world for my coming.

"I requested that this video be circulated, as a test of your faith in me; a test that some of you failed. After watching it, a few of you lost confidence in my leadership. You questioned my authority and considered following the destructive path of the Imperfectives.

"I warn you: do not provoke my hand of justice.

"But to those of you who are listening, I am merciful. I choose to treat you as my children; heirs to the Perfect World.

"You demand a sign of my divine nature. But remember: blessed are those who have not seen and yet have believed.[183]

"How many signs will be necessary for you of little faith? The great "t" in the sky should convince you that Titan will protect you all.

"Huntington Cyst's death was also a sign. You see, Dr. Cyst willingly died so that I would raise him from the dead. Don't you remember? I resurrected him and even replaced his severed feet so that he would become greater than before. He was a walking miracle, proclaiming my divinity.

"How can I be accused of murder, when I gave him the gift of life?

"Such will be the blessings of those who follow me: the gift of eternal life.

"However, today I must also speak with you about the penalty of eternal punishment for those who reject the Perfect World Agenda. At this moment, rebellious armies are approaching Jerusalem, against my wishes. They ignored my proclamation of peace and, instead, chose the path of defiance and war."[184]

The broadcast video changed, briefly, to a telescopic satellite view of Jerusalem, its surrounding valleys, and the highways that lead into them. The areas were all congested with caravans, transporting soldiers from all directions. The invading troops appeared to scurry over the holy land like ants on a carcass, and the awesome display of manpower seemed the most powerful army on earth.[185]

It was an image of overwhelming force, more powerful than anyone had ever imagined.

So, when Evan's makeup-plastered face returned to the broadcast, most viewers suspected that the diminutive leader might be completely out of his depth. His distracting Titan eye patch and pretentious papal costume diminished him, in their eyes, and his pretended superiority over the incalculable power of the invading armies seemed laughable.

Who is he to challenge them?

Still, Evan appeared to maintain complete confidence. Inwardly, however, he seethed at Melnikov's increasing audacity in recent months. Yes, the Russian had been instrumental in Evan's rise to supreme power.[186] However, his supporting role had clearly gone to his head. Now, rumors were circulating that the plump little toad had even begun professing his shared divinity with Pope Jesus.

So, aiming a barb at Melnikov's leadership, Thas advised his viewers, "Beware of false Christs. For false Christs and false prophets will appear and perform signs and miracles to deceive even the elect – if that were possible."[187]

Then he continued,[188]   "I declare to the invaders: I am against you. I will turn you around and drag you along. I will bring you from the far north and send you against the mountains of Israel. On the mountains of Israel you will fall, you and all your troops and the nations with you. I will give you as food to all kinds of carrion birds and to the wild animals. You will fall in the open field, for I have spoken."

So, like an emperor dismissing a slave, Evan passed the back of his hand through the air and added, "Let us see the consequences of your sin against me."

Around the world, viewers witnessed a live broadcast of the invasion of swarming soldiers, converging on Jerusalem like hungry locusts on a fertile field. They watched truck convoys approach their destination with complete coordination. Over the highways and through the mountain passes, filling the valleys and covering the plains, a tide of invaders washed over the land. The beige sands of Israel darkened as the belligerent forces descended on Jerusalem, the city of peace.

Suddenly, however, the smooth flow of troops disrupted and one convoy after another convulsed into anarchy. Drivers appeared blinded as vehicles began to drive off the roads or crash into each other. Soldiers jumped out of their trucks and ran in all directions, as if attempting to escape from some unseen attacker. Many vehicles reversed course, forcing a disorganized retreat eastward toward the Dead Sea.

As Evan's Glass Andalusian poured forth his wrath, the tumultuous panic on the ground grew, and horrified television viewers watched the merciless extermination with a mesmerizing sense of nightmarish detachment.

To some, the massacre seemed to drag on endlessly. To others, it was over in the blink of an eye. Regardless, within twelve minutes of the first sign of difficulty, it had ended. As the satellite scanned over Jerusalem, the Kidron Valley, the Jezreel Valley, and the world's largest graveyard at Tel Meggido, nothing moved.[189] It would appear that the video had switched to a still picture if not for the rivers, now turning blood red.

That day, Glass Andalusian's electromagnetic beam leveled the invading army, and all nearby life, with acute radiation poisoning. In the history of warfare, nothing like it had been seen before.

They had been spared during the Darkness. They had been warned by the awesome Cross in the sky. Still, they placed their faith in the mark of Titan and, because of that, they received no protection on the day of wrath.

The Battle of Armageddon had not advanced like a movie scene, exploding with thunderous fireballs. Still, the lack of theatrics did not diminish its awesome death toll.[190] The lives of 200 million soldiers were terminated.[191] None of the invaders were spared. Not even two leaders of the Legion of Babylon, or the one ambitious general named Melnikov.[192]

For twelve mesmerizing minutes it seemed that the planet had descended into quiet shock as mankind watched the unprecedented inhumanity to man. The soldiers on the sands of Israel experienced the same vicious vengeance that had been inflicted on the martyred saints of the Sistine Chapel except, this time, everyone observed the horror.

To each witness, the televised images of the silent slaughter would be unforgettable. However, an unsettling sound had also transmitted, and it would be just as memorable. It was the disturbing gurgling of Evan's sinister laugh.[193]

This is the plague
with which the Lord will strike
all the nations that fought against Jerusalem:
Their flesh will rot while they are still standing on their feet,
their eyes will rot in their sockets,
and their tongues will rot in their mouths.
Zechariah 14:12

I am against you, O Gog…
I will bring you from the far north
and send you against the mountains of Israel….
On the mountains of Israel you will fall,
you and all your troops and the nations with you….
I will send fire on Magog
and on those who live in safety in the coastlands….
On that day I will give Gog a burial place in Israel…
It will block the way of travelers,
because Gog and all his hordes will be buried there.
So it will be called the Valley of Hamon Gog.[194]
For seven months the house of Israel
will be burying them
in order to cleanse the land.
Ezekiel 39:1, 2, 4, 6, 11, 12

They will trample the holy city
for forty two months.
Revelation 11:2

FORTY ONE MONTHS LATER

At any given moment,
there is a sort of all-pervading orthodoxy –
a general tacit agreement
not to discuss some large and uncomfortable fact.
George Orwell

Chapter 34
The Perfect World
February 13

IN THE TWENTIETH CENTURY, deaths caused by governments exceeded a quarter billion.[195] It was the bloodiest century on record. Nazis attempted to organize a totalitarian society on the basis of race, and failed. Fascists attempted to organize a totalitarian society on the basis of nationalism, and failed. Communists attempted to organize a totalitarian society on the basis of class, and failed.

Yet, Evan Thas had learned from them all and the twenty first century was already proving even more deadly. Now, Perfectives were organizing a totalitarian society on the basis of secular religion, and succeeding.

Hitler once observed, "Without the loudspeaker, we would never have conquered Germany."[196] Without control of the media, the Internet and the faith, Thas would never have conquered the world.

With obsessive determination, he had prioritized strategic objectives and then focused his forces against all opposition. He dealt with his opponents like a boy wielding a magnifying glass to sizzle an ant in the woods. It made little difference to him whether the effort ignited a forest fire, as long as the ant was eliminated.

Initially, Evan's entertainment division had produced non-stop movies, game shows and video games that celebrated hunting and killing Imperfectives. But, eventually, the global audience grew bored with the redundant themes, especially when the victims praised Jesus, even to the death. Instead, audiences increasingly preferred the sexually explicit programs that XBC Entertainment Networks offered.

Lately, the priority of eliminating peaceful Imperfectives had lessened. Like mammals in the Age of the dinosaurs, they survived as long as they remained unnoticed. Patrollers had lost interest in them particularly because they no longer possessed anything worth stealing.

Materially, Imperfectives lived without access to modern technologies. They grew their food, built their shelters, and even protected and educated themselves. Still, they never seemed to mind. Their small communities were peaceful and even joyful. Around the world, they had learned from the teachings of the Latter Day Apostles, and they spread their knowledge from believer to believer, by word of mouth.

The most fortunate of the prayerful communities secretly harbored priests and other clergy so that their Sacraments were still available them. Other members of religious Orders also were highly prized, even though their presence could be dangerous for any group that hid them. Still, even in this tumultuous world, they had been able to organize communities that were exemplary islands of faith, hope and love, resembling the monasteries of the Middle Ages.

These days, however, widespread difficulties complicated daily survival for everyone. In every country, even Perfective Patrollers endured a relentless struggle for the fulfillment that had been promised by the Perfect World Agenda. Perfectives were becoming perpetually frustrated because, no matter how faithfully they cooperated, the Perfect World remained just out of reach.

Evan had cleverly responded to many of the challenges that the Darkness had presented. Though his most valued associates had not survived, the world's reduced population had allowed him to play Santa Clause, supervising the aftermath and taking credit for redistributing wealth. So, at first, the massive transfer of property had acted as an anesthetic on the world's wounded economy. Painful realities, now, however, were no longer so easily masked.

Consequently, Thas felt he had no choice but to drive Perfectives harder, even to the brink of their endurance. The world's workers had to return to their former productivity. Increasing demands coupled with decreasing rewards, however, were beginning to take a toll on his popularity.

Still, no one complained openly. Terrible things happened to those who did.

With the Titan global digital currency now in place, Thas had begun hammering social behavior to his liking.[197] He had designed and implemented a global social caste system that segmented populations and provided rewards based on contributions to the Perfect World Agenda.

Class 1 Perfectives included those with minimal skill or talent. Consequently, they received Titan credits that afforded only the most basic in food, clothing and shelter. Their disintegrating neighborhoods were populated by workers in the most dangerous and dirty jobs. Everyone, no matter how infirm or disabled, was required to work. So, because money and possessions were scarce there, crime and suicide rates were high.

However, by enlisting their service in Evan's wars and distinguishing themselves in battle, Class 2 Perfectives would be promoted to better jobs and gain enough credits to move to safer communities with greater access to health care, police protection, and sanitation. Still, no one at this rank achieved personal fulfillment. They lived only for the respite that sleep provided.

The next level of promotion allowed Class 3 Perfectives to earn enough Titan credits to dress and groom themselves attractively. This was considered vitally important because they were now admitted into the social circles of the Patrollers, attending their social and sporting events. Because of that, no one made it to this stage without first gaining the eye of a Perfective Patroller. Sponsorship was required, so briberies and sexual favors became popular means of ascent. Consequently, jealousies began corroding order and morale.

Class 4 Perfectives were few in number, well compensated and highly esteemed. They were chosen by Evan, himself, for demonstrating excellence, particularly in intellectual, artistic, or athletic pursuits. They were the teachers and indoctrinators that everyone was required to watch on the XBC Education channels, the athletes on the XBC Sports channels, and the porn stars on the XBC Entertainment channels.

Usually, promotion to this level required an attractive on-screen appearance and an outstanding effort in hyping the cult of Highest Holiness. "Quads" as they were respectfully called, became the faces and voices of the Perfect World movement, the only ones regularly featured on the omnipresent XBC networks. In fact, Brother Daniel Mitchum – Chief Global Correspondent for XBC News – had become a role model for everyone who sought fame at any cost. His flamboyant lifestyle, on air, gave every Perfective hope that if he could become such a successful Quad, anyone could.

Finally, Class 5 Perfectives were the rarest breed. They did not necessarily possess talent, skill, beauty or even intelligence. They were the Patrollers. They had been aggressive enough to join the movement in its earliest days and clever enough to demonstrate ruthless zealotry for the cause. Consequently, they had also reaped the richest rewards, so far, and were not ashamed to flaunt their wealth and superiority.

But their positions were not maintained without effort. Patrollers had been responsible for organizing the global corpse disposal, first, after the Darkness and, then, after the invasion of Jerusalem. The second effort, alone, had taken seven months.[198]

According to the Perfect World scientists who were regularly featured on XBC News, Class 5 Perfectives were the enlightened elites who had integrated their lives with the transcendent insights of Highest Holiness. Their slavish devotion to their leader was proof of their unparalleled wisdom and their lifestyle of Perfect Virtue.

No one questioned such tenets of the Perfect World Faith, out loud, even though most of the claims on the XBC networks did not seem to mirror reality. Brother Daniel Mitchum's reports on increasingly positive data were abundant, but the global economy seemed to be in depression. Year after year, scientists on XBC News professed that Highest Holiness had brought mankind to the brink of the Perfect World ... if only Imperfectives would stop sabotaging his brilliant and beneficent efforts.

So, societies around the globe had become polarized. Most sided with Evan, submitting to his laws in the hope that his bold promises of pleasure and comfort in this world eventually would come true. Others, clung to a belief in God's Law and gravitated to Pope Peter II, no matter what religion or denomination they had previously professed. After all, no one could escape the fact that the miraculous object in the sky had forced a decision for every person: do you believe in the "t" of Titan, as Evan professed, or do you believe in the Cross of Christ, as Jesus' Beloved Apostle professed?

The deck was stacked in Evan's favor, though, because he took full advantage of his media monopoly. So, with each passing day, he tried to further limit anyone's ability to choose against Titan. He encouraged Perfectives, themselves, to report or even attack Imperfectives whenever they committed violations against the Perfective Agenda or the Perfect Speech Code. Even children were taught by the XBC Education Network that they would be rewarded for reporting their parents' violations.

For those Perfectives who sought refuge in the temporal pleasures of Cardinal Sins, truth was not a priority and confusion became their way of life.[199] So, over time, the atmosphere of pervasive personal spying resulted in widespread allegations without support. Many faithful Perfectives were falsely accused and imprisoned or eliminated and abuses of power became commonplace as revenge motives caused them to spiral out of control. Consequently, the social machinery of the Perfect World began to break down. But no one could admit it, publicly.

Since Perfect World promises had never actually come true, blame continued to be necessary, and XBC Networks were the preferred tools and weapons in that regard. Specifically, Evan focused his attacks on the three most famous Imperfectives because he believed they were ideal scapegoats.

XBC regularly highlighted the antics of the two so-called proph-ets of Jerusalem who fancied themselves Elijah and Enoch.[200] Along with their equally laughable leader, "The Pretending Pope," the two lunatics had become the greatest source of comedic humor on the XBC comedy shows. Bearded and unwashed, the prophets had spent years, now, begging the world for repentance, prayer and sacrifice as they smeared ashes on the foreheads of followers. They claimed that the Mark of God would never be erased, once accepted.[201]

At first, Evan had dispatched assassination squads to eliminate the pesky, outspoken prophets. The Patrollers, however, not only failed in their missions, but never returned.[202] So, Thas eventually chose a different strategy. He decided to let them live and even pro-mote them as the alternative to his point of view. He believed that he could not have dreamed up a more incompetent group of opponents and imagined that everyone would be repulsed by their preaching.

He was wrong.

Regularly, Evan's commentaries accused Imperfectives of insane-ly preferring ashes over a Perfect World. As far as he was concerned, those comedic clowns – along with that pope in Italy who was still embracing the ruins of the old Catholic Church – were symbols of all that had been misguided in world history.

His charges were not just inaccurate, they were bold, audacious lies.

He called the most charitable institution in human history a cess-pool of greed. He claimed the Catholic Church was anti-science and anti-education even though it had educated more individuals than any other institution, and could claim an unprecedented record of scholastic achievement and university development. He even labeled it a despotic dictatorship, ignoring that Church teachings had helped form the foundations of free-market economics and the Western rule of law.[203] Thas wanted the Church gone, even if that meant closing its hospitals, orphanages and AIDS hospices around the globe. To his thinking, Catholicism was just too narrow-minded, though its clergy and congregation had arisen from every race and every country, over the past twenty centuries.

So, to drive home his point even more clearly, Evan's news division regularly staged and broadcast violent protests against Imperfectives and manufactured interviews of man-on-the-street outrage against them. Someone had to be blamed for the promises that remained unfulfilled.

Thas produced numerous news programs that sharply contrasted his philosophical and theological differences with theirs. He believed that few would fall for their evangelizing efforts, especially when his experts all judged the pretending prophets insane.

Especially in this increasingly gritty world, the law of the jungle had become the rule. So, Evan was comfortable with promoting his preference for rough justice. When the crazy duo emphasized loving enemies, Thas emphasized killing them. If they asked for self-restraint, Thas encouraged self-indulgence. Whenever they shunned materialism, Thas flaunted it. How else could one gauge the glory of his achievements?

In every way, Evan's pride had ballooned in recent years.

Ripping a page from the history of Caesar Augustus,[204] Evan took measures to insure that his widely circulated image was now digitally enhanced so that a youthful and attractive appearance would be broadcast. However, his lifestyle had become so decadent that he hardly resembled his old form. He was now bloated from gluttony and sloth.

His mother had not been helpful in curbing his addictions. Faridah had feared that he would some day demand her life in exchange for his physical restoration. So, she numbed his rages with vodka and delivered to his bed a different woman every evening. Consequently, he devolved into loving only pleasure, despised everyone who failed to delight him, and respected only himself.[205]

Time after time, Faridah selfishly hoped that one of his concubines would conceive for her a grandson. Yet, none had.

The hard work of organizing communities around the globe had been accomplished, by now, in large part because of the Patrollers. They had been controlled by a stern code of justice: manage your area of responsibility, exactly as dictated, or die. In this world, there was no place for former Patrollers. They knew too many secrets.

They knew, for example, the awesome power of the XCyst satellites. Four of them – along with their associated sub-satellites – offered Evan more power than any leader had ever possessed.[206] The satellite code named White Appaloosa allowed him to broadcast his soothing messages of peace and security to 184 countries, while simultaneously translating his words into 62 languages. The orbiting transmitter also overrode every other frequency so that no other broadcasters could operate.

Red Thoroughbred was designed to dominate 21st century warfare. It would scan the battlefield and detect every weapon, including weapons of mass destruction. It would then determine the balance of forces, first-strike opportunities, as well as optimal attack and retreat routes.

At long last, the orbiter named Black Arabian was fully operational. In association with the Cyst-Blanc supercomputer, it processed every Titan financial transaction as quickly as cars pass through RFID detectors on toll roads. So, for those who rejected the primitive life of an Imperfective – independent of money – this satellite was their salvation from starvation.

Finally, Glass Andalusian was the most powerful satellite, delivering death to anyone Evan wished. This mysterious source of the so-called N1656 virus, however, continued to be a closely guarded secret. If word got out, Evan's indiscriminate slaughter could subject him to War Crimes charges.

Certainly, Vasiliy Melnikov would have pressed for those prosecutions … if he had lived. Evan mused that the Russian had been entrusted with control of the satellite named Red Thoroughbred. The bloated toad, however, should have demanded Glass Andalusian.

Yet, in a way, Melnikov exacted his own revenge from the grave.

To Evan's great dismay and fury, the holocaust of Armageddon had exhausted the battery banks of Glass Andalusian. In his lust for vengeance, Thas could not restrain his attack and had foolishly failed to retain a base charge in the battery banks. Now, the satellite's sophisticated solar array was unable to recharge them. Consequently, Evan's lack of self-control had reduced XCyst's multibillion dollar orbiter to the status of worthless junk, floating in space. He, himself, had neutralized the greatest weapon in his arsenal.

Still, Thas was never one to let a setback slow him down. In a major worldwide address, he dramatically commanded nature to end the pandemic plague of the N1656 virus.

Nature listened to the miracle worker and the world experienced a resurgence of hope.

> Of all the animals,
> the boy is the most unmanageable.
> Plato

A DAM CROUCHED QUIETLY on the bend of an old oak branch that leveled off eight feet above the trap. He wore only underwear, and mud covered his red hair, freckled face and pale little body. He planned that the sludge would prevent his scent from wafting in the summer breeze. After all, he knew that wild boar have a keen sense of smell.

Adam looked down on his work with pride, eagerly anticipating his first trapping. Yet, he resisted fidgety boyish impatience and remained perfectly still.

Below him was the hefty animal trap that he had made from chopped branches and vines. To construct it, he had needed only a hatchet and his knowledge of knot tying. Then he found the perfect location for the trap. There, he had discovered signs of boar activity: hoof prints, rooting holes, and missing bark at the base of pine trees. So, he place the cage under the oak tree, near a watering hole, where he suspected boar wallowed in the late afternoon mud to cool off and kill parasites. Under this tree, they probably also enjoyed munching on acorns. But, inside the trap, Adam had placed a large pile of what they craved even more: hickory nuts.

With little training, the blue-eyed prodigy already had devised techniques that rivaled experienced trappers. He absorbed everything he observed and applied his knowledge creatively. He was a serious child, driven by purpose.

In many ways, Adam was his father's son. There was no doubting his advanced development, regardless of whether his prodigious nature had been inherited or nurtured from the human growth hormones of Eden Village.

So, he set his mind on attaining what he wanted most: meat. His growing little body's need for protein did not appreciate that it had become such a rare commodity. So, as dusk approached, the boy imagined how excited the community would be if he dragged a dead boar into camp. He'd be a hero.

Suddenly, Adam tensed when he heard grunting and shuffling in the bushes. He clutched his hatchet more tightly, and his eyes widened as the massive animal emerged from the leaves.

It was big, perhaps bigger than any he had seen. This one was dark, almost black, and probably weighed over 300 pounds.

The boar dipped its long snout and tusks into the pool to slurp up refreshment. But when it lifted its head, it sniffed repeatedly, appearing to have caught a scent.

Frozen above, Adam worried that the wild pig may have sensed his presence. However, it was soon clear that it had become aware of the hickory nuts in the trap.

The animal cautiously approached the cage and began sniffing from the side. Adam observed as the animal's snout nudged the cage wall and it longed to get at the treats.

The boy wanted to scream out, "The door is open!" But he remained quiet, instead.

Looking down, he marveled at the size of the hog and wondered if his cage was big enough.

The answer soon came as the boar found the door, wandered in and began munching on the hickory nuts.

But the door remained open. The hog had not knocked over the stick that supported it.

With increasing frustration, Adam watched as the boar finished every last nut.

He's gonna escape! the boy thought.

He couldn't wait any longer.

"Hey!" Adam shouted from above.

The massive boar jerked with fright, knocked over the stick, and the door slammed shut.

"I got him!" Adam screamed. "I got him!"

The boar squealed its confusion, then its surprise, then its rage.

It began kicking and butting the walls of the cage. It ripped its tusks into the door and jerked its snout upward, tearing vines and breaking branches.

"Stop it!" Adam screamed from above as he brandished his hatchet.

The boar backed as far as it could and charged ahead, slamming its snout into the yielding door. Its head burst through and then it twisted and jerked until it forced its body out.

Now it was wounded, bloodied, and shrieking its fury.

But the boy was also mad. He stood on the branch and waved his ax at the hog.

"You tore up my cage!"

The wild boar snorted back its anger and raised its tusks, inviting the boy to come after him.

I'll jump from here, Adam calculated.

One quick blow and I'll have him.

He won't know what hit him.

The angry little boy prepared to pounce.

The enraged wild boar prepared to welcome him.

MERCEDES DARE blew on the brown leafy twigs and nodded when flames came to life. Then she reached into a nearby woodpile, covered the kindling with a pyramid of logs and stepped back to watch the dense smoke rise.

The young woman had changed over the past few years. Her hair was short and choppy, the result not only of her attempt to disguise her appearance but the inevitable consequence of cutting hair with a knife. She was also thinner from her meager woodland diet and voluntary fasting.

"It's not quite dark, yet," Father Thomas said as he stepped up to help.

"I know," Mer said, "but Adam's not back."

In this remnant community, they rarely built fires before dark for fear that daytime smoke might be seen by Patrollers many miles away. Unfortunately, this community could remain safe – and Father Thomas alive – only as long as they remained unnoticed. But Mer thought that young Adam might need a fire to find his way back to camp. So, the lanky young priest did not object.

"You want me to look for him?" he asked.

"He's been gone all day." Mer sighed. "But let's give him a little more time. He's smart ... wise beyond his years."

"Yes he is," the priest laughed. "They call him the inventor. Quite a kid."

She didn't disagree.

Mer often wished that her son would have found young friends to play with, here, but there were none. The other boys were older. Still, this group's diverse adults had been loving and accepting of her son. In fact, Thomas had become almost like a natural father to Adam; teaching him the ways of the woods and the ways of the world in order to hone his survival instincts and mold his character.

The priest was the leader of this remnant community. He administered the sacraments regularly and led Bible studies, from memory. Though this holy group knew that each day could be their last, none of them had fear. Their constant prayers expelled fear.

Still, each of the twenty four committed Christians often wondered: *How many remnant communities are left? Are we the last one?*

Mer had trusted only Thomas with the knowledge that their great persecutor was the boy's father. He, alone, knew what would happen to the mother and son if they were discovered.

Nearby, people sat on rough hewn picnic tables, diligently chopping root vegetables and mushrooms for tonight's soup. Unfortunately, venison, squirrel or rabbit would not be included. Still, no one complained. They thanked God for every little blessing.

A dozen colorful tarps dotted the campsite, under a leafy forest canopy. They had been donated to the group by a canvass shop owner who had joined them shortly after his conversion. The fabric had been ideal for making the simplest of small tents.

"You know, Father," Mer said as she jabbed a stick into the campfire, "if anything ever happens to me…"

"Stop it," he interrupted. "How many times do you have to bring this up? I'll do it. Okay?"

"I know. I just want to make sure that…"

He interrupted again. "Look!"

The priest pointed at the crying boy who emerged from the bushes. He was covered with mud and wearing only his little white undies. In one hand, he held his hatchet. With the other, he dragged the rest of his clothes.

"Adam!" she shouted. "What are you doing?"

"Mom, I almost caught a boar."

Some nearby campers applauded the little boy's heroic efforts while Mer frowned at their misplaced but good natured encouragement.

"Adam, they're dangerous. You stay away from wild boars."

He dropped his hatchet and clothes next to the fire. He groaned, "I chickened out."

"Oh, look at you. I have to bathe you, now."

"I can bathe myself."

"No you can't, little man. It's dark. You're not going into the stream without me."

"Mom, I can…"

"March down there, right now!" She handed Thomas the stick. "Father, can you look after the fire? I'll be right back."

As she followed the muddy little hunter through the community, campers hardly restrained their laughter. Mer, however, glared back at them with stern frowns. She resented that they encouraged his boyish schemes, making him imagine that he could accomplish almost anything.

Still, the young mother could not be too angry at them. After all, she knew that Adam offered, every day, the community's most amusing distraction.

> The voice of the parasite
> will be more agreeable to them
> than the melody of the harp
> touched by the sage's finger.
> St. Columbkille

Chapter 36
Capernaum, Israel
February 18

CAMERAS PANNED the rugged terrain and the looming red Cross as jackhammers roared their *tat-tat-tat*. Evan and Faridah watched from their portable thrones on a nearby, rocky hillside. Still, even though two dedicated Patrollers shaded them with large, colorful umbrellas, Evan felt hot in his papal vestments. These days, he was uncomfortable wherever he went.

"Cut," he shouted. Three cameramen immediately complied, but the hammering continued.

Thas fanned his bloated face and observant Patrollers took his cue. Within seconds they rushed up the incline and delivered fans, facial tissues, and icy Bloody Mary's.

"Keep the rocks small!" Thas shouted to the demolition workers who were widening the entrance into the Cave of Secrets.[207]

They paused their noisy labor for a moment and one nodded.

"Is the net holding up?" Thas yelled.

A worker looked into the hole and responded, "Yes sir, Highest Holiness."

"Good. I don't want any big rocks damaging the altar."

This was the meticulously choreographed extraction of the *mizbach ha'olah* – the Altar of Holocausts – prescribed by God in the Book of Exodus.[208] It would be the focus of tonight's XBC News documentary in which Brother Daniel Mitchum will gush that Highest Holiness had discovered another great treasure: the first of all altars.

According to Scriptures, God commanded Moses, "You shall make an altar of earth unto Me, and you shall offer upon it your holocausts and peace offerings, your sheep and oxen, in every place where the memory of my name shall be: I will come to thee and bless thee."[209]

The altar was later moved to Solomon's Temple in Jerusalem, and animal sacrifices had been consumed by the perpetual fire that burned on it, as directed by God.[210] That fire served more purposes than just for the holocaust offerings. Its coals were used to smolder the holy incense at the Temple's Altar of Incense and those were the only flames that could be used to reignite the light of the ancient *menorah*.

At the destruction of the first Temple, the altar was secretly transported to Capernaum's Cave of Secrets, the cavern that had played a significant role in Evan's decades-long efforts to ally with evil.[211] Both as a boy and as a young man, Thas had been laid on the cave's historic altar slab. The first time led to the end of Evan's boyhood years with his mother. The second time led to the end of Huntington Cyst's life.

Perhaps it had been a fitting place for Cyst's death because he had been largely responsible for finding the Cave of Secrets. Back then, as their college days were ending, Cyst and his colleague, Henri Blanc, deciphered the location of the legendary mystery. Then they eventually located and removed the boulder that had concealed the entrance to the cavern for many centuries.

Huntie had never forgotten his archeological triumph. Henri eventually wished he could.

During the early days of the discovery, Blanc had been quietly amused that Cyst's bizarre research had apparently panned out. Huntie, however, was wildly ecstatic, not with reverential pride, but with defiant conquest. After all, the monumental discovery would be known, forever, as his.

On one of their first days in the cave, after surveying the interior with flashlights, Cyst said he wished to thank the one who had led him there. Blanc knew not to argue with his buddy whenever he had that look in his eye. So, he watched with amusement as Cyst pulled a small pick ax out of his backpack. Then, for ten minutes, Huntie furiously hammered the top of the altar.

When the frantic effort was over, Huntie wiped the stone free of dust and rock slivers, and Blanc stepped up to view his work. He could only laugh when he saw the result of Huntie's mischievous artistry: a Satanic pentagram.

It amused Henri, but meant little to him. In those days, Blanc had no concern for religion of any type. So, as long as Huntie covered the bills, Henri would be happy to travel the world with him. He felt that a little vandalism, here and there, was to be expected from a rebellious adrenaline junkie, like Cyst.

However, only years later would he understand that Cyst's disfiguring prank had possibly caused more than just graffiti. Eventually, Blanc learned of God's role in human existence and the altar's role in human history. But by then, he had forgotten the location of the cave and even the town under which it was hidden. That memory lapse was very unusual for a mind that rarely let any detail escape. Perhaps there had been a providential reason for it.

WHEN EVAN AND FARIDAH finished their Bloody Mary's, under the shade of their umbrellas, they handed their fans, tissues and tumblers to waiting Patrollers. Then Thas resumed his role as director of Perfective movie productions.

"Okay, everyone. Take your positions.... Action!"

The video cameras resumed taping and the jackhammers resumed pounding.

Soon, the thumping stopped and the foreman examined the enlarged hole. Then he turned to Thas and announced, "Highest Holiness, we're ready to extract the antiquities."

Playing a digitally enhanced Pope Jesus for the cameras, Evan nodded with regal calm. Then the foreman signaled for a small construction crane to be moved into place.

Inside the cave, Patrollers scurried to remove the rope net that had protected the altar. Now containing fallen rocks, the heavy mesh required the effort of six men. But, eventually, they stripped away the net and secured the crane's steal cable around the top of the altar. Then, very slowly, the ancient slab rose into the sunlight as cameras recorded the historic moment.

Evan raised his hands and proclaimed a prayer: "God almighty, my father, my equal,[212] thank you for helping me show our children our mercy. Together, we shall teach them the perfection of our wisdom. Together, we shall teach them the imperfection of their superstition. Together, we shall teach them to become like gods."[213]

As the slab ascended toward the enormous Cross, Evan slowly turned.

Suddenly, however, his regal calm vanished.

"Are you kidding me?!" he screamed.

The cameras stopped taping.

"What the hell are you people doing?"

No one was brave enough to respond.

"I told you that the pentagram must stay out of view!"

All eyes rose to the dangling slab, displaying its blasphemous graffiti.

"I need a drink," he complained as he stormed back to his portable throne.

There, under his umbrella, a Patroller quickly delivered another Bloody Mary.

Evan sipped on it while the crew practiced raising the slab.

"Don't worry," Faridah soothed. "It's going well."

These days, placating his frequent rages seemed to be her primary responsibility.

"This is an important shot," he complained between gulps. "This altar is one of the fundamental proofs of my mastery over all Judeo-Christian history. It's the altar upon which God's finger kept the fires lit."[214]

"And you now have it in your possession," she added.

"But possession is not enough. I can't have anyone claim that the altar has lost its value before God."

"Why would they think that?"

"Mother," he groaned. "We have to learn how our enemies think, before we can destroy them." He continued, "Scripture says that God warned about the delicate power of this altar, '...thou shalt not make it of carved stone, for if thou lift a tool upon it, it shall be defiled.'"[215]

"So, Huntie's prank with the pick ax was not helpful."

"Obviously."

Then the foreman yelled that his crew was ready for another take.

From that point on, the documentary progressed flawlessly, becoming a film of unprecedented religious importance.

To the delight of a worldwide audience, the historic altar slab was raised with all the reverence it deserved. However, the filming stopped before revealing an even more impressive antiquity that Evan insisted must remain secret until the time of a more impressive unveiling.

The camera crews left to prepare the documentary for that night's global broadcast. Only Patrollers remained on the grounds. Then, the greatest holy relic in Judaic history was secretly unearthed. For the first time in twenty six centuries, the golden Ark of the Covenant glistened under the morning sun.[216]

**It is dangerous to be right
when the government is wrong.**
Voltaire

Chapter 37
Shenandoah Valley
Virginia
February 19

"A DAM?" Mer yelled into the forest. "It's getting dark. Come back to camp."

She heard no response. So, the concerned mother reluctantly headed into the woods to find him.

She grumbled, "Probably trying to catch that boar again," as she pushed back small branches and shuffled through the least encumbered path.

Indeed, her smart, little son had not given up on his game-hunting dreams. His active and growing body craved protein, and he knew that meat was the best way to get it. So, Adam designed and deployed one trap after another. His schemes, however, had only produced one failure after another.

Yet, he had refused to give up. He modified his strategy by recruiting two older boys who could help with more labor-intensive designs. The progress seemed to delight him and she had laughed when he came home, one night, bragging that he liked being the boss.

Now, though, she failed to find humor in his hobby. So, Mer pushed ahead, farther and deeper into the darkening forest.

She had learned the habit of keeping prayers in her thoughts, always. However, this time, she placed them on her lips. "Lord, please protect him. He has so much more to give."

She shouted, again, "Adam?"

Mer heard nothing but the sound of water rippling over valley rocks and, so, she made her way towards it. There, at least some of the remaining dusk light might penetrate through the overgrowth to help her see farther.

When she arrived at the bank of the stream, though, Mer saw no sign of the boy.

She considered wading through the shallow water but decided, instead, to investigate the area that she had declared off limits for Adam. So, Mer headed toward the oak tree where the boar liked to wallow in the mud and nibble on acorns.

She whispered, "Please keep him safe, Lord. I'd give anything to protect him."

As she treaded deeper into the woods, she did not realize that Adam and his friends had made it back to camp, by now.

So, as she arrived at the oak, her heart sank when she saw no boar and no boys.

Then, as she turned to head back to camp, she also did not see the trip wire.

Suddenly, a sharpened branch unleashed its bowed resistance and whipped across her path.

"MER? CAN YOU HEAR ME?" Father Thomas whispered loudly as he pushed his way through the dark and dense foliage.

He had waited until he could put the boy to sleep. He had not told anyone, around camp, that his mother was missing because Thomas did not want to unnecessarily alarm the campers, especially Adam. But, as soon as he could slip away, he left to look for her, still confident that he would find the young mother, lost and disoriented in the woods.

Thomas carried with him a backpack with miscellaneous tools and ropes that might prove useful in the wild. He wished he owned a flashlight but artificial light, these days, was just a fond memory for Imperfectives. So, he continued to fumble forward, in the dark.

"Mer, where are you?"

Still, no response.

He pushed even farther and deeper into the woods.

Then he squinted at what was laying, up ahead, on his path.

FATHER THOMAS sat next to an earthen mound, exhausted. He looked through the trees, into the sky, and could see that the sun would be rising soon. However, he did not welcome it. He knew that with the morning would come mourning.

The priest had concluded a brief funeral service for Mercedes Dare. But, before that, he had spent most of the night digging her grave with just his hands and a trowel. It was the least he could do for the trusted friend that he had come to know and love. They had shared so many stories about their lives and he had been amazed at her secret past.

Thomas had decided that he would not allow loose lips, around camp, to further traumatize the boy. After all, Adam's spear-like booby trap had pierced his mother's abdominal aorta, causing massive blood loss and death within seconds.

If only we could all go that way, he thought as he dug. *So quickly. So painlessly.*

So, he buried her, along with Adam's handiwork, and he would claim that a snake bite had killed her.

As he sat there, staring at a lonely full moon in the expansive sky, the priest dreaded what he would have to do with the boy, tomorrow. After all, he had sworn that he would abide by Mer's wishes if anything happened to her. He had always found her words disturbing and had refused to believe that this day would ever come. Still, he could not dismiss her warning that Adam was the son of Evan Thas, the greatest murderer in history, the Antichrist.

Woe to those who call evil good and good evil,
who put darkness for light and light for darkness...
Isaiah 5:20

Chapter 38
Rome and Jerusalem
March 5

R ARELY, DID THEY WATCH TELEVISION. But today was a special occasion. John and Evie sat on simple, fold-up chairs in the modest living room of their Roman safe-house, awaiting the momentous event. Around the world, almost every TV had tuned to the live broadcast that promised to document the historic entrance of Jesus II into Jerusalem.

Before the documentary began, however, viewers endured another lengthy barrage of promotions for the Perfective Agenda. These days, one could hardly escape from the relentless messages that promised, "Equality for all!" and "The Perfect World is our right!"

Already, Evie had grown bored. So, she slid out of her chair, shuffled over to the bookcase and brought back her children's Bible. It was one of the few that had escaped the confiscations of the Patrollers.

On TV, amidst colorful balloons and falling confetti, a commercial celebrated that Titan would soon be the world's sole currency. The attractive announcer gushed about the benefits of digital money, warning that those who delayed converting their money would be left with worthless paper.

Next, Perfective Patrollers who had joined the movement in the early days offered testimonials regarding how they had become rich beyond their wildest dreams. Each of them thanked Highest Holiness for achieving the glorious redistribution of justice that he had promised.

Then, more ominous news was reported regarding the outrages

of the week. As usual, the conduct of Imperfectives was highlighted as the dangerous and destructive cause of the world's economic and social ills. Those who had refused to receive Titan implants were accused of undermining the path to a Perfect World.

The focus of the outrages changed weekly, with a different class of alleged victims each time. This week, it was the children: a hungry little girl at the grocery store, crying in front of empty shelves; a sick boy at the hospital, unable to find a doctor; a baby in a crib, shivering from lack of heat. The clear message was that these problems would not exist, if only Imperfectives would cooperate.

However, as the commercials had rattled on, John paid no attention to the television. He was too busy helping Evie pronounce words from her Bible.

At the back of the room, a lone nun, Sister Francis, pointed out, "There he is, Holy Father. It's starting."

The grand spectacle began with Brother Daniel Mitchum offering viewers a long commentary, overflowing with fawning superlatives. Once again, he proved that no sycophant could surpass his flair for toadying up to the boss.

On camera, the antipope's dazzling approach toward Jerusalem would have made Cleopatra blush. Leading the parade, up a rocky hill on a recently constructed road, twelve hundred trumpeters announced his arrival, as twelve hundred beautiful maidens peppered his path with rose petals. Then twelve hundred cherubic children followed, while singing their praises for the Perfect World and the one who was creating it.

Next, six virile, shirtless Patrollers appeared, supporting the antipope's golden throne at shoulder height. On it, Evan sat comfortably, wearing his triple tiara and white papal regalia. The patch over his right eye and the staff in his hand displayed three concentric circles: the mark of Titan.

Evan's carriers dressed as ancient Egyptian Pharaohs and Mitchum explained to television viewers that they symbolized that even kings, emperors, presidents and pharaohs would serve Highest Holiness in the holy city. Perhaps the comment irritated national leaders as they watched from around the world. But they knew better than to complain.[217]

Evie asked, "Who's that, Papa?"

"A very bad man."

"I think the children like him."

John smiled.

"Today," Mitchum gushed, "heaven and earth rejoice as Highest Holiness fulfills prophecy by entering Jerusalem through the double-arched Golden Gate. On the first Palm Sunday, Jesus of Nazareth passed through this gateway on a donkey, and mystics have foretold that that the Messiah will enter here at the beginning of a new Age, when He returns to bring justice to the world.

"Until recently, however, no one passed through this entrance. In 1541, Suleiman the Magnificent sealed it off with thick concrete. He even placed a cemetery in front of it so that neither the Messiah nor Elijah would dare pass through, as prophesied."[218]

Along his parade route, the broadcast showed thousands of people waving palm fronds and cheering, but without sincere enthusiasm. Like every player in an Evan Thas production, they were just props, assigned to applaud his wisdom and laugh at his jokes. Still, they provided the images that Evan wanted conveyed, regardless of their motivations.

John, himself, had witnessed similarly unrestrained hubris many centuries before, when godlike emperors led triumphal parades of conquered slaves and exotic animals through the Forum of ancient Rome ... right up to the time of their destruction.

As Evan gestured a royal wave with the back of his hand, Mitchum continued, "An army of Perfective engineers and workers have made this prophetic entrance possible. They worked tirelessly, not only on the construction of the new Temple, but on the palace of Highest Holiness, where he and his holy mother shall reside. From their balconies, the views of the Temple are absolutely stunning!"

Mitchum's tone became more respectful. "Unfortunately, though, the break-neck pace of demolition and construction resulted in the deaths of fourteen Perfective laborers." Then rejoicing, again: "Still, everyone who was allowed to labor for this highpoint in human history felt blessed. They all say that they deserve no credit for these accomplishments. All praise and thanksgiving are due to Highest Holiness!"

"Ahhh," Sister Francis sighed, "it almost makes me ill. Please, Holy Father, let me take her now."

"Yes, you're right," he said. "Wouldn't want Little One to get the wrong idea." But then he waved a halt to the nun. "Wait. There they are."

Pedro and Alonzo were shown standing with the crowd inside the Golden Gate. The mournful pair wore coarse robes and appeared unshaven and unwashed. Instead of waving palm fronds in the air, they were beating them against their own backs.

The camera focused on the two prophets as Mitchum read Evan's script. "Every celebration deserves clowns, so I see that our crazy prophets have arrived to amuse us. How anyone could take them seriously is beyond me. Look at how filthy and disgusting. Yet they think Perfectives will believe their lies. It would be hilarious if it weren't so sad."

The pontiff then nodded for the nun to take Evie but, before the little girl would leave, she sidled up to his chair and closed her eyes.

John responded to her unspoken request by stroking a Cross on her forehead and blessing the little saint.

"Love you, Papa," she said as she stretched up on her toes and kissed his cheek.

IN JERUSALEM, the broadcast lingered on the panoramic view of the prophesied third Temple.[219] XBC News Networks had also positioned one particular camera to provide continuous live coverage on a dedicated channel. So, from now on, the newest wonder of the world could be viewed from any place at any time.

The architectural marvel stood 90 feet long, 30 feet wide, and 45 feet high. Two features, however, particularly dazzled the eye. Inside and out, the structure had been overlaid with the glimmering gold that Evan's satellites had located for him in recent years. Also, at the entrance, two immense bronze pillars – known as Jachin and Boaz – flanked gold-covered, fir doors.

Though space limitations in modern Jerusalem had prevented the clearing of all the acreage of the original Temple grounds, still, pilgrims could now congregate at the entrance, either on the raised marble porch, or the courtyard below.

"Here," Mitchum explained to his viewers, "Solomon built the first Temple in the 10th century BC. It had served as Judaism's center of worship for 410 years before Nebuchadnezzar II destroyed it in 587 BC. Then all Jews were exiled to Babylon.

"The second Temple was built on the same site by Herod the Great after Cyrus the Great of Persia allowed the Jews to return to their homeland in 538 BC. The architectural wonder stood for 420 years, but was leveled by the Romans in 70 AD after a Jewish revolt."

Brother Daniel inserted, sagely, "That is just one of history's many examples of terrible consequences for those who rebel against the established order."

He continued with the script. "For almost twenty centuries, Jews prayed daily for the construction of the third Temple, and Highest Holiness is the one who has answered their prayers. He has now accomplished for the Jews what only Solomon and Herod the Great could claim!"

Even if grudgingly, Jews had to accept that the claim was correct. Prophecies were being fulfilled as Jews from around the globe returned to the Promised Land in record numbers.[220] They came for healings or for blessings from God. So, naturally, they began to wonder if this strange but powerful man truly could be their prophesied Messiah.

Observing from the Temple courtyard with disgust, however, Rebekah Emunah was not misled. The former prime minister was now a private citizen. She was pleased to be in retirement even though Evan Thas had deviously engineered her ouster, along with control of Israel's Knesset. Now, her impossible ambition to save Israel – or even the world – had been reduced to a more achievable goal: saving her own soul.

Who could blame Israel for embracing Evan's leadership? After all, Thas had miraculously delivered the Jewish state from 200 million enemies.

However, Rebekah and others from the remnant House of Israel knew – just as devout Christians had discerned – that Evan Thas was the embodiment of modern evil. They had wisely judged him with Spiritual eyes, not by the senses of the material world.[221]

When the costumed antipope, Jesus II, rose from his throne, he motioned for the welcoming courtyard crowd to let him speak. Just as instructed, however, they refused to silence their cheering. So, he continued to accept their praise while slowly circling a large, covered object that had been placed on Solomon's porch, between the pillars of Jachin and Boaz, in front of the golden doors. The object appeared to be sitting on the Altar of Holocausts, covered with the finest silk fabric.

Evan smiled at the grand irony of this event as he soaked up their enthusiastic approval. Every one of these applauding Jews would have been dead today if his strategy had executed as originally planned. However, when Melnikov betrayed him with a coalition army of communists and Islamists, Evan turned his deadly fury on them, instead. So, Thas was now pleased to take credit for annihilating Israel's enemies.

As the crowd finally quieted, his amplified voice could be heard over all Jerusalem. "How do you like my Temple?"

Again, his paid lackeys whipped up the audience to scream their approval.

After a few moments, he continued. "We are standing on the most hotly contested 35 acres on the planet: the Temple Mount. Here, I have fulfilled prophecy.

"This is where we asked Abraham to sacrifice his son, and where we instructed Solomon to build our Temple. Here, during my first coming, I was presented as an infant, I taught the elders as a child, I overturned the moneychangers' tables as an adult. This is where my father asked me to rebuild my Temple!"

Again, they cheered.

He shouted, "And this is where my father asked me to return the Ark of the Covenant!"[222]

Trumpets blared, children sang and a flurry of rose petals filled the air as a Patroller removed the cover, revealing the object on the altar.

The courtyard crowd became almost unmanageable in their excitement as they marveled at the golden Ark of the Covenant. Viewers, around the world, were mesmerized by the surprise.

When the tumult died down, he continued. "As you can see, the Dome of the Rock and the al-Aqsa Mosque remain standing in Jerusalem. After centuries of fighting, I alone found the true site of the first Temple, a site that did not interfere with those places of worship. I alone found a way to unite all faiths in Jerusalem … because I am the one, true god of all faiths.

"To the Jews: I am your Messiah. To the Muslims: I am the Islamic Caliph. To the Christians: I am the second coming of Christ.

"To anyone with ears to hear and eyes to see, I proclaim: Behold your Savior!"[223]

When prompted, the crowd erupted again and, this time, Evan allowed the cheering screams to continue without interruption as he marveled at the ancient Ark and remembered Huntie's intense description of it.

Cyst had warned young Evan about the incredibly traumatizing jolt he had experienced when he first touched it in the Cave of Secrets. He said that few could survive such contact. But he never explained to the boy that Henri Blanc had touched it also, but without consequence.

Soon, the crowd grew weary of plastic adoration and their enthusiasm trailed off.

Then someone in the crowd shouted, "Touch it!"

"No one may touch the Ark of the Covenant," Evan responded, sagely. "Even I, in my human state, do not dare touch it. For no one, in human form, is holy enough to make contact with the sacred Ark."

"I will!" came another shout from the audience.

Thas tried to maintain his sense of calm. He scanned his audience to see who was heckling him. Then he saw Pedro Lopez shout again, "I will touch it!"

Thas pretended delight. "Ohhhh, I see. Our crazy little prophet wishes to embrace the Ark."

The crowd responded with mocking laughter. The worldwide television audience responded with increased interest.

Then, from another area in the crowd came the shout, "We'll touch it if you do!"

Thas jerked in his direction, saw Father Alonzo, and dropped his pretense of humor. "No," he growled. "You wish to embrace the Ark, and so you shall." He snapped, "Bring them to me!"

Evan's security detail quickly waded through the crowd, roughly dragged the prophets to the anti-pope, and threw them down at his feet. The holy pair did not resist, nor did they appear afraid as they rose from the marble steps.

When they turned to the crowd, Alonzo pointed to the sky and thundered, "Witness the glorious Cross of our Lord and Savior, Jesus Christ!"

Thas shouted, "Punish his blasphemy!" and two Patrollers advanced on Alonzo.

Suddenly, a torrential fire shot out of Pedro's mouth and the two attackers immediately incinerated into an ashen pile.[224]

The crowd gasped their shock and the sight of such awesome power stunned Evan Thas into silence.

So, Alonzo continued. "Repent and reject this false Christ. Pray for God's wisdom and mercy … as if your life depends on it … because it does."

Thas desperately wanted to shout the prophet down but he had become paralyzed. It seemed everyone was being forced to watch.

Faridah could hardly contain her horror as she observed from the distant balcony of their newly constructed palace. "Stop them!" she screamed.

Perhaps, no one heard. Certainly, no one listened.

Frozen cameramen continued filming. Patrollers remained immobile. Even viewers at home seemed mesmerized before their television sets.

The two prophets stepped to the Ark and laid their hands on it.

"Thank you almighty God," Pedro prayed, "for your miraculous signs that show the end of the Age is near. Lord Jesus Christ, we await and welcome Your glorious return."

They removed their hands and Alonzo announced a warning: "Follow no man who cannot touch the sacred Ark."

He glanced at Thas, whose frozen expression revealed only fear and embarrassment. Then they walked to him and began to circle the petrified leader as his security forces observed helplessly.

Pedro began, "Lawless man of sin; son of perdition; bloody, deceitful beast…"

Alonzo continued, "…wicked man of the earth; vile, willful little horn; you are Antichrist, the enemy, the adversary, the liar!"[225]

Slowly, they circled him as Pedro added, "Faithfully, you have followed your god, the Father of Lies. You have deceived and, so, you have been deceived. From this day forward, receive your father's reward."

"May the ground you trod be cursed," Alonzo said. "Above your head, may the clouds dry up; below your feet, the land yield no life."

Pedro said, "The blood of saints is on your hands and, so, it shall be in your cup."

Alonzo cried out, "Holy God, if it be Thy will, strike this reprobate with consuming plagues so that he may end his days on earth contemplating the consuming fires of his eternal damnation!"[226]

The costumed criminal could convey no response, except terror in his eye.

With an aura of authority that seemed to transcend his small frame, Pedro shouted, "Now, suffer as you have made others suffer! For years, you have dedicated every moment of your life to this day. You worked tirelessly to rebuild the Temple. Proud fool! You think prophecy was fulfilled for your glory? Your vanity mocks you! You shall never enter the Temple. You desired to defy God but, instead, you served His will. Your life, your labors, your Temple all belong to Him, the God of Abraham, Isaac and Jacob. Now you shall begin to learn that His justice never dies and you shall not escape it!"

Evan cowered on the marble floor and began trembling and whimpering, in a fetal ball.

The two prophets had nothing more to say. So, they turned, walked down the steps and departed, unencumbered by the stunned audience.

Moments later, the quiet crowd watched as Evan rose to his feet and tried to recover from his breakdown. He studied his audience and saw doubt in every eye. He wanted to say something but couldn't find the words.

Then someone shouted "Touch it!"

He didn't know how to respond.

Another voice: "Yeah, touch the Ark!"

Looking small, afraid and alone on the porch of the magnificent Temple, he did not answer. He could not answer.

"Touch it," more of the disillusioned crowd demanded, "if you want us to believe you!"

For all to see, this unsightly coward was not the digitally enhanced media celebrity that had conquered the world's fascination.

Before a global audience, he screamed an anguished cry to his Patrollers: "Make them leave!"

Suddenly, dozens of thugs stormed into the peaceful crowd, mercilessly beating them with clubs and stampeding them out of the Temple square. In the crushing exodus, many were injured and some were killed. Still, from Evan's perspective, a lesson had been learned: Pope Jesus takes orders from no one.[227]

"BRING ME A VODKA!" Evan growled from the gilded bed in his golden bedroom. Alcohol, he thought, might calm his addled mind.

This was not how he had expected to spend his first day in Jerusalem. Everything had been planned to the slightest detail. His grand palace, his historic temple, his triumphant arrival — all of them should have made this day a dream come true. Instead, it had become a nightmare.

Everywhere, his body itched and, every time he scratched, his fingernails shredded the skin.

So, he rolled out of bed and yelled again, "Mother! Where's my drink?"

"I'm coming," she answered testily as she entered with a crystal tumbler.

Evan snatched the glass from her and gulped. Then he frowned and spit it out on the bedroom's silk Isfahan rug. Thas held up the tumbler and examined its contents: thick and red.

"I said vodka, not a Bloody Mary!"

"It is vodka."

Evan examined the red contents of the glass again. He reached in and fingered out ice. Before his eyes, the cube became red and opaque.

Thas threw down the glass, rushed into the bathroom and slammed the door.

"Evan?" Faridah asked from the bedroom, "Are you okay?"

He stared at himself in the mirror, squirming from the incessant itching.

Then he reached for the sink faucet, turned the lever and watched as the water flowed – clear, at first – then red, blood red.

He squirmed from the unrelenting itch and growled into the mirror. But when he could no longer resist scratching his forehead, he watched as blood drizzled down, covering his Titan eye patch.

Evan reached for a hand towel that hung next to a flowering orchid plant. He wiped the blood from his face. Then, when he examined his new cut in the mirror, something else caught his eye. The flowers were suddenly wilting.

> The martyrs were bound, imprisoned, scourged,
> racked, burned, torn apart and butchered.
> Still, they multiplied.
> St. Augustine

Chapter 39
White House Oval Office
March 9

FOR MORE THAN THREE YEARS, Angela had nagged Evan to visit her in the White House, only because she expected him to reject her persistence. Today, however, he arrived without advance notice. So, even though the visit was a surprise, she knew she could not refuse to see him.

Still, Angela nearly gasped when he entered the Oval Office.

"Evan? What happened?" she asked as her receptionist shut the door, leaving them in private. "Please, have a seat."

She stared, but did not extend her hand.

"Oh, stop your gawking," he complained as he plopped onto an upholstered sofa in the middle of room. "You're not much to look at, these days, yourself."

She knew it was true. Her hair had grayed, wrinkles were setting in, and she rarely wore makeup, anymore. The stressful demands of her job in recent years had taken priority over her previously glamorous lifestyle. Now, she was all business.

Perhaps that was why she had won a second term so easily. This time, she had even succeeded honestly, without Evan's manipulations. Her path to victory, though, had proceeded without much serious opposition. Lately, few opponents wished to lead the collapse of American supremacy. They were satisfied with letting her hold power, for now, as long as she took the blame.

Indeed, she knew she looked bad. But Evan was absolutely hideous. Since she last saw him, Thas had deteriorated into a mass of dying flesh. His eye patch and burn-scarred face were no longer his most unsightly attributes. Now, he was bloated and covered with scabbed cuts that oozed foul smelling pus.

"I need your help," he said, getting down to business immediately. "I think I've been targeted with a bio weapon ... either that or some kind of poison."

"Why do you say that?"

"Look at me!" he shouted.

From a deliberate distance, Angela observed that Evan had changed in many ways. Instead of ostentatious dress, he wore cheap, navy blue, cotton sweats. His manner of maintaining charismatic control had disappeared, and he twitched and squirmed on the sofa as if itching, but unable to scratch. Even in his eye, she could see that he appeared sleepless and exhausted.

Privately, she relished his torments.

She remembered his last XBC broadcast and asked, "Well, do you think the two prophets have something to do with…"

"They're not prophets!" he snapped. "They're just pretending! They're absolutely crazy!"

To Angela, his overreaction revealed more of his hope than his belief. So, she backed off quickly.

"What do you need me to do, Evan?"

He launched into a lengthy description of the specific steps he felt would be necessary in order to attack his problem. His medical facilities on the island of Nauru were still inoperable. So, he wanted complete access to the Centers for Disease Control and the National Institutes of Health.

As he continued to talk, Angela rose from her chair and wandered to the fireplace, behind him. There, she reached down and removed a heavy brass poker from its stand.

He continued speaking, but she was not listening. She could only hear her memory of the time she met Mercedes Dare in the Rose Garden. *If you want him to stay away, beg him to come back to Washington,* she advised. Angela asked, *But what if he does?* Mer did not hesitate. *Kill him.*

Now, as Thas babbled on with orders and requirements, he had no idea that his life was in danger. Angela stroked the shaft of the heavy poker and felt an odd kind of power from the cold, deadly object. Then she remembered Agent Anderson's words: *If I were in your shoes, I would kill him.*

Evan began naming the specific doctors and scientists he wanted assigned to his research and recovery project and their specific skill sets that had impressed him. As always, he had done his homework.

It could be messy, she thought as she loomed behind him. *But I'll never have an opportunity like this again.*

Still uncertain, she wandered to the window and gazed out to the Rose Garden. Immediately, she was struck by the uncommon view: flowers were beginning to loose their petals and the meticulously manicured lawn was browning. At the far end of the garden, through the wrought iron fence, a protester also caught her eye. He was walking the property perimeter with a small boy. He carried a bright yellow poster. Perhaps she would never have noticed them, if not for the words on his sign: "Times Square lights are out."

Those were the words that Mercedes Dare had used, years ago, to get her attention; the same ones that had been originally uttered by Dr. Huntinton Cyst when he first met Angela.

The president interrupted Evan's unrelenting stream of instructions, shouting, "Betsy? Anderson?"

Thas was clearly irritated.

The office door opened and the president's administrative assistant looked in.

"Yes ma'am?"

"Get Doctor Burkelton at CDC and Doctor Ipsley at NIH on the phone. Tell them I am ordering their full cooperation with the requests of Dr. Evan Thas. I will provide formal notice through the proper channels, shortly, but these urgent matters require their focused and immediate attention."

Thas rose from his sofa.

"Evan, Betsy will take care of you, now."

Thas nodded, satisfied that he still pulled all the levers of power in America.

When they left the Oval Office, Agent Anderson peaked in. "Madame president?"

"Yes, Anderson," she pointed the poker out the window. "There's a man with a boy, protesting outside the Rose Garden fence. He's carrying a yellow poster board sign. Bring them to me. I want to speak to them."

"Yes ma'am."

She caught him before he closed the door. "And Anderson…"

"Yes?"

She pointed the poker at the residue-stained furniture. "Trash that sofa as soon as possible."

"SO, YOU'RE ADAM," Angela marveled.

"Yes ma'am," the little redhead whispered, his feet dangling from his chair, kicking back and forth.

"You've grown quite a bit since I last saw you."

He nodded, trying to be agreeable.

"And Thomas, you're a priest?"

He shrugged his admission.

"I appreciate your honesty. It's a dangerous profession, these days."

"I was told you can be trusted."

"Lately, trust can also be dangerous." She sighed, but then perked up. "So, you obviously wanted my attention, and now you have it. You must have a message for me from Mercedes Dare."

"Madame president, she is…" he hesitated, "…in heaven."

Angela groaned softly. The boy continued kicking his feet, seemingly tuning out the conversation.

"What happened?"

"For the past few years, we've been living in a remnant camp. She … uh … may have been snake bit. Anyway, she told me everything."

He looked more deeply into her eyes. "Everything."

The president nodded. She knew that the grand secret in Adam's family was that his father would carve him up for spare body parts if he ever learned of his existence.

He continued, "She made me promise that, if anything happened to her, I would bring Adam to you. Mer said you know someone who can protect him."

Angela's eyes widened at the unexpected request.

"It's taken us a long time and a lot of effort to get here."

Still, she hesitated to agree.

"We hiked all the way up the Shenandoah Valley and then east to Washington."

Again, she sighed. "I don't know."

"He needs protection."

Angela studied the boy and then addressed him. "Adam? What do you think?"

"'Bout what?"

"Would that be okay? Would you like to live with a real nice man who'll take care of you?"

Continuing to kick his feet, he thought for a moment. "Is he in heaven?"

She smiled. "No ... not yet."

"I dunno. I kinda like Thomas." Then he started to open up. "Thomas taught me how to hunt... and build a fire... and forge..." he asked, "forge?"

"Forage," Thomas corrected.

"...and forage for mushrooms. You know, you gotta be careful, 'cause some mushrooms taste good, but some will make you go to heaven."

Angela was amazed at the boy's intelligence.

Father Thomas smiled. "I taught him everything I know."

"And he obviously learned well."

Angela addressed the boy again. "So, how about we let that nice man take care of you?"

"Will we live in a tent?"

"Oh, no," she grinned, "it'll be a much nicer place than that."

He began kicking his feet again. "I guess so."

The two adults were pleased with the response. Father Thomas rose from his chair and kneeled next to Adam's chair.

"Okay, big guy, you're off on another adventure."

"I like adventures."

"I know, and this will be the best one yet."

"Are you comin' with me?"

"No, Adam. I have to go back to camp and take care of our friends. But you'll be making new friends on your adventure. And, maybe some day, you'll take care of them. Would that be good?"

He nodded enthusiastically.

The priest leaned over and hugged the boy. "Now, you remember everything I taught you."

Again, he nodded.

The priest rose to his feet and extended his hand to Angela. "Madame president, thank you for doing this…"

"Thomas?" Adam interrupted. "I can't go adventuring without a blessing!"

The priest softly whispered as he stroked a Cross on the boy's forehead.

Then the child gave an enthusiastic "Amen!" and resumed kicking his feet.

MOMENTS LATER, Angela struggled to organize her thoughts for executing her unexpected, new responsibilities. As Adam ran to a Remington bronze at the far end of the office, she pecked on her computer keyboard, preparing a confidential message.

The president glanced up at the rambunctious boy. "Don't knock that over, honey,"

"Yes ma'am," he mumbled as he stroked his hand across the cold, metal horse.

One last time, she scanned her computer monitor, quietly reviewing the wording of her orders to Doctors Burkelton and Ipsley:

1. Quickly conduct a superficial examination of Evan Thas, including taking blood samples;
2. Assure him that he has become your highest priority, but warn that this research will take time;
3. Send him on his way;
4. Return to your previous responsibilities.

Everything looked in order, so she clicked to send the communication over the White House's secure intranet.

Angela continued to meditate on the message, however, wondering how long she would be able to stall Evan. Then she flinched when she heard, "Hey lady?"

The president turned and grinned at the active tyke who had snuck up behind her.

"Mind if I ask you a question?"

She marveled at how much the charming little redhead had inherited Evan's features, but not his bad manners. *Doesn't miss a trick,* she thought.

Angela responded, cheerfully, "Certainly, Adam. How can I help you?"

"Oh, I don't need help. I was just wonderin.'"

"Yes?"

He pointed at the door. "Who's that scary man I saw out there?"

> **Come, let us go down and confuse their language
> so they will not understand each other.**
> Genesis 11:6-7

EVAN'S PALACIAL BEDROOM was dark, but his mood, darker. As he shivered under silk sheets, thirsting and itching, Thas realized he was losing control of events and, perhaps, even his mind. Still, his steady eye remained transfixed on the faint outlines of his ornately coffered ceiling even as his thoughts wildly careened through sinister contemplations that confused credible threats with paranoid delusions.

Every betrayal replayed in his troubled mind like a scratched record, ripping back to the same incomplete lyric, again, and again, and again.

First, Huntie had abandoned him in Russia.

Then Mercedes attacked him.

Next, Melnikov and the Legion's other Judases tried to destroy him.

Only Angela had proved trustworthy, revealing that his own mother had been communicating with John Malek.

What was that all about?

Now, the so-called prophets had made a mockery of his power and influence by continuing to evangelize in Jerusalem, after humiliating him before a global audience. At one time, he was certain they were not converting anyone. Now he was not so sure.

XBC News execs insisted that they had tried everything, but had been unsuccessful at stopping the continuous live broadcast of their preaching. Evan fumed that his own news division either could not or would not stop providing global publicity for his enemies.

Are they lying to me? Why can't they stop it?

Thas longed for the day when he would repay these indignities and he imagined that his luck would turn, the moment the two preachers were silenced.

Certainly, they had become another high priority problem to solve. But infuriating him most of all, Evan realized that his own body was betraying him. In his mind, the Nauru tragedy had crippled not only his own body, but also his grand plan for the immortal man. Now, as his workers busily reconstructed XCyst's biotechnology capabilities on the island, he obsessed over finding a suitable donor for the reconstruction of his own body.

Laying quietly, Evan summoned the demons of the Abyss for solutions to his problems and he sensed that, tomorrow, the Beast would be with him. But his incantations were suddenly disturbed by a knock on the door.

Outside, he heard, "Evan, I need to speak to you."

"Go away, Mother."

She opened the door, anyway, and entered with a lit candelabra – the only light he now allowed in his bedroom. "These priority reports were just delivered."

Thas barely acknowledged her presence as she tossed a folder onto his golden bed. He remained under the covers and refused to look at her.

"Evan, this is no time to sulk."

"Get lost."

"You need to know what's happening. This is when we're most vulnerable."

"You read them."

Faridah picked up the folder, took it to a chair near the bed, sat down and began skimming under the candle light.

Faridah had become Evan's closest aide, largely as a result of President Concepcion's mischievous meddling. Angela had planned to divide and conquer the powerful pair by planting lies in their minds. She warned Evan that Faridah was communicating with

John Malek. She cautioned Faridah that Evan wanted her body for transplants and skin grafts. The lies, though, had backfired. Instead of breaking them apart, Faridah chose to ensure her survivability by becoming invaluable to her son, making her services indispensable. Evan accepted her increasing assistance cautiously, at first, plotting a strategy of keeping his enemies closer. Still, he would never again trust her even though, now, they had become inseparable.

She flipped through page after page. "Evan, people are getting restless."

"Tell me something I don't know," he groaned.

"Look," she lectured, "I'm giving you all the news: the good and the bad. You don't need a sugar-coated version."

He pouted. "Go on."

"Your security force has been alerted to assassination plots and have taken extra measures for your protection."

"A week ago they cheered me. Now they want to kill me?"

"Evan, the crops around Jerusalem are dying. It could be for lack of rain but, regardless, people are beginning to blame your presence here. Some are predicting famine and plagues until you leave."

He changed the subject. "What about the broadcast at the Temple?"

"We can't stop it. We've tried everything but... our engineers are baffled."

"The two lunatics?"

"Still preaching. I keep thinking they'll eventually need to sleep or eat, but they just keep smearing idiots with those damn ashes."

"And the whole world is watching."

She nodded and changed the subject. "We've got a bigger storm building. Looks like Malek's friend, Blanc, has been organizing a fighting force."

"I'm not worried. They're powerless without the Church."

"You should have used Glass Andalusian on them when you had the chance."

He was in no mood to listen to lectures. He knew he had been responsible for exhausting the power of his most lethal weapon. "Well, it's too late now. Isn't it?"

She ignored his sarcasm and continued with the reports. "He's not as harmless as you think. Blanc established a global communications network in Avignon."

"Patrollers have been monitoring it. He's setting up a religious Order. Big deal. Let 'em pray themselves to death."

She skimmed more pages. "His new Catholic Order has three divisions: warriors, priests and hoteliers.[228] According to this, they are fearlessly devout. They wear red Crosses on their chests."[229]

"Good. Makes it easy to identify who to kill."

"Evan, this is serious," she said. "They wouldn't be a problem for us now if you had listened to me and attacked them with Glass…"

"I did!" he finally admitted.

"What? Then, why aren't they dead?"

"I don't know," he groaned. "We targeted them at the Avignon Palace. But it had no effect."[230]

"We? Evan, your Patrollers must be letting you down. Most of them are incompetent. All of them are corrupt. You can't delegate anything that important."

He grumbled a curse at his underlings as she returned to the file reports.

Faridah asked, "What's this?" as she read from a newspaper article that she found in the file. "A French referendum has been called to restore the monarchy. Yesterday, all possible claimants to the future throne agreed to renounce their rights in favor of crowning Henri Blanc."

"What?"

"His reputation at Avignon is spreading around France… maybe even the world."

Thas continued to sulk, under the covers. In the past he would have simply ordered the elimination of anyone who gave him problems. Now, however, no murder could change the fact that his body was in a death spiral. His enthusiasm for conquest had waned because no victory could postpone his inevitable defeat. He was losing all hope.

Faridah stood and tossed the file on the foot of his bed. "You need to snap out of it. Our lives are on the line, here!"

She wanted to storm away. But then something in the flung file caught her eye. Faridah reached down and picked up a photograph from among the scattered papers. It appeared to be just another of the many thousands of pictures from White House pool photographers. Obviously, however, a Patroller had included it in the report for a reason.

Faridah studied the date stamp at the bottom of the picture: four years ago.

"Evan," she gasped, "what's this?"

He snatched the picture and examined the image. It was Angela Concepcion in the Rose Garden.

Then he noticed to whom she was talking.

"Wait a minute…" he mumbled. "That's Mer."

"Look at the date," Faridah prompted with amazement.

Then he saw something even more baffling. "Who is that?"

They both examined the boy in Mer's arms: pale complexion, freckles, and bright red hair.

Evan rolled out of bed and carried the picture to his balcony's French doors and studied the photo. Then he remembered the crib he had seen in Mer's cabin, just before he torched it.

She survived the fire, he thought, *and so did he!*

His hope returned.

Evan turned to his mother and growled, "You get me that kid."

"Wait." She knew what he wanted. "That's something you should do, yourself."

He turned back toward the Temple and viewed the tireless prophets continuing to preach while blessing the pilgrims.

"No," he responded firmly. "You bring him to me. I can't do everything." His eyes never left the despised prophets. "But I'll fix two problems tomorrow."

> The deaths of the vanquished
> are necessary for the tranquility of the victors.
> Genghis Khan

Chapter 41
Various Bedrooms
March 12

THAT NIGHT, the concept of life would not leave Angela's mind. As she tossed in bed, she wondered: *What is human life? If we accept that life is a gift from God, then who has the right to take it? If we reject that it is a gift, then who deserves to keep it?*

She was unable to reconcile her past blindness with what seemed so clear to her now. In her long political career, she had found political reasons to denounce one industry after another. Yet, she had disregarded her own significant role in establishing America's abortion industry. That leadership role had placed her on the slippery slope of marginalizing all human life. Now, abortion had become the celebrated sacrament of the Perfect World Agenda.

As her career advanced and her contacts widened, she had championed partial-birth abortion bills, mass-sterilization projects, and the approval of abortion-inducing drugs. She had attacked the Born Alive Infant Protection Act, limitations on euthanizing senior citizens, and protections against the growing problem of gendercide. She had ignored the horrific human research of XCyst Industries, including embryonic stem cell research, human cloning and trans-humanist genetic experiments.

She, essentially, had supported every initiative of Evan Thas and, now, he was loading dissenters into boxcars, headed for the frozen wilderness.

Merciful God, please forgive my blindness. I offer you the rest of my life, atoning for it.

Angela rolled over, and then drifted off to sleep.

§§§

THAT NIGHT, the concept of life would not leave Faridah's mind. As she tossed in bed, she wondered: *Evan will kill that child. But who can blame him? It's his life or the boy's.*

Faridah considered how she might find the child. She knew that President Concepcion was her only lead.

Angela's too smart to trick. I'll have to level with her.

She'll understand. She knows my own life's in danger if I don't find him.

Evan trusts her now.

Surely she'll help.

Faridah contemplated how the sudden turn of events had opened new opportunities for both of them. The medical facilities on Nauru would soon be operational and Evan had found a donor. Now, each could count on a long, healthy life.

Still, there was that unsettling task, ahead, of facilitating the kidnap and murder of the child. But his death would ensure her life.

So, who can blame me? It's my life or the boy's.

Faridah rolled over, and then drifted off to sleep.

THAT NIGHT, the concept of life would not leave Rebekah's mind. As she tossed in bed, she wondered: *Why was Israel reborn, if You want it to die? How could You breathe life into its dry bones, and then let it suffocate? Where are You, Holy One of Israel?*

Rebekah reflected on Yahweh's covenant with Abraham – some 4,000 years ago – in which He had ensured the Israelites a Promised Land.[231] There, Rebekah had been blessed to govern His people. But their journey had been long and hard, just as the prophecies had foretold. First, Yahweh dispersed the Jews, as He had predicted.[232] However, He had also promised that He would protect the survival of their race during those difficult times.[233] Then, after thousands of years, He fulfilled another promise: to gather His people together, again.[234] Perhaps, the most miraculous of His prophetic promises: Yahweh restored the nation of Israel.[235] And, since then, He had preserved the state of Israel against repeated threats to its survival,[236] and had protected its prosperity.[237]

Prince of Peace, the increase of Your government and peace shall have no end. Come, reign on David's throne and over his kingdom, establishing it and upholding it with justice and righteousness, now and forever more.[238]

Rebekah rolled over, and then drifted off to sleep.

THAT NIGHT, the concept of life would not leave John's mind. As he tossed in bed, he wondered: *Lord Jesus, is Your Church dying? How can You remain silent? Protect the life of Your Church!*

Lord, You see their evil goal. Just as Saul once plotted, they are scheming to destroy Your Church.[239] *But You granted him wisdom, in time, and Paul then reminded us to be shepherds of the Church, which You purchased with Your own blood.*[240] *Guide and protect Your shepherds so that we may guide and protect Your flock!*

Sacred Scriptures declare that Your Church is God's household, the pillar and foundation of Truth.[241] *Defend Your Church, as we defend your Truth.*

Your Word taught us that it is better to edify the Church than ourselves.[242] *Edify Your faithful as we edify Your Church.*

Come, Lord Jesus! The Church is Your Body, here on earth.[243] *Let not the gates of hell prevail against it!*[244]

John rolled over, and then prayed the rest of the night.

THAT NIGHT, the concept of death would not leave Evan's mind.

How many times
has the renewal of the Church
sprung from the shedding of blood?
This time, it will not be any different.
Pope John Paul II

WATCHING FROM HIS BALCONY, under the bright morning sun, Evan tried to control his rage at the many thousands who had come to Jerusalem to be blessed by the prophets. It appeared that the orderly queue below him wound through the narrow streets of Jerusalem for miles.

Surely, those pilgrims knew that they were defying his authority, within view of his own palace. Surely, they realized the danger.

The betrayals were unforgivable. The solution was clear.

"You should have done this a long time ago," Faridah complained from behind him.

Evan ignored her.

He glared up at the flames that raged in the heart of the looming Cross, and offered a derisive snort at its pretended importance, but actual impotence. Today, the so-called prophets would need more than symbols of protection.

During the entire rebuilding of the Temple, they had pestered his efforts in Jerusalem. Every day – wearing only course robes and refusing to bathe or shave – they had made fools of themselves, preaching idiocy with their ashes.[245] They had not been able to entice many followers. But now, their words were being broadcast around the world – and no one had been able to stop it. They had become too big of a problem to ignore.

Something had to be done.

So, Evan raised his semi-automatic rifle and nestled its butt onto his right shoulder.

As he squirmed to position his good eye – the left one – in line with the sights, he realized how unusual this act would be, for him. Normally, he had always delegated such tasks. Lately, however, he had learned to trust no one but himself.

For this accomplishment, he would accept no excuses, he would share no credit.

Evan heard shouting as he sighted down the barrel. He mumbled a baffled, "What are you doing?" Then Highest Holiness summoned the Beast of the Abyss, and squeezed the trigger.[246]

MOMENTS EARLIER, pilgrims were continually shuffling forward in two very long lines that led to the persevering prophets. Miraculously, none of them seemed hungry or tired, not even Pedro Lopez or Michael Alonzo.

Time and again, the prophets recited, "Remember that you are dust and to dust you shall return." The words penetrated to the soul of each pilgrim, not as a morbid prediction, but as an affirmation that this life – no matter how successful – is nothing compared to the next.

Many of these Christians had slipped back, after the Darkness. The Illumination of Conscience had awakened them, but only for a while. Then, the worldly pursuits of the Perfective Agenda gained influence over them. Initially, they had not comprehended the subtle power of the enemy. They did not realize that the only way to gain the next life is to be a contradiction to this one. Now, they had even cut out their Titan implants and destroyed them. Their forehead scars, in the shape of crosses, would now condemn them to lives of poverty, or worse.

Here in Jerusalem, a large and growing number of converts were Jews who had come to accept that the giant Cross in the sky was from Jesus Christ, their promised Messiah. For them, the prophets offered Baptism, along with their blessing with holy ashes. The profound experience also Confirmed them in the faith. Now, they eagerly awaited the Messiah's return in kingly glory.

Each blessing was accompanied by a Spiritual gift. Some received a word of Knowledge that comforted or instructed; many were healed, either physically or Spiritually; others heard a prophetic utterance that prepared them for challenges or opportunities in their lives.

Now, as the holy ashes dwindled down with each blessing, pilgrims were struck by the realization of the Spiritual gifts that they, themselves, had not used or even wanted throughout their lives. They longed to spread those gifts to family, friends and loved ones.

The constant procession seemed unending, until Pedro reached into his pocket and, for the first time, found no ashes. Immediately, he knew what that meant: they had blessed the last of 144,000 Jews. They would be the first fruits of Christ's Kingdom, descendants from every Tribe of Israel, entering with the Seal of God on their foreheads.[247]

Then a woman, in line, stepped closer and drew their attention. She pulled back her delicate white veil and whispered, "It is time."

Pedro and Alonzo gasped when they recognized the blazingly beautiful face of Sister Clarita.

She turned her head toward Evan's palace balcony.

Their eyes followed her glance.

They watched as Thas lowered his rifle barrel.

"Please step back!" Alonzo shouted to the crowd.

"Everyone, move back now!" Pedro pleaded.

Then, as the crowd descended the marble steps, into the courtyard, the two prophets turned to face the Son of Perdition. Side by side, they raised their arms, striking crucifixion poses.

Pedro whispered, "I love you, brother."

But before Alonzo could respond, rifle shots echoed through the streets of the holy city, along with bitter, anguished screams.

In one hour,
such great wealth
had been brought to ruin!
Revelation 18:17

Chapter 43
NASA Heliophysics Division
Boulder, Colorado
March 13

RESEMBLING AN OLD MARRIED COUPLE, the two young physicists had grown comfortable but bored with each other. Their days of mutual admiration, infatuation and exploration had long passed. Now, everything was routine – dull, monotonous routine. In fact, the pair rarely spoke, anymore.

At first, Doctors Tilda Lars and Chad Boyle had felt privileged to be recruited into the Solar Terrestrial Relations Observatory program. The anorexic-thin blond and the Australian rugby fan also had felt a curious attraction for each other. However, he soon learned to resent her air of superiority and she, his slobbery. Their fleeting thrill was gone after seven years of graveyard shifts, dutifully monitoring solar plasma and solar radiation, along with their effects on earth's magnetosphere.

In a way, they had come to accept that their work resembled that of airline pilots or assassination snipers: 99% boredom, 1% terror. So, they had learned to occupy their down time with reading. She enjoyed her suspense thrillers. He preferred his men's magazines.

Earlier this year, the two scientists had represented their Division at the Perfect World Environmental Conference. There, they had predicted record solar activity. However, since then, the season had progressed normally.

That was fine with them. The less work, the better.

The respite, also, was a welcome development for Perfectives around the globe. After all, the world had been slammed with one crisis after another, lately. They didn't need another.

However, missing the mark so profoundly in forecasts did not auger well for their program's continued funding. So, in periodic reports, the clever couple always credited Highest Holiness for the miraculously positive deviations. It did not matter to them that he was a good news credit glutton. They would gladly give him the glory, as long as they could keep their jobs.

Tonight, they had ignored each other while some of the world's most sophisticated technologies quietly continued collecting and displaying atmospheric and space data. When Chad went to the coffee pot for another cup, he no longer asked if Tilda wanted a refill. When she left for the restroom, she no longer paid him the courtesy of mentioning her absence. Fortunately, however, the sun was beginning to rise and their shift was almost over.

Then, a softly ringing alarm triggered. It was the same signal that was often used for their periodic training tests, requiring a response, but only to ensure that they were not sleeping at their stations.

When Tilda emerged from the restroom, she saw Chad wiping spilled coffee from a keyboard.

"What did you do?" she groaned.

"Get off my back! It started ringing before I spilled it!"

The senior scientist stepped over to her computer and began entering the code that would shut off the signal.

"You know," she complained, "you'd be more helpful if you spilled less coffee."

Then another alarm began buzzing.

"*Crikey!* Just do your job and stop blaming me!"

Unfazed, she continued to enter code. This had happened twice before. "I am doing my job. And if you'd bother to learn how to do this, you could do more than just watch!"

He began lecturing. "Hey, Tilda, if they paid me what they pay you, I'd learn your job! Why should I bust my butt to help you? I mean, I spend as much time as you, around here. Did you ever think about that? Huh?"

She wasn't listening. Her brow tightened as she focused on her monitor. "This is big," she mumbled while continuing to peck on the keyboard.

Then a third alarm began dinging loudly – one they had never heard before.

"What's happening?"

Suddenly, her face revealed panic. "Emergency channel broadcast!" she barked.

He ran to his computer station. "Which departments?"

"All of 'em!" she screamed. "International, too! Anybody ... everybody. I've never seen anything like it. This thing's a monster!"

"How much time do we have?"

"Thirty minutes, tops ... No ... maybe less." She continued typing frantically and evaluating whatever hit her screen. "Much less.... What? This is unbelievable."

"Okay, it's going everywhere. I'm ready."

"Oh, man…" she whispered, mesmerized by the data.

"What do I send?" he screamed.

She dictated, "Urgent. Immediate action required. Unprecedented X Class solar flare approaching. Early estimate is electromagnetic pulse equivalent of X36. Tangential impact projected for western Europe, Atlantic and most of continental U.S."[248]

Staring at a new stream of data, she interrupted herself. "No, that can't be."

"What?" he pleaded.

She stopped typing and slumped back in her chair. "It's not coming from the sun." Her tone lost its urgency. "Send it."

But before he could press the key, every light went out, every circuit fried.

**…the kingdom of heaven
belongs to such as these.**
Matthew 19:14

**Chapter 44
The Secret Archives
Vatican City
March 15**

"YOU GO FIRST," John instructed as he slammed the steel door behind them. Adam darted down the shadowed metal stairs, ignoring the haunting echo of the trio's footsteps in the cavernous stairwell. Deeper and deeper he descended, into the darkened abyss while John followed, close behind, with Evie in his arms.

As John alternated from watching his step to studying her countenance, he could tell that the little one was trying to manage a brave face. Still, he detected fear in her eyes.

"It's okay, little one. You'll be safe, down here."

Adam, on the other hand, exhibited no hesitation. The little redhead loved adventure and craved to lead. Perhaps oddly, John had learned to trust the lad's judgment. Even though the wise, old apostle had only met Adam a few days before, he had concluded that the boy was mature, well beyond his years.

When they reached the bottom – sixty meters below ground – Adam paused at another door.

"Go ahead," John prompted. "It's not locked."

The boy swung it open and led them into the anteroom of the Vatican's secret storage vault. There, they saw the empty table that had been manned around the clock, in the past, by armed Swiss Guards.

John reached for the stainless steel vault door and was pleased to see that it remained open, just as he had left it. The discovery was a relief, for him, because he knew that if anyone had closed the door the vault's biometric security system would have prevented them from using it for refuge.

The ancient apostle gave it a tug and was surprised at how easily the fourteen inch thick door swung open. He tried to put the best face on the situation as he led the children into their bunker.

John clicked on the light. "Oh, this will be nice." He pointed at a wall of supplies. "Look at all the food and water they stored. That's perfect."

He did not voice his disappointment in seeing, again, the empty shelves that had once stored the collection of 1,782 inspired scrolls that he had provided Church leadership over twenty centuries. Right now, the less said about the rampaging Patrollers, the better. But he was pleased to see, at least, that his final epistle was still rolled up on a shelf.

Evie asked, "Papa, why do we have to come down here?"

"Sweetie, right now, it's dangerous out there. This is where we'll be safe."

Adam had wandered into a side room and started laughing. He pointed at a toilet. "Look Papa, they've got a potty. This is even better than camping."

"Right. We'll have everything we need, no matter what happens outside."

Indeed, John knew that this vault had been designed, primarily, to preserve his scrolls. However, it was also planned as a bunker for a few members of Church hierarchy if World War III ever threatened. Here, generators maintained the power supply and the air was conditioned, dehumidified, and even filtered for possible attacks from weapons of mass destruction.

No safer place on the planet existed.

"Don't worry, Evie," Adam volunteered. "This'll be an adventure."

John smiled at the precocious little soldier and then remembered that the anteroom's stairwell door had been left open. He wanted the benefit of every layer of protection, so he told the children, "Wait here, kids. I'll be back."

John stepped out of the vault and headed past the guard's table. At the far end of the anteroom, he heard Adam say, "It's dangerous out there, Evie. I'll shut the door."

John turned with a jerk and immediately bolted toward the vault. But just as he reached for the door, it slammed shut. Then he heard its massive deadbolts grind into their locked position.

"Nooo!" John screamed.

His eyes darted around the door. He pounded his fists on its smooth, stainless steel.

"Dear God, no!"

He strained with all his might to turn the locking wheel on the vault.

"Please God, Evie's in there!"

He reached toward the guard's table, picked up a chair and crashed it against the unyielding barrier.

"Please, please, please." He collapsed onto the floor. "Not yet, Lord. Not yet."

Over the next few hours, John repeatedly revived himself with new plans of attack until he eventually accepted that he had exhausted every possibility.

Then, at the limit of his endurance, the lights went out.

What happened? he asked himself.

John slid his hands across the cold, steel door that he could no longer see.

"I understand," he finally groaned. "It is time."

There was nothing more Papa could do, except weep bitterly in the dark.

"LET'S PRAY THE ROSALY," Evie said as she pulled her ruby-red rosary out of her pocket. John had taught her to treasure the prayer beads, not only because they could bring her closer to Blessed

Mother and Baby Jesus, but because they had been passed down to her through three generations: from Elizabeta – the grandmother she never knew – to Angela – the mother she had not seen for years – to herself.

Their first day in the vault, Adam had insisted on the incorrect pronunciation and he had claimed to know how to lead rosary prayers. Evie knew better, but she did not want to argue. So, she let Adam lead. After all, he made her feel safe and she made him feel important.

"Okay," Adam said, still scrounging through the food supplies on the top shelf.

Then he paused. "Hey, look at this," he said as he pulled out John's scroll and unrolled it. "It's big as a book."

"Can you read it?"

"Sure," he claimed with more confidence than certainty. "I can read anything."

Adam continued skimming the scroll. Then his voice took on a tone of awe. "Maybe its a adventure story."

"Yeah!" she cheered. "Read it to me after the rosaly."

"Okay." The boy tossed the scroll down to the floor and then hopped down, himself.

He sidled up to her and they sat together on the concrete floor, softened only by the sleeping bags that they had previously found on the storage shelves.

"Evie?" he asked, "When's Papa coming back?"

"Don't know," she shrugged. "But he said he'll be back, so we just have to wait. Papa always said Baby Jesus is coming back, too."

"When?"

"I don't know, silly." She repeated, "We just have to wait."[249]

Adam frowned at being called down. He moped, "That's what they said about my mom: I gotta wait." But he soon recovered. "You want me to hold the beads?"

She handed them over, politely.

Then he began with: "Hail Mary, full of grace."

She repeated, "Hail Mary, full of grace."

Again, he said, "Hail Mary, full of grace."

She repeated.

Unfortunately, he did not know many of the prayer's words, nor did he realize that the beads should have helped him count the prayers. So, after a couple dozen repetitions, he arbitrarily changed to "Our Father, Who are in heaven…"

Then they exchanged glances, but neither knew how to continue. So, he quickly concluded with the Sign of the Cross.

It was not quite "by the book" but, still, the best they could do. So, God was pleased.

They were in their third day of refuge in the vault but, already, their daily patterns were being established.

She loved hearing his adventure stories about how he had hunted boar in the forest, built campfires and harvested edible plants in the wild. He told her about how much Father Thomas had taught him when they ventured along the Shenandoah River on their long journey to Washington.

She laughed at his story about meeting the president of the United States and how she asked him to fly – for the very first time – in a big, fancy plane. He said he flew so high that cars looked like ants. He thought he was almost alone on the plane but a real nice man, named Agent Anderson, told him that some pilots were in the front driving it.

Adam also loved hearing her stories about Papa because she had been with him so much longer. She even told him tales from her children's Bible that Papa and the Sisters had read to her.

Unfortunately he had never seen a Bible.

So, as Adam unrolled the large scroll on the sleeping bag, they fidgeted with excitement over the new story they could share.

Before he started, they gazed at each other and smiled with anticipation.

Then he began reading slowly, struggling with the first word: "Neo-gen-e-sis… chapter one…"

Out, out, brief candle!
Life's but a walking shadow,
a poor player that struts and frets
his hour upon the stage
and then is heard no more:
it is a tale told by an idiot,
full of sound and fury,
signifying nothing.
From *Macbeth*
by William Shakespeare

O N A CANDLE LIT TABLE, Faridah reviewed their most recent reports. Flipping through page after page, she absorbed whatever she could while he paced the darkened room with a knife in hand. She did not feel comfortable revealing the extent of their setback.

"Well?" Evan demanded. "What's happening?"

She continued searching for a small scrap of good news to help balance the voluminous bad.

"Hmmm," Faridah mumbled as she leafed through more pages. "Power grids are down across most of the continental U.S."

"Secure communications?" he prompted.

She skimmed through pages. "No, still down…. They're evaluating possible satellite damage now." Faridah drew a heavy breath. She could not stall any longer. "Translators are out. CyBot is inoperable…"

"Are you saying the supercomputer has been…" He interrupted himself. "Titan. What about Titan?"

She flipped through a few more pages.

"Ohhh, this is not good," she mumbled.

"What?" he shouted as he paced faster and clutched his knife tighter.

She read, "Significant loss of Titan data... possibly unrecoverable."

He jerked the knife toward her. "No way. Give me that!"

She handed him the folder and he began violently ripping through the pages under the candle light.

"We have redundant backup systems," he argued.

"Yes. They're spread across the east coast. They were all hit."

"This can't be!"

But his torment was made even more intolerable by incessant itching and unrelenting thirst.

"Water!" he yelled as he squirmed for comfort.

"Are you sure..."

"Get it!" he demanded.

She put the candelabra on this bed table and went to the bathroom as he continued leafing through the reports.

When she returned, he was violently stabbing his mattress as he uttered animalistic grunts.

She handed him a glass and cringed as she saw the liquid turn blood-red just before he gulped it down.

Then he snatched the reports up again, still clutching his knife.

The macabre scene became all the more disturbing for her as candle flame shadows danced across his ravaged face. She turned her head, but found nothing to focus on except dead plants that once decorated his room.

"We're losing our advantage," he mumbled to himself. "Vast technologies have been neutralized: power grids, the Internet, control of the money supply."

He threw the reports down on his bed. "The universal translator is out!"

"You still have your forces," she tried to reassure, "the Patrollers."

He collapsed onto the bed. "We can't communicate," he cried. "We can't communicate."[250]

This heaven I've forfeited
I know it full well.
My soul, once true to God,
Is chosen for hell.
From *The Pale Maiden*
by Karl Marx

Chapter 46
Thas Palace
Jerusalem
March 15

FARIDAH SLAMMED the door of her bedroom and groped in the dark to find her mahogany dresser. On it she patted around until she found matches and lit a large candle. As she stared at herself in the mirror while removing her jewelry, she sighed deeply over her son's incapacitating depression.

Then the mirror revealed something that startled her. She jerked around and barked, "What are you doing here?"

Barely visible, near her bed, John sat calmly in an upholstered chair. "Do not be afraid."

"Afraid? You're the one who should be worried. If I…"

"Go ahead. No one will hear you."

She paused for a moment and then shouted, "Security!"

Nothing happened.

"Security! Help!"

No one responded.

She studied John's appearance. He did not look threatening. But she could see that he was bedraggled and tired. Though he had sailed the Mediterranean many times in the past, this had been his record pace. He knew time was running out.

Softly, John continued. "I have a message for you. We won't be interrupted."

"A message from who?"

"You know."

"Why would God communicate with me?" She snorted a derisive laugh. "I hate Him."

"Yes," John responded flatly. "Still, He loves you even though you despise everything, even yourself."

The truth silenced her.

"You resented the gift of your Jewish heritage. So, you rebelled, hoping that impiously taking the vows of a Catholic nun would prove your rejection of God's chosen race as well as God, Himself. But He forgave your defiance and even offered you a Spiritual gift."

"What gift?" she sneered.

"Prophecy…. You know how it all ends."

"I know how to change how it all ends!"

"That is your pride speaking. You can only control your own destiny."

She growled, "You're here to trick me, to tempt me to betray Evan. I'm no Judas!"

"But you will share his fate if…"

"In Beirut," she interrupted, "why did you pull me out of the rubble?"[251]

"The God you hate is patient and merciful. You have another opportunity to repent."

She was defiant. "You want me to betray my son."

"Time is running out. You know the prophecies. St. Malachy foretold that Peter II would be the last reigning pope.[252] The Jews have returned to their homeland.[253] The Temple has been rebuilt. [254] The apostasy flourished."[255]

She interrupted, with pride, "Your God did not fulfill those prophecies. My son did."

Undaunted, he continued. "Satan's century is expiring. From Fatima, to Garabandal to Medjugorje, Blessed Mother has warned us of what is and what shall be. The century of Satan's freedom is coming to as close.[256] Evan's time is running…"

"Enough!" she shouted. Her face contorted from the light of the flickering candle in her hand. She approached his chair and glared down at him. "You are such a fool." She radiated hatred, as if wanting to attack or even kill him. "Do you not realize that the night you pulled me from the convent wreckage, I was pregnant with Evan? You saved not only my life, but his."

Unafraid, John rose from his chair.

She did not retreat. Staring intensely, she growled at him, "All this blood is on *your* hands."

He walked around her and headed for the door. He knew he was speaking, now, only to the demons that possessed her.

But just as he reached for the door knob, the demons left, her tone changed, and John heard her whimper, "You should have left me in the rubble."

I have come to bring fire on the earth,
and how I wish it were already kindled! ...
Hypocrites! You know how to interpret
the appearance of the earth and the sky.
How is it that you don't know how to interpret
this present time?
Luke 12:49 and 56

Chapter 47
Jerusalem
March 16

INEXPLICABLY, the Temple's live video had continued – even in homes where the blackout persisted. Cars had been abandoned in the streets, utilities had been unable to operate, even police and fire protection had disappeared. But, for the past three days, XBC cameras had broadcast the Temple view, including the bodies of Pedro Lopez and Father Michael Alonzo.

Patrollers had deemed the pair unworthy to remain on Solomon's porch and undeserving of a proper burial. So, they had dragged the corpses down the steps and left them on the cobblestone street.[257] Brother Daniel Mitchum, had declared that no one was permitted to touch the so-called prophets except the vultures of the air and the dogs of the street. He hoped that their gruesome deterioration would serve as a lesson to all Imperfectives.

Some wondered, *Why were they so hated?* But they knew better than to speak the question.

The bold warnings of the prophets had shined the light of truth on the sins of modern man. So, initially, Christians mourned their deaths while Perfectives celebrated.[258] Like lions and lambs, they gladly separated, each to be with his own kind. As always, God embraced them in their prayers, or abandoned them to their sins, honoring their freedom to choose.

Now, however, the tide was decidedly turning on Evan's

popularity, and no one was more disillusioned and upset about recent developments than Faridah Shabaan. She stormed into his bedroom without bothering to knock.

"Get up!" Faridah demanded. "It's broad daylight, out there, and you're sleeping again!"

"You have no idea what I'm going through!" he groaned from bed.

"Stop feeling sorry for yourself. If you don't get back in control of the situation we'll all be dead, soon."

"What are you talking about?" he said as he tightened blankets around his shivering shoulders and squirmed from incessant itching.

"Henri Blanc's troops have been overwhelming our strongholds!"

"Where?"

"Europe, Asia, Africa, North America, South America," she screamed, "everywhere!"

"That's impossible!"

"Evan, a lot of power grids are down. Even where people have electricity, they haven't been able to access their Titan accounts. They can't buy or sell anything. Our people feel tricked. They aren't even defending your outposts, anymore. Blanc's men are taking over without a shot fired."

Evan had been informed that all Titan records had been destroyed and that the Cyst-Blanc supercomputer had been disabled.[259] "How are they communicating… coordinating their offensive?"

"Mostly by word of mouth. But, somehow, they protected their computers and generators from the electromagnetic radiation."

"Where did the pulse come from? Do we know, yet?"

She did not answer him directly. "We ruled out a solar flare."

"Then what?"

She wanted to avoid the obvious conclusion but had tired of pretending ignorance. "Evan, you saw it."

"What?"

"The fire is gone from the center of the Cross in the sky."

"It's not a Cross!"

"Whatever it is, a lot of people saw the flames burst toward earth when you shot the prophets. Then the power went out."

He had hoped that the timing was a coincidence. Now, he was forced to accept that his technological advantage had been neutralized by a supernatural intervention.

She continued, "Mitchum has tried his best to continue broadcasting messages of hope from the Temple's live feed. He keeps playing for time, announcing everything is under control."

"And?"

She couldn't lie. "People don't trust Mitchum, not even your Patrollers."

"Why not?"

"They're desperate. They think they're broke."

"It can't be as bad as you say. Look at all I've done for them. I redistributed justice. They're rich beyond their wildest dreams."

"Evan," she reasoned, "every Patroller who gained a penthouse apartment under your leadership was thrilled, at one time. But now his electricity is out, his elevators don't work, and he has to lug his food and water up dozens of flights of stairs. It's amazing how quickly some people can become barbarians without some of their modern conveniences."

Thas appeared to be ignoring her, but she continued anyway.

"It's only been three days but, already, people are trashing grocery stores and stealing everything in sight. Newer cars won't drive because their computer chips are inoperable and older cars can't find gas. Modern conveniences are gone. It's almost as if Western Civilization has been set back two centuries but nobody is prepared to return to an agrarian society."

He sighed. "Except the damn Imperfectives."

"Evan, you still have your Temple broadcast getting into homes around the world. Nobody understands how it is happening but that is your one trump card. You need to play it. The people need you, now more than ever. Take control. Get on camera and encourage them to hold together under your leadership." She tried cheerleading. "The Perfect World is our right! The Perfect World is almost here!"

Thas grumbled to himself, "I need somebody to blame."

Suddenly, Faridah felt very uncomfortable.

He sat up and stared at her.

"Mitchum!" she offered.

His expression did not change.

She begged. "Blame everything on him. Evan, you need to rule by fear. I'll have him shot… on camera, if you like."

He mulled her suggestion for a moment and then nodded. "Yeah. He'll do."

She breathed a sigh of relief and then asked, cautiously, "And if that isn't enough, what next?"

After an unsettling moment of reflection, he remembered Plan B. "Mother, some assets are always protected against electromagnetic radiation." He added, calmly, "I still have access to Israel's nuclear launch codes."

**Abandon all hope,
ye who enter here!**
Sign over the gates of hell,
according to Dante

Chapter 48
The Temple Porch
Jerusalem
March 16

THOUGH HE HAD NEVER dared to enter the Temple, nor touch the Ark of the Covenant, Evan lectured the world confidently from the Temple steps. He had finally pulled himself together and was hoping that television, once again, would elevate his image and bolster his sagging popularity. Without that entrancing invention of the 20th century, he would never have mastered his special talents: turning doubt into faith, making black seem white. Today, television could be his savior.

Stretched out below him, were the bodies of the two prophets that had been laying in the street for three and a half days. Around them, a few dozen Patrollers had gathered, following orders to listen to Evan's words of wisdom. But even though Thas effervesced with optimism, their interest was waning.

So, Faridah felt compelled to inject some enthusiasm from her balcony. Every time Evan offered a promise or pronounced a victory, she applauded, prompting the dutiful but bored Patrollers below to follow her lead. Still, with the right camera angles, Evan was confident that audiences at home would be sufficiently deceived regarding his support.

He began his remarks by pretending heartfelt sympathy for all those who were struggling through the difficulties of the day. Then he listed his own accomplishments before blaming Brother Daniel Mitchum for the recent problems that had developed. He explained that Mitchum's guilt over his recent failures had overwhelmed him.

"Brother Daniel meant well," Thas explained, "but just wasn't up to the task." Then he added, "Tragically, he was found in bed this morning, dead of a heart attack."

Around the world, nobody mourned. In fact, no one would be watching Evan's broadcast if not for the fact that people were desperate to hear any possible fragment of good news.

"Fortunately for us all," Thas continued, "I will now take control of…"

"You murdered him," a voice interrupted from the small crowd.

His eye jerked to the dead prophets, fearful that they were humiliating him again, even from the dead. Then he noticed his Patrollers backing away from a white-robed man in the crowd. It was John Eben Malek.

"Just like you murdered Enoch and Elijah," John added.

"Kill him!" Evan pleaded with Patrollers.

None of them responded.

Calmly, John ascended the steps. Evan appeared fearful.

"You are on your own, now," John warned.

"Shoot him!" Faridah screamed frantically from her balcony. "Kill him!"

John ignored her, as the global broadcast continued. He walked to the Ark of the Covenant and placed his hands on its golden top. He spoke toward the camera. "You have been told to follow no man who cannot touch the Ark. Today, you shall follow no man at all. You shall follow God Almighty."

John elevated his hands toward Pedro and Alonzo. Then his voice thundered, "In the name of God – the Father, the Son, and the Holy Spirit – rise holy prophets."

The Spirit of God entered them and a worldwide audience witnessed Pedro Lopez and Michael Alonzo rising to their feet, illuminated by a supernatural glow.

The Patrollers, nearby, became terrified that the men who had incinerated their cohorts had risen from the dead. So, they fled in panic, to the safety of their homes.[260]

Faridah Shabaan was outraged that no one was confronting John. "Kill him, Evan!" she shouted from her balcony.

But her son seemed impotent from fear.

Then John raised his hands to the looming red Cross in the sky and prayed, "Almighty God, Your holy prophets await their reward."

Then a voice, more profound than any they had heard before, filled the air and reverberated to the depths of their souls: "Come to Me, now."

Everyone gazed in amazement as a luminous cloud slowly engulfed the ecstatic prophets who stared at John with heartfelt appreciation. The ancient apostle nodded back his profound joy for them. Then the cloud transported them up and they disappeared into the heart of the awesome Cross in the sky.[261]

For a moment, everyone continued to watch, silently. Then Faridah screamed, "It's all trickery! They're frauds!"

John returned to the Ark, closed his eyes, and again placed his hands on it.

"Thy will be done, Lord."

Immediately, a streak of lightning flashed across the eastern sky, crashing on the Mount of Olives with a thunderous roar.

Then the ground started shaking.

Suddenly, Jerusalem jolted as never before.

Thas tumbled off the Temple porch like a rag doll.

Faridah cursed at the sky as she clutched her balcony's railing for support.

Homes, one after another, were leveled by the unprecedented earthquake, but only those that were occupied by Evan's 7,000 Patrollers.[262]

As the ground around him shook, Thas crawled across the cobblestones toward the Temple steps. They seemed the only stable ground, nearby. But before he reached them, his attention was diverted. Mixed with the deafening cacophony of crashing destruction, he heard Faridah scream for help.

Thas turned toward his grand mansion and caught a glimpse of horrified eyes just as her balcony collapsed. Then, as if in slow motion, he watched the palace crumble like a sand castle and bury her under a mountain of rubble.

It was over in a matter of seconds.

Evan could do nothing, except tremble.

Faridah could do nothing, except perish.

GROVELLING IN THE STREET, Evan's mind raced. His Patrollers, his palace and his mother were gone. But his instincts were not. He remembered what Huntie had taught him: no matter how bad circumstances appear, there is always a bargain to be made. So, as he watched John pray at the Ark, he quietly conjured every demon from hell.

Suddenly, he knew what to do. But he needed to get on camera, first. It was the only way he could communicate with his Patrollers.

When the rumbling finally ceased, Thas shouted to John, "Have mercy, holy one."

The ancient apostle continued praying.

Evan's voice echoed through the empty streets of Jerusalem, "Have mercy on me, a sinner."

It seemed that the holy city had been emptied of everyone, but themselves. However, viewers, worldwide, were mesmerized by the miraculous events.

"Christian, can you not forgive when I beg for mercy?"

John opened his eyes and removed his hands from the Ark. "My mercy is of little concern for you now."

"Then let me earn God's mercy. Let me confess my sins. Let me witness to the world what is right and true."

"Come," John said as he motioned for him to approach. "I want you to see something."

Thas rose to his feet, brushed himself off, and ascended the steps. He was pleased that he would now be in view of the camera.

When Evan reached the top, John pointed to the east and said,

"Welcome your jailers."

Evan's gaze extended across the Kidron Valley to the Mount of Olives. There, the land was covered with soldiers, on foot and on horseback. They were advancing on Jerusalem just as a similar force had done almost four years earlier. Now, however, Evan had no satellite to assist him. He had only his demons.

Leading the forces down the road to the Golden Gate – the one that Evan, himself, had ordered reconstructed – was a man on a white stallion. His standard was a large crucifix, in his right hand, and he wore a white tunic with a large red Cross on his chest.

"Henri Blanc is leading them," John said proudly. "The Great Monarch."

I need my Patrollers! Evan thought.

"Today," John advised, "you shall choose between prison or death."

Suddenly, the diminutive Thas exploded with demonic rage. He grabbed John's robe and hurled the apostle off the Temple steps. John landed with a thud as his head slammed onto a cobblestone paver, knocking him out.

Thas looked into the camera and played his only remaining card. He ordered, "Israel N-Class Patrollers: Mayday, Mayday, Mayday. Prepare to initiate launch sequences immediately. Pre-set target: Avignon France. Repeat: Initiate launch sequences immediately. Target: Avignon, France. Begin sequence: Zulu; Bravo; Niner; Five; Niner; Three; Delta; Tango…"

As John regained consciousness, Evan continued shouting the launch code sequence into the camera. Then he said, "Prepare to launch on my order."

John rose to his feet, on the street, below.

Thas demanded, "You stop them in the valley. Tell them that if they don't back off, immediately, their families in Avignon will be incinerated in seven minutes."

John did not move.

"Now!" Thas ordered.

"Henri Blanc will not take orders from you."

"I have nuclear missiles at my disposal. You have men on foot and horseback." Evan sneered, "Who do you think will win?"

"I know who will win."

"I swear, if you don't force them to back off, I'll wipe out Avignon!"

John did not move.

Evan's voice was cracking from panic. "I have 174 nukes in my arsenal! You do what I say or I'll start launching them everywhere!"

With that televised threat, nuclear launch teams around the globe began to scramble. They knew that preemptive strikes might be required.

Though most technologies had been neutralized in the Western Hemisphere, nuclear delivery systems were the weapons that had been most protected against the detrimental effects of an electromagnetic pulse. These days, most Western populations could not even feed themselves, but they could still kill each other.

John pleaded, "You don't have to do this. It is possible to turn your life around in prison."

"Target Avignon, launch!" Thas shouted to the camera. "I repeat: launch target Avignon."

Upon hearing that alarming order, military commanders in nuclear silos and submarines around the globe began arming their Automatic Decapitation-Response Protocols. They could no longer count on the sanity of the mercurial Evan Thas. So, now, calculating but uncaring computers would execute pre-planned orders, even if their commanders were dead.

Evan gazed into the valley at the enormous advancing army and shouted, "Israel N-Class Patrollers: Mayday, Mayday, Mayday. Prepare to initiate launch sequences immediately. Pre-set target: Vatican City..."

Then, with the aid of his brilliant mind, he again recited the appropriate launch codes from memory.

However, before the sequence was completed, the world responded with nuclear hair-triggers. France was first, attempting to counter Evan's attack. Pakistan was next, unwilling to tolerate any nuclear launch from Israel. Then India reacted to their enemy, Pakistan.

Within thirty seconds, the dominoes had fallen and enough firepower had been launched to incinerate the earth seven times over. The U.K., the U.S., Russia, China and North Korea had responded to defend their interests. By doing so, everyone would soon be dead.

It was a major miscalculation by Evan … but not by the demons who had inspired him.

AS THE SECONDS TICKED AWAY, viewers from around the world perceived the impending disaster, but felt helpless. Some cursed whoever they blamed. Others realized their impotence, raised their gaze to the awesome Cross in the sky and placed their trust in God.[263]

The world's Imperfectives, though, had no televisions to watch. So, they did not know about the looming catastrophe. However, they did not need to know. They were already prepared.

In Jerusalem, John had simply lowered his head in prayer. But Evan had continued lecturing into the camera, not realizing that countries had launched against him.

"You forced me to rule by fear," he said, demanding the world's grudging respect. "Your disobedience must be punished."

Then he paused, staring at a vapor trail in the eastern sky. He jerked around and saw, in the distant west, another missile streaking toward him.

His boastful pride vanished. Thas realized that only one man could save him, now.

He turned to John. "Do something," Evan pleaded.

The ancient apostle ignored him, continuing in prayer.

"Do something," he screamed, "or we're both dead!"

John finished his prayer, raised his head, and smiled.[264]

Then they both heard why.

> ... the Lord knows
> how to rescue the devout
> from the trial
> and to keep the unrighteous
> under punishment
> for the day of judgment.
> 2 Peter 2:9

Chapter 49
The World
Judgment Day

ACROSS CONTINENTS and oceans, cities and farms, valleys and deserts, the wail of the Resurrection Trumpet reverberated to the depths of every soul.[265] Like a thief in the night, the day of justice had arrived. God's merciful patience had ended for those who had ignored it.

In Jerusalem, Evan Thas stumbled to the street as he watched the sky roll open like a scroll, behind the looming red Cross. He no longer feared incoming nuclear missiles. They had stopped in midflight. He did not care about the army of Henri Blanc. They were merely human. Now, he was more concerned with the battalion of angels that were streaming from the sky, led by Michael the Archangel.

Thas marveled in fear at the luminescent creatures as they streamed toward him, seemingly unconcerned about anyone else. The winged warriors appeared delicately beautiful but deadly powerful. He knew not to challenge them. So, instead, he tried to bargain.

As Michael landed before him, Evan rose to his feet on the cobblestone street.

"Look, I can explain…"

The angel held up his hand and Thas choked into silence.

Then Michael turned to John, as hundreds of angels fluttered behind him. They all offered him a slight but respectful bow.

"Beloved Apostle," Michael said, "what do you ask that we do with him."

John did not hesitate. "God's will be done."

Slowly, the angels began to back away from Evan.

"Wait," he pleaded, "what are you gonna do? I mean, everybody deserves mercy. Look, I'm really sorry. I, uh, I'm asking for forgiveness."

Thas began to back down the street.

He continued to beg. "You gotta show forgiveness. I mean, Jesus forgives everybody, doesn't He? You know, even on the Cross, He forgave the people who crucified Him. I mean, I had nothing to do with that."

Michael began to raise his hand.

"Wait! You need to hear me out before you make a rash decision. Please!"

Thas stumbled, backward.

Before he could return to his feet, however, Michael pointed his finger at Evan and levitated him ten feet above the cobblestones.

"What are you doing?" Thas screamed.

Then Michael dropped his hand toward the ground, causing Evan's body to slam onto the street with a thud.

As soon as he regained consciousness, Thas realized that the angel had punished him for throwing John to the pavement earlier that day.

Thas wanted to sit up, but felt too battered to try. So he continued to lay there. But his defense continued: "Okay. I deserved that. I'll be good from now…"

Evan felt his body rising again.

"Hey, wait! You already punished me!"

Then Michael removed his sword from its scabbard.

As Evan's bloated, bruised and bloody body helplessly dangled above the street, he watched the angel point the sword at the ground and slash it through the air.

Immediately, a huge, gaping chasm opened in the earth below

him. Thas screamed but no one listened. Out of the darkness, flames leaped to taunt his body, while sulfuric smoke filled his nostrils.

"Please! I'm begging you! I'll change!"

From the flames, Evan heard voices mocking him. "I'm begging!" "Please!"

Then he heard familiar voices ascending from the flaming pool, far below. First, he thought he detected Faridah and Melnikov, crying out for him. Then he recognized the screams of his twin step brothers, members of the Legion of Babylon and officers from XCyst Industries. Most agonized of all, however, was the voice of The Prophet of Technology, his mentor, Huntington Cyst.

It struck him that these were the people with whom he had been closest … and they were all in hell.

Still, negotiating had never failed Evan before.

"Look," Thas pleaded as he dangled above the flaming cavern, "John Malek made me an offer. He said I can choose between prison or death today. He said I can change my life around in prison. He practically begged me to show mercy."

The archangel turned to John, who was observing from the Temple porch without sympathy.

"It's true," Evan choked and coughed, "isn't it? You made me that offer!"

Calmly John added, "And you rejected it."[266]

The archangel turned, dropped his hand and watched Evan plunge, screaming, into the lake of fire.[267]

Then Michael waved his sword through the air, again, and the smoking cavern slammed shut.

SUDDENLY, the angels descended to their knees and lowered their faces to the street. John turned to see that they were anticipating the approaching army, entering through the Golden Gate of Jerusalem.

At the front of the forces was Henri Blanc. But he was walking, not on horseback.

"Henri!" John shouted at first glimpse.

Blanc beamed with pride as he held the reigns of his white stallion, leading it through the historic gate.

John raised his gaze to see that a man was seated on the stallion. Then he gasped as a million memories flooded his mind.

"My Lord!" he shouted.

What had been done before, was being done again.[268] In His first coming as a humble servant, Jesus Christ had entered that gate on a donkey, shortly before his humiliating death. Now, in His second coming as an almighty King, He was entering on a white stallion, shortly before His glorious victory.

John ran down the steps and through the street as Jesus dismounted. He could feel the Lord's Spiritual presence radiating toward him and his soul soared to the heights of ecstasy as he approached Him. Every eye was on Jesus, every heart felt His love.

Smiling, Jesus stretched His arms toward John when he approached. But the Beloved Apostle did not embrace his Savior. Instead, John dropped before Him and began kissing His feet.

"Oh Lord, have mercy on me, a sinner," John prayed.

Jesus reached down and gently lifted John by the shoulders. Then, face to face, tears filled John's eyes.

With deep affection, Jesus said, "Well done, good and faithful servant."

John was overcome with emotion and could not respond.

"You once asked Me," Jesus continued, "to sit at My right hand in Paradise."[269]

John lowered his eyes, embarrassed that he had ever been so impudent.

Jesus added, "Today, you shall."

The Savior turned to the archangel and nodded. Then Michael led hundreds of angels toward the Temple. There, they opened the golden doors, lifted the Ark and its altar, and respectfully transported the sacred objects into the inner sanctuary, the Holy of Holies.

Jesus then followed them, but only to the base of the steps.

John could not wait any longer. He asked Henri, "You assembled this enormous army?"

"You give me too much credit," Blanc said with a smile. "With a flash of lightning, the Lord appeared and descended on a cloud. When His feet touched the Mount of Olives,[270] the earth quaked furiously, the winds howled and the angels of heaven delivered this awesome multitude to join our small force."[271]

John felt embarrassed that he had been so distracted by his confrontation with Evan Thas that he had missed the moment of Christ's glorious arrival, even though he had anxiously awaited it for almost two thousand years.

"Now," Jesus announced, "you all join Me as the first fruits of the resurrection. Today, I shall present you to My Father."[272]

John turned to the crowd and, immediately, his jaw dropped.

"James!" he shouted as he ran to embrace his brother. Then he saw his mother, Salome, and his father, Zebedee. The loving family had never before experienced such joy, as they laughed and hugged.

Then someone tapped him on the shoulder. John turned and was shocked to see Peter and the other apostles converging on him, as they playfully shoved and hugged him.

That was only the beginning.

The Latter Day Apostles eventually filed through the gate, singing joyfully. Following Worthington's booming lead, the nearby angels and saints joined in the chorus: *Praise God from Whom all blessings flow; Praise Him, all creatures, here below; Praise Him above, ye heavenly host; Praise Father, Son and Holy Ghost.*[273]

As the mass of humanity continued through the Golden Gates, John embraced his friends and welcomed many thousands of Christians that he had loved throughout the centuries. Particularly honored were those who were dressed in white. They were the souls who had been beheaded because of their testimony for Jesus. They had refused to worship the Beast and had rejected his mark.[274]

At the base of the Temple steps, Jesus welcomed every passing saint by offering them their first incredible encounter with His infinite love. Their souls swooned from the touch of His hand and, for the first time, each of them experienced the awesome knowledge of the Holy Trinity. The overwhelming encounter produced tears of joy in every eye.

Then, with the prompting of the angels, they all knew where to go. In a joyful but orderly procession, the holy ones – both living and resurrected[275] – filed up the Temple steps, through the golden doors, and into Paradise.

JOHN HAD NO IDEA how long the amazing procession had lasted. It seemed he had begun to enter into God's eternal time in which so much could be accomplished in the blink of an eye. He had been enthralled by the unbounded joy of history's faithful — especially his loved ones. So, as they were lovingly welcomed by their Savior, he completely lost track of time, in awe of the multitudes who had fought the good fight throughout the centuries. These holy souls had been delivered here, by God's angels, to receive their unimaginably generous, but just reward.

Near the end of the line, however, John saw two more familiar faces. They approached him with joyful peace.

"I want to thank you for protecting Adam," Mercedes Dare offered. Then she added, "especially considering … his father." John nodded his thanks but could not bring himself to tell her that her son had locked himself in the Vatican vault.

He simply responded, "Every child is a child of God."

Then Angela Concepcion smiled, "Evie and I cannot thank you enough."

John's eyes welled with tears. Her words reminded him that he had not yet seen the children in the incredibly long procession.

He choked out a response: "She was … the love of my life."

Angela tried to lighten his mood. "You know, there was something about you I liked, from the very first time we met."

John rubbed his forehead. "You had a strange way of showing it."[276]

"Sometimes," she said, "I'm a slow learner."

"Better late than never," Mer added, speaking from experience.

The two women smiled at each other and offered a respectful nod to John. Then they continued in procession, entering the Temple, near the end of the line.

Jesus had observed John's emotional exchange with tender appreciation. However, His demeanor became solemn as the last holy soul filed past Him.

When the final saint had disappeared into the Temple, the angels emerged from it carrying a large, golden throne. They placed it on the Temple porch.

Jesus turned to John and warned, "This will be disturbing. Do you wish to stay with Me or enter, now, into Paradise."

"Lord," he answered, "I want to be with You, always."

Jesus nodded and more angels emerged from the Temple with another, smaller throne that they placed at the right side of the first. Then the angels closed the Temple's thick doors with a resounding slam.

Once they were seated, John became amused at the fluttering wings of hundreds of angles around them. But he nearly lost his breath when, behind him, Michael blasted the Resurrection Trumpet again.

Without explanation, Jesus pointed to His left, at the street. Michael obeyed the unspoken order, pulled out his sword and slashed it through the air. Again, with a grinding roar, the ground ripped open, exposing the fiery chasm to hell.

Jesus gestured toward the Abyss and, suddenly, the air resonated with the squeals and shrieks of delighted demons. As nauseatingly hideous creatures began flying out of the earth, John closed his eyes and covered his ears. His sensitive Spirit was greatly disturbed and he could not understand why the devils had been released.

The ancient apostle turned to Jesus, seeking solace. But he

detected no joy in the eyes of the Lord, only justice.

Soon, John watched as devils began returning, bearing people of every description. With sadistic satisfaction, demons howled happily as they swooped with their screaming prizes, into the flaming Abyss of eternal ruin.

Examining the terrified faces of each doomed person, John asked, "What is happening, Lord?"

Jesus answered, "These have chosen their own ways and taken pleasure in their own abominations. Therefore, I will show them that they loved what they should have hated, and hated what they should have loved. They surrendered to these demons, in life. Now they shall spend eternity with their chosen gods."

Snatched from streets, homes or graves, it made no difference. From the farthest reaches of the earth, the swarm arrived and darkened the sky. In every language known to man, the damned begged or shouted obscenities while struggling with their clutching and clawing captors. The air reverberated with a rumble of demon wings and a *crescendo* of curses.

The proud learned humility. The strong learned weakness. The persecutors learned persecution. No matter how powerful the condemned had been, they discovered what it was like to be powerless as they plunged with their demons to their eternal doom.

FOR JOHN, the sad demise of so many souls was excruciatingly regretful. He felt responsible for failing to make them understand the truth. But, then again, he knew from twenty centuries of experience that some people are determined to choose the path to hell. Deep down, he realized that there was nothing more he could have done.

When the last lost soul had plunged to her doom, Michael waved his sword through the air and the chasm to hell abruptly closed.

John could see that Jesus was very moved by the horrible Day of Judgment. So, for a moment, they were silent.

Then he saw tears roll down Jesus' cheek.

John could not hold back anymore. "Lord, Jesus, there was nothing more You could have done. You gave everything to save them. People like that tortured You to death. Through the centuries they mocked, harassed, imprisoned and tortured millions of your faithful. They lived only for themselves, spreading hate and wrecking lives. They mocked Your love and despised Your gifts. Lord, there is no other way to say it: deep down, they hated You, the Creator of all that is good."

Jesus turned to John. "I know," He said, softly. "But it is still sad … so sad. I had hoped to save every one."[277]

The solemn pair continued to sit quietly for a few moments longer. Then Jesus sighed deeply and offered, "But, soon, you will see a new heaven and a new earth."[278]

John smiled. "When, Lord?"

"I will begin to show you, now."

They rose from their thrones, the angels opened the Temple doors, and Jesus led John through the portal to Paradise.

A MOMENT LATER, airborne nuclear missiles resumed their flight, reached their targets and engulfed the earth with fire.[279]

> Then I saw a new heaven and a new earth,
> for the first heaven and the first earth had passed away,
> and there was no longer any sea.
> Revelation 21:1

Chapter 50
The World
Seven Days Later

Neogenesis
Chapter One

In the beginning,[280] God created the heavens and the earth. Now the earth was formless and empty, darkness was over the surface of the deep, and the Spirit of God hovered over the waters. And God said, "Let there be light," and there was light. God called the light "day," and the darkness he called "night."

There was evening the first day and God saw that it was good.

And God said, "Let there be an expanse between the waters to separate water from water." And it was so. God called the expanse "sky."

There was evening the second day and God saw that it was good.

And God said, "Let the water under the sky be gathered to one place, and let dry ground appear." God called the dry ground "land," and the gathered waters he called "seas." Then God said, "Let the land produce vegetation: seed-bearing plants and trees on the land that bear fruit with seed in it, according to their various kinds." And it was so.

There was evening the third day and God saw that it was good.

And God said, "Let there be lights in the expanse of the sky to separate the day from the night, and let them serve as signs to mark seasons and days and years," God made two great lights—the greater light to govern the day and the lesser light to govern the night. He also made the stars.

There was evening the fourth day and God saw that it was good.

And God said, "Let the water teem with living creatures, and let birds fly above the earth across the expanse of the sky." And it was so.

There was evening the fifth day and God saw that it was good.

And God said, "Let the land produce living creatures according to their kinds: livestock, creatures that move along the ground, and wild animals, each according to its kind." And it was so.

And God said, "Let us make mankind in Our image – male and female – and let them have dominion over the fish of the sea and the birds of the air, over the livestock, over all the earth, and over all the creatures that move along the ground." And it was so.

And God blessed them and said, "Be fruitful and increase in number.[281] Enjoy this paradise and the life and love that are My gifts to you."

There was evening the sixth day And God saw that it was good, until it was not.

Chapter Two

On the first day of Recreation, God passed judgment according to the truths He had revealed. And God said, "Those who lived according to Our love – even imperfectly – shall have life eternal. Those who defied Our love, shall be delivered to the death they chose."[282] And it was so.

There was evening the first day of Recreation, but God saw that it was not yet good.

And God said, "Let Us seize the Angel of Iniquity, and all his minions, and imprison them in the Abyss. They shall have no influence over mankind for a thousand years." And it was so.

There was evening the second day of Recreation, but God saw that it was not yet good.

And God said, "Let Us create a new heaven, for the former heaven has passed away.[283] And Let us share this heaven with all who had chosen to live according to Our love." And it was so.

There was evening the third day of Recreation, but God saw that it was not yet good.

And God said, "Let Us create a new earth, for the former earth has passed away. Let there be fields and forests, teaming with flora and fauna."[284] And it was so.

There was evening the fourth day of Recreation, but God saw that it was not yet good.

And God said, "Let there be a new Jerusalem – a holy city of pure gold, yet clear as glass – adorned with jasper and every precious jewel. Let Us dwell among the human race there, where those who seek Us shall never again experience mourning or pain." And it was so.

There was evening the fifth day of Recreation, but God saw that it was not yet good.

And God said, "Let there be a river of life-giving water, sparkling like crystal, flowing from Our throne in Jerusalem. And Let there be trees of life, growing on either side of the river, bearing bountiful fruit throughout the year, along with leaves of medicinal value." And it was so.

There was evening the sixth day of Recreation, but God saw that it was not yet good.

And God said...

"ADAM, DON'T STOP," Evie said as she nudged her sleepy best friend.

"Come on," he whined. "I'll read more tomorrow."

"You're just getting to the best part."

"I know, but I'm tired." Adam rolled up the scroll and set it aside.

"Okay," Evie said as she fluffed her sleeping bag and turned off the nearby lamp. "We'll do it tomorrow, after the rosaly."

He didn't respond. He was already dozing.

A few moments later, Evie said, "Adam?"

"Yeah," he mumbled.

"Thanks for reading to me."

He nudged closer to her, enjoying the warmth they shared. "Okay."

Moments slipped away in the darkened vault of the Vatican Archives.

"Evie?" he asked.

"Yeah."

"I'm glad you're here with me."

She smiled. "Me too."

Then, they snuggled tighter and their innocent hearts rewarded them with peaceful dreams.

THE NEXT MORNING, Adam woke Evie with a persistent nudge.

"Evie, wake up. I gotta tell you something."

"What?" she groaned, still half asleep."

"I saw her again."

Evie sat up. "What did she look like?"

"I don't know how to describe her. She's *really* beautiful."

"It's Mary Grace!" she squealed.

"She was holdin' a baby."

Evie's brow tightened. "Baby Jesus?"

He nodded enthusiastically.

"So, what did she say?"

He pulled her closer. "We're goin' on a adventure."

They joyfully squirmed and bounced around on their sleeping bags.

"Where?" she begged.

"To Jerusalem."[285]

She reminded him of the story in Neogenesis that he had read to her. "That's where He built everything out of gold and jewels and …"

"Mary Grace said Baby Jesus is there now. When we get there, she'll be with Him … and Papa, too!"

She could wait no longer. Evie stood up and looked around. "What are we gonna bring?"

Adam clutched the scroll to his chest. "She said to just bring the story. Everything we need to know is in here."

Evie clapped her hands and hopped around. Then she slowed and finally stopped. "But how are we gonna get out?"

They turned toward the vault door.

It was ajar.

Suddenly, their excitement settled into reverential awe.

They imagined all the things, both good and bad, that they might find outside.

Like a dutiful mother, preparing themselves for a big event, she stepped over to the boy and examined him closely. Standing face to face, she admired his bright blue eyes and freckled face. She fingered his wispy red hair into place, then straightened the red collar on his colorfully striped polo shirt.

When they were ready to go, she repeated what she had said, dozens of times before: "I love you, Adam."

Likewise, he responded with what he had said, dozens of times before: "I know."

It was not exactly what she had hoped to hear, but close enough.

THAT DAY, Adam and Eve set out to find God. When they made their way out of the Archives, however, they found nothing on the surface of the New Earth that remained familiar.[286] Now, the world was covered with the natural beauty of an immense botanical garden. Lush greenery surrounded them and the fresh air carried the scent of the colorful flowers that seemed to bloom everywhere.

As she looked around, Evie worried, "Which way do we go?"

"Don't you remember?" Adam asked, confidently. "The story said that Jesus appeared in the east."

Evie frowned, "Which way's east?"

Adam looked at the morning sun. "The sun always rises in the east." He pointed. "We'll go that way."

His training in the wilderness and trek across the Shenandoah Valley would prove valuable for this new adventure. So, they headed east and soon approached where the Tiber River once flowed. Now, however, it contained bright sparkling water. On either side of it, healthy trees bore the largest fruit the children had ever seen.

"Look, Adam," Evie prompted. "That's the river of life-giving water. See the fruit trees?"

"Yeah. We'll follow that river. It'll take us straight to Jerusalem."

As they approached a fruit tree, Evie asked, "How long will it take us to get there?"

"Mary Grace said something about a day, in God's time.[287] She told me not to worry if it takes longer."

Adam reached up for a luscious apple and plucked it from a low-hanging branch.

He continued, "It can't be as far as Washington was. That took forever!"

Then, as he raised the apple to his mouth, Evie screamed, "Wait!"

Adam frowned.

She asked, "Are you sure we can eat that?"

"Yeah," Adam said confidently.

They remembered the story that she shared about the Garden of Eden.

He added, with less certainty, "I think so."

Her glare melted his confidence, he threw down the apple, and she led him to an orange tree.

ON THE BANKS OF THE TIBER RIVER, Adam and Eve dedicated themselves to live according to the Book of Neogenesis. They understood that God had provided new Scriptures for the new earth because the sacred writings of old had been destroyed.

Before proceeding on their long journey to find Jerusalem, the two children committed themselves, first, to The Holy Trinity and, then, to each other. So, they agreed to become husband and wife in a sacramental ceremony that had been prescribed by their holy scroll.

And God witnessed the faithful union and saw that it was good.

Then, the loving little pair set off on an adventure that would span a thousand years.[288]

Throughout their long lives, they were fruitful and multiplied, just as God had asked. The couple grew into a family, the family into a tribe, the tribe into a nation, and the nation into a race. Adam and Eve treasured every blessing that God bestowed upon them and they raised their family with unshakeable faith.

What had been done before, was being done again. In the Age of dinosaurs, God wiped away the predators and began again. Likewise, in the days of Noah, Lot and Thas, God sustained on earth only those most precious in His eyes.[289]

This time, God preserved a new Adam and a new Eve who appreciated His loving generosity.

This time, they treasured His wisdom.

This time, God's love triumphed.

Adam and Eve rejected the foolishness of trying to become like gods. This time, they chose to become like God's children.[290]

Led by Jesus, Mary and John, the saints and angels in heaven cheered the loving innocence of Adam and Eve every day of their long lives.

And God saw that it was good … very good.

BECAUSE YOU HAVE KEPT
MY MESSAGE OF ENDURANCE,
I WILL KEEP YOU SAFE
IN THE TIME OF TRIAL
THAT IS GOING TO COME
TO THE WHOLE WORLD
TO TEST THE INHABITANTS OF THE EARTH.
I AM COMING QUICKLY.
HOLD FAST TO WHAT YOU HAVE,
SO THAT NO ONE MAY TAKE YOUR CROWN.

REVELATION 3: 10-11

1. This cataclysm is known as the Cretaceous–Paleogene extinction event which resulted in mass extermination of plant and animal species over a geologically short period of time, 66 million years ago.

2. The Catechism of the Catholic Church (hereinafter CCC) 390 informs us "The account of the fall in Genesis 3 uses figurative language, but affirms a primeval event, a deed that took place at the beginning of the history of man. Revelation gives us the certainty of faith that the whole of human history is marked by the original fault freely committed by our first parents."

3. "So God created man in His own image, in the image of God He created him; male and female He created them." Genesis 1:27.

4. This paragraph is paraphrased from CCC 340.

5. "God saw all that He had made, and it was very good." Genesis 1:31.

6. Paraphrased from CCC 374.

7. CCC 1777 states, "When he listens to his conscience, the prudent man can hear God speaking." Also, 1776 says, "His conscience is man's most secret core and his sanctuary. There he is alone with God whose voice echoes in his depths."

8. From CCC 1730, we read that St. Irenaeus wrote, "Man is rational and therefore like God; he is created with free will and is master over his acts."

9. CCC 1733 reads, "There is no true freedom except in the service of what is good and just. The choice to disobey and do evil is an abuse of freedom and leads to 'the slavery of sin.'" This concept is from Romans 6:17 which states, "But thanks be to God that, though you used to be slaves to sin, you wholeheartedly obeyed the form of teaching to which you were entrusted." So, with that in mind, CCC 1734 adds: "Freedom makes man responsible for his acts *to the extent that they are voluntary.*" [Author's emphasis.] This limitation presents us with one of the great uncertainties of life, the question of how God chooses to balance His justice with His mercy.

10. Genesis 1:28-30 reads:

> "God blessed them and said to them, 'Be fruitful and increase in number; fill the earth and subdue it. Rule over the fish of the sea and the birds of the air and over every living creature that moves on the ground.'
>
> "Then God said, 'I give you every seed-bearing plant on the face of the whole earth and every tree that has fruit with seed in it. They will be yours for food. And to all the beasts of the earth and all the birds of the air and all the creatures that move on the ground – everything that has breath of life in it – I give every green plant for food.' And it was so."

11. "… you will be like gods…" was Satan's first temptation, described in Genesis 3:5.

12. In the 19th century, the Ecstatic of Tours prophesied, "There will be earthquakes and signs in the sun. Towards the end darkness will cover the earth." Around that time, Blessed Anna Maria Taigi predicted, "There will come over all the earth an intense darkness lasting three days and three nights…. All the enemies of the Church, secret as well as known, will perish over the whole earth during that universal darkness, with the exception of a few…"

13. Some prophecies predict unseasonably cold temperatures during the Three Days of Darkness.

14. CCC 377 points out how Angela had embraced a lifestyle that was at odds

with God's purposes: "The first man was unimpaired and ordered in his whole be-ing because he was free from the [triple tendency toward sin] that subjugates him to the pleasures of the senses, covetousness for earthly goods, and self-assertion..."

15. St. Pio of Pietrelcina (Padre Pio) urged, "Love the Madonna and pray the Rosary, for her Rosary is the weapon against the evils of the world today."

16. In the 19th century, St. Caspar del Bufalo prophesied, "The death of the impenitent persecutors of the Church will take place during the Three Days of Darkness."

17. In 1945, four girls from Heede Germany claimed these words from Jesus Christ: "Humanity has not heeded My Blessed Mother, who appeared in Fatima, to exhort everyone to penitence. Now, I have come, in this last hour, to admonish the world. The times are grave. Men should do penance for their sins…. The earth will tremble and will suffer. It will be terrible, a minor judgment. For those not in a state of grace it will be frightful…. Men do not listen to My calls. They close their ears, resist My graces and refuse My mercy, My love and My merits. They will agonize in the blindness of their faults…. The world sleeps in a dense darkness. This genera-tion deserves to be annihilated, but I desire to show Myself as merciful. Great and terrible things are being prepared. That which is about to happen will be terrible, like nothing ever since the beginning of the world."

18. See Matthew 24:29.

19. See Luke 17 and Matthew 24.

20. The seven cardinal sins are: lust, gluttony, greed, sloth, acedia (joyless apathy), wrath, envy, pride, and vainglory (boasting). A case can be made that the sinful pleasures and comforts that modern technologies have enabled are unprec-edented in human history.

21. Garabandal is in Spain. Medjugorje is in Bosnia-Herzegovina, the former Yugoslavia. From those obscure villages world-renowned apparitions, with warn-ings for the future, have been reported. In each case, a visionary will come forward and announce before prophesied calamities occur.

22. "There is no fear in love. But perfect love drives out fear…" 1 John 4:18.

23. "He who outlives the darkness and the fear of these three days will think that he is alone on earth because the whole world will be covered with cadavers." (St. Casper del Bufalo) Also in the 19th century, Blessed Mary of Jesus Crucified predicted, "During a darkness lasting three days the people given to evil will perish so that only one fourth of mankind will survive." For the purposes of this novel, however, the Darkness is not so deadly.

24. In the 20th century, Blessed Elena Aiello prophesied, "…the punishment will be the most terrible ever known in the history of mankind. It will last 70 hours [three days]. The wicked will be crushed and eliminated. Many will be lost because they will have stubbornly remained in their sins." However, regarding all private revelations from saints, it should be noted that Father Benedict Groeschel, CFR, points out in his book, "A Still, Small Voice" the following: "For centuries it has been a clear papal teaching that even a canonized saint who has reported a private revelation which has been approved by the Church for acceptance by the Faithful may have introduced some personal element that is subject to error or distortion."

25. "At that time those slain by the Lord will be everywhere—from one end of the earth to the other. They will not be mourned or gathered up or buried, but will be like refuse lying on the ground." Jeremiah 25:33.

26. "Woe to those who call evil good and good evil, who put darkness for light and light for darkness, who put bitter for sweet and sweet for bitter." Isaiah 5:20.

27. Author's personal note: On the subject of calling good evil and evil good, The American Library Association has issued its "Guidelines and Considerations for Developing a Public Library Internet Use Policy" which initially states:

> "... Libraries that raise barriers to access damage their credibility with their users. By providing information across the spectrum of human interests, and making them available and accessible to anyone who wants them, libraries allow individuals to exercise their First Amendment right to seek and receive all types of expression, from all points of view. Materials in any given library cover the spectrum of human experience and thought, even those that some people may consider false, offensive, or dangerous. In the millions of Web sites available on the Internet, there are some—often loosely called "pornography"—that parents, or adults generally, do not want children to see. A very small fraction of those sexually explicit materials is actual obscenity or child pornography, which are not constitutionally protected. The rest, like the overwhelming majority of materials on the Internet , is protected by the First Amendment."

Therefore, the American Library Association is actively resisting responsible efforts to filter even "false, offensive, or dangerous" content on library computers. In essence, they argue that the First Amendment requires taxpayers to provide a welcoming environment of air-conditioned comfort to those who seek sexual thrills in our public libraries, even if it jeopardizes the safety of those who work and visit there, particularly women and children. They suggest that treating pedophiles or terrorists, for that matter, otherwise would "damage their credibility with the users."

This is not a theoretical argument. Enter the search words "sexual assaults near public libraries," and the search engine Bing delivers 58,600,000 results. How can reasonable people ignore such a crisis?

28. A permanent sign from God has been prophesied at Garabandal and Medjugorje, but the exact description of it has not been revealed. At Garabandal, the visionaries said that it will be visible over an area called "The Pines" at Garabandal and that it will be a "thing" never before seen upon the earth that can be photographed but not touched. In St. Faustina's Diary, she described the sign as a Cross in the sky in which light streams from the places where nails once pierced Jesus Christ in the hands and feet.

29. In August of 1987, Brother David Lopez said that the Virgin Mary informed him of the following: "Before the great Tribulation, there is going to be a sign. We will see in the sky one great red cross on a day of blue sky without clouds. The color red signifies the blood of Jesus Who redeemed us and the blood of the martyrs selected by God in the days of darkness. This cross will be seen by everyone: Christians, pagans, atheists, etc., as well as all the prepared ones (understand for prepared ones not only the Christians, because there are people who have never heard the Gospel, but also for those who have the voice of God in the sanctuary of their consciences) who will be guided by God in the way of Christ. They will receive grace to interpret the significance of the cross."

30. In many Marian apparitions, Blessed Mother pleads for everyone to pray constantly. Prior to 1938, an anonymous Bernardine sister claimed that the Virgin

Mary told her that hell had been let loose on the earth and that prayers were necessary in order to call upon the heavenly legions to fight against the foes of God and men. "But my good Mother," she replied, "you who are so kind, could you not send them without our asking?" "No," Our Lady answered, "because prayer is one of the conditions required by God Himself for obtaining favors."

31. "The wolf will lie with the lamb, the leopard will lie down with the goat, the calf and the lion and the yearling, together..." Isaiah 11:6.

32. Revelation 6:9-11 predicts, "When he broke open the fifth seal, I saw underneath the altar the souls of those who had been slaughtered because of the witness they bore to the word of God. They cried out in a loud voice, 'How long will it be, holy and true master, before you sit in judgment and avenge our blood on the inhabitants of the earth?' Each of them was given a white robe and they were told to be patient a little while longer until the number was filled of their fellow servants and brothers who were going to be killed as they had been."

33. Previous information implied that Jin would become the Judas of the modern-day Apostles.

34. Regarding the timing of Christ's second coming, in Zagreb, Yugoslavia, a woman named Julka claimed that Jesus Christ told her, "As it has been foretold, so it will be. But one cannot postpone one incident without postponing all other events. If I have extended one happening there, I have also extended the others, and especially through the intercession of Mary, the Mother of God, many postponements have been granted. Through this the whole purification process has been significantly extended, but because of this, the great catastrophe will not be as severe as prophesied."

35. Matthew 24:29-30.

36. Matthew 24:33.

37. At the time of this writing, the Vatican investigation into the alleged apparitions of Medjugorje is reportedly nearing a conclusion. The author and publisher recognize and accept that the final authority regarding miracles, prophecies and apparitions rests with the Holy See of Rome, to whose judgment we willingly submit.

38. This is described in Hebrews 11:5. Enoch was the greatx4 grandson of Adam (through Seth). See Genesis 5:3-18. Enoch "walked with God: and he was not; for God took him. Genesis 5:22-29. In some apocryphal works, Enoch is claimed to be the inventor of writing. That belief makes his role in this fictional tale even more appropriate.

39. 2 Kings 2:11.

40. See CCC 966 and 974.

41. The Illumination of Conscience (aka Illumination of the Soul) was foretold to St. Catherine Laboure' in 1830. It was also predicted by St. Faustina Kowalska in the 1930s and told to the four young seers of Garabandal Spain. Some suspect that it is also included in one or more of the so-called ten secrets of the Medjugorje visionaries.

42. "Now the Spirit expressly says that in the latter times some will depart from the faith giving heed to deceiving spirits and doctrines of demons." 1 Timothy 4:1.

43. The scar of three concentric circles that the Titan implant causes has been

identified previously as the Mark of the Beast from the Book of Revelation.

44. Blessed Anne Catherine Emmerich (19th century) prophesied, "I saw how baleful would be the consequences of this false church. I saw it increase in size; heretics of every kind came into the city (Rome).... Whole Catholic communities were being oppressed, harassed, confined, and deprived of their freedom. ... I saw a strange church being built against every rule.... No angels were supervising the building operations. In that church, nothing came from high above.... There was only division and chaos. It is probably a church of human creation, following the latest fashion as well as the new heterodox church of Rome.... There was something proud, presumptuous, and violent about it, and they seemed to be very successful. I did not see a single angel nor a single saint helping in the work."

45. "Then many false prophets will rise up and deceive many .... For false christs and false prophets will rise and show great signs and wonders to deceive, if possible, eve the elect. See, I have told you before hand." Matthew 24:11, 24-25.

46. The martyrs included Pope Innocent and four cardinals from the papal conclave that had been irradiated by Evan's satellite, known as Glass Andalusian. Helen Wallraff (d. 1801) foretold: "Some day a pope will flee from Rome in company of only four cardinals and come to Cologne." Also, Jane le Royer, aka Sister Mary of the Nativity, (d. 1798) foretold that "Antichrist will kill the pope." She also predicted, "When the reign of Antichrist draws near, a false religion will appear which will deny the unity of God and will oppose the Church. Errors will cause ravages as never before." Today, as we find undermining schemes within Church leadership, defiance in the religious leadership of nuns, sexual scandals in the priesthood, loss of faith in historically Catholic countries like Ireland, and on and on, we can see that such errors may be causing ravages as never before.

47. On October 1, 1822, visionary Anne Catherine Emmerich said, "We must pray that the pope may not leave Rome, for unheard-of evils would result from such a step.... If the pope leaves Rome, the enemies of the Church will get the upper hand. They are now demanding something from him.... I now see that in this place [Rome] the [Catholic] Church is being so cleverly undermined, that there hardly remain a hundred or so priests who have not been deceived.... A great devastation is now near at hand." Also, in the 13th century, John of Vatiguerro predicted: "The pope will change his residence. The Church will not be defended for the duration of twenty-five months, and more, because during all this time there will be no pope; no emperor of Rome and no ruler of France." Finally, even St. Pope Pius X said: "I saw one of my successors by name fleeing over the corpses of his brethren. He will flee to a place for a short respite where he is unknown, but he himself will die a cruel death."

48. No previous pope has ever taken the name of Peter, the first pontiff. However, St. Malachy predicted short descriptions for the 112 popes who would reign after his time. The final name on his list is Peter ("Petrus Romanus"). This is how the prophecy translates, from the original Latin, regarding that pope and his times: "In the extreme persecution of the Holy Roman Church, there will sit Peter the Roman, who will pasture his sheep in many tribulations: and when these things are finished, the city of seven hills will be destroyed, and the terrible judge will judge his people. The end." An ominous warning comes from the fact that Pope Benedict XVI is described as the last pope before the reign of Peter the Roman. Other prophecies claim that toward the end of the Age, apostasy will be ascendant, forcing a pope to flee from Rome to Cologne and, there, he will die a terrible death.

Therefore, prayers are in order for the protection of Pope Benedict XVI, who is German and has served as a consultor to the archbishop of Cologne.

49. Westphalia has been predicted to eventually become an area of great victory for the Great Monarch in his battles against the Antichrist.

50. Sister Ludmilla of Prague (cir. 1250) prophesied: "Hardly three generations will pass after the world war, when one will also endeavor to prevent the pope from exercising his sacred office, which will be a sign that the fall of Rome and the end of the world is near."

51. Brother John of the Cleft Rock (ca. 1340) prophesied, "Toward the end of the world, the pope with the cardinals will have to flee Rome under trying circumstances to a place where he will be unknown. He will die a cruel death in this exile. The sufferings of the Church will be much greater than at any previous time in her history."

52. A saying from the Greek Stoic philosopher, Epictetus.

53. In 1524, a book titled Liber Mirabilis was published that contained the prophecies of St. Caesarius. It states:

> "When in the entire world, and in a special way France ... shall have been laid waste by the greatest miseries and trials, then the provinces shall be comforted by a prince who ... shall recover the crown of the lilies [the House of Bourbon]. This prince shall extend his dominion over the total universe.

> "At the same time, by the will of God, a most holy man shall receive the papacy, who will be most perfect in every spiritual perfection. This pope will have with him the great monarch, a most virtuous man, who shall be an eminent leader of the holy line of French kings. This great monarch shall assist the pope in the reformation of the whole earth. Many nations and their princes that are living in error and impiety shall be converted, and an admirable [peace shall reign among men during many years, because the wrath of God shall be appeased through their repentance, penance, and good works. There will be one common law, only one faith, one baptism, one religion.

> "All nations shall recognize the Holy See of Rome, and shall pay homage to the pope. But after extended period of time, fervor will cool, iniquity will abound, and moral corruption shall become worse than ever before, which shall bring upon mankind the last and worse persecution of Antichrist, and the end of the world."

54. The following overview of prophetic warnings is drawn from prophecies that are too numerous to cite, here, but can be found in books that are listed in the Sources section of Book One of this trilogy. Of course, many of the specific prophecies are included in the end notes of all three books of this trilogy.

55. One set of prophecies is from St. Senanus (d. 560) who seemed to aptly describe the world of 15 centuries after his death. Here, he identifies lying politicians, a litigious society, clerical abuses, the family breakup, the disappearance of virtue, and even the mortgage meltdown that has left beautiful homes unoccupied:

> "Falsehood will characterize that class of men who will sit in judgment to pass sentence according to law. Between a father and his own son, litigations will subsist. The clergy of the holy church will be addicted to pride and injustice.... Women will abandon feelings of delicacy,

and cohabit with men out of wedlock. They will follow those practices
without secrecy, and such habits will become almost unsuppressable. All
will rush into iniquity against the will of the Son of the Blessed Virgin
Mary.... Full mansions will be deserted and unpleasant will be the tid-
ings concerning them."

56. A lengthy prophecy attributed to St. Nilus is particularly prescient. Though its date of origin could be the 4th, the 14th or the 17th century, there is more certainty regarding its predictive accuracy. (It should be noted, however, that wherever great evil exists, greater good remains, even if hidden.)

"After the year 1900, toward the middle of the 20th century, the
people of that time will become unrecognizable. When the time of the
advent of the antichrist approaches, people's minds will grow cloudy
from carnal passions, and dishonor and lawlessness will grow stronger.
Then the world will grow unrecognizable.

"People's appearances will change, and it will be impossible to dis-
tinguish men from women due to their shamelessness in dress and style
of hair. These people will be cruel and will be like wild animals because
of the temptations of the antichrist. There will be no respect for par-
ents and elders, love will disappear, and Christian pastors, bishops, and
priests will become vile men, completely failing to distinguish the right
hand from the left.

"At that time the morals and traditions of Christians and of the
Church will change. People will abandon modesty, and dissipation will
reign. Falsehood and greed will attain great proportions, and woe to
those who pile up treasures. Lust, adultery, homosexuality, secret deeds,
and murder will rule in society.

"At that future time, due to the power of such great crimes and licen-
tiousness, people will be deprived of the grace of the Holy Spirit, which
they received in Holy Baptism, and equally of remorse. The churches of
God will be deprived of God-fearing and pious pastors, and woe to the
Christians remaining in the world at that time; they will completely lose
their faith because they will lack the opportunity of seeing the light of
knowledge from anyone at all. They will separate themselves out of the
world in holy refuges in search of a lightening of their spiritual suffer-
ings, but everywhere they will meet obstacles and constraints.

"And this will result from the fact that the antichrist wants to be
lord over everything and become the ruler of the whole universe, and
he will produce miracles and fantastic signs. He will also give depraved
wisdom to an unhappy man so that he will discover a way by which one
man can carry on a conversation from one end of the earth to the other.
At that time, men will also fly through the air like birds and descend to
the bottom of the sea like fishes. And when they have achieved all this,
these unhappy people will spend their lives in comfort without knowing,
poor souls, that it is the deceit of antichrist. And the impious one! -- he
will so complete science with vanity, that it will go off the right path and
lead people to lose faith in the existence of God.

"Then God will see the downfall of the human race and will shorten
the days for the sake of those few who are being saved, because the en-
emy wants to lead even the chosen into temptation, if that is possible ...."

57. Maria Valtorta (d. 1961) is responsible for 15,000 handwritten pages that were eventually distilled into a lengthy work known as "The Poem of the Man God." Initially, Pope Pius XII expressed approval for its publication but Pope John XXIII later placed it on the Index of Forbidden Books. Though the Index is no longer in use, Catholics continue to argue over these stories that are reputed to be about the life of Jesus Christ as dictated by Himself. So, with that warning in mind, we observe that Valtorta predicted today's climate change debate well before Global Warming alarmists:

> *"Hunger will arise from the stoppage, by God's will, of the cosmic laws: cold will be bitter and drawn out; heat will be scorching and not moderated by rain; the seasons will be turned around and you will have drought in the rainy seasons and rain when the crops are ripening; plants and trees will be tricked by unexpected warmth or unusual coolness, plants will bloom out of season and trees, after having already produced, will cover themselves with new, useless flowers that will exhaust them fruitlessly.... [H]unger will cruelly torment this haughty race hostile to God."* Also, a thousand years earlier, St. Columbkille foretold: *"The changes of the seasons will produce only half their verdure.... The trees shall not bear their usual quantity of fruit, fisheries shall become unproductive and the earth shall not yield its usual abundance. Inclement weather and famine shall come... Dreadful storms and hurricanes shall afflict them. Numberless diseases shall prevail."*

58. The three, young, peasant visionaries of Fatima did not know the meaning of Our Lady's plea to pray for Russia. They guessed that "Russia" was a woman's name.

59. In Revelation 12:3-4, we read, "Then another sign appeared in heaven: an enormous red dragon with seven heads and ten horns and seven crowns on his heads. His tail swept a third of the stars out of the sky and flung them to earth." In the 1980s, more than a third of the world's population was under communist rule. Many have interpreted Revelation's "red dragon" to represent communism.

60. Reagan was the first serving US President to survive after being shot in an assassination attempt. The agent who saved Reagan's life went on to become a pastor. Reagan went on to defeat Soviet communism.

61. On 5/2/82, Our Lady of Medjugorje (aka, The Queen of Peace) said, "I have come to call the world to conversion for the last time. Later, I will not appear any more on this earth." She reaffirmed that prediction just seven weeks later. On 6/23/82, she said, "These apparitions are the last in the world."

62. Quoted from Jeremiah 6:14 and again at 8:11.

63. One might argue that global control is the agenda of Islamists, radical secular humanists, and even the United Nations. Of course, all of them believe that their governance would offer utopia to all of mankind... or at least to their ruling class.

64. Along with her appeals for conversion, prayer and fasting, Blessed Mother has promised to give ten secrets to the six visionaries of Medjugorje. Many already have been told, but not all. Though they remain mostly secret, some information known. They include information regarding a permanent sign from God and chastisements for mankind, if we do not change our ways.

65. A promise from Our Lady of Fatima.

66. Matthew 13:40.

67. See Mark 4:1-20.

68. Ephesians 6:12.

69. Paraphrased from Ephesians 6:13-17.

70. Jesus warned: "That servant who knows his master's will and does not get ready or does not do what his master wants will be beaten with many blows. But the one who does not know and does things deserving punishment will be beaten with few blows. From everyone who has been given much, much will be demanded; and from the one who has been entrusted with much, much more will be asked." (Luke 12:47-48)

71. This is a quote from James 2:24. In light of the second chapter of James, fundamentalist Christians have an impossible task of reconciling the inerrancy of the Bible with one of the founding doctrines of the Protestant Reformation known as Sola Fide, or justification by faith alone. Scripture is clear: "faith without works is dead". James 2:26.

72. There are at least 13 prophecies, through the centuries, predicting that the Antichrist and his mother will become possessed, some of which claim that he will then lose his conscience and guardian angel. For example, St. Jerome (d. 420), predicted, "Antichrist will be born near Babylon. He will win the support of many with gifts and money. He will sell himself to the devil and thereafter will have no guardian angel or conscience."

73. John of Vatiguerro (13th century) foretold, "Spoliation, pillaging, and devastation of that most famous city which is the capital and mistress of France will take place when the Church and the world are grievously troubled. The pope will change his residence and the Church will not be defended for twenty-five months or more because, during all that time, there will be no pope in Rome...."

74. The Ecstatic of Tours prophesied: "The revolution will spread to every French town. Wholesale slaughter will take place. The revolution will only last a few months but it will be frightful; blood will flow everywhere because the malice of the wicked will reach its highest pitch. Victims will be innumerable. Paris will look like a slaughter-house. Persecutions against the Church will be even greater, but it will not last long. Many bishops and priests will be put to death. The archbishop of Paris will be murdered..."

75. In the 18th century, Father Nectou, S.J., predicted, "During this revolution, which will very likely be general and not confined to France, Paris will be destroyed so completely that twenty years afterwards fathers walking over its ruins with their children will be asked by them what kind of a place that was; to whom they will answer: 'My child, this was a great city which God has destroyed on account of her crimes.' Yes, Paris will certainly be destroyed but, before this happens, such signs and portents will be seen that all good people will be induced to flee away from it."

76. "The coming of the lawless one will be in accordance with the work of Satan displayed in all kinds of counterfeit miracles, signs and wonders, and in every sort of evil that deceives those who are perishing. They perish because they refused to love the truth and so be saved. For this reason God sends them a powerful delusion so that they will believe the lie..." 2 Thessalonians 2:9-11.

77. Benjamin Franklin famously said, "Those who would sacrifice freedom for security deserve neither."

78. Revelation 13:11 describes the pretense of peace that the Antichrist will

offer saying that he "had two horns like a lamb, but he spoke like a dragon."

79. The Antichrist "will oppose and will exalt himself over everything that is called God or is worshipped..." 2 Thessalonians 2:4.

80. St. Hildegard of Bingen (12th century) prophesied: "The Son of Corruption and Ruin will appear and reign for only a short time, towards the end of the days of the world's duration; the period which corresponds to the moment when the sun has disappeared beyond the horizon; that is to say he shall come at the last days of the world. He will not be Satan himself, but a human being equaling and resembling him in atrocious hideousness."

81. From Luke 2:14.

82. Matthew 21:9.

83. "While people are saying, 'Peace and safety,' destruction will come on them suddenly, as labor pains on a pregnant woman, and they will not escape." 1 Thessalonians 5:3.

84. Pope Saint Gregory ("the Great") declared, "I do confidently say that whosoever called himself universal bishop; or is desirous to be called so, in his pride, is the forerunner of Antichrist because, in his pride, he prefers himself to the rest [of the bishops].

85. "His [Antichrist's] armed forces will rise up to desecrate the temple fortress and will abolish the daily sacrifice [the Mass]." Daniel 11:31.

86. In the 17th century, Venerable Sister Marianne de Jesus Torres said the Blessed Virgin revealed to her that beginning in the 20th century a corruption of virtue will occur, even in some members of the clergy:

> *"The sacred Sacrament of Holy Orders will be ridiculed, oppressed and despised, for in doing this, one scorns and defiles the Church of God and even God Himself, represented by His priests. The demon will try to persecute the ministers of the Lord in every possible way, and he will labor with cruel and subtle astuteness to deviate them from the spirit of their vocation, corrupting many of them. These [corrupted priests] who will thus scandalize the Christian people, will incite the hatred of the bad Christians and the enemies of the Roman Catholic and Apostolic Church to fall upon all the priests. This apparent triumph of Satan will bring enormous sufferings to the good pastors of the Church, to the great majority of good priests, and to the Supreme Pastor and Vicar of Christ on earth, who ... will shed secret and bitter tears in the presence of his God and Lord, beseeching light, sanctity and perfection for all the clergy of the world, of which he is the king and father.*

> *"Moreover, in these unhappy times there will be unbridled luxury which, acting thus to snare the rest into sin, will conquer innumerable frivolous souls who will lose themselves. Innocence will almost no longer be found in children, nor modesty in women, and, in this supreme moment of need of the Church, those whom it behooves to speak will fall silent."*

Similarly, in the 20th century, Sister Agnes of Akita predicted:

> *"The work of the devil will infiltrate even into the Church in such a way that one will see cardinals opposing cardinals, bishops against other bishops. The priests who venerate me [the Virgin Mary] will be scorned and opposed by their confreres, churches and altars sacked; the*

Church will be full of those who accept compromises and the demon will press many priests and consecrated souls to leave the service of the Lord.

"The demon will be especially implacable against souls consecrated to God. The thought of the loss of so many souls is the cause of my sadness. If sins increase in number and gravity there will be no longer pardon for them."

87. On the heels of a recent public relations blitz (The "Nuns on he Bus" tour") by the Leadership Conference of Women Religious, rebelling against Church authority, as well as a leaked document scandal -- that some have characterized as civil war -- at the Vatican that may implicate one or more cardinals, Venerable Father Bartholomew Holzhauser's 17th century prophecy appears prescient:

"When everything has been ruined by war, when Catholics are hard-pressed by traitorous coreligionists and heretics, then the hand of Almighty God will work a marvelous change, something seemingly impossible according to human reason... There will arise a valiant king, anointed by God."

88. Early Christian author, Lactantius (d. 320), prophesied: "This impious man ... will give orders that he himself shall be worshipped as God. For he will say he is Christ, though he will be His enemy."

89. Blessed Anne Catherine Emmerich (d. 1824) prophesied, "I wish the time were here when the pope dressed in red will reign. I see the apostles, not those of the past, but the apostles of the last times, and it seems to me, the pope is among them."

90. Jesus said, "I tell you, you are Peter, and on this rock I will build my church, and the gates of hell shall not prevail against it." Matthew 16:18. Jesus continued: "I will give you the keys of the kingdom; whatever you bind on earth will be bound in heaven, and whatever you loose on earth will be loosed in heaven." Matthew 16:19. These are Jesus Christ's founding declarations for the almost 2,000 year old institution of the Roman Catholic papacy. Protestant arguments that Jesus used two different words are in error. Jesus spoke Aramaic, a language that did not have masculine and feminine versions for the word "rock." Only in later translations were two different words used.

91. The Ecstatic of Tours predicted that, after revolution and slaughter in every French town, "the French people will turn back to God and implore the Sacred Heart of Jesus and Mary Immaculate..."

92. In the Catechism of the Catholic Church, we find the following:

•   *"Already the final age of the world is with us, and the renewal of the world is irrevocably under way ... for the Church on earth is endowed already with a sanctity that is real but imperfect." (670)*

•   *"Before Christ's second coming the Church must pass through a final trial that will shake the faith of many believers." (675)*

•   *"The Church will enter the glory of the kingdom only through this final Passover, when she will follow her Lord in his death and Resurrection." (677)*

93. The ancient Chinese philosopher Lao Tzu observed, "The virtuous man promotes agreement; the vicious man allots the blame."

94. Jeremiah 8:16. The significance of this verse will soon be explained.

95. This is a quote from Revelation 13:9-10. It is a verse that leads the author to believe that "The Rapture," as popularized in modern Protestant writings, is fully supportable, Biblically, only if it is interpreted as a Post-Tribulation Rapture.

96. From Revelation 13:8.

97. From Matthew 5:11-12.

98. In the second book of this trilogy, Henri injured his leg while jumping out of the pope's medi-vac rail car in Cologne, Germany. Supporting that fictional circumstance, in the 19th century, Blessed Anne Catherine Emmerich foresaw:

> "When Mass was ended, [the Virgin] Mary came up to Henry [the Great Monarch] and she extended her right hand towards him, saying that it was in recognition of his purity. Then, she urged him not to falter. Thereupon, I saw an angel, and he touched the sinew of his hip, like Jacob. He [Henry] was in great pain, and from that day on he walked with a limp."

99. Mass fish and wildlife deaths have been documented in many news reports but the citations for many of them are conveniently located at https://maps.google.com/maps/ms?ie=UTF8&hl=en&oe=UTF8&msa=0&msid=201817256339889828327.0004991bca25af104a22b

100. See Revelation 6:1-8.

101. Three years after the author conceived this fictional plot, he was surprised to find a similar scenario proposed as possibly unfolding now. Assuming that a weaponized satellite may be causing the massive fish and wildlife deaths that have occurred, a typical satellite path is shown at: http://img811.imageshack.us/img811/9162/170967486138497615556422.jpg

102. Revelation 13:13 says that the Antichrist "performed great and miraculous signs, even causing fire to come down from heaven to earth in full view of men."

103. In Book Two, the Legion of Babylon was the secretive, evil organization of global power players who hoped to divide the world into ten regions and centralize power under their governance. It was started by Henri Blanc as a philanthropic entity after he withdrew from XCyst Industries, many years earlier. However, the group's mission was soon perverted from serving others to controlling others. Evan Thas had become its leader. At the time the Book of Revelation was written, such a powerful, global, non-governmental entity would not have been understood as anything other than a city-state or country. So, it is conceivable that the Apostle John would have referred to something like the Legion of Babylon (or, for that matter, the United Nations) as Babylon the Great. Relevant prophecies in the Book of Revelation include: "God remembered Babylon the Great and gave her the cup filled with the wine of the fury of His wrath..." (16:19) "With a mighty voice he shouted, "Fallen! Fallen is Babylon the Great!" (18:2) "...Babylon the Great, the mother of prostitutes and of the abominations of the earth..." (17:5) "Fallen is Babylon the Great, which made all the nations drink the maddening wine of her adulteries.... Babylon the Great has fallen!" (14:8)

104. St. Columba (6th century) prophesied, "Hearken, hearken to what will happen in the latter days of the world! There will be great wars, unjust laws will be enacted, the Church will be despoiled of her property, people will read and write a great deal, but charity and humility will be laughed to scorn, and the common people will believe in false ideas."

105. In Revelation 6:1-2, we read of the first horseman of the Apocalypse: "I watched as the Lamb opened the first of the seven seals. Then I heard one of the four living creatures say in a voice like thunder, "Come and see!" I looked, and there before me was a white horse! Its rider held a bow, and he was given a crown, and he rode out as a conqueror bent on conquest." The XCyst satellite that is code-named White Appaloosa represents this horse. Here, Evan Thas is the rider. He is on a white horse, as if pretending to be good. (Later verses in Revelation make clear that this rider is, in fact, evil.) He carries a bow but no arrows, indicating the power to make war, but preaching peace. His crown, of course, was usurped from the Catholic Church. He is also bent on conquest.

106. Saint Ephrem (d. 375) foresaw, "Antichrist will use worldly goods as bait. He will entice many Christians with money and goods to apostasize. He will give them free land, riches, honor and power."

107. Two books are very helpful in describing the causes of the 2008 financial crisis as well as the folly of the U.S. Federal Reserve Bank and the dangers of fiat currency (i.e. money produced at will, without the backing of a store of value, such as gold). The first is "Meltdown" by Thomas E. Woods Jr. (Regnery Publishing 2009) and the second is "The Creature from Jekyll Island" by G. Edward Griffon (American Media 2008).

108. The Titan implants were previously described as consisting of radio frequency identification devices (RFID), miniaturized using nanotechnology, and providing a transmittable identification capability that is even more rigorous than finger prints or DNA sampling. Of course, this is a work of fiction. However, ulterior motives have accompanied vaccinations in the past. For example, leading up to the assassination of Osama bin Laden in Pakistan, the CIA conducted hepatitis vaccinations to obtain DNA samples that could locate bin Laden and his family. (Source: Time Magazine, "Why the Taliban is Banning Polio Vaccines," August 6, 2012) Still, the author of this trilogy hopes that readers will not be diverted down a trail of Internet conspiracy theories but, instead, focus on the true prophetic warnings on which this fictional tale is based.

109. Revelation 13:16-18 states, "He [Antichrist] also forced everyone, small and great, rich and poor, free and slave, to receive a mark on his right hand or on his forehead, so that no one could buy or sell unless he had the mark, which is the name of the beast or the number of his name. This calls for wisdom. If anyone has insight, let him calculate the number of the beast, for it is man's number. His number is 666." Previous footnotes have described the prophecies that say that possible names for the Antichrist will be "evanthas" and "titan." Also, some reports claim that the word "computer" also corresponds to the number 666.

110. Ezekiel 7:19-20 says, "They will throw their silver into the streets, and their gold will be an unclean thing. Their silver and gold will not be able to save them in the day of the Lord's wrath. They will not satisfy their hunger or fill their stomachs with it, for it has made them stumble into sin. They were proud of their beautiful jewelry and used it to make their detestable idols and vile images. Therefore I will turn these into an unclean thing for them."

111. The Titan analyses are supercharged versions of what the Church of Scientology calls "auditing." One report, after the marital breakup of Tom Cruise and Katie Holmes, described the process as follows: "The auditing process requires members to be hooked up to an electropsychometer, or E-meter, a kind of an old-fashioned lie detector that measures bodily changes in electrical resistance, as one

answers personal questions posed by the auditor. It is like a spiritual counseling session, its purpose is to clear the mind and blockages so you can become totally free.... But this includes very, very personal questions, and to get rid of the blockage, you have to 'declare'. But this is not in confidence; the auditor logs everything. I would not be surprised if Katie's declarations are used against her." From: http://www.foxnews.com/entertainment/2012/07/03/former-scientologist-says-katie-holmes-answers-during-church-qa-sessions-will/?intcmp=features

112. Along with many others, Former Clinton administration official and economist Robert Reich has predicted, "There will be a time – I don't know when, I can't give you a date – when physical money is just going to cease to exist."

113. CCC 1794 states, "A good and pure conscience is enlightened by true faith, for charity proceeds at the same time 'from a pure heart and a good conscience and sincere faith.'" (See also 1 Timothy 3:9; and Acts 24:16.)

114. CCC 1793 adds that "one must work to correct the errors of moral conscience."

115. This quote is from 1 Timothy 3:15. It is a verse that fundamentalist Christians should consider because it reminds us that the Roman Catholic Church preceded the Bible. Further, the Bible that fundamentalists exclusively rely on was compiled and preserved by the Catholic Church. No other faith can reasonably lay claim to the four distinctive marks of the Christian Church that even Protestant denominations profess: one, holy, catholic and apostolic. To argue that the Roman Catholic Church eventually lost its God-given authority is to deny Jesus Christ's assurance that the gates of hell shall not prevail against it. (See Matthew 16:18) Consequently, Catholic doctrine has always embraced sacred Scripture, but also sacred Traditions that were established in the Church by Jesus Christ and his holy apostles.

116. "He [Antichrist] will show no regard for the gods of his fathers or for the one desired by women..." Daniel 11:37. There has been disagreement over the interpretation of his disregard for "the desire of women," as it is sometimes translated. Some, claim he will be asexual, others homosexual. Perhaps more intriguing is the suggestion that "the desire of women" refers to the natural inclination to become a mother. Consequently, some have suggested that the Antichrist will be a strong advocate of contraception and abortion.

117. To some, this may sound like a crazy proposition. However, reducing the earth's human population by 95% is a goal that billionaire atheist Ted Turner once advocated. Now, though, he has softened his position, only proposing that we reduce global population by a mere 5 billion people. More on Turner's radical agenda can be found at http://www.lifesitenews.com/news/video-ted-turner-reduce-population-by-five-billion-people

118. One might think that it would be impossible for someone as demonstrably evil as Evan Thas to maintain popularity with the masses. But history is littered with mass murderers who accomplished that deception. Even in the gulags, prisoners mourned the death of "Papa Joe" Stalin, the man who had been responsible for 40 million deaths and countless imprisonments. Mao Zedong was responsible for 77 million deaths, yet his cult followers were led to believe that he had accomplished miracles, including even healing the deaf and raising the dead. Perhaps less well known is the fact that the notoriously evil Nero also died popular. According to Rev. Joseph M. Esper's "Defiance!," in which he details the lives of various antichrists of history and their doomed war against the Church, Nero murdered his

mother and brother. He executed one of his wives and kicked another to death. He became a perverse, cross-dressing exhibitionist who fancied himself a great actor. However, whenever he played the role of a murderer, on stage, his victim was not acting. Among many other cruelties and murders, he excelled at sadistic tortures of Christians, even dipping them in pitch, alive, and setting them aflame to serve as torches for his dinner parties. Still, according to Esper, "The policy of appeasing the mobs with 'bread and circuses' proved wildly successful, and long after Nero's death, many of the members of the lower classes (in contrast to the nobility) remembered him with fondness." In "The Most Evil Men and Women in History," author Miranda Twiss notes that for years after Nero's death, flowers were put at his burial place and funerary busts of him were commissioned. His edicts continued to be treated with special reverence, as if he would some day return to take vengeance on his enemies. All of this, even though his cruelty, violence and grotesque appetite for self-indulgence had brought the Roman Empire to the brink of financial ruin.

119. "… those will be days of distress unequaled from the beginning, when God created the world, until now—and never to be equaled again. If the Lord had not cut short those days, no one would survive. But for the sake of the elect, whom he has chosen, he has shortened them." Mark 13:19-20.

120. From Acts 2:17 and Joel 2:28.

121. Saint Paul wrote, "…we urge you, brothers, to progress even more, and to aspire to live a tranquil life, to mind your own affairs, and to work with your [own] hands, as we instructed you, that you may conduct yourselves properly toward outsiders and not depend on anyone." 1 Thessalonians 4:10-12.

122. A Church tradition describes John in his latter days, in Ephesus. Nearing 100 AD, he had become so frail that the old man had to be carried to the church by his disciples. There, he often said no more than, "Little children, love one another!" After a while, the disciples wearied of hearing the same words and asked, "Master, why do you always say this?" He answered, "It is the Lord's command, and if this alone be done, it is enough!"

123. Caligula, Nero and Domition professed their divine nature during their lifetimes. Other emperors were recognized as divine after death.

124. This is one of the reasons that Catholics profess the importance of Apostolic Tradition in shaping their beliefs. Both from history and Sacred Scripture, itself, we are informed that the Bible is not meant to be our sole source for instruction.

125. Paraphrased from Matthew 12:30.

126. Regarding the world's malignant tumor, note that Evan's rise to power was enabled by a man named Cyst and his multi-national conglomerate is named XCyst Industries.

127. Blessed Anne Catherine Emmerich predicted, "A man who will subsequently be known as a great saint will ultimately be elected pope near the end of the Chastisement. He will be heavily responsible for the French acceptance of a king to be their military and civil leader…"

128. Brother John of the Cleft Rock (d. 1340) prophesied: "The White Eagle [Great Monarch], by order of the Archangel Michael, will drive the crescent [Muslim warriors] from Europe, where none but Christians will remain…. There will no longer be Protestants or schismatics…. [T]here shall be one faith, one law, one rule of life, one baptism on earth. All men will love each other and do good, and all

quarrels and war will disappear."

129. A quote from Saint Cataldus of Tarentino (ca. 500).

130. Saint Hippolytus (d. 235) wrote: "The Great French Monarch who shall subject all the East shall come around the end of the world."

131. Blessed Catherine of Racconigi (d. 1547) prophesied, "...a descendent of Francis I of France will rule Europe like Charlemagne."

132. Quoted from a prophecy by Telesphorus of Cozensa (d. 1388), regarding "A powerful French monarch."

133. Restoration of the French monarchy is repeatedly prophesied for the Latter Days and not an impossible event. Though France is now a republic, the monarchy was restored as many a four times in the 19th century, depending on how one defines it. A return to monarchy could be accomplished by a French referendum.

134. This ancestry of the Great Monarch was described by Josefa von Bourg (d. 1807). He also said the leader would "...have the sign of the Cross on his breast and besides being a religious man, will be kind, wise, just and powerful. Under him the Catholic religion will spread as never before."

135. Blessed Catherine of Racconigi (d. 1547) predicted this ancestor of the Great Monarch.

136. Venerable Bartholomew Holzhauzer (d. 1658) predicted that the Great Monarch will be a Catholic descendant of Louis IX, yet also a descendant of an ancient imperial German family.

137. According to Rev. R. Gerald Culleton's *The Prophets and Our Times,* an old German prophecy predicts, "When the world becomes Godless... revolutions will break out... dogma will be perverted; men will try to overthrow the Catholic Church; mankind will be lovers of pleasure. A terrible war will find the north fighting the south. The south will be led by a prince wearing a white coat with a cross on the front; he will be lame afoot."

138. Venerable Bartholomew Holzhauser (d. 1658) prophesied, "When everything has been ruined by war; when Catholics are hard pressed by traitorous co-religionists and heretics; when the Church and her servants are denied their rights... then the hand of Almighty God will work a marvelous change, something apparently impossible according to human understanding."

139. In the Catholic Catechism (2309), the conditions for a just war are laid out. They are as follows: The damage inflicted by the aggressor must be lasting, grave and certain; All other means of putting an end to it must be shown to be impractical or ineffective; There must be serious prospects for success; The weapons used must not produce evils and disorders graver than the evil to be eliminated.

140. Paraphrased from Matthew 18:20.

141. Dionysius of Luxemberg (d. 16820 prophesied that the Antichrist will "teach that the Christian religion is false, confiscation of Christian property is legal, Saturday is to be observed instead of Sunday, and he will change the Ten Commandments."

142. In the 19th century, Anne Catherine Emmerich predicted, "I saw again a new and odd-looking Church which they were trying to build. There was nothing holy about it..." Reverend Frederick William Faber (d. 1863) foretold that his teaching will be "an apparent contradiction of no religion, yet a new religion."

143. Saint Cyril of Jerusalem (d. 386) prophesied, "Antichrist will exceed in

malice, perversity, lust, wickedness, impiety, and heartless cruelty and barbarity all men that have ever disgraced human nature. ... He shall through his great power, deceit and malice, succeed in decoying or forcing to his worship two thirds of mankind; the remaining third part of men will most steadfastly continue true to the faith and worship of Jesus Christ. But in his satanic rage and fury, Antichrist will ... exceed all past persecutors of the Church combined."

144. As previously noted, two different prophecies identify 'Titan' and 'Evanthas' as names that match the Antichrist's number of 666. Also, just as prophecy often uses the number 3 to indicate completeness – i.e. The Trinity – the three concentric circles are meant to represent three zeroes, or complete nothingness.

145. As the author rushed to finish this novel, he was informed but not surprised to read that Russia, China, Syria and Iran were preparing to engage in the largest war games in Mideast history. See: http://www.timesofisrael.com/iranian-news-agency-reports-joint-syria-iran-russia-and-china-wargames/

146. The author speculates, for this fictional story, that Babylon the Great could be a global non-governmental entity (i.e. the Legion of Babylon) that has built its power base on "the maddening wine" that we call oil, a uniquely modern necessity that had little value until the 20th century. After that, however, oil was responsible for catapulting humanity into a world of previously unimagined travel conveniences and commercial opportunities. From Revelation 18:2-3 we read: "With a mighty voice he shouted: 'Fallen! Fallen is Babylon the Great! She has become a home of demons and a haunt for every evil spirit, a haunt for every unclean and detestable bird. For all nations have drunk the maddening wine of her adulteries. The kings of the earth committed adultery with her, and the merchants of the earth grew rich from her excessive luxuries.'"

147. Red Thoroughbred was the code-name of the second powerful satellite that represents the second horse of the Apocalypse. It's purpose was for waging war. "When the Lamb opened the second seal, I heard the second living creature say, 'Come and see!' Then another horse came out, a fiery red one. Its rider was given power to take peace from the earth and to make men slay each other. To him was given a large sword."

148. To make candidates fully Titanized, Cyst and Thas designed a psychological testing system that detected minute brain responses to audio and video stimuli. Particularly, they monitored changes in adrenaline and endorphin output. Their goal was not to determine intelligence or knowledge in a candidate, but rather the individual's capacity for blind allegiance. The battery of tests also revealed hidden, even subconscious, motivators and fears.

149. St. Jerome prophesied: "Antichrist will be born near Babylon. He will win the support of many with gifts and money. He will sell himself to the devil and thereafter will have no guardian angel or conscience."

150. Though this fictional tale was conceived long before this date, on August 25, 2012, reporter Peter V. Milo reported on what might be called a primitive forerunner to the Titan Analysis: "Researchers from the University of California and University of Oxford in Geneva figured out a way to pluck sensitive information from a person's head, such as PIN numbers and bank information. The scientists took an off-the-shelf Emotive brain-computer interface, a device that costs around $299, which allows users to interact with their computers by thought." (See: "Scientists Successfully 'Hack' Brain To Obtain Private Date" at seattle.cbslocal.com.)

151. In Revelation 9:21, we read, "Nor did they repent of their murders, their

magic arts, their sexual immorality or their thefts." Here, the original Greek word for "magic arts" is pronounced "pharmakon," which is more accurately translated into the phrase "drug use." Similarly, Revelation 18:23 states, "Your merchants were the world's great men. By your magic spell all the nations were led astray." Here, the Greek word is pronounced "pharmakeia," indicating drug dealing. So, two millennia ago, the Apostle John foresaw that in the End Times a major cause of sin would be drug use and drug dealing. Considering that only in the modern age have drugs become such a widespread source of personal destruction and violent turf battles, those prophecies are all the more impressive.

152. Saint Anselm (d. 1109) foresaw, "Antichrist will rule the world from Jerusalem, which he will make into a magnificent city." Also, Rabanus Maurus (d. 856) prophesied that the Antichrist will "rebuild the temple of Jerusalem and make Jerusalem the capital of the world with the vast wealth from hidden treasure." Similar predictions were also made by St. Hippolytus, St. John Damascene, St. Irenaeus, St. Ephrem and St. Ambrose.

153. Revelation 20:9.

154. Estimates suggest that a third of the manuscripts preserved in the world are found in Italy and most may be kept in Roman libraries which contain millions of books, both rare and antique. The most outstanding and prestigious of the Roman libraries is the *Vaticana* which was established in 1475 to preserve the papal archives.

155. Dionysus of Luxembourg (d. 1682) prophesied: "Antichrist will be an iconoclast [a destroyer of religious images]. Most in the world will adore him. He will teach that the Christian religion is false."

156. The Secret Archives of the Vatican is a restricted part of the Vatican Museums. It houses so many documents and books from Christian history that 52 miles of shelving are required to store them.

157. Revelation 1:10-11.

158. The Catholic Church teaches that the Bible is the General Revelation that is the foundation of our beliefs. No Private Revelation – even when investigated and judged worthy of belief – carries the same mandate of trust. Further, any alleged Private Revelation that contradicts sacred Scriptures is immediately disqualified from being judged, by the Church, worthy of belief.

159. St. Thomas Aquinas said that at death we all become like we were at thirty three, the age at which Christ died and the one at which humans are at the height of their powers.

160. When St. John of the Cross was imprisoned by the Carmelite brothers who opposed his reforms of their wayward order, he wrote "The Dark Night of the Soul." In it, he described what many of the most holy saints have experienced, the devastating feeling of abandonment by God. The trial, however, is never without Spiritual reward.

161. In "Defiance!" Reverend Joseph M. Esper writes, "More European Christians were enslaved over the centuries by Islam than the total number of black Africans sent as slaves to North and South America combined." In fact, in some Muslim-controlled countries, slavery is still tolerated.

162. Jonathan Cahn's book, "The Harbinger," describes our human foolishness regarding the 9/11 Twin Towers terrorist attack in New York. He cites Old Testament prophecy from Isaiah 9:10 that reads, "The bricks have fallen, but we will

rebuild with hewn stone; the sycamores have been cut down, but we will plant cedars in their place." Similarly, rather than focusing on God's warning to change our sinful ways, we have vowed to rebuild the Freedom Tower, even bigger and better.

163. Blessed Anne Catherine Emmerich prophesied, "I saw the fatal consequences of this counterfeit church. I saw it increase; I saw heretics of all kinds flocking to the city.... Again I saw in a vision St. Peter's undermined according to a plan devised by the secret sect whilst, at the same time damaged by storms; but it was delivered at the moment of greatest distress." Another time, she predicted, "I saw a strange church being built against every rule... No angels were supervising the building operations. In that church, nothing came from high above. There was only division and chaos.... Everything was being done according to human reason.... There was something proud, presumptuous, and violent about it, and they seemed to be3 very successful. I did not see a single angel nor a single saint helping in the work."

164. Jane le Royer, aka Sister Mary of the Nativity (d. 1798), prophesied, "When the time of the reign of the Antichrist is near, a false religion will appear which will be opposed to the unity of God and His Church. This will cause the greatest schism the world has ever known. The nearer the time of the end, the more darkness of Satan will spread on earth, the greater will be the number of children of corruption, and the number of Just will correspondingly diminish."

165. In Mark 10:35-45 we read:

> *Then James and John, the sons of Zebedee, came to him. "Teacher,"*
> *they said, "we want you to do for us whatever we ask."*
>
> *"What do you want me to do for you?" he asked.*
>
> *They replied, "Let one of us sit at your right and the other at your*
> *left in your glory."*
>
> *"You don't know what you are asking," Jesus said. "Can you drink*
> *the cup I drink or be baptized with the baptism I am baptized with?"*
>
> *"We can," they answered.*
>
> *Jesus said to them, "You will drink the cup I drink and be baptized*
> *with the baptism I am baptized with, but to sit at my right or left is not*
> *for me to grant. These places belong to those for whom they have been*
> *prepared."*
>
> *When the ten heard about this, they became indignant with James*
> *and John. Jesus called them together and said, "You know that those*
> *who are regarded as rulers of the Gentiles lord it over them, and their*
> *high officials exercise authority over them. Not so with you. Instead,*
> *whoever wants to become great among you must be your servant, and*
> *whoever wants to be first must be slave of all. For even the Son of Man*
> *did not come to be served, but to serve, and to give his life as a ransom*
> *for many."*

166. Jesus had nicknamed John and James "the sons of thunder" in an apparent reference to their tendency toward anger.

167. This is the reminder that priests give when they place ashes on the foreheads of Catholics every Ash Wednesday.

168. Many have claimed that the two prophetic witnesses from Revelation, chapter 11, will be Enoch and Elijah, particularly in light of ancient Jewish teaching – especially in the last chapter of Malachi – that Elijah will return before

the coming of the Messiah. However, some prophecies claim that Saints Peter and Paul will return before that glorious day. For example, Blessed Anna Maria Taigi (d. 1837) predicted, "After the three days of darkness, Saints Peter and Paul, having come down from heaven, will preach throughout the world and designate a new pope. A great light will flash from their bodies and will settle upon the cardinal, the future pontiff." Both scenarios, conceivably, could be fulfilled. However, for the purposes of this story, the author chose to include only Enoch and Elijah.

169. General Gideon is a fictional character but the seemingly miraculous Israeli victories in the Six Day War and the Yom Kippur War are true. The general's name is from Judges, chapter 7, in which Gideon accomplishes an amazing war victory by remaining true to God's direction, no matter how absurd it seemed.

170. "He [Antichrist] will confirm a covenant [of peace?] with many for one 'seven' [seven years?]. In the middle of the 'seven' he will put an end to sacrifice and offering [the Mass?]." Daniel 9:27..

171. In Daniel 11:31-32, we read: "His armed forces will rise up to desecrate the temple fortress..." (Thas led the group that ravaged Vatican City, including St. Peter's Basilica.) "...and will abolish the daily sacrifice..." (When Thas seized control of the Catholic Church, he suspended the administration of Sacraments, including the offering of the Mass.) "Then they will set up the abomination that causes desolation. With flattery he will corrupt those who have violated the covenant, but the people who know their God will firmly resist him." Daniel 11:31-32.

172. This trilogy identifies the prophecy of the land of Magog (from Ezekiel chapters 38 and 39) as Russia. That conclusion was first popularized in the Scofield Reference Bible from the early 20th century. However, Joel Richardson – author of The Islamic Antichrist – asserts that modern scholarship identifies Magog as squarely in modern day Turkey. He makes a strong case that leader of the apocalyptic war against Israel will be Islamic. Supporting his view that Magog refers to modern day Turkey, he cites the following sources: The New Moody Atlas of the Bible, The Zondervan Atlas of the Bible, The Holman Bible Atlas, and the IVP Atlas of Bible History. However, Revelation 20:7 identifies Gog and Magog as nations from the four corners of the earth.

173. The following verses are from chapter 16 of the Book of Revelation.

174. The colossal Ataturk Dam is controlled by Turkey and is capable of causing the Euphrates River to dry up. This is a fulfillment of prophecy in a way that was unimaginable two thousand years ago.

175. Armageddon is the Greek name that was derived from the Hebrew Har Megiddo: the "mountain of Megiddo." An interesting note, however, is that there is no mountain in the vicinity. The ancient fortress town of Megiddo was situated on a small mound, known as a Tel, on the plain of Megiddo. However, the plain is located at the foot of Mt. Carmel, the mountain on which that Elijah resided in a grotto, according to Jewish, Christian and Islamic traditions. Regarding that prophet, Malachi 4:5 identifies God's last promise in the Old Testament: "See, I will send you the prophet Elijah before that great and dreadful day of the Lord comes."

176. Luke 21:20-22.

177. Matthew 24:15-19.

178. These countries have all been identified as the modern day nations that are prophesied to participate in the battle of Armageddon, particularly in the Book of Ezekiel, chapter 38.

179. Revelation 20:7-9 prophesies: "When the thousand years are over, Satan will be released from his prison and will go out to deceive the nations in the four corners of the earth – Gog and Magog – to gather them for battle. In number they are like the sand on the seashore. They marched across the breadth of the earth and surrounded the camp of God's people, the city he loves."

180. Ezekiel 38:15-16: "You will come from your place in the far north, you and many nations with you... a mighty army. You will advance against my people Israel like a cloud that covers the land. In days to come, O Gog, I will bring you against my land, so that the nations may know me when I show myself holy through you before their eyes."

181. This is a saying from the ancient Athenian general, Chabrias.

182. This reference to John the Baptist preparing the way for the Lord's First Coming is found in all four Gospels, including John 1:23; Luke 3:4; Mark 1:3; and Matthew 3:3. The False Prophet is foretold in Revelation, chapters 16, 19 and 20.

183. John 20:29.

184. Ezekiel 38:8 addresses a prophecy to the apocalyptic forces: "After many days you will be called to arms. In future years you will invade a land that has recovered from war, whose people were gathered from many nations to the mountains of Israel, which had long been desolate."

185. Revelation 20:8 describes the troops: "In number they are like the sand on the seashore." Also, Ezekiel 38:9 says, "You and your troops and the many nations with you will go up, advancing like a storm; you will be like a cloud covering the land."

186. Daniel 7:23 predicted that the Antichrist's kingdom will devour the whole earth, and Revelation 13:7 foretold that he would have power over all kindreds, tongues and nations (a feat that would have been almost unimaginable before the rise of modern technologies, including simultaneous translations.)

187. From Mark 13:22 and Matthew 24:24.

188. The following speech is paraphrased from Ezekiel 39:1-6, except it is Evan who apes the words of the Lord. However, this story reminds us that God may use whoever He wants – even evil people – to accomplish whatever He wants.

189. Ezekiel 38:15-16 states: "You will come from your place in the far north, you and many nations with you … a mighty army. You will advance against my people Israel like a cloud that covers the land. In days to come, O Gog, I will bring you against my land, so that the nations may know me when I show myself holy through you before their eyes.

190. Revelation 16:1-17 predicts:

"Then I heard a loud voice from the temple saying to the seven angels. 'Go, pour out the seven bowls of God's wrath on the earth.'

"The first angel went and poured out his bowl on the land, and ugly and painful sores broke out on the people who had the mark of the beast and worshiped his image.

"The second angel poured out his bowl on the sea, and it turned into blood like that of a dead man, and every living thing in the sea died.

"The third angel poured out his bowl on the rivers and springs of water, and they became blood. Then I heard the angel in charge of the

waters say:

"'You are just in these judgments, you who are and who were, the Holy One, because you have so judged; for they have shed the blood of your saints and prophets, and you have given them blood to drink as they deserve.'

"And I heard the altar respond: 'Yes, Lord God Almighty, true and just are your judgments.'

"The fourth angel poured out his bowl on the sun, and the sun was given power to scorch people with fire. They were seared by the intense heat and they cursed the name of God, who had control over these plagues, but they refused to repent and glorify him.

"The fifth angel poured out his bowl on the throne of the beast, and his kingdom was plunged into darkness. Men gnawed their tongues in agony and cursed the God of heaven because of their pains and their sores, but they refused to repent of what they had done.

"The sixth angel poured out his bowl on the great river Euphrates, and its water was dried up to prepare the way for the kings from the East. Then I saw three evil spirits that looked like frogs; they came out of the mouth of the dragon, out of the mouth of the beast and out of the mouth of the false prophet. They are spirits of demons performing miraculous signs, and they go out to the kings of the whole world, to gather them for the battle on the great day of God Almighty.

"'Behold, I come like a thief! Blessed is he who stays awake and keeps his clothes with him, so that he may not go naked and be shamefully exposed.'

"Then they gathered the kings together to the place that in Hebrew is called Armageddon.

"The seventh angel poured out his bowl into the air, and out of the temple came a loud voice from the throne, saying, "It is done!"'

191. Various researchers estimate total world population, in the first century AD, in the range of 150 to 300 million. So, the 200 million troop count that St. John specifically names in Revelation 9:16 would have been almost impossible for someone of his era to comprehend. Yet, China, today, has announced that it alone can put 200 million troops into combat. Further, because China's one-child policies have created an excess of around 40 million young Chinese males, there is actually a strong incentive to eliminate this excess, if political and economic stability are to be maintained in the country. Some bible scholars claim that the "red dragon" of Revelation 12 is actually communist China or a coalition of China and Russia.

192. Daniel 7:8 predicts that a boastful "little horn" – the Antichrist – will rise from among 10 kings, which is the number of leaders in the Legion of Babylon. That verse also says that he will displace 3 of those kings in his rise to full power. Also, Daniel 2:41-43 foretold that the ruling world government near the end of the Age would not remain united, just as iron and clay do not bond well together.

193. From Revelation 13:2-4 we interpret: "The dragon [the Russian, Vasiliy Melnikov] gave the beast [Evan Thas] his power and his throne and great authority. One of the heads of the beast seemed to have had a fatal wound, but the fatal wound had been healed. [From the blast shrapnel that penetrated Evan's eye in the Nauru disaster.] The whole world was astonished and followed the beast. Men

worshiped the dragon because he had given authority to the beast, and they also worshiped the beast and asked, 'Who is like the beast? Who can make war against him?'" Finally, Daniel 11:44 predicts, "But reports from the east [Middle East and Asia] and the north [Russia] will alarm him, and he will set out in a great rage to destroy and annihilate many."

194. The Valley of *Hamon Gog* translates to "the valley of Gog's hordes." In this story, Vasiliy Melnikov is Gog, based on God's words to Ezekiel (ch. 38, v. 2), "Son of man, set your face against Gog, of the land of Magog, the chief prince of Meshech and Tubal..." Bible scholars believe that Gog's homeland and cities, named here, are all in modern day Russia.

195. In the twentieth century, deaths caused by governments are estimated to be 262 million. They are meticulously cataloged at http://www.hawaii.edu/powerkills and the toll for the twentieth century is found at http://www.hawaii.edu/powerkills/20TH.HTM.

196. Quoted from "Liberal Fascism" by Jonah Goldberg, Doubleday, 2007, p. 56.

197. "... no one could buy or sell unless he had the mark, which is the name of the beast or the number of his name." Revelation 13:7.

198. "'Men will be regularly employed to cleanse the land. Some will go throughout the land and, in addition to them, others will bury those that remain on the ground. At the end of the seven months they will begin their search. As they go through the land and one of them sees a human bone, he will set up a marker beside it until the gravediggers have buried it in the Valley of Hamon Gog. And so they will cleanse the land.' Ezekiel 39:14-16.

199. The Cardinal Sins are: lust, gluttony, greed, sloth, wrath, envy and pride.

200. Revelation 11:3 states: "I will commission my two witnesses to prophesy for those twelve hundred and sixty days, wearing sackcloth." Also, in Malachi 4:5, we read, "I will send you the prophet Elijah before that great and dreadful day of the Lord comes." Finally, Matthew 17:10-11 informs us, "The disciples asked him, 'Why do the teachers of the law say that Elijah must come first?' Jesus replied, 'To be sure, Elijah comes and will restore all things.'"

201. In Revelation 9:3-5, we read: "...out of the smoke locusts came down upon the earth and were given power like that of the scorpions of the earth. They were told not to harm the grass of the earth or any plant or tree, but only those people who did not have th seal of God on their foreheads. They were not given the power to kill them, but only to torture them..."

202. "If anyone wants to harm them [the two witnesses], fired comes out of their mouths and devours their enemies. In this way, anyone wanting to harm them is sure to be slain." Revelation 11:5.

203. For much greater detail regarding humanity's extraordinary debt to Catholicism, read "How the Catholic Church Built Western Civilization" by Thomas E. Woods, Jr. (Regnery Publishing, 2005).

204. The statues of Caesar Augustus always represent the image of him as a young man. That was the way he ordered it.

205. Daniel 11:37 (KJV) reads: "Neither shall he regard the God of his fathers, nor the desire of women, nor regard any god; for he shall magnify himself above all."

206. In Revelation 6:1-8, we read:

> *"I watched as the Lamb opened the first of the seven seals. Then I heard one of the four living creatures say in a voice of thunder, 'Come!' I looked, and there before me was a white horse! Its rider held a bow, and he was given a crown, and he rode out as a conqueror bent on conquest. [These references may symbolize a powerful conqueror but, since no arrows are seen, one who deceptively professes peace.]*

> *"When the Lamb opened the second seal, I heard the second living creature say, 'Come!' Then another horse came out, a fiery red one. Its rider was given power to take peace from the earth and to make men slay each other. To him was given a large sword. [Indicating its purpose is war.]*

> *"When the Lamb opened the third seal, I heard the third living creature say, 'Come!' I looked and there before me was a black horse! Its rider was holding a pair of scales in his hand. Then I heard what sounded like a voice among the four living creatures, saying, 'A quart of wheat for a day's wages, and three quarts of barley for a day's wages, and don not damage the oil and wine!' [Indicating the ability to make food too expensive for survival.]*

> *"When the Lamb opened the fourth seal, I heard the voice of the fourth living creature say, 'Come!' I looked, and there before me was a pale horse! Its rider was named Death, and Hades was following close behind him. They were given power over a fourth of the earth to kill by sword, famine and plague, and by the wild beasts of the earth." [Indicating the ultimate killing machine or being.]*

207. This is the cave in which an occultic Black Mass involved Evan as a child and, again as a young man. St. Hildegard of Bingen warned, "…fly from those who linger in caves and are cloistered supporters of the Devil. Woe to them, woe to them who remain thus!"

208. See Exodus 30:28.

209. Exodus 20:24.

210. See Leviticus 6:5 in NAB or Exodus 20:24-25 in other translations.

211. Saint Hildegard also said of cave dwelling supporters of the devil: "They are the Devil's very viscera, and the advance guard of the son of perdition."

212. In 2 Thessalonians 2:4 we read that the Antichrist will proclaim himself to be God.

213. Regarding the Antichrist, Dionysius of Luxembourg (d. 1682) predicted, "He will teach that the Christian religion is false, confiscation of Christian property is legal, Saturday is to be observed instead of Sunday, and he will change the Ten Commandments …. He will read people's minds, raise the dead, reward his followers, and punish the rest."

214. Leviticus 6:12-13.

215. Exodus 20:25.

216. In 2 Maccabees 2:5-7 we read: "And when Jeremias came hither he found a hollow cave, and he carried in thither the Tabernacle, the Ark, and the Altar of Incense, and so stopped the door. Then some of them that followed him, came up to mark the place, but they could not find it. And when Jeremias perceived it, he

blamed them, saying: 'The place shall be unknown, till God gather together the congregation of the people, and receive them to mercy.'" For the purposes of this fictional account, we substitute a similarly historic altar, the Altar of Holocausts, in place of the Altar of Incense, which was smaller and layered by gold over wood.

217. St. Vincent Ferrer (d. 1419) predicted, "The temporal lords and ecclesiastical prelates, for fear of losing power or position, will be on his [Antichrist's] side, since there will exist neither king nor prelate unless he wills it."

218. Wikipedia indicates that this belief was premised on the Islamic teaching that Elijah is a kohen, or priest, and therefore not permitted to enter a cemetery. However, Suleiman's extensive efforts were founded on incorrect information because there is no such limitation for priests entering a cemetery where mostly non-Jews are buried, such as is the case outside the Golden Gate.

219. Ezekiel chapters 40 to 42 provide a detailed description of the third Temple of the future.

220. Regarding Israel in the End Times, Isaiah 43:5-6 prophesied, "I will bring your children from the east and gather you from the west. I will say to the north, 'Give them up!' and to the south, 'Do not hold them back.'" Similarly, Jeremiah 31:8 predicted, "See, I will bring them from the land of the north and gather them from the ends of the earth. Among them will be the blind and the lame, expectant mothers and women in labor; a great throng will return."

221. "With flattery he will corrupt who have violated the covenant, but the people who know their God will firmly resist him." Daniel 11:32.

222. In 587 B.C., Jerusalem was sacked and burned by King Nabuchodonosor and the Jews were then led into bondage in Babylon. At that time, the Temple was destroyed and, according to the Second Book of Maccabees, the prophet Jeremiah transported the Altar of Incense and the Ark to a cave in Mt. Nebo and hid it. There is no mention of the Ark of the Covenant in Scriptures, after that. For the purposes of this fictional account, the author chose to locate the cave in Capernaum, the location of the early years of Jesus Christ's ministry.

223. "He shall regard neither the God of his fathers nor the desire of women, nor regard any god; for he shall exalt himself above them all." Daniel 11:37.

224. "If anyone wants to harm them [the two witnesses], fire comes out of their mouths and devours their enemies. In this way, anyone wanting to harm them is sure to be slain." Revelation 11:5.

225. All of these descriptions have been used for the Antichrist in the Bible.

226. Revelation 11:6 prophesies, "These men [the two witnesses] have power to shut up the sky so that it will not rain during the time they are prophesying; and they have power to turn the waters into blood and to strike the earth with every kind of plague as often as they want." For the purposes of this fictional tale, the author chose to direct these powers directly against Evan Thas.

227. In 1846, the Virgin Mary appeared to two children in La Salette, France. She warned, "The Church will be eclipsed, the world will be in consternation. But there are Enoch and Elias, they will preach with the power of God, and men of good will shall believe in God, and many souls will be comforted; they will make great progress by virtue of the Holy Ghost and will condemn the diabolical errors of the Antichrist."

228. From the prophecies of St. Francis de Paul (d. 1507), we read that the Great Monarch "shall be the founder of a new religious order different from all the

others. He will divide it into three strata, namely military knights, solitary priests, and most pious hospitalliers. This shall be the last religious order in the Church, and it will do more good for our holy religion than all other religious institutions."

229. St. Francis de Paul also prophesied, ""These devout men will wear on their breasts, and much more in their hearts, the sign of the living God, namely the cross.... [T]he Great Monarch... shall be a great captain and prince of holy men, who shall be called 'the holy Cross-bearers of Jesus Christ'.... He shall reform the Church of God by means of his followers, who shall be the best men upon the earth in holiness, in arms, in science and in every virtue.... They shall obtain dominion over the whole world, both temporal and Spiritual...."

230. Henri Blanc had protected the Avignon palace by adding lead to the rooftop and by surrounding the premises with chain link wire that effectively turned the papal apartment into a Faraday Cage, protected from the radiation of Evan's satellites.

231. "On that day the Lord made a covenant with Abram and said, 'to your descendants I give this land, from the river of Egypt to the great river, the Euphrates...." Genesis 15:18. Perhaps this promise is the reason Israel's Arab neighbor's are so hostile towards them. The land mass between the Euphrates and Nile Rivers could conceivably include parts of Egypt, Iraq, Turkey and Syria, as well as all of Kuwait, Qatar, UAE, Oman, Yemen, Saudi Arabia, Jordan Lebanon and, of course, Israel.

232. "I will scatter you among the nations and will draw out my sword and pursue you." Leviticus 26:33.

233. "As a shepherd looks after his scattered flock when he is with them, so will I look after my sheep. I will rescue them from all the places where they were scattered on a day of clouds and darkness." Ezekiel 34:12.

234. "I will save my people from the countries of the east and the west. I will bring them back to live in Jerusalem; they will be my people, and I will be faithful and righteous to them as their God." Zechariah 8:7-8. "I will restore them to the land I gave their forefathers." Jeremiah 16:15. "I will bring them out from the nations and gather them from the countries, and I will bring them into their own land." Ezekiel 34:13.

235. "I will take the Israelites out of the nations where they have gone. I will gather them from all around and bring them back into their own land. I will make them one nation in the land, on the mountains of Israel. There will be one king over all of them and they will never again be two nations or be divided into two kingdoms." Ezekiel 37:21-22.

236. "I will plant Israel in their own land, never again to be uprooted from the land I have given them..." Amos 9:15. "He who scattered Israel will gather them and will watch over his flock like a shepherd." Jeremiah 31:10. "If you follow my decrees and are careful to obey my commands, ... you will pursue your enemies, and they will fall by the sword before you. Five of you will chase a hundred, and a hundred of you will chase ten thousand, and your enemies will fall by the sword before you." Leviticus 26:3, 7-8.

237. "...the Lord your God will restore your fortunes and have compassion on you and gather you again from all nations where He scattered you." Deuteronomy 30:3.

238. Paraphrased from Isaiah 9:6-7.

239. "But Saul began to destroy the church. Going from house to house, he dragged off men and women and put them in prison." Acts 8:3.

240. "Keep watch over yourselves and all the flock of which the Holy Spirit has made you overseers. Be shepherds of the church of God, which He bought with His own blood. I know that after I leave, savage wolves will come in among you and will not spare the flock. Even from your own number, men will arise and distort the truth in order to draw away disciples after them. So be on your guard!" Acts 20:28-30.

241. "Although I hope to come to you soon, I am writing you these instructions so that, if I am delayed, you will know how people ought to conduct themselves in God's household, which is the church of the living God, the pillar and foundation of the truth." 1 Timothy 3:14-15.

242. "He who speaks in a tongue edifies himself, but he who prophesies edifies the church. I would like every one of you to speak in tongues, but I would rather have you prophesy. He who prophesies is greater than one who speaks in tongues, unless he interprets, so that the church may be edified." 1 Corinthians 14:4-5. "Since you are eager to have spiritual gifts, try to excel in gifts that build up the church." 1 Corinthians 14:12.

243. "And God placed all things under His feet and appointed Him to be head over everything for the church, which is His body, the fullness of Him who fills everything in every way." Ephesians 1:22-23.

244. "And I tell you that you are Peter, and on this rock I will build my church, and the gates of Hades will not overcome it." Matthew 16:18.

245. "And I will give power to my two witnesses, and they will prophesy for 1,260 days, clothed in sackcloth." Revelation 11:3.

246. "Now when they have finished their testimony, the beast that comes up from the Abyss will attack them, and overpower and kill them." Revelation 11:7.

247. In Revelation 7:3-4, John writes that an angel from the east proclaims, "'Do not harm the land or the sea or the trees until we put a seal on the foreheads of the servants of our God.' Then I heard the number of those who were sealed: 144,000 from all the tribes of Israel."

248. History's highest rated solar flare was estimated at X28. But since the numbers in the scale escalate in geometric proportions, X36 would be spectacularly more powerful.

249. CCC 672 reads, "Before His Ascension, Christ affirmed that the hour had not yet come for the glorious establishment of the messianic kingdom awaited by Israel which, according to the prophets, was to bring all men the definitive order of justice, love, and peace. According to the Lord, the present time is the time of the Spirit of witness, but also a time still marked by "distress" and the trial of evil which does not spare the Church and ushers in the struggle of the last days. It is a time of waiting and watching."

250. "If as one people speaking the same language they have begun to do this, then nothing they plan to do will be impossible for them. Come, let us go down and confuse their language so they will not understand each other." Genesis 11:6-7.

251. In "The Rise," more than three decades ago, John saved Faridah's life by pulling her from the rubble of her Beirut convent after an errant Israeli missile struck it.

252. St. Malachy predicted every future pope – sometimes with remarkable

accuracy – from the twelfth century to "the end of time." Typically, he used a short phrase that described the particular pontiff's coat of arms, his past or his gifts. In more recent years, for example, he described John Paul II with the phrase *"De Labore Solis,"* which can translate, "Of the Eclipse of the Sun." Solar eclipses occurred both on John Paul's day of birth and the day of his funeral. The next pontiff is described as *"Gloria Olivae,"* which translates "The Glory of the Olive." Pope Benedict XVI took his name from St. Benedict who established the Benedictine Order, known as the Olivetans. St. Benedict, himself prophesied that before the end of time his Order will triumphantly lead the Catholic Church in its fight against evil. The final pope is described as *"Petrus Romanus"* or "Peter the Roman," who would be known as Pope Peter II. Malachy prophesied: "In the final persecution of the Holy Roman Church there will reign Peter the Roman, who will feed his flock among many tribulations; after which the seven-hilled city will be destroyed and the dreadful Judge will judge the people. The end."

253. Among other prophecies, see Isaiah chapter 43 and Jerimiah 31.

254. See Ezekiel 37:26-28.

255. See 2 Thessalonians 2:3.

256. Among other similar prophecies, Medjugorje visionary, Mirjana Dragicevic-Soldo, explained a message from the Queen of Peace: "The Virgin told me God and the devil had a conversation, and the devil said that people believe in God only when life is good for them. When things turn bad, they cease to believe in God. Then people blame God, or act as if He does not exist. God therefore allowed the devil one century in which to exercise an extended power over the world, and the devil chose the twentieth century."

257. "Their bodies will lie in the street of the great city, which is figuratively called Sodom and Egypt, where also their Lord was crucified. For three and a half days men from every people, tribe, language and nation will gaze on their bodies and refuse them burial." Revelation 11:8-9.

258. "The inhabitants of the earth will gloat over them and will celebrate by sending each other gifts, because these two prophets had tormented those who live on the earth." Revelation 11:10.

259. For many centuries, an interesting parlor game has been to find words and names that correlate with the number 666. If one assigns numeric values to the English alphabet in the following way: A=6; B=12; C=18; etc., then the sum of the numeric values for the word "computer" equals 666.

260. "But after three and a half days a breath of life from God entered them, and they stood on their feet, and terror struck those who saw them." Revelation 11:11.

261. "Then they heard a loud voice from heaven saying to them, 'Come up here.' And they went up to heaven in a cloud, while their enemies looked on." Revelation 11:12.

262. "At that very hour there was a severe earthquake and a tenth of the city collapsed. Seven thousand people were killed in the earthquake, and the survivors were terrified and gave glory to the God of heaven." Revelation 11:13.

263. "At that time, the sign of the Son of Man will appear in the sky, and all the nations of the earth will mourn." Matthew 24:30.

264. Regarding "Dying in Christ Jesus" the Catholic Catechism teaches: "To rise with Christ, we must die with Christ..." (1005); "For those who die in Christ's

grace, it is a participation in the death of the Lord, so that they can also share his Resurrection." (1006); "...remembering our mortality helps us realize that we have only a limited time in which to bring our lives to fulfillment..." (1007); "Bodily death, from which man would have been immune had he not sinned is thus the last enemy of man left to be conquered." (1008); "The obedience of Jesus has transformed the curse of death into a blessing." (1009); "Because of Christ, Christian death has a positive meaning: 'For to me to live is Christ, and to die is gain.' The saying is sure: 'if we have died with him, we will also live with him.'" (1010).

265. "...the trumpet will sound, the dead will be raised imperishable, and we will be changed." 1 Corinthians 15:52.

266. Venerable Mary of Agreda noted in "The Mystical City of God" that, even on the night of His betrayal, Jesus offered Judas love and forgiveness, if only Judas would reject his diabolical plan. From Mary of Agreda's visions, we read that Jesus said to Judas, "I assure thee, that we love thee; for thou art yet in life, where there is hope and where we will not deny thee our friendship, if thou seek it. But if thou refuse it, thou wilt merit our abhorrence and eternal chastisement and pain."

267. "But the beast was captured, and with him the false prophet who had performed the miraculous signs on his behalf. With these signs he had deluded those who had received the mark of the beast and worshiped his image. The two of them were thrown alive into the fiery lake of burning sulfur." Revelation 19:20.

268. "What has been will be again, what has been done will be done again; there is nothing new under the sun." Ecclesiastes 1:9.

269. Again, we are reminded of John's lesson from Mark 10:35-45:

"Then James and John, the sons of Zebedee, came to him. 'Teacher,' they said, 'we want you to do for us whatever we ask.'

"'What do you want me to do for you?' he asked.

"They replied, 'Let one of us sit at your right and the other at your left in your glory.'

"'You don't know what you are asking,' Jesus said. 'Can you drink the cup I drink or be baptized with the baptism I am baptized with?'

"'We can,' they answered.

"Jesus said to them, 'You will drink the cup I drink and be baptized with the baptism I am baptized with, but to sit at my right or left is not for me to grant. These places belong to those for whom they have been prepared.'

"When the ten heard about this, they became indignant with James and John. Jesus called them together and said, 'You know that those who are regarded as rulers of the Gentiles lord it over them, and their high officials exercise authority over them. Not so with you. Instead, whoever wants to become great among you must be your servant, and whoever wants to be first must be slave of all. For even the Son of Man did not come to be served, but to serve, and to give his life as a ransom for many.'"

270. "On that day his feet will stand on the Mount of Olives, east of Jerusalem, and the Mount of Olives will be split in two from east to west.... You will flee as you fled from the earthquake in the days of Uzziah king of Judah. Then the Lord my God will come, and all the holy ones with him." Zechariah 14:4-5.

271. "For as lightning that comes from the east is visible even in the west, so will be the coming of the Son of Man…. The will see the Son of Man coming on the clouds of the sky, with power and great glory. And he will send His angels with a loud trumpet call, and they will gather His elect from the four winds, from one end of the heavens to the other." Matthew 24:27-31.

272. "But Christ has indeed been raised from the dead, the first fruits of those who have fallen asleep. For since death came through a man, the resurrection of the dead comes also through a man. For as in Adam all die, so in Christ all will be made alive. But each in his own turn: Christ, the first fruits; the, when He comes, those who belong to Him. Then the end will come, when He hands over the kingdom to God the Father after He has destroyed all dominion, authority and power. For He must reign until He has put all His enemies under His feet. The last enemy to be destroyed is death." 1 Corinthians 15:20-26.

273. Hymn lyrics by Thomas Ken, 1674.

274. This is a description from Revelation 20:4. It also says, "They came to life and reigned with Christ for a thousand years."

275. In CCC 998, the Catechism cites John 5:29 and Daniel 12:2 in supporting that, "All the dead will rise, 'those who have done good, to the resurrection of life, and those who have done evil, to the resurrection of judgment.'"

276. In "The Rise," Angela becomes so exasperated with John, in their first meeting, that she throws a pitcher of water at him.

277. From the visions of Blessed Anne Catherine Emmerich, we read that Jesus' agony in the garden, before His death, was especially painful because He had hoped that His sacrifice would save all mankind.

278. "I will create new heavens and a new earth. The former things will not be remembered, nor will they come to mind. But be glad and rejoice forever in what I will create, for I will create Jerusalem to be a delight and its people a joy." Isaiah 65:17-18.

279. "For with fire and with his sword the LORD will execute judgment upon all men, and many will be those slain by the Lord." Isaiah 66:16. "His winnowing fork is in his hand to clear his threshing floor and to gather the wheat into his barn, but he will burn up the chaff with unquenchable fire." Luke 3:17.

280. Adapted, for this work of fiction, from the Book of Genesis.

281. "Be fruitful and increase in number…" is God's first commandment to mankind. Genesis 1:28.

282. "For the wages of sin is death, but the gift of God is eternal life in Christ Jesus our Lord." Romans 6:23.

283. Citing Ephesians 1:10 for support, CCC 1043 states: "Sacred Scripture calls this mysterious renewal, which will transform humanity and the world, 'new heavens and a new earth.' It will be the definitive realization of God's plan to bring under a single head 'all things in [Christ], things in heaven and things on earth.'"

284. "But in keeping with His promise, we are looking forward to a new heaven and a new earth, the home of righteousness." 2 Peter 3:13.

285. CCC 1044 references Revelation 21:4 in stating, "In this new universe, the heavenly Jerusalem, God will have his dwelling among men. 'He will wipe away every tear from their eyes, and death shall be no more, neither shall there be mourning nor crying nor pain anymore, for the former things have passed away.'"

286. Referencing the writings of St. Irenaeus, CCC 1047 states, "The visible universe, then [at the time of the new heavens and new earth], is itself destined to be transformed, 'so that the world itself, restored to it original state, facing no further obstacles, should be at the service of the just,' sharing their glorification in the risen Jesus Christ.'"

287. "But do not forget this one thing, dear friends: With the Lord, a day is like a thousand years, and a thousand years are like a day." 2 Peter 3:8.

288. Sin brought death into the world. "For the wages of sin is death, but the gift of God is eternal life in Christ Jesus our Lord." Romans 6:23. The original Adam lived 930 years, according to Genesis 5:5.

289. "Just as it was in the days of Noah, so also will it be in the days of the Son of Man. People were eating, drinking, marrying and being given in marriage up to the day Noah entered the ark. Then the flood came and destroyed them all. It was the same in the days of Lot. People were eating and drinking, buying and selling, planting and building. But the day Lot left Sodom, fire and sulfur rained down from heaven and destroyed them all. It will be just like this on the day the Son of Man is revealed." Luke 17:26-30. This description gives strong backing to support why the Catholic Church has never embraced the concept of a pre-Tribulation Rapture.

290. "… you will be like gods…" was Satan's first temptation, described in Genesis 3:5.

The Trials and Triumph Trilogy:
The Rise
The Rebellion
The Return

www.VeroHousePublishing.com